SOME RISE

Richard Snodgrass

Book Two of the Furnass Towers Trilogy

Calling Crow Press

Pittsburgh

Published by Calling Crow Press
Pittsburgh, Pennsylvania

Book design by Book Design Templates, LLC
Cover design by Jack Ritchie

Printed in the United States of America
ISBN 978-0-9997249-5-8
Library of Congress catalog control number: 2018904108

This book is for Jay and Holiday Tuttle

who helped to keep me going, all those years;

and, as with everything,

for Marty.

Some Rise

Prelude

As Dickie Sutcliff hammered the last nail into the piece of plywood that he used to cover the basement transom window, particles of soot rained down on him, flecking the sleeves and shoulders of his white shirt.

"You'll ruin your shirt," his mother said.

"It was ruined three nails ago." A final blow sent another shower of black specks over him.

"I didn't mean for you to fix that window right this minute and ruin your good clothes."

Of course you did. Mean for me to fix it for you right this minute. And you knew I'd do it for you right this minute too, whether I was in my good clothes or not. Dickie sighed. The smell of the soot—oily, sulfurous, slightly fecal—brought back memories of growing up here, memories of the house when he was a child and what the town was like before the mills shut down.

Suspended with clothesline from the basement ceiling were the bicycles and tricycles and wagons and pedal cars that he and his brother and sister had played with once upon a time. As she watched Dickie on the step stool, Kitty, his mother, reached up and batted the pedal of one of the bikes; the pedal spun on its axis, whirring on its bearings, causing a stir among the other suspended toys.

"I've always thought of this as tricycle heaven," Kitty said. "The place where tricycles and bikes go after their life is over."

"Dead tricycles," Dickie said. And immediately wished he hadn't.

"Yes, dead tricycles, if you will."

She appeared to be okay with it. Dickie, never one to backtrack or to take things for granted, decided to push it further, to see if she was at peace with the subject as much as she seemed.

"Just so you don't have any dead bodies strung up there to go along with them."

"Smarty," she said, and poked him in the ribs.

Satisfied, he gave one last whack to the nail and climbed down from the step stool, bending over and fanning his hand across his brush-cut dark hair to clean away the soot. As Dickie turned toward her in the faint afternoon light coming through the ground-level windows, she dissolved in giggles.

"What?"

"Your face is covered with soot. You look like you've got black freckles."

As Dickie reached for his face, Kitty grabbed his hand to stop him—and let it go just as quickly. They both seemed awkward with the touch.

"Don't smear them, you'll only make them worse. Wait till you get some soap and water."

Dickie carried the stool over to the cellar steps to be taken back upstairs and returned the hammer to the picnic basket where she kept her tools. Kitty gave the pedal another whir. It was his brother's Schwinn Black Phantom; the chrome fenders were rusted now and one side of the belly tank was missing. Kitty spun the pedal again, then grabbed it and gave it a couple of cranks, sending the flabby rear tire humming against the frame, the chain clanking. The adjacent bikes and wagons bobbed violently on their clothesline tethers—they acted as if they were all connected to the same line—as if ready to break free and set sail around the room, or come crashing down to the floor. Kitty covered her head in mock terror at what she had started, then, as things settled down again, smiled happily, as if pleased with herself.

Dickie waited for her at the bottom of the steps; he was anxious to get back to the office and wanted to keep things moving.

"That plywood over the transom should help keep out any barbarians at the gate."

"Thank you, kind sir," she said, brushing past him. As she climbed the steps, without looking back at him, she added, "Oh, I don't think I told you. Harry Todd's coming."

"For a visit?"

"Won't that be nice?"

"For how long?"

"You know, he didn't say."

Dickie stared after her, watching the aging woman in the long denim jumper climb the steps. "No, you didn't tell me."

"I didn't think I had," she said, and disappeared beyond the door.

He stood there for a moment in the murkiness of the basement. In the corner the hot-water heater *whooshed!* into life; the glow of the flames flickered against the cement floor. Slowly he climbed after her, forgetting to take the step stool with him. He found her in the kitchen washing her hands.

"And what brings Harry Todd back to this part of the country?"

"I don't know. Maybe he finally decided to see his decrepit old mother. Before she gets any older and decrepiter."

"Yeah, I'll bet."

Kitty dried her hands on her apron and with two hands, a long-practiced gesture, lifted her shoulder-length gray hair off the back of her neck to reset it. "I know you and your older brother don't get along very well. . . ."

"We get along fine, as long as he stays at his end of the country and I stay at mine."

"That's what I wanted to talk to you about, Dickie my love. I was wondering if you would mind not coming around for a little while once he gets here, until he gets settled in and all."

And isn't that the way it goes? Here I do everything I can to help her, and she's excited about the prodigal who will come back and take as much from her as he can. One son still can't do anything wrong in her eyes, and the other still can't do anything right. But Dickie didn't say anything. He walked out on the back porch and flicked at the loose material of his shirtsleeves. Some of the black spots jumped off like fleas; most of them stayed there, wedded to the crisp white cloth.

"You don't have to worry," he said through the screen door. "If Harry Todd's here, I wouldn't come around anyway. I'll send Jennifer over once in a while to see how things are going and find out if you need anything."

"That'll be nice. I don't get to see her much since she's been away at school. And this way she'll have a chance to get to know her uncle."

Dickie went back into the kitchen to get his suit coat, draped over the back of a chair.

"I'm not sure that's such a good idea," he said, kissing her on the cheek. She smelled of glycerin soap and Oil of Olay. As she squeezed his arm affectionately, she whispered in his ear.

"Don't forget to wash your face, Freckles. You look like a car mechanic."

Dickie pulled back from her. Kitty pretended to gasp in horror. Dickie shook his head and headed through the downstairs of the old house toward the front door. Kitty followed him.

"You're always so serious about everything, my young son. You were that way even as a baby. You should learn to relax more. Let things go."

He stopped in the vestibule and looked back at her. In the darkness that filled the big house even in daytime, she was coming down the hallway in graceful sliding steps, pointing the toes of her sandals from one side to the other as she glided along.

"My glissades. Have to keep in practice, you know, in case the Rockettes ever call me back." She stopped in front of him and gave a little curtsy, spreading her apron.

"And you wonder why I worry about you," Dickie said and pushed out through the screen door, squinting in the sudden sunlight as he headed down the front steps and across the lawn. Why would Harry Todd decide to come back now? He made a mental note to have a talk with Jennifer about her uncle, he didn't want her to get too friendly with him, he didn't want Harry Todd to get too friendly with her. Maybe I'm overreacting . . . no, I know my brother, I've seen what he's capable of, remember? Time doesn't change somebody like Harry Todd. Nor did he want Harry Todd bringing up the past; Dickie had worked too hard to make things right, to help his mother get over it, to put it all behind her. Okay, big brother. What's on your mind after all this time? Why can't you leave well enough alone?

As Dickie reached his car in the driveway and looked back at the house, Kitty called from the front porch, "Don't be a stranger."

PART ONE

. . . the smoke rises from the mills along the river, streaming from the tall smokestacks like guidons of an army at war, billowing up in gigantic shapes, steam whiter than white, from the blast furnaces and the coke ovens . . . the smoke surges from the flaming mouths of the Bessemer converters as they loll in their berths, escaping in rust-gray clouds from the roof vents of the soot-blackened buildings that house the open hearths and later the BOP Shop, the smell of the smoke always there in the town, the particles of soot drifting down at times like black snow, like black rain (it was a game when they were kids standing at the corner, holding out their hands to see who collected the most black spots before the school bus came) . . . the smoke drifts through the streets of the town, becoming entangled in the branches of the trees along the streets and in the narrow backyards; it rolls over the rooftops and along the porches of the small frame houses stacked up the slope on this side of the valley, it lingers along the brick storefronts of the main street on the days when the sky is heavy and it's going to rain and the smoke can't rise above the horizon of the hills, the smoke and the clouds on those days covering the valley like a lid . . . though that was years ago during the glory days of steel, when steel was king, the glory days of the town, when he was a child here; now the smoke covers the town only in his mind. . . .

1

The first time Harry Todd saw her, he was outside on the lawn. When he came downstairs after sleeping to almost noon, he had found the big house empty, his mother gone somewhere on an errand. In the kitchen he fixed himself a bowl of cereal—he hadn't had Cheerios since he was a kid—and ate it while standing at the sink, looking out the window at the backyard. Then he stepped out the back door to take a walk around the yard, down to the old tennis court, to see how things looked now, his first morning home in twenty-five years.

It turned out to be a day of many revelations. The tennis court behind the garage looked as if it hadn't been used since he left. Dead leaves and debris were blown into piles along the bottom of the fence; the hard surface, even though his mother said it had been a rainy spring, in summer was webbed with cracks like a dry creek bed. The net was long gone, the posts left leaning at opposing angles. He could barely make out the lines of play. It was sad to see the court in such bad condition, he had thought that he might pick up his game again while he was here.

Harry Todd stood in the center of the empty space, still protected from the outside world by the tall wire fence, though its forest-green paint had long since turned to rust, and looked around. How many hours he and Kathleen had spent here as kids. The curious muffled ring of the balls hitting the racquets, the rustle of the leaves of the trees along the edge of the bluff, the sounds—and smells—of the mills below in the valley along the river. His sister laughing, pleased with herself, whenever she won a point. Whenever she beat him . . . Come on, Harry Todd, don't pout. It's only a game, remember? I'll race you to the house. Winner gets to shower first. . . . Start thinking about that stuff, old friend, he reminded himself, and they'll be coming to take you away. Then he sang to himself, a little singsong to amuse himself, his hands tucked down into the pockets of his relaxed-fit jeans, under the loose tails of his short-sleeved madras sport shirt—he was proud that it was surfer-boy blue, a reminder of his recent California heritage—the words of an old popular song, totally forgotten until now, They're coming to take me away, away, they're coming to take me away. . . . As he walked across the ridged and crackled asphalt he stumbled, surprised at the pain and stiffness in his ankles, his feet in loafers without socks, also in the California style, unused to any surface not leveled and maintained.

Harry Todd Sutcliff, pushing fifty as he had begun to say of himself, liked to think he was still fit enough to take up tennis again, or could be fit without too much effort, but the fact was that his athletic days were far behind him, the athletic frame and bearing that came naturally to him as a young man—in high school he looked so much the image of a football hero that the coach made him quarterback of the Furnass Stokers even though Harry Todd wasn't that good at the position—absorbed now by too much flesh, his golden-boy good looks softened to the point of puffiness, blurred beyond repair by too much alcohol and fun drugs before he was able to dry out through AA, though by then of course the damage was done; his trademark blond hair looked surprisingly like it did in high school, curled back in a natural wave above his forehead though now the front of the wave tended to look ready at any time to break away into a Bill Haley spit curl. As he left the tennis court, conscientiously latching the gate behind him, the way he'd found it—I wonder who or what Mother is trying to keep out; or maybe she's trying to keep something in, the Kitty Sutcliff Collection of Ill Winds and Imagined Beasts—and headed across the large side yard toward the front of the house, his mother's white Cadillac pulled up the driveway and parked in front of the garage. With his mother was a young woman who appeared to be in her early twenties, wearing a straw Stetson, her long auburn hair down her back, probably his brother Dickie's daughter. He waved to them but kept going, across the lawn, and they went on into the house.

He wasn't ready to speak to anyone quite yet today, if he could avoid it. Having arrived late yesterday afternoon, he was still trying to unwind from the long drive across the country, to get used to the idea of being here, as well as to get used to the way he found things here. He had come back to his hometown expecting to find the place much as he left it twenty-five years earlier, all fire and brimstone, the mills spewing out great clouds of smoke and steam that drifted through the narrow streets of narrow frame houses, the furnaces and coke ovens lighting the sky at night all orange and red and yellow, ready-made scenes from a hell. He hadn't known, or hadn't realized, living in California, that the mills were shut down now, that Furnass was a very different place now.

He circled around the side of the house and on across the wide front lawn, his quick shuffling busy walk—his ankles aching again at the slight uneven grade, the pock holes in the grass; Christ, what's happening to me, I come back home and fall apart—to stand at the tree line at the edge of the bluffs. The house sat on the edge of Orchard Hill, a hill within the valley's hills, a plateau really, at what most people who lived here considered the north end of town (it was actually more to the east). From where he stood, through the branches of the red oaks and scrub maples and trees of heaven that covered the hillside, he could see the rest of Furnass below, the cramped streets layered up the slope on this side of the valley, and the largest mill in town, the Allehela Works of Buchanan Steel, or what was left of it, dull black husks of industrial buildings, along the S-curve of the river. Beyond the river were the tree-covered hills on the other side of the valley; beyond the valley was a glimpse of more tree-covered hills, hiding more steep valleys, each with its own little mill town tucked away among the folds, rolling away toward the horizon.

It was the color of the place that surprised him, that unhinged him in a way. He hadn't remembered how green southwestern Pennsylvania could be in early summer. This hard dull unrelenting green. Standing in the tall grass at the edge of the lawn, looking down through the woods that clung to the bluffs—the stairway of a hundred steps to the main part of town, the criss-cross trails across the face of the slope where they played as children—brought back memories of warm sunny days, he and Kathleen playing pioneers among the trees, afraid of Indians and ambushes, the time on the lawn they played tunnel in the boxes for the new refrigerator and dishwasher, their little brother, Dickie, left on the outside pounding on the sides . . . Get away, Dickie. I want to be in there too, I want to be with Kathleen too. Leave us alone. We sat together in the cardboard darkness, the little rays of light spotlighting through the holes so I could barely see her, huddled up against each other like twins in a square womb, our knees drawn up under our chins, and I leaned over and kissed her bare knee and she giggled and she tasted like sweat and grass and something else I couldn't name then and Dickie kept thumping on the sides like it was a drum and wouldn't go away, I want to play tunnel of love too. . . .

That was Dickie, Harry Todd thought. Always a pest. And now I better get in the house and fulfill my obligations as a loving son and dutiful uncle . . . or is it dutiful son and loving uncle . . . I guess I wouldn't know, having never been much of either one. I hope the great karma-bookkeeper-in-the-sky is keeping track of all this. . . .

He turned away from the woods and the bluff and started back across the front lawn, hands tucked in his pockets, scuffling along. It's easier on my ankles going up rather than down, what does that tell you about the world? The house was still impressive—at least *that* was the same as he remembered. It was a redbrick Victorian, a mixture of Gothic Revival and Queen Anne, a three-story hodgepodge of geometrical shapes, with a large veranda encircling the front and side toward the end of the dead-end street, a tall slate roof broken up with dormers and gables, and the distinctive round tower. The Big House on the Hill, as most people in town referred to it. The Big House with the Tower. Father's castle, and she was his queen . . . though she turned into his pawn, his damsel in distress holed up in his dungeon, Father the dragon at the gate, the bullheaded minotaur sitting at the end of his maze of tricks, or was that a centaur, never could keep them straight, should have paid more attention when I was at Cal, a good opportunity wasted, oh well. Certainly not the first time, a lot of history there. You're the Sutcliff boy, aren't you? He heard that a lot when he was growing up, You're one of the big people up on the hill. He felt like one of the big people, growing up here. Since then, not so much.

As he neared the house, despite his earlier admonition to himself, he thought again of the scene he remembered at the tennis court, when he and Kathleen were teenagers, the last time Harry Todd ever played tennis with her, with anyone.

. . . we raced back from the tennis court to the house and I let her beat me there too so she could take her shower first and I stayed downstairs in the dark house listening to the sound of the distant water and then the water stopped and the house grew silent again and I thought of going upstairs and just happen to walk into the bathroom while she was drying herself but before I could she came and stood on the landing of the stairs and I could see her from where I was sitting on the old straight-backed rocking chair in the living room, she was wearing only a white towel and the sunlight came in through the stained-glass window behind her and the colors all green and blue washed over her soft soft skin and then she came on down the stairs—Stop it!

He glanced up at the tower, at his room in the attic. There was someone at the window, looking down at him, a woman. Kathleen? For a second his breath caught, he started to run, then looked again. There was no one at the window now.

He stopped, his hand on his chest, swallowing hard. It must have been a reflection on the glass, the clouds or the trees. Or maybe it was his mother, or maybe Dickie's daughter, up in his old room poking around. He hurried on toward the house, taking the front steps two at a time, to catch whichever one it was when she came downstairs, to ask her what she was doing up there, though the idea that it was one of them snooping around was certainly better than what he first thought. That's all I need, to think I see Kathleen's ghost floating around.

. . . and smoke fills the house, it drifts through the high-ceilinged rooms of the first floor, along the dark cherry wainscoting and the built-in bookcases, the heavy floor-length drapes the color of dried blood that cover the windows, across the faded Oriental carpets and scatter rugs placed like fringed life rafts on the hardwood floors, under the fake beamed ceilings, though this is when he is no longer a child, it is during his first visit back here, a few months after graduating from college, his first visit home after he began his exile, after he was sent into exile: he thinks there must be a fire one morning when he comes in from a walk and finds the downstairs of the house slowly filling up with smoke though his father and mother continue with their breakfast as if there is nothing wrong or out of the ordinary, a gray haze settling over the rooms that traces the path of anyone who walks through it, the smoke lifting and swirling and tumbling about the unseen afterimage until it settles into place again, and he follows the trail of smoke looking for its source as it drifts toward him through the front hallway and curls along the ceiling of the staircase and he goes upstairs cautiously as if exploring deeper into a cave and down the hall to where the smoke is coming from: his sister sits crosslegged on her bed, not quite in the lotus position, an old Ouija board on her lap for a tray, hunched over a large ceramic ashtray shaped like an outstretched hand, the palm of which contains a mound of slowly burning powder, a line of tiny glowing embers ringing the slopes of the earth-colored powder like the line of a forest fire seen from a great height, Kathleen inhaling open-mouthed the plume of smoke that rises genie-like before her. . . .

2

His mother and the auburn-haired girl, standing at the table in the dining room, looked up at him, somewhat surprised, as Harry Todd burst into the front hall. He forgot his concern that someone had been poking around in his room—How could she get down here so fast? Was I imagining someone in the window?—with his concern that he appeared foolish. He smiled, trying his best to be charming.

"And this must be my niece," he said, walking into the room, arms outstretched in welcome.

"It must be," the girl said without expression. "And you must be my uncle Harry Todd."

When she made no movement toward him, no further acknowledgment, Harry Todd stopped short. He looked around uncomfortably, wondering what to do next; he patted his jeans pockets as if he had forgotten something.

"Come have a look, Harry Todd," Kitty said, smiling from one to the other. Her glasses were hanging from a chain around her neck, lenses aimed downward as if they were peering down the front of her dress; she lifted them to gaze at the photograph she was holding, then dropped them back into place again. "I was showing Jennifer pictures of the last time you came back for a visit, after you graduated from Berkeley. Remember?"

He looked at the snapshot his mother was holding. It showed him and his girlfriend at the time standing in front of the van they had driven across the country, a beat-up VW bus with peace stickers on the crumpled bumpers and an imitation tie-dyed paint job. His girlfriend was dressed in a fringed shirt and Indian boots; he was wearing a headband, his brush-cut blond hair grown long and pulled back into a ponytail.

"What was her name, Harry Todd?" his mother said.

"I don't even remember now." Laurel.

"Laurel," his mother said.

If she knew why did she ask me? Another game?

"Everything that summer was sort of in a haze, if you know what I mean," he said, tilting his head toward Jennifer as if to a fellow conspirator, thinking the vague drug reference might give them a common bond. Jennifer gave no indication that she knew what he was talking about.

Other photographs were spread across the table like a hand of playing cards. He was chagrined to have the photos brought out for the girl's benefit—he didn't know what she'd think of them, he was afraid she would think they were funny.

"What are you looking at these for?"

Jennifer met his eyes, not unfriendly, but as if throwing his gaze right back at him. "I asked Grandmother to show them to me."

Why would she be interested? "They seem awfully dated now."

"They are," Jennifer said, unflinching. "They're totally weird. But that's what's so great about the sixties, isn't it?"

Weird. But weird can be good.

She was a tallish girl in her early twenties with skin the color of the moon and eyes that seemed variously green or gray. Her hair was long and straight like her grandmother's, but he had misjudged its color when he thought it was auburn; though it might be called reddish, it was dyed a shade never seen in nature, almost metallic.

I'll tell you what's weird. Me standing here talking to my mother and my niece. . . .

"I've got all sorts of things in here," Kitty chirped, rummaging around in a chest open on the table. The chest was somewhat larger than a shoebox, with a domed lid and molded straps and buckles; it was made to look old, stained and weathered, an imitation treasure chest that might have been dug up by pirates. "All sorts of things. . . ."

"I don't doubt it in the least," Harry Todd said.

"Your uncle doesn't approve of the way I keep house," Kitty said without rancor, sweeping her hand to encompass the clutter of the room. "He never did, even as a little boy."

"What did I say?"

"I think the term he used the last time he was here was," his mother said, rocking back and forth on her heels, gazing up at the chandelier, the cut-glass pendants slightly fuzzy from accumulated grime, as if she were reading the words there, "the world's largest collection of meaningless junk."

"That was harsh," Jennifer said.

"Whatever could have possessed me to say such a thing?" Harry Todd said. He wagged his head, pretending to be regretful, as he looked around the room. The smile he elicited from Jennifer was blank.

The downstairs of the house was dark even at midday; a few flame-shaped bulbs, the ones that weren't burnt out, glowed feebly in the chandelier over the table, but their light was canceled out by the dim sunlight filtering in through the venetian blinds and the heavy velveteen drapes. Every flat surface of the room, the tops of the bureau, sideboard, window seat, mantel, table, chairs, was covered with knickknacks, magazines, pill bottles, hair ribbons, gloves, mail, more magazines, more knickknacks—the accumulation seemingly of decades. His mother shuffled through a new stack of photographs she took from the chest, her glasses momentarily perched on the end of her nose, looking for other photos to lay out as she talked.

"Your uncle tends to be very hard on people. Very judgmental. He demands a lot, he has very high standards. I'm afraid none of us around here have ever quite measured up."

"He doesn't sound like a very nice person," Jennifer said, not looking at him, looking instead over her grandmother's shoulder at a photograph. After studying the picture for a moment,

Jennifer and his mother looked at each other and wrinkled their noses and shook their heads.

"I'm afraid he would be totally insufferable," Kitty said, dropping the glasses onto her chest and rooting around in the chest again, "except that he's as hard on himself as he is on everyone else, probably even harder. I've always thought he is more disappointed with his inability to measure up to his own standards for himself than he is with ours."

"If you want to talk about me, I'll be glad to leave the room," Harry Todd said pleasantly.

"No, no, you can stay. What's the fun of talking about someone behind their back if he can't hear what you say?" Kitty smiled perfunctorily and went on.

"I picked up Jennifer and took her with me to the hairdresser's. I was thinking of doing something wild with my hair like she does, a different color or something. But I decided for a woman my age, my hair is outlandish enough the way it is. What do you think, dear?"

Harry Todd was leery; he didn't want to step into another trap, he didn't want to appear any more foolish than he was afraid he already had. "I think it looks fine the way it is."

The old woman twisted back and forth girlishly within the loose gown she was wearing, setting up a slight counter-rhythm with the garment, as she held up her latest find. The photograph showed his father stretched out on a chaise lounge on the front lawn, in his sport clothes, as sporty as he allowed himself to get— gray gabardine trousers and putty-colored silk shirt, a gambler's string tie around his neck—looking benign and placid, as much as his bloated, blowsy, bulldog face ever did, his smile the one he wore when he tried to show pleasure (it never quite worked, it always came off a bit forced and toothy, as if he had gas). Kitty stood on the front steps of the house some distance behind him, looking at the camera, her arms at her sides, fingers pinching the

edges of her apron as if she were about to curtsy; from this perspective and the angle from which the photo was taken she appeared to be a diminutive woman perched on the arm of his chaise
like a puppet. Farther in the distance, Kathleen, in a long white
summer dress, floated in the shadows of the front porch as if
tethered to the railing, only a vague image, as if she were being
absorbed into the darkness of the house. He wondered who'd
taken the photo; it must have been himself. What did he know
even then? Doesn't she realize what she's showing me? Doesn't
she see it? No, of course not. . . .

"And here's what your father looked like at the time."

"That's my dad? Oh wow." After staring at the photo for a
moment, Jennifer passed it on. Dickie, in a polo shirt, cutoff
jeans, and Docksiders, was looking dubiously at Harry Todd's
van, while Harry Todd was in the driver's seat hunched over the
wheel as if speeding furiously away, already gone. Wonder what
I thought I was so anxious to get away from, Harry Todd asked
himself, but he knew the answer to that too. For a brief instant
he remembered the scene, the last night he was here, that sent
him back to California earlier than he expected, that kept him
from seeing any reason to come back here before now . . . Kathleen looked at me like I was a monster and cried Why would you
think I want to leave here? This is my home, my home and buried
her head in Mother's lap and Father said Well, looks like you
don't know so much about this family after all. . . . He shook his
head once to clear the scene from his thoughts. His mother was
watching him, a concerned look on her face, as if she could read
what he was thinking. When he focused on her, she shifted moods,
smiled brightly.

"You haven't said anything about my dress," Kitty said.

Harry Todd smiled noncommittally; he had been hoping to
avoid the subject.

"Don't you like it?" It was a purple gown trimmed in gold and white lace, high-waisted, with short puffy sleeves and flowing skirt. She held out her arms to show it off as she did a flat-footed pirouette. Her arms looked thin and frail, the muscles flaccid, hanging loose; she seemed lost inside the garment as if she had shrunk within it. He didn't like to think how old his mother was.

"You look like the Queen of Hearts," he said, directing the comment to Jennifer to get a laugh. The girl gave no reaction.

"That's because I'm the queen of *your* heart," she smiled sweetly.

It's like a quagmire, he said to himself, amazed, even a bit admiring, you take one step too many, and it sucks you down. She leaned over and patted him twice, pat pat, on the cheek.

Or maybe it's like a revolving door, where you start in one direction and then spin around so that pretty soon you don't know which way you're headed or even the direction you started from.

"I think I better get going," Jennifer said, "so you two can get on with whatever it is you're going to do."

"So soon, dear?"

"It's time I got back."

"I'll get my keys," his mother said, looking around on the table.

"I can take you," Harry Todd said quickly. "Where do you have to go?"

"Downtown," Jennifer said, a smile playing on the edges of her mouth.

"No problem."

"Would you mind, Harry Todd?" Kitty said. "That would be a help. Here, take my car."

"Mine's right out back in the garage," Harry Todd said, digging for his keys in his pockets.

"Mine's already sitting out," Kitty said brightly. "And you'll be more comfortable."

"There's nothing wrong with mine."

"I never said there was, dear."

"Then we'll take mine."

"Don't argue with your mother."

He felt like he was eighteen again. Here I am, a grown middle-aged man, having the same kind of discussion I used to have with her when I was a kid. I had forgotten how quickly this place can tie you up in knots. Jennifer stood there like a spectator at a match, watching the exchange of remarks as if following a ball hit back and forth between them.

"Poor Harry Todd," his mother said, tilting her head, looking at him fondly, though directing her remarks to Jennifer. "He never knows what to think of his mother. He always thinks I have some deep dark ulterior motive for everything. And yet, if I came right out and told him, 'I killed your sister,' he wouldn't believe me. It's a real problem for him."

"Whatever," Jennifer said, as if totally unconcerned. She took her straw cowboy hat from a stack of magazines and headed toward the back door.

I killed your sister, where the hell did that come from? Harry Todd gazed at his mother, enchanted, swaying slightly back and forth, experiencing new respect for the snake in the basket before the charmer. The girl must think I'm an idiot, the way I'm just standing here. How did this happen, turned around so I'm the bad guy? At the same time he realized he must have left his keys upstairs; his mother must have realized that he realized it too. She held out her keys. Shit, I couldn't take her in my car anyway, I haven't unloaded it yet, there's no room. Double shit. He took the keys docilely, mirroring his mother's sympathetic expression—aged mother and aging son, smiling measure for measure at each other—and followed his young niece.

"Drive carefully, my sweet patootie," his mother called after him.

Outside on the back steps, he shook his head, an attempt to clear it, ran his hand through his blond hair, to get himself on track again, then quick-stepped down the walk and across the driveway, working to get his energy level up again, to appear, for the girl's benefit, that he wasn't bothered in the least by the little scene with his mother. Jennifer was waiting for him beside the Cadillac, having guessed how the discussion would turn out.

"Ready?" he said as he headed for the driver's side, trying to be jovial. The girl was watching him under the brim of the Stetson, her eyes deep in shadow with the bright sunlight, as if she were gauging him on something. A warm wind stirred briefly in the branches of the sycamores.

"You didn't know my name in there, did you? Until Grandmother said it."

He looked at her over the car roof, uncertain what to say.

"It's okay," she said. "I'm not hurt or anything. I was just wondering, that's all. I didn't think you did."

She shrugged and gave him an enigmatic smile and ducked inside the car. She was right, of course, he hadn't known her name, or wasn't sure enough to attempt to say it—Jennifer? Jessica?—until his mother said it first. Tell me again why I decided to come back here? he asked himself. If I needed pain this badly I could have slammed my hand in a car door. He looked up at the house, to make sure there were no ghostly faces watching him from the upper windows, and climbed in behind the wheel.

3

"And exactly where, milady, in this bustling metropolis, am I taking you?" Harry Todd asked gallantly, turning onto Orchard Avenue and heading down the hill toward the main part of town. He was working to be his charming best; he wanted to establish himself, or rather, reestablish himself, with Jennifer, after what she had seen of him when he was with his mother. He made a face, laughed at his own befuddlement. "God, this car is bigger than some places I've lived in. It's like trying to pilot a living room down the street."

A faint smiled passed across Jennifer's face; she looked away, out the side window. "The Allehela Works of Buchanan Steel. Down by the river. Or what used to be the Allehela Works. Now it's called Furnass Landing."

Harry Todd felt a little easier, that he got at least some reaction from her; he had been afraid she was going to ignore him completely during the ride, sitting in stony silence. Relax, don't let her get to you, she's probably used to intimidating people with this attitude of hers. No different than if she was one of your employees. One of the waitresses. Turn on the manager charm. Maître d' of Smiles.

"That's right. Mother said your father was involved in taking down the old mill."

"Sutcliff Realty is handling the site preparation and developing the property."

"That should make Dickie happy. He always liked to have a hand in everything that was going on." . . . *I want to play tunnel of love too.*

"I don't know about that. I do know he's excited about the new industrial park that's going to be built there, and what it will do to help the town."

"I probably shouldn't have said it like that. It sounded like a put-down and I didn't mean it that way."

"Of course you meant it that way," she said, glancing at him from under the brim of her straw Stetson, as if amused that he would try to tell her such a thing. "I know how you and Dad feel about each other."

"Yeah, I guess you're right. I did mean it as a put-down."

He rolled down the electric window—he wasn't going to attempt to figure out how to turn on the air-conditioning—and stuck his elbow into the warm breeze. Give it a rest. Why am I giving myself such a bad time today? Must still be tired from the long trip. Culture shock. Late morning sunlight glinted through the branches overhanging the tree-lined streets, diamonds, gun flashes among the leaves. Near the foot of Orchard Avenue, they passed the site of what had been the Cork Works before it was demolished and cleared away; instead of the brick industrial buildings and towering smokestacks he remembered, there was only empty space, an unexpected view of the bluffs across the river, the green wall of the valley. While they waited at a stoplight he said, "As a matter of fact, your dad always enjoyed building things as a kid."

"You don't have to try to say something nice about him or anything."

"No, it's true. He was always in his room building model planes and ships and things when he was growing up. He was pretty good at it."

"What were you good at?"

"Back then?" Tennis? No, not after that day. . . . "Nothing, I guess." Her directness took him aback; he thought a moment. "Chasing girls. Cruising up and down the main street."

He meant it as a joke. She looked away, but he caught a glimpse of her knowing smile, as if something suspected had been confirmed.

As the light changed and they started up again, he said, "Does that fit with what you've heard about me?"

"Pretty much."

"Did they tell you to stay away from me?"

"Not in so many words. But it was implied. I was told to be careful."

"Your father told you that?"

"Hmm."

Harry Todd cocked his head to look at her, as if peering over the top of a pair of glasses. "And what do you think now, after you've met me?"

"I think I'm safe enough. For the time being."

Christ, Dickie, what did you think I was going to do, ravish your daughter? Thanks a lot.

They continued to descend through the narrow streets, the rows of narrow frame and Insulbrick-covered houses stacked up the slope of the valley, the poor neighborhoods at the foot of Orchard Hill; as they sank farther into the town, the hills across the river pushed the horizon above the normal sightline.

"Is your dad or someone else there at the Buchanan Works to give you a ride home?" he said after a moment.

"My bike is there."

"You're going to pedal all the way out to Highland Hills?"

"My motorcycle."

"Oh." Of course she'd have a motorcycle. . . .

"I work at Furnass Landing. That's where my office is."

Harry Todd looked more puzzled than ever.

"Dad hired me for the summer as a consultant. I'm studying to be an architect and he thought it would be good experience for me."

Of course he would hire her. A Sutcliff family tradition: hire your daughter. A little nepotism never hurt anybody. "And is it? Good experience?"

"Sure, it's invaluable being involved with a major project like this. I only wish he'd listen to some of the recommendations he's paying me for."

And of course he wouldn't listen to her. Another Sutcliff family tradition. Dickie never listened to anyone in his life. Except Father. "Give me a for instance."

"For instance: I think it's a mistake not to save more of the old mill buildings. Some of them are perfect examples of turn-of-the-century industrial architecture, a few date back all the way to the Civil War. My idea is that we should renovate some of them to add character to the new project, rather than just level everything in sight and start over. That's Dad's idea."

"As I was saying about your father. . . ," he inclined his head toward her.

"Yeah, right," she said and wrinkled her mouth, making fun of herself.

This is what it must be like to have a daughter, Harry Todd thought, smiling to himself. Having a nice conversation with an attractive young woman, without all the sexual business that happens: if I'm not thinking about it they are. Dickie must have talks with her like this all the time. It makes you feel like you have a real place in the world. Makes you feel special. I guess I do have a place in her world too: Uncle Harry Todd. He's my uncle Harry Todd. Good old Uncle Harry Todd.

When they entered the business district, he turned left at Fifteenth Street and headed down the steep side street toward the river. Some of the buildings of the mile-long steelworks were still intact, though most had been leveled. When he was growing up in Furnass, the mill was an exciting, forbidding place, a walled city set apart from the rest of the town where people like the Sutcliffs didn't go, a world of its own full of smoke and flames leaping up, rumbling machinery that had been known to crush a man in seconds, a source of endless activity with rail cars being shuttled back and forth and cranes raising and lowering against the sky and workmen coming and going at all hours of the day and night. Now the place seemed desolate, sad even—a ghost mill. Beyond the cyclone fence a large billboard showed an architect's rendering of new industrial buildings surrounded by trees and grass. The billboard read:

Richard Snodgrass

THE FUTURE HOME OF
FURNASS LANDING INDUSTRIAL PARK
REPRESENTED EXCLUSIVELY BY
SUTCLIFF REALTY

Jennifer directed him along Third Avenue to the contractor's gate. He turned in and headed toward an office trailer. A motorcycle was parked out front, along with a flint-gray Lincoln Town Car.

"Go straight, if you want to take a little tour before you drop me off."

Harry Todd did as he was told, glad—he was surprised; it was almost like he was grateful—for the chance to be with her a little while longer. *Maybe she likes me a little after all.*

They crossed some abandoned railroad tracks and approached the old mill buildings, bumping slowly along the dirt access road, avoiding the ruts left by the heavy trucks and bulldozers, the standing pools of water left by the sprinkler trucks and men with fire hoses trying to keep the dust down.

"I worked here one summer," Harry Todd said, "on a labor gang. Our job was to move a set of railroad tracks exactly eight and three-quarter inches to the west. Well, actually I only worked here a week. Three days."

"What happened?"

"I couldn't stand the noise and confusion, if you can believe that. All that banging and clanging, and the dust."

She thought a moment. "My dad worked here too, a couple summers. It must have been on the same labor crew."

"Probably," Harry Todd said. *Meaning? That Dickie could do something I couldn't? That he's stronger than I am? I guess she'd be right, for that matter. Fact was I didn't want to be bothered when I was a kid, I didn't see the point, getting all dirty and* sweaty in the mill didn't fit the image I had of myself back in high school. I was Harry Todd Sutcliff. Yeah, well, we saw how far that got me. . . .

There were piles of debris everywhere, mounds of twisted metal, sections of I beams, metal sheeting torn from the roofs and sides of the buildings, jumbles of metal pipes and flooring. Mammoth ladles lay on their sides as if they had spilled there; piercer shells used in the manufacture of seamless pipe were scattered about like leftovers from an artillery duel. Incongruously, sumac and trees of heaven were sprouting from the innards of the rusting metal buildings.

"This used to be the BOP Shop," Jennifer said, holding up her hand for him to stop.

"As in bebop?"

"As in *B-O-F*, for 'basic oxygen furnace,' but everyone called it BOP. They tell me that a furnace during a heat used enough liquid oxygen to send a rocket to the moon. And when the mill was going full blast, they could do one heat an hour. Now we're taking it all down."

The building, two city blocks long and a block wide, towering eight stories above them, was slowly being cut apart lengthwise, layer by layer, bay by bay, as if eaten away by a giant cancer, the structure's cross sections shamefully exposed. On the ground in front of what was left of the building, workmen wielding long-barreled acetylene torches were cutting hunks of metal into smaller sizes. Comet tails of sparks lit up pockets of the dreary scene; laborers moved through the clouds of smoke like phantoms, carrion eaters.

She leaned forward to peer up through the windshield, looking at something high on the building, studying the structure or design. After a moment she said, "Can I ask you a question?"

"Sure. Fire away," Harry Todd said, returning to his earlier gallantry.

"Why did it take you twenty-five years to come back for a visit?" She got a mischievous look on her face. "Someone might think you don't you love us anymore."

Anymore? he almost said, trying to make a joke, but caught himself. Careful, you don't know why she's asking, who asked her to ask that, who she'll tell what you say. Remember who you're trying to be now. "It's complicated, there was a lot going on. . . ."

"I guess I can understand why you didn't come back for Grandpap's funeral. I've heard you two didn't get along very well. . . ."

Harry Todd snorted, a short blast of air. *Grandpap?* I guess it would be. . . . "Yeah, you can certainly say your grandfather and I didn't get along. I figured he wouldn't care one way or the other whether I was there."

"I don't know. It would have meant something to Grandmother though. Your mom."

Harry Todd raised his eyebrows, wagged his head, to say he wasn't so sure.

Jennifer looked at him quizzically for a moment, before going on. "But you didn't even come back for Kathleen's. I thought you two were close when you were growing up."

So much for trying to be nice.

Jennifer took off her straw Stetson and shook out her hair; she leaned back against the door, bringing her knee up on the seat between them, giving him a glimpse if he so desired of the inside of her Levi'd thigh, her crotch, waiting for his reply.

"Why do you ask?"

"Grandmother mentioned the other day about your not coming back for the funeral and it got me thinking. I remember thinking at the time it was strange." She turned her head to look out the windshield, then back at him. "I also remember I was disappointed. I had heard I had an uncle but I never met him."

I'll bet you heard about me. But he was touched in spite of himself. He pictured a little girl, a doll held by one arm dangling beside her, looking sad at the news her uncle wasn't coming.

"You're right, Kathleen and I were close, at one time. But again I didn't think my coming back for her funeral would do her any good."

"And again, it probably would have done some good for Grandmother. And even Grandfather."

He gave a little shake of his head.

"It might have done *you* some good. To say good-bye to her."

Nothing was going to do any good, then. "We already said good-bye, years before."

"When you went away to California?"

She's not going to let me off easy on this, is she? Because that's the kind of girl she is. Ballsy. Serves me right for offering to drive her down here. For wanting to hang out with her a little longer. What's that song about a restless heart. . . ?

"It was during that visit you saw in the photographs. And it didn't start out as good-bye. I thought she was coming with me, back to the West Coast. I thought Kathleen wanted to get away from here like I had, to go someplace else and start a new life on her own. That's what she told me she wanted, anyway."

He looked away from her, away from the mill buildings. From here on the flatland close to the river, he had a full-frontal view of the town stacked up the hill, the rows of narrow peaked roofs like the teeth of so many saw blades; above the trees on top of the bluffs of Orchard Hill, the tower of his family's house, the house of the big people on the hill, stood like a battlement. He became lost in thought momentarily, remembering glimpses of the scene with the family during his last visit here, the night Kathleen turned on him, turned away from him . . . She told me she wanted to get away from here, I didn't imagine that, she told me that afternoon sitting on the porch with the sunlight coming through the railing like gold bars across the floor, she said she dreamed of going back to school, of going to graduate school at the University of Arizona to get her master's in speech therapy, she told me she wanted to work with disadvantaged kids and go someplace where the air was cleaner and she seemed so happy and full of hope and I thought I knew how to arrange it. . . . When he didn't say anything for several moments, Jennifer said, "So what happened?"

"When it came time to do it, she turned on me, like I was trying to make her do something against her will. She left me hanging there like I was an idiot or something. I figured after that, there was nothing I could do for her. She was on her own."

"So you just wrote her off?" She looked at him, giving him a chance to say something, but he found he had nothing to say. "Grandmother's right, you are hard on people."

He waited until a giant front-end loader trundled across the road, then put the car in gear and continued slowly on. The big car floated dreamlike among the abandoned mill buildings, spongy over the bumps and ruts. He maneuvered carefully around a six-foot choker of steel rope lying in the road like a mammoth black snake.

"What did Grandmother mean when she said you think she always has an ulterior motive for everything? It sounds like you blame her for a lot of things."

Maybe the song wasn't about a restless heart, maybe it was a foolish heart. I'm afraid that would apply as well. . . .

"Yeah, I'm afraid I do. Blame her for a lot of things. I blame her for not standing up to Father when she had the chance."

"Such as?"

He sighed, as if he found it difficult to talk about; but in fact he was pleased that someone wanted to hear his side of the story. "I got into some trouble at the end of high school with a girl, and Father sent me away to school in California on account of it. And

Mother didn't do anything to stop it or try to change his mind. She let it happen. She just went on with all her crazy business, filling up the house with knickknacks and going to her women's club meetings."

"Wow, what a punishment. Sent away to school in California. Most people I know would consider that the prize for good behavior—Stop here," she interrupted herself. "This is one of the buildings I'm trying to save."

When he pulled over, she popped out of the car and was gone, heading toward the building.

Maybe it wasn't foolish heart either. Maybe it was lonesome heart. What the hell am I wasting my breath for? What could she know, she's a child. She's had everything she ever wanted, Father undoubtedly spoiled her rotten just like he did Kathleen, to say nothing of her own father. Why would she care about my feelings about the family?

He got out of the car and scuffled after her. It was an orange-brick building with a cupola running the length of the roof. Diamond-shaped designs in maroon brick were laid among the courses; some of the courses near the top protruded from the others, creating texture and casting small shadows down the sides. The windows were so grimy they appeared painted over. With one of the keys from the crowded ring on her belt she unlocked a door built into a larger door. She raised her eyebrows at him, parodying her own excitement at showing him something that was special to her, and led the way inside.

The air in the church-like structure was still, dead, the light coming down from the clerestories seeming to hang in space. In the gloom the forges and power anvils stood like industrial sculptures; the casting beds on the floor still held the impressions of the last machine parts cast in the sand. Droplets of metal glinted dully here and there like spilled coins. Everything was covered by a dark gray dust, thicker than powder; wherever they stepped they left footprints, kicked up little clouds.

"This used to be the forge and casting shop. It was built before the turn of the century, some of the equipment dates from that era. Look back here."

He followed her through a doorway into an area that the men had used to change their clothes. Inside a tall cabinet, leaning against the wall, were the tools used around the hot metal, long-handled hooks and prods and pinchers. The doors to the men's abandoned lockers were standing open, revealing faded pinup pictures, family snapshots, pictures from magazines, taped to the insides. Hanging from a hook was a heavy canvas jacket, pitted and scorched from the molten metal; a pair of bulbous-toed work shoes sat on a bench, metal splash guards tied in place over the laces; a half dozen hardhats were tossed about the room, the top of each one crusted with slag. In the corner a pair of goggles stared up from the floor, as if the man who had worn them was buried there, had sunk into the floor as if in quicksand, or had melted away. Farther on were the offices, the desk drawers left open, papers thrown everywhere, as if the place had been ransacked.

"The last day here must have been a real blowout," Harry Todd said, in order to say something.

"Some of the men had worked in this same building for twenty, thirty years. And a lot of them got screwed out of their pensions, when the mill closed the way it did."

Harry Todd poked with the toe of his loafer among the scattered time cards and ledger sheets and calendar pages on the floor. He tried not to think how isolated they were here, that he was alone in a deserted, out-of-the-way building with an attractive young woman. Or maybe it was plain old horny heart. Does she ever think what it really means, when she uses a word like *screw*? Out the grimy window, a phalanx of a dozen smoke stacks stood close to the river, left standing by themselves after the buildings around them had been cleared away. Pillars of a giant's walkway. Remains of a world larger than life.

"What do you think the chances are that your father will keep these buildings?"

"Pretty good. I can be persuasive when I want to be."

Yes, I'm sure you can. Harry Todd turned back to the window; he brushed his hand back and forth through his hair to reset it. What's wrong with me? Here she is, so proud of this building she's hoping to save, full of high-minded sentiments, and all I can think about is that I'm alone with her. All I can think about is that I would like to kiss her. He could see her walking into his open arms, see her bent over one of these dusty desktops, leaning on her elbows among the scattered papers, as he tugged her jeans down over her ass, came into her from behind. How can I think things like that? I'm an old man to her. She's my niece, for Christ's sake. Stupid heart, evil heart. . . . It was a relief when she turned to go.

As they got back in the car and continued the drive, she said, "What you were talking about, the family and all and how your father sent you away, is that why you aren't nicer to Grand-mother?"

He was surprised she brought up the subject again. So she was listening after all. "I thought I was being very nice."

"No, you're very sarcastic with her. It's like you're making fun of her all the time for somebody else's benefit."

"I had to do something to handle all that crazy business with those old photographs."

"See? That's what I mean. You thought her looking at the photographs was some 'crazy business.' I just thought we were having a nice time looking at some old photographs. Grand-mother's right, you always think she has an ulterior motive for everything."

"Most people do."

"Oh wow. I wonder what you think my motives are."

"I think somebody, probably your dad, asked you to find out why I came back here and how long I intend to stay."

"You have to admit, when you come for a visit all the way across the country and your car is packed to the gills, as Grandmother put it, people might be curious what you're up to."

"Well, you can tell 'people,' and especially your father, I'm having such a good time back here that maybe I'll decide to stick around a while. Maybe a good long while."

"I'll tell him, if that's what you want. But you should know there was nothing 'ulterior' about why I asked you. Nobody asked me to find out anything. I just wanted to know for my own curiosity. What I can't understand is with all the anger you have about this place and your family, why you'd want to come back at all."

They had circled the mill and were back at the office trailer. Harry Todd pulled in beside the gray Town Car. That must be Dickie's Lincoln Continental. He must be inside the trailer. Yoo-hoo, brother, here I am. Wonder what he'll think if he sees me with his daughter. There's Harry Todd up to his old tricks. . . .

"Okay, now can I ask you something?" Harry Todd said.

Jennifer shrugged, putting her Stetson back on her head.

"What did your grandmother mean back at the house when she said she killed Kathleen? When she said it, I thought she was using it as a figure of speech, just to be shocking or outlandish or something. But the more I think about it, I don't know."

"It sounded weird to me too. But I figured you must know what she was talking about, that it was more of the stuff between the two of you."

"I always thought Kathleen died of her asthma, maybe a heart attack or stroke brought on by it."

"You don't know how your own sister died?"

"Well, no. I was in California, remember? I don't think anybody ever said for sure what happened, and I guess I just assumed, the way they found her and all. . . . Do you know how she died?"

"No, but she wasn't my sister." She seemed to think that was a bit harsh, and softened a bit. "But you're right, nobody talked about it at the time. Whenever the subject came up, everybody got all hush-hush about it. In fact I heard Julian Lyle bring it up again last week and Dad shut him up about it right away. I didn't hear the whole conversation, I only came in on the tail end, but you know how my dad can be when he wants to shut somebody down."

"Oh yes," Harry Todd said, looking across the desolate fields, the piles of debris, stretching away toward the river and the hills of the valley beyond. "What do you suppose all the mystery is about?"

"I don't know, it's all too morbid for me." Before Harry Todd could say anything more, Jennifer leaned over and kissed him lightly on the cheek. "And I don't care what anyone says about you, Harry Todd. I'm glad you're here."

Then she was gone again, slamming the car door behind her. He watched her walk up the wood steps to the trailer, watched the line of her buttocks and thighs in her tight jeans, her long reddish hair spilling down her back from under her hat. She turned at the top step as if she knew he was watching her, gave a little wave, like wiping a spot clean on a dirty window, and disappeared inside. As he backed the car out of the space and headed toward the gate, he thought, Funny. She said she's glad I'm here. Wonder what she meant by that?

4

Dickie had just dialed Pamela's number and was listening to the message on her answering machine, leaning his elbows on the plan table as he looked out the window, when his mother's Cadillac went by the trailer headed into the mill site, his brother, Harry Todd, driving and his daughter, Jennifer, sitting beside him. They appeared to be laughing as Jennifer pointed out something to Harry Todd. Dickie's first thought as he straightened up and dropped the phone back onto its cradle was What do you suppose that son-of-a-bitch is up to? His second thought was What do you suppose she's up to? You'd think I know better, telling her to be careful around her uncle. It only made her more curious about him. And she knew I'd probably see them drive by. Together. This is not what I need today.

Dickie and Harry Todd had never been close. Growing up the two boys almost seemed to belong to different generations, though there was only a few years' difference between them; definitely, they were worlds apart, Harry Todd in one orbit, Dickie in another, with Kathleen looping between them. But if Dickie was suspicious of his big brother now, it was a suspicion, a wariness, born of experience. He had spent a good part of his growing up watching Harry Todd in action. It did not take much, given what he knew of his older brother—given what he knew of the family, for that matter—to imagine the trouble Harry Todd could get himself into, with an attractive girl like Jennifer or in some other way. Dickie hadn't seen or talked to Harry Todd in more than twenty years; nonetheless, he felt he knew him all too well.

Dickie had his own memories of his older brother's visit home in the mid-sixties. The visit had been strained, to say the least, between Harry Todd and the family. His father was openly annoyed at Harry Todd's hippie clothes and long hair, though he liked Harry Todd's hippie girlfriend well enough; his mother's response to the changes in her oldest son was to start wearing long peasant dresses, sandals, and a headband; and Kathleen retreated more into herself, having one of her attacks and filling up the house with the smoke from her asthma cure. Meanwhile,

Harry Todd acted as if everyone in Furnass were the odd ones
out. The two brothers had little to say to each other—the differences between them had become more apparent as they grew
older, in more than modes of dress—and little opportunity to say
it; Dickie, home from Penn State for the summer, spent his days
working on a labor gang at the mill, and his evenings with his
girlfriend, Tinker. On what turned out to be the last evening of
Harry Todd's visit, Dickie had just walked in the front door after
a date with Tinker when he heard crying in the living room,
Kathleen's voice, a kind of wail, and his father saying something
about Harry Todd not knowing so much about the family after
all. Harry Todd shuffled out of the room, shaking his head, an
uneasy, embarrassed smile on his face, and almost ran into Dickie
in the front hall.

"Crazy people. It's like trying to talk to crazy people," Harry
Todd said. He was trying to appear in control of himself but his
eyes looked as if he might break out crying any moment. He continued down the hall and out the front door, into the night.

Dickie looked into the living room, wondering what he was
going to find there. Near the door the old straight-backed rocker
was rocking back and forth on its own, an indication of where
Harry Todd must have been sitting. His father was in his favorite
overstuffed chair, one leg thrown over the chair arm as he liked
to do, watching a Western on TV; his mother was sitting on the
sofa, comforting Kathleen who was huddled against her, crying,
head in her mother's lap. His mother looked up at him and smiled
sadly.

"Dickie dear, please go after him. Maybe you can talk to him."

"I'll punch him in the mouth," he said and thought, For doing
this to Kathleen.

"No, please don't. Promise me you won't. Just see that he's
okay. He needs someone to talk to."

The last thing Dickie wanted to do at that point was to talk to Harry Todd, but he did what his mother asked; he retraced his steps back outside and across the porch and down the front steps into the summer evening. In the dew-soaked grass a pair of silvery footprints headed across the dark lawn toward the line of trees along the edge of the bluff.

Good, maybe he'll fall off the edge and I won't have to worry about him anymore.

Clippings from the recently cut lawn stuck to his trainers as he made his way across the yard; fireflies lifted around him. Dickie entered the dark treeline along the edge of the bluff as if entering a wall; inside was a world full of its own eerie light. The light from the furnaces below in the valley cast a yellowish glow under the canopy of leaves; as he started down the hillside, through the underbrush and brambles, the crisscross trails below him across the face of the slope, winding in and out like strips of genetic code, glowed luminescent among the trees.

They had played here on the bluffs as children, though not together; Harry Todd and Kathleen had had their own games here, games that Harry Todd said Dickie was too young to join in, and Dickie had learned to play by himself. And here I am wandering around the hillside in the middle of the night, still trying to follow my older brother. When am I going to learn? The town below was visible through breaks in the trees, the grid of lights spread across the slope of the dark valley. At the foot of the town the furnaces of Buchanan Steel flickered against the backdrop of the hills on the other side of the river; in the distance the furnaces of the mills at Wyandot and Aliquippa and Pittsburgh glowed like cities in flame beyond the dark rolling hills. Dickie continued along the trail.

He heard Harry Todd before he saw him. Harry Todd was singing, in what sounded like an imitation of Gene Kelly or Fred Astaire; in the distance, farther up the wooded slope of the valley, several dogs were barking and howling in response, a commotion in the night. The only place Dickie could think of where his brother might go was the old spring. Orchard Hill was a smaller hill within the valley, an upper level of the valley floor on this side of the river; the spring was on the backside of the hill, emerging from the slope on a small ridge overlooking Walnut Bottom Run. Someone in the past had installed a cast-iron pipe to channel the water from the underground spring, but the pipe had rusted away badly so that only a stub remained, sticking out obscenely from between the rocks. From the few houses on the other side of Walnut Bottom, scattered through the dark woods up the valley wall, the dogs still carried on.

As Dickie came over a little rise, he found Harry Todd in an open space close to the spring, a wide shelf of sandstone below the edge of the bluff; he was gliding from side to side, the not-very-graceful steps of a pretend tap routine, singing the few lyrics he could apparently remember about putting on a top hat, brushing off his tails. He tried to include Dickie in a few steps, but Dickie brushed him off, though he smiled in spite of himself, Harry Todd was obviously having a good time. He could always do that, couldn't he? He could always make us smile, Kathleen and me, he could brighten any day, win us over to his side, all he had to do was turn on his charm or do one of his funny routines. He must have known I would follow him here, this little show is for my benefit. In the glow of the evening Harry Todd's blond hair, which he had taken down from its ponytail so it fell free about his shoulders, looked as if it were on fire.

"What was all that about, back at the house?" Dickie said.

"That was about two minutes," Harry Todd said, gliding left, gliding right. "That's all it took for Kathleen to set me up and make me look like a fool. Well, so be it." Heel and toe; heel and toe. "If that's the way she wants it, she'll get no more help from me. Bye-bye dear, and amen." He spun slowly around, tipped an imaginary top hat.

This was a different Harry Todd from the one Dickie had met in the hallway a short time earlier, or was trying hard to appear that way. Dickie didn't know what to make of him.

"Kathleen's been sick a lot lately. . . ."

Harry Todd stopped. He looked suddenly concerned, sad. "You just don't get it, do you, Dickie? You just don't see what Father and Mother are trying to do to you and Kathleen, how they're trying to suck you into their comfortable middle-class life-style, how it's ruining your sense of yourself as an individual, your sense of value. Everything is oh so 'nice' here, everything is oh so easy. But there's a whole new world opening up these days, little brother, a revolution of the spirit, a new freedom, you hear it in the music, you see it in how people are opening up about their sexuality, how people are standing up to the government about Vietnam and taxes and drugs." Then he started dancing again. "But you do whatever it is you're going to do. Do your own thing, little brother. Stay here, go into the firm, marry the girl they want you to, have yourself a nice little life." Shuffle, shuffle. Quickstep. "I wish you well. You have my blessing to do whatever you want."

Dickie watched his brother dancing on the ledge, against the darkness beyond the edge of the bluff, the dark wall of the valley climbing to the dark sky. Along Walnut Bottom, the lights of a car swept across the overgrown trees and bushes that crowded the back road. From the hillside came the occasional bark of a dog that wouldn't give up; from the foot of the bluffs, from the loading dock of the Allehela Tool & Die Company, came the whine of a forklift hustling back and forth, stacking empty pallets. Otherwise, the only sound was the gurgle of the spring, the sound of the water running down the trough worn into the surface of the rocks and over the edge of the bluff, Harry Todd shuffling through a few steps.

And that's the same too, isn't it? It's only about him, he can only see things in relation to himself. When Father sent him away to California to school, it was the end of the world, Harry Todd thought his life was over. Now he comes back here all full of California hippie-dippie talk ready to change the world. How can he blame the way we live here for messing up Kathleen's life, when he did that to her years ago?

After tripping through one last buck-and-wing, Harry Todd laughed at himself and came over to him, a different Harry Todd again. "Hey, I've got an idea. Let's go for pizza. Is Shine's still out there toward Indian Camp?"

"Yeah. . . ."

"Greatest pizza in the world. I've been dying to have some since I've been home but I don't have any money. We'll go back to the house and pick up Laurel."

He'll let me treat him and his hippie chick. Isn't that nice? "I don't think so."

"Why not?"

Harry Todd was looking at him with a puzzled, searching smile. It was a smile Dickie also remembered all too well, full of Harry Todd's eagerness at his own idea, whatever it was, and total bewilderment that anyone would go against it, that anyone would have an idea of their own. It was the smile that Harry Todd had always used to get his way. Dickie didn't bother to explain. He gave a little shake of his head and left him standing there, walked past his brother without a word, heading back through the woods to the house. At one time in his life he would have done anything to get his big brother to like him. But now he found he didn't care.

So how did those sixties hippie-dippie ideas work out for you, big brother? They didn't last very long as I recall when Father cut off your allowance after you graduated and you found you had to do something to earn a living, didn't last when you started that string of training programs that were supposed to lead to management positions in one fancy resort or hotel after another and ended up in dead-end jobs as a desk clerk somewhere no one else wanted to be, all those failed attempts to start one restaurant after another, I think there was a franchise shoe store in the mix somewhere, you ended up as a manager of a Denny's for Christ's sake. And now you're back here, back here, I wonder what you want now, what you're up to now. At least you *were* a manager at Denny's, did you lose that job too? Wait a minute, you don't suppose . . . no, he wouldn't dare, would he. . . ? Dickie wasn't aware of it, but fifteen minutes had gone by and he was still standing at the plan table, staring out through the narrow slats of the blinds, when the white Cadillac reappeared and pulled into a parking space in front of the trailer. Dickie took a step back so they wouldn't see him; he watched as Harry Todd and Jennifer sat there a few moments talking about something, watched while Jennifer leaned forward and gave her uncle a quick kiss on the cheek before bounding out of the car. When she came into the trailer she looked at Dickie with a sly smile on her face.

"What?"

She's watching to see how I handle this. She's watching to see how I react. She's as bad as her mother. Now he wanted to see Pamela more than ever, and he wasn't going to wait till she was home. As he took his suit coat from the back of the chair and headed out the door, Jennifer called after him, in a voice all sweet and light, "You don't have to worry, Dad. Uncle Harry Todd doesn't like you either."

5

As Dickie drove up steep Downie Hill Road out of the valley, he was no longer thinking about Harry Todd; in fact he was angry at himself for letting the presence of his older brother get to him as much as it had. So what if Harry Todd was around, he wasn't worth the energy. There were more important things for Dickie to be thinking about, much more important. He slouched behind the wheel of the Town Car, his left knee wedged up against the door so he could support his elbow to support his chin, and thought about the visit he had had a couple of days earlier from Julian Lyle. A visit that, unbeknownst to Julian, promised to open a whole new world for Dickie.

At the time, however, the visit had seemed only one more aggravation in a day filled with change orders, subcontractor delays, and scheduling conflicts. On top of everything else, he had received a call that morning from a preservationist group in Pittsburgh asking him to save the blast furnace at the old mill so it could be turned into a monument, a tribute to the fallen steel industry or some such thing; Dickie told the caller he would consider it, without bothering to mention that the dynamite charges for the furnace's demolition were being set even as they spoke. So, when he looked out the window and saw Julian coming toward the trailer, Dickie thought Groan . . . my day is complete. Dickie had been dreading talking to him ever since Julian's own development project in town, the ten-story Furnass Towers, was abandoned and the S and L that was funding the project went belly-up, ever since Julian's assets were frozen and it was said he was teetering on the brink of bankruptcy. But, regardless of whether Dickie wanted to talk to the man or not, here he was, pacing up and down the narrow confines of Dickie's office trailer, making small talk about the weather as he worked up the courage to say whatever it was he had come to say.

There are those of us in this world who are the Kickers. That's our function in life. And then there are those who get kicked. The Kickers and the Kickees, as it were. Julian Lyle is definitely of the Kickee persuasion. . . .

Dickie washed his hand down over his face, rubbed first one eye and then the other until they both hurt. At least Jennifer was out of the office, making one of her tours of the project; he didn't want to embarrass Julian in front of her. He reset the stud in his French cuff as he broke into Julian's monologue about diurnal temperature changes.

"I think I know why you're here."

"You do?" Julian said, stopping in midsentence and midstep.

"It's about Furnass Towers, right?"

Julian looked relieved. He was in his late forties, a thin lanky figure in an ill-fitting suit, a pilled oxford-cloth white shirt that was too loose around the collar, with close-cropped salt-and-pepper hair and a close-cropped graying beard. He patted the top of his head a couple of times, cupping it, as if reassured by the feel of it in his hand, then reached for the chair across from Dickie's desk like a man caught in a current who was trying to make it to shore, holding on to the chair with two hands as he sat down as if afraid it might slide out from under him.

"You may have heard that they're planning to have the sheriff's sale for the Towers soon, within a few weeks I'm told. . . ."

"I heard something to that effect," Dickie said.

"I also heard they're concerned because no one has shown any interest in bidding on it. They're afraid they may get stuck with it. I mean, who would want a half-finished multistory building in a dying mill town, right?"

"Who indeed?"

Julian chuckled, thinking he and Dickie shared a joke.

Dickie looked away toward the window. From here on the flats beside the river, the town mounted up the hillside like the tiers of an auditorium, and sticking up in the middle, an unfinished pillar to the sky, was the skeleton of the abandoned ten-story building. Out of sight, on the street behind the Towers, was the apartment building where Pamela lived when Dickie first started to see her. In his mind's eye he imagined Pamela in her old place padding around half-dressed as she got ready for work, in only her slip and bra, her black curls brushing her bare shoulders. . . .

But it's more than that too, it's not based necessarily on who likes to kick or who is particularly good at it. If you're one of the Kickers, you can even try to be decent to them, and the Kickees will seek you out and insist on bending over in front of you.

"You want me to bail you out so you can finish your Towers project, is that it?"

Julian cleared his throat. "Here's what I'm thinking: we form another limited partnership to buy back Furnass Towers. Only this time, we reverse the terms of the partnership. You'll be the general partner and I'll be the silent partner. That way it'll look more like a new corporation so we can attract new investors."

"If you recall, the reason I was the limited partner in the original agreement was because you needed a letter of credit to get your financing."

"And so you could get your forty-nine percent of the profits, don't forget that," Julian said, trying to be cagey.

Dickie sighed. The man's an idiot, he always was. For an instant he had the image of Julian and the other kids from Orchard Hill playing basketball in the alley behind Sonny Rourke's house, Julian standing with the ball tucked under his arm as he expounded on the physics of trajectories or something of the sort, the other guys rolling their eyes and yelling, "Just shoot the ball, Julian!"

Dickie had agreed to be the silent partner for Julian's Furnass Development Corporation out of some misplaced loyalty to someone he had known while growing up, to someone his father had helped when Julian started his law practice; he had hoped that maybe, just maybe, Julian could make something of the project, both for Julian's benefit and for that of the town. But now Dickie wished he had never heard of Furnass Towers. Or of Julian Lyle, for that matter. The investigation into the questionable dealing between Julian and the failed Sycamore Savings and Loan was still going on; meanwhile, the unfinished building was an eyesore, a ten-story monument to foolishness and bad planning and misplaced dreams.

It's not even that they bend over and asked to be kicked. They put your foot on their ass, and if you still won't do it, they start tapping you on the knee with one of those pointy little hammers doctors use to get a reflex. . . .

"Let me ask you something. Why do you think I'd be interested in finishing the project with you?"

"Because you're a good businessman," Julian said. "And because you're always on the lookout for new opportunities. Furnass Landing will not only attract new business to this town, it will attract a new class of professional people. And they're going to be looking for office space and places to live. Or, if you think it would make the place more viable, we could promote it as housing for the elderly. There might even be government loans and grants for such a project. . . ."

Julian's face was full of excitement and hope. *The man's not only an idiot; he thinks I'm as much an idiot as he is.* For a moment Dickie saw again the scene of the basketball game in the alley; he saw himself sitting on an upturned garbage can watching Sonny Rourke feed the ball to Harry Todd and, as Julian stood there flat-footed, waving his arms like a useless semaphore, his brother, hardly one of the best players of the group, drive past him for the lay-up.

"You're not hearing what I asked you. I said: Why would I want to finish the project . . . with you?"

Julian continued to sit there, the anticipatory smile still on his face; but now he was blinking, as if a light were dawning in front of him and it was beginning to hurt his eyes. "I'm not sure I follow you. . . ."

"Why would I want you as a limited partner? What do you bring to the table?"

Julian laughed uneasily. "Well, you see. . . ."

"No, *you* don't see. Why would I want you as a partner at all? You certainly don't have any finances of your own at this point. And you've demonstrated that you're incapable of handling a project of that size. Otherwise you'd never let it get to a point where the original contractor refuses to come back on it even if the finances get straightened out. And as far as that goes, I doubt if we've heard the end of your creative bookkeeping with Sycamore Savings and Loan."

"You're a fine one to talk. Everyone knows you're involved in shady deals all over this county."

"Everyone knows that, do they?" Dickie said.

It was obvious that what Dickie had said wounded Julian; and he knew he should leave Julian alone at this point, that wounded creatures, even otherwise timid, ineffectual ones, can turn dangerous when backed into a corner, all eyeballs and teeth. But he wanted to make a point, once and for all, he was weary of people like Julian Lyle thinking the worst of him, thinking they were better than he was. He got up and moved around to the front of his desk, sitting on the edge so he was looking down at Julian.

"Let me tell you what I find ironic about all this. I know that 'everyone,' as you say, thinks I'm in a lot of shady deals. But the fact is I've built this business to what it is today by operating on a strict ten percent margin. That's all. No wild speculations, no attempts to make a killing. I did it by keeping my eyes open to make sure I was at the right place at the right time, and that I knew what I was looking at when I got there. You, on the other hand, thought you could make a killing in the real estate game, and thought you could be clever by doing it with other people's money. The problem is, you didn't know what you were doing, you made mistakes, and you got caught."

Julian got slowly to his feet, chuckling to himself. "It seems a little funny, hearing Dickie Sutcliff talk to me about morality. You seem to forget who you're talking to, Dickie. You seem to forget that I've been cleaning up your family's dirty little messes for years."

"Whatever business dealings you had with my father were over a long time ago. . . ."

"It wasn't all business, if you remember, and it wasn't all with your father. There was that little matter of your sister's death, for one thing, and then Donna Bruno—"

"Be careful what you say, Counselor." Dickie stood in front of him, inches from his face. "If you ever mention any of that again, to anyone, in any context, I'll crush you like a bug."

He heard a noise. Jennifer was standing in the doorway of the trailer, watching the two of them.

"I can come back . . . ," Jennifer said.

"No, come on in. Mr. Lyle was just leaving."

"Yes, I guess he is," Jennifer said, a curious smile on her face. Julian nodded and muttered something and hurried past her out the door. As Jennifer came into the trailer and went to her desk, Dickie watched her.

"How much of that did you hear?"

"Not very much. Mainly the 'bug' part."

"Julian and I had some things to get settled."

She shuffled a few papers on her desk and grinned at him. "Offhand, Pops, I'd say you settled them."

Dickie smiled to himself—She does get a kick out of her old man now and then—but he knew the situation wasn't funny. He couldn't have Julian Lyle going around talking about such things, bringing up the whole business of his sister's death and other little secrets he might know about the family. That Julian had even brought up the subject meant that he was suspect and Dickie would have to keep an eye on him. Wonderful, something else to be concerned about. But some good had come from the visit regardless. Julian, unwittingly, had given Dickie an idea, the makings of a larger deal, something that Dickie had been trying to put together for weeks but which had so far eluded him. Until now. Thank you, Julian. You poor sad bastard. You silly twit. As he gained the top of the long hill and popped free of the confines of the valley, turning right onto Seneca Road and speeding along the rolling hills into the suburbs, he rolled down his window and let a rush of warm air into the air-conditioned interior. The sleeve of his white dress shirt ballooned about him as he straight-armed the wind. Yes sir, even with Harry Todd being home again, or maybe in spite of it, things seemed to be looking up.

*

When Pamela came out of the Racquet Club, she didn't notice Dickie at first, sitting in his car in the parking lot. She was with two other young women, other nurses at the hospital, Dickie thought, laughing and talking about something, making plans for another day perhaps, before she came across the lot between the parked cars, her black hair still damp from her shower—she had had it cut sometime in the last few months, since the last time he saw her; before, it was a thick mane down to her shoulders, she knew how much he liked it that way, but now it was short, a kind of curly shag, though this was nice too—her sport bag slung over her shoulder. When she did finally recognize his car, parked a few spaces from her midnight-blue Corvette, she stopped, looking to make sure it was the car she thought it was, looking to see if he was in it. Dickie remained where he was, slouched behind the wheel, his jaw resting on his upturned fist, watching her. Watching to see what she'd do. Pamela gave him a quizzical look, then smiled and held up a finger, indicating for him to wait a minute. Well, at least it wasn't *that* finger. After she put the sport bag in her trunk, she came over and climbed in beside him.

"Hey," she said.

"Hey, yourself."

"What's up?"

"Nothing. Just sitting here."

"I got your message. I called your office this morning but your secretary said you were out."

"Yes, she told me. When you weren't at your place, I thought maybe I'd find you here."

"You've just been sitting here? How long?"

"Not very long." Dickie's conscience started to bother him. That's no way to try to start it up with her again. Idiot. "Actually, I have to tell you, I called the club. They told me your court time."

"That's a little scary. That they give out information like that."

"I'm part owner of the place, remember?"

"You're right, I'd forgotten. Still."

"Still, you're right. I'll make sure they don't make a practice of giving out information like that." Dickie grinned. "To anyone except me."

Pamela didn't smile; she was thinking about something. She was wearing blue shorts and a white halter. Her olive skin had a slight sheen to it, from the workout or her shower or the heat of the summer day; she smelled fresh, a mix of soap and shampoo and cinnamon.

"Why didn't you come in?" she said after a moment. "If you knew I was there."

"I wasn't sure you'd want to see me." He added, trying for a smile, "I didn't want to throw you off your game, one way or the other."

"And?"

"And what?"

"There are usually a couple reasons involved with anything Dickie Sutcliff does."

She knows me well. "I didn't know if you were there with some guy."

"If I had been, if I had come out with a guy, would you have driven away?"

Dickie pursed his lips and shrugged. "Probably. Though I might have run him over first. Depending on who it was."

"That sounds like the Dickie Sutcliff I know." Pamela smiled and looked at her hands. "How's Tinker?"

"Tinker is Tinker. Tinker is always the same. Tinker's been the same since high school." He waited a moment. "If you wanted to kick me in the balls, why didn't you just kick me in the balls?"

"We're sitting down. I couldn't get a good shot at them from here." She waved her leg ineffectually, to show she couldn't get a good swing.

"I'm sorry I haven't called. . . ."

"Dickie, it's all right. We said there were no commitments here. That was supposed to be the beauty of it."

"I know, but I've wanted to see you. Believe it or not. Things have been a little crazy lately, that's all. . . ."

"Dickie Sutcliff is a busy man. I know that. It's part of your charm."

He reached over and put his hand on her knee, felt the incredible softness of her skin. How can I live without this softness in my life? "But I think things are finally going to open up for me."

"Really."

"Really. I'm putting together a special deal."

"There's always a 'special deal' with Dickie Sutcliff too."

"No, I mean it, this is a really special one. It's going to put me in a position to do the things I've been wanting to do." Does she know what I'm telling her? Does she know I'm talking about us? "I'll tell you all about it as soon as I finalize the details . . . I don't want to jinx it."

"Does it have anything to do with your brother?"

"Harry Todd? No, why would it?"

"I didn't know. I heard he was back in town."

"News travels fast." Not always good news.

"Furnass is a small town. Your mother was in for some blood work, she was talking about it to one of the nurses. I wondered if he was back to get involved with the business or something. Maybe claim his share."

"No. Harry Todd won't be making any claims on the business. You can be sure of that." Wish I was sure of that. Did she hear something from Mother?

She nodded and smiled tight-lipped and they were silent for several minutes. That was another thing, he thought. The silences with Pamela were always as comfortable as the talk. When they finally spoke, they spoke at the same time—she asking if he wanted to see her place, he apologizing for not being able to spend more time with her right now.

"I've got to get some figures together. For a meeting later this afternoon."

"No, that's okay."

"I do want to see your townhouse. I haven't seen it since you moved in."

"It probably doesn't look that much different from the last time you saw it. Or the first time you took me there to show it to me. But I've got some of my new furniture now. And I'll be getting more soon."

"I'll call you, maybe later today when I know my schedule. Okay?"

"I'd like that."

"I missed you."

"Dickie Sutcliff, you never missed anyone in your life."

She swatted at him good-naturedly and got out. He watched as she went back to her car—Like I said, she knows me well—watched as she unlocked the door and, with a coy smile, aware that he'd be watching her, toodled her fingers at him over the roof—She's right in a way, at least it's been a long time since I missed anyone—before climbing in and driving away. But that's the point, isn't it, I did miss her. I think I'm missing her right now.

6

In the photograph, Harry Todd is only eighteen months old, if that, dressed in white shorts with crisscross straps over his little shoulders like a jumper, a white short-sleeve shirt and white socks and shoes. He is standing looking in the cellar window at the side of his grandparents' house in downtown Furnass, no taller than the window frame itself, able to stand inside it as he peers into the depths of the house. Against the black pool of the window, his blond curls down to his neck, the little boy all in white looks like a young god, a small Adonis. My beautiful beautiful boy. After gazing at the photograph a moment longer, Kitty placed it in its proper order with the others she had taken from the chest and placed on the table.

"It's almost like laying out the tarot, isn't it, Merry Anne?"

At the sound of her name, the brown tabby cat lying on the throw rug in the doorway to the dining room lifted her head slightly and said, "Meowr."

"Except this might reveal the past, instead of predicting the future."

"Meowr."

Kitty clasped her hands to her breast, one hand folding the other back upon itself, and considered the row of photographs before her, naming them out loud. "Father. Mother. Oldest son. Daughter. Youngest son. There are even the two cats we had at that time, Gabriel and Michael; Kathleen's Scotty dog, Shiva; and a picture of the house itself. You'd be here too, Merry Anne, except this was all before you came along."

"Meowr."

"Yes, just like the tarot."

"Meowr."

"Except I wonder which one is the Seven of Hearts? And which one the Fool?"

Merry Anne gazed up at Kitty and blinked and rolled painfully on her side.

"It all depends on how you look at it, doesn't it? I guess I better go freshen up, Harry Todd will be back soon. It never occurred to me to use these old photographs for our little plan. But he seemed interested despite himself in the ones I showed him earlier. So we'll try a few more. It certainly can't hurt."

The cat closed her eyes and didn't say a word.

. . . the house sits on the edge of the bluff on a hill among the valley's hills, sits on the edge but not too close . . . from certain perspectives appearing to hang back, almost as if it were peering over the edge at the town below, afraid to get too close, either because it might slip over or because something from the town might reach up and grab it . . . the house is a landmark, a guide for directions and a steady presence, distinguished by its corner tower not its gables (there are three) . . . it was built in the 1880s for a descendant of the founder of Buchanan Steel but not to be lived in as such, becoming instead a kind of gaming house, a playhouse with gambling and pool tables and rooms for mistresses until Prohibition dampened its spirits and the place fell into disrepair, for a time during the Depression being divided into low-rent flats until Harry Sutcliff restored it for his wife and growing family and it became known around town as the Sutcliff House . . . the house carries the memory of the family in its very

structure, carries their weight and measure in the memory of the wood . . . the sound of their voices is still present in the rooms and hallways, a child's giggle, the mother calling the children for dinner, the weeping from a farther bedroom . . . the presence of the family is part of its molecular structure, contained in the warp and weave of its subatomic fibers, so that a tread on the staircase recognizes a particular footfall though it hasn't felt its distribution in decades, the timbre of a voice twenty-five years later echoes among the like sound waves still resonant in the walls . . . it holds the memory of a young woman sitting on her bed inhaling the smoke from a smoldering mound of asthma cure, and the time her beloved older brother came home for a visit after being away almost five years and finds her that way, the look he gives her from the doorway of pity and repulsion sucking the breath from her deeper than the illness ever did . . . it holds the memory of a thirteen-year-old boy peeking around the post at the top of the staircase to watch his sister wearing only a towel after her shower go downstairs to get something from the laundry and on her way back upstairs as she walks past the doorway to the living room Harry Todd sitting in the room in the old straight-backed rocking chair stretches out and pulls the towel from her body leaving her naked and in the process his sister is pulled on top of him and they end up on the floor rolling around and Dickie runs back to his room and buries his head under his pillow crying, "I hate him I hate him I hate him" . . . the memories of the family live on in the house . . . within its electromagnetic currents and fields a daughter stands forever in her underwear before the full-length mirror in her bedroom, studying the image of this thin but ripe young woman, bewildered that no one seems to appreciate her, when she hears him cough as he comes up the stairs, his footsteps as he starts down the hall, and she watches in the glass as she unfastens her bra and slips out of her panties and prepares to open her bedroom door and step out into the hall . . .

within its fields of force dancing around their axes it will always
be a certain late afternoon when a mother in search of her daugh-
ter comes in the front door and hears the murmur of voices from
the second floor, follows the trail of the voices up the stairs and
down the hallway to the open door of the bedroom and witnesses
a scene unfold between her husband and daughter as if it were a
tableau or morality play being performed in her honor . . . in
some way beyond understanding it will always be an early July
morning when a father wearing only his pajama top and under-
pants stands in the hallway moaning and a mother keeps her hand
clutched in the pocket of her robe as if somebody's life depends
on it as the attendants from the funeral home struggle down the
stairs with something terrible in a long black rubber bag . . . many
years later the darkness that fills the house on this sunny after-
noon in June is alive with shadows and glimpses of things not
quite seen and sounds from distant rooms . . . at times the smoke
from the daughter's asthma cure still seems to be visibly present
in the rooms, a haze that has settled over the furniture and pic-
tures on the wall and countless knickknacks, so that everything
seems slightly out of focus . . . at times a wisp of the smoke still
seems to linger in the house, a vapor that travels restlessly from
room to room, looking for something or someone . . . but all of
that remains in the future of our story, and the past. . . .

7

As Harry Todd came in the back door of the house through the
kitchen and into the dining room, his heart caught: something
stirred in the corner, the drapes covering the windows parted,
letting a shaft of light into the darkened room . . . but it was only
his mother's skin-and-bones tabby cat. The drapes fell into place
again, the light was gone; the cat moved slowly, quietly as a
whisper, a shadow among shadows, along the window seat among
the pots and jars of raggedy, untended houseplants. Geezus, no

wonder I thought I saw Kathleen in the tower window this morning, this place is creepy. Even the living look dead.

He flicked the wall switch to turn on the overhead, the grimy chandelier hanging above the dining room table. On the table was a neat row of photographs, a picture of each member of the family, including the pets and the house itself. What's this, he said to himself, all but out loud. A rogues' gallery? The cast of characters? The list of the usual suspects?

He picked up a photo of a blond-haired child dressed all in white who was staring in a basement window. Though he couldn't recall having seen the picture before, something told him it was of himself; he studied it for a moment, but there was nothing in the image of this one-and-a-half-year-old that he could acknowledge as his own and he put the snapshot back in its place again. It's like they are in order. . . . Another photo showed a giggling blond-haired two-year-old in his mother's arms, being carried in what almost appeared as triumph through an adoring collection of people at a picnic. But what he first assumed to be another picture of himself turned out to be a picture of Dickie; Kathleen was at her mother's side, joining in this apparent makeshift celebration of the child—What's the occasion? A birthday party? Wonder what he did to get such attention, but they always made a big fuss over Dickie—and standing by himself off to one side was a seven-year-old, looking appropriately disapproving and pouty, whom he recognized as himself. No surprise. I was jealous of my little brother. I was human, wasn't I? The question is why did he end up so angry at me? I was the one with the right to hold a grudge. I was the one pushed out of the picture. Harry Todd replaced the photo and glanced over the other photos of his family, then continued on through the dining room.

In the front hallway he stood for a moment, absorbed in the shadows and the dark wood paneling, listening to the stillness of the old house. That any house could be this dark in the middle of a sunny summer day. An amazing feat, a masterful job of blocking out. It's a talent in a way, I guess it's her art form. Housekeeping or lack of it as a performance piece. On the landing of the stairs to the second floor the stained-glass window glowed dully without illumination, in shadow from the sun just past its zenith. It was a long, narrow window, more like a transom than a window, a pattern of interwoven gold cords on a background of blue and green diamonds. When I was a kid I used to love standing here looking at that window, the colors glowing in the darkness of the house. I thought the fact that we had such a window showed what a special family we were. That we lived in a world of glowing colors and that it would never change, the big people on the hill. Well, so much for that.

He went on into the living room and sat down in his grandfather's old straight-backed rocker inside the door, rocking slowly back and forth, one foot extended. He had been sitting in the rocker that evening during his last visit here when Kathleen turned against him. Why didn't you come back for Kathleen's funeral, Jennifer asked and I told her I said good-bye to Kathleen years before. That night Kathleen looked at me like I was a monster and started to cry and Father said Well, looks like you don't know so much about this family after all . . . He had been sitting in the rocker that day as a teenager when Kathleen beat him at tennis and they ran to the house and he waited downstairs while she took her shower.

. . . I stayed downstairs in the dark house listening to the distant water rushing through the walls as she was upstairs in the shower and then the water stopped and the house grew still again and then she came and stood on the landing wearing only a white towel with the sunlight against the stained-glass window behind her and the colors all green and blue washing over her soft soft skin and then she came on downstairs to get something from the laundry and on her way back I thought it would be funny and as she passed the door to the living room I pulled the towel from her and as she tried to hold on to the towel I pulled her toward me and we fell on the floor and I thought her body was the most beautiful thing I had ever seen in my life but then I ran from the house and got in the car and spent the rest of the day and every day for the rest of the summer driving around. . . .

From upstairs he heard his mother moving about, whistling to herself, a song he remembered her whistling around the house when he was a child, "When I Grow Too Old to Dream," warbling the mellow, high-pitched vibrato of which she was so proud, sounding like a broadcast of the Hartz Mountain canaries. Whistler's Mother, he thought; no, Whistler's son, Mother the Whistler. Whistle and I'll come; you know how to whistle, just put your lips together and blow. When he heard her start down the stairs, he pushed himself up from the rocker, stretched . . . and froze. Across the hall in the side sitting room, in the chiaroscuro from the shrouded windows, he noticed next to the baby grand piano a bucket of blood, the remains of an abortion, or body parts. No, it wasn't that at all, it was only the red cover of a *Time* magazine, sitting in an old coal scuttle. He laughed to himself, shook his head at his foolishness, but felt a trickle of sweat down his backbone. Watch it, Harry Todd, keep it together, you can't afford to lose it now.

<h1 style="text-align:center">8</h1>

"You look like you've seen a ghost," his mother said, coming down the last step of the front stairs, her hand cupped familiarly over the top of the newel-post. She had changed from the purple gown she wore that morning into a kaftan-like cotton maxi dress, floor length, in a multicolored print, dabs of colors like flowers underwater on an earthy background, her long gray hair around her shoulders. She raised her eyebrows at him, as if expecting an answer, but then answered for him.

"Well, it's no wonder, this old house is enough to spook anyone. Do you remember when you were a boy, you'd never go down to the basement by yourself. I don't know what you thought was down there."

"I'm not sure I'd want to go down there now," Harry Todd said.

"And you used to have a lot of fun scaring Dickie about the house too," Kitty went on. "You had him convinced there was a secret stairway in the walls. He used to walk around for hours knocking on the wood paneling trying to find it."

"Dickie was always pretty gullible."

"Only in regards to you. That was because he looked up so much to his older brother."

Harry Todd started to say something but caught himself. Watch it, don't let her get started, keep it light. A moving target. As if she recognized the conversation was going in a questionable direction, his mother patted the newel-post a couple times before removing her hand and smiled at him anew.

"Well, you're undoubtedly hungry. I'll fix us some lunch, if we wait much longer it'll be time for dinner. There's some nice tuna salad in the refrigerator. Made the way you like it with celery and onions, I have some good rye bread too. Or I'll tell you what, how about I fix you a Spam sandwich, that was always your favorite."

Ohmygod. Is she serious? Spam? He laughed a little. "No, no, that's okay. I've got some bread and peanut butter and honey in the car, that's what I've been eating across the country, so I wouldn't have to stop during the day. I'll get that. . . ."

"Don't be silly, that can't be very good for you. I thought you California types were into eating well. I'll fix you a sandwich."

Before she could start toward the kitchen, Harry Todd brushed past her. "No, Mother, I said I'd get my food from the car." He hurried on through the kitchen and out the back door to the garage.

Spam. Are you kidding me? That's healthy? She's going to save me from peanut butter and honey with processed meat? Lord help me, I haven't sunk that far. Not yet anyway.

He chugged along the flagstone walk across the yard and into the three-stall garage at the end of the long driveway beside the house. His Honda Civic was sitting in the last stall where he left it when he arrived the day before. As his mother had described it to Jennifer, the car was indeed loaded to the gills and contained everything he owned in the world. Everything he had left. Before leaving California he had stayed the last few weeks with Emily at her apartment, the girl he was seeing, one of the waitresses at his restaurant. Or what used to be his restaurant, before he went against company policy once too often, this time instructing the cooks to serve the famous Grand Slam breakfast in a smiley face that came out looking positively lewd, a great joke as far as Harry Todd was concerned but was enough to get him fired. He ended up staying with Emily because, as luck would have it, the day before getting fired he gave up his apartment, on a vague notion that he might be able to find something better. Emily took him in okay, but after a few weeks, on what seemed another whim, he decided to come back to Furnass, the car already loaded except for his toiletries and a change of underwear, it wasn't certain that Emily would welcome him back. Even if he wanted to be.

He opened the car door and was taken aback by the musty odor, the smell of dirty clothes, old food, and cardboard boxes. Woof! Better leave the windows down to air things out before I start taking them upstairs. Yeah, that should get people thinking, after I unload all this stuff in the house, that should get them wondering. After rolling down the windows, he rooted around on the front seat to find the jar of peanut butter and his honey bear; he held up the plastic bag of Wonder Bread, but even in the dim light of the garage he could see mold beginning to form on the few remaining slices. Well, it made it all the way across the country, I guess I can't complain. Surely Mother has some bread among all the other stuff in that kitchen. He took the plastic bag with him as he left the garage and dumped it in the garbage can outside the back door, then took his peanut butter and honey on into the house. His mother was just carrying a plate with a Spam sandwich into the dining room.

"There you are, my sweet patootie. Perfect timing. I went ahead and put ketchup on it, like you used to. What would you like to drink?"

On the stove was a greasy skillet cooling down; on the drainboard a de-canned block of Spam with a couple slices missing. Harry Todd followed her to the doorway of the dining room, looking after her as if caught in her wake. How did she do that? I couldn't have been out there more than five minutes, ten at the most. What is she, a witch? A genie? His mother put the plate at his old place at the table and came back to the kitchen, moving him aside with the back of her hand, smiling at him as she passed.

"I'll bet you've outgrown drinking milk with your meals like you used to. At least I hope you have, they say that's bad for you—and shows you haven't really grown up. I'll get you a Coke. I'm sorry I don't have any beer, but I'll get some."

In a minute she was back with a glass of Coke. She put her free hand on his shoulder and moved him on into the room. "Come on, don't be shy. Get yourself seated, I'll take your peanut butter and honey on out to the kitchen." She took the containers from his hands and nodded for him to come on into the room. He moved as if dazed around the table and got settled. The photographs that earlier had been laid out on the table had been cleared away since he went out to the garage, another act of magic, put away he supposed in the small metal chest at the end of the table. On reflex he took a bite of sandwich. Damn, that tastes good. How did she know I would like it if she fixed it?

In a moment his mother was back with a container of cottage cheese, a large spoon, and a glass of red liquid; she sat across from him, in Kathleen's and Dickie's usual spots when they were growing up, not at her usual place at the end of the table across from her husband. When she noticed him looking at her glass, she held it up toward the lights of the chandelier over the table.

"Blood," she intoned. "No, sorry to disappoint you. It's only cranberry juice. Good for the aging plumbing. I suspect you'll be looking for plumbing remedies yourself pretty soon, if you're not doing so already."

"Mother!"

"Well, that's interesting. So I can still embarrass my oldest son."

He was embarrassed that he was embarrassed. "I'm eating, you know," he said, holding up his sandwich, latching on to the first thing he could think of.

She held up her spoon and waved it in circles a couple of times before dipping into the container. She went on, without rancor or sadness, just matter-of-fact, not looking at him, watching as she stirred the cottage cheese. "I always seemed to embarrass you, in one way or another, while you were growing up, I was never quite sure why. Do you remember, when I'd come to your school programs in grade school, you'd never look at me, you'd never even look my direction. You'd pretend I wasn't there." She looked up at him then and smiled.

"I was afraid to look at you," he tried to laugh. "All the other moms would be sitting there in their nice little dresses or something and you'd be all gussied up like a showgirl."

"Hmm," Kitty said, pulling the spoon slowly between her lips. "Well, maybe so. I did tend to dress pretty fancy in those days. My Broadway-Comes-to-Small-Town-America period. But I always thought there was something else going on with you back then. Dickie, on the other hand, always seemed to get a kick that his mom didn't look like everybody else's mom. But I guess Dickie was always better suited to roll with the punches. Some would probably call that opportunistic, and I suppose he was and is, but it seems to work well enough for him. When you took Jennifer to work, did she show you what all her father is doing with the old mill? That's something, isn't it?"

He wanted to hurt her. She was obviously bringing up what Dickie was doing to make him feel bad, to make the point of how successful Dickie was and Harry Todd wasn't. He wanted to wound her the way he felt wounded. He wiped his mouth with a paper napkin and put the half-eaten sandwich back on his plate.

"Jennifer said something in the car that got me wondering. I never heard how Kathleen died."

Kitty held the spoon suspended halfway to her mouth and cocked her head at him. "How she died?"

"I realized I never heard the actual cause of death. That morning when you called, you said the doctor didn't know for certain what caused it. And I guess we didn't talk much about it after that."

"No, we didn't talk much after that." Harry Todd started to say something but she added quickly, "It's okay, I understand, you don't have to try to explain. That's all behind us now. And you're right, you wouldn't have had any way to know what caused it."

She put the spoon down beside the cottage cheese container on the table, sat back against the chair with her hands folded in her lap. She thought a moment before proceeding.

"It all happened so quickly, so quickly. Kathleen was here with us that evening and went to bed, and the next morning she was gone. Jennifer was the one who actually found her."

"How did she do that?"

"She was staying over here at the house, her father and mother had gone somewhere, she was only six or seven at the time. She was sleeping in Dickie's old room and heard Kathleen fall out of bed and went to see what happened."

"I didn't know."

"She was the last one Kathleen spoke to. Kathleen told her to come get me. But by the time I got there she was pretty much gone." She thought about something for a moment, then pushed whatever it was away. "I can forgive Jennifer a lot on account of it. That would be a terrible shock for a little girl that age, to have your treasured aunt die right in front of you. I've always thought it made her wise beyond her years, as well as a little unruly."

They sat in silence for a few minutes. It was the first time since he was back that he really looked at the woman who was his mother, focused his attention on her, not just look and look away. He was surprised at how attractive she actually was, distinguished even in her old age, the beauty of the girl who had been a Rockette—Good grief, my mother really was a Rockette, no wonder I didn't know how to act around her when she came to my school functions—still visible in her features though mitigated with age now, worn away, blurred as if undermined from within, her beauty collapsing slowly in upon itself as much as she tried to shore herself up. If Harry Todd didn't know better he would have said the change in her looks came from sadness, grief even, but that didn't fit the image, the profile he had of his mother. He could see, though, that she was troubled now at the topic of their discussion. He hated that he brought it up, but he couldn't help himself, he started it and was curious. After another moment, he said, "You still haven't said how Kathleen died."

She blinked several times, coming back to the present. Smiled wistfully. "It was a coronary thrombosis. That's when there's a blockage—"

"I know what it is," Harry Todd said, then wished he hadn't been so hasty. "I'm surprised. I always thought it must have had something to do with her asthma."

"I think it surprised us all. She must have had the heart condition all along, it just never showed up before. I guess we were so busy looking at the one problem that we missed the other. But it does no good to overthink it now. It can be a dangerous thing, thinking."

"I try to avoid it at all costs."

"Thinking was never your strong suit."

"Thank you."

She looked up at him. Smoothed the wrinkles from the tablecloth in front of her. "I meant it nicely, whether you believe it or not. You were always the one who felt things the most, rather than think about them. I think it was always a big problem for you, you had your father's rugged good-looks and demeanor, no one expected you to be the sensitive type. If anything you felt things too much, too strongly—you always made yourself uncomfortable."

"I've done what I could to change the over-feeling part," Harry Todd said, smiling, making a joke to himself, thinking, Rainier Ale, Red Mountain Burgundy, Jack Daniel's, to say nothing of grass, a little mescaline, peyote, LSD. . . . I wonder what she'd think of her first-born if she knew he used to play around with drugs, so many years ago. . . .

"There were times after your sister died when I could have used some drugs myself," Kitty said.

Did she just read my mind?

"Finish your sandwich, dear, before it gets cold," his mother said. Harry Todd did what he was told.

"It was a bad time for all of us, I'm afraid," she went on, smoothing wrinkles again from the tablecloth as if expecting something to be placed there. "I don't think your father ever recovered from the shock. And Dickie took it very hard too."

"Why would Dickie take it so hard?"

She studied him a moment. "I'm afraid you never appreciated how close Kathleen and Dickie were. You and Kathleen had a special relationship, because you were so close in age and all, but Dickie and Kathleen had their own special relationship. And it grew stronger after you were no longer here."

"Forgive me if I don't feel overly sympathetic toward Dickie. He was never one to let his feelings—or anyone else's, for that matter—get in his way. And his broken heart at Kathleen's death certainly hasn't stopped him from doing very well for himself in this town."

He regretted saying it even as he was saying it. He sounded jealous and weak, and he couldn't afford to come off that way now. Not now. Fortunately, his mother seemed to gloss over what he said, as if she didn't hear it or didn't want to. As he finished the last bites of his sandwich, his mother prattled on.

"Getting back to what you asked earlier. If you're interested, I have an excellent article on coronary thrombosis."

"That's okay," Harry Todd said, "I know enough."

"It's really an excellent article. It's where I learned all about it."

When he didn't reply, she went on.

"It was in *Reader's Digest*." She paused again. "I probably never would have known myself what took our Kathleen if I hadn't read about it there. It described her condition perfectly—there were even some little drawings."

It was a full minute before what she said sunk in. He stopped and looked at her. "You read an article in *Reader's Digest*?"

"I know what you're going to say," she said primly, chasing a wrinkle in the tablecloth. "But it's really a very informative magazine. I've learned all sorts of things there. . . ."

"The doctor didn't say it was a coronary thrombosis?"

"Oh no, dear. What gave you that impression?"

"What did he say? If there was some question about how she died, wasn't there an autopsy? What did the death certificate say?"

"I don't know if there was an autopsy or not. And as for the death certificate, I wouldn't know what it said, dear." Kitty looked at her hands, then looked at Harry Todd again, head canted to one side, and smiled, a picture of innocence. "Your father took care of those details, he and Julian Lyle. You know your father would never tell me about things like that. He didn't think I was smart enough to understand. The poor man, he was always afraid I was going to embarrass him about one thing or another."

From the dark corner came a loud *Thump!* Harry Todd jumped, looked around the room wide-eyed but his mother didn't flinch. Merry Anne stepped out from under an antique magazine rack, looking up at the two humans looking at her as if she was the one surprised.

"Good grief," Harry Todd said. "It's only the cat."

"Of course, dear. What did you think it was?"

"Like we were saying, you can certainly think you hear or see a lot of things in this old house," Harry Todd said, trying to laugh at himself but not succeeding, thinking back to the image of the girl he thought he saw earlier in the tower window.

His mother grew reflective. "I often think I hear somebody moving about."

"You do?"

"Oh yes. Sometimes I pretend it's you boys, playing in another part of the house. Other times I think maybe it's Kathleen, or your father."

He didn't dare ask her if she meant alive or dead. "Are you okay with that?"

"Of course. It's really quite a comfort, thinking you're all still around." His mother took a drink of her cranberry juice, then looked quizzically at Harry Todd. "Maybe you should go lie down, dear. You must not be rested up from your trip. You look all tuckered out."

9

"Nice view," Charles Selby said, tearing off a hunk of Italian bread from the half loaf delivered to their table with the antipasto, ignoring the knife that came with it on the platter. "I've never seen the project from this side of the river before."

"I thought you might find it interesting," Dickie said, looking to where his companion across the table was looking, out the large picture window beside them, at the view across the Allehela.

It was called the Riverside Inn, though, technically, it was neither an inn—it was a bar and restaurant—nor by the side of the river. It was built on an outcropping of rock, on the road that climbed out of the valley across the face of the bluff, across the river from the town, close to the top of the valley wall; from this height there was a sweeping panorama looking toward the end of the valley, following the curve of the river, of the mill buildings of Buchanan Steel on the opposite bank, what was left of it now that it was being demolished, and the town of Furnass crowded up the slope behind it. Dickie wanted a piece of bread himself, but decided to pass after the way Selby manhandled it; he took a piece of prosciutto wrapped around a slice of melon and followed it with a sip of Johnnie Walker Black.

"Gives you an appreciation for the size of the old mill, doesn't it?" Selby said, continuing to stare at the view.

"In a way, it's hard to believe it's not going to be there, even though we're the ones who are taking it down. It seemed as much a part of this valley as the hills and the river."

Selby turned to him, looking genuinely nonplussed. "Ten years ago—five years ago—if you had told me that we'd be razing a mill like the Allehela Works, or that I'd be the one in charge of getting it done, I would have said you were crazy."

Dickie nodded, commiserative, though he was feeling anything but. It was such remarks that encouraged him to think Selby would be interested in what Dickie was going to propose. Selby was a tall, ramrod-stiff man in his late fifties, at least ten years older than Dickie, with a silver mustache, silver hair, and flinty eyes behind small metal-framed glasses, dressed in an expensive hard-finish suit. Dickie didn't particularly care for him personally—Selby was too corporate, too much a company man, for Dickie's taste, though he would like to meet his tailor—but he respected him, he thought he could do business with him. From their dealings so far, Dickie had determined that Selby had enough power within his corporation to make things happen, at least in regard to this project; and he was banking on his read of the man as someone who, because of his years in the steel industry—Selby told him that he had worked his way up from the mill floor to the executive suite, that he had spent his entire professional life making steel, until this project came along— strongly disliked, found particularly distasteful, his role in taking down the mill.

Selby had recovered his aplomb. He wiped a piece of bread across the butter in the dish and popped it into his mouth, fingered the black olives in the dish before choosing one. Dickie decided he wasn't hungry after all.

"But somehow, Dickie, I get the feeling that you didn't ask me here to admire the view. Not after the way you reamed the owner of this place a new asshole."

"We had an understanding, and he didn't honor it, that's all."

"Whatever, it worked. It must be important, if you wanted all these tables around us empty so we'd have some privacy."

Dickie smiled ruefully. "Furnass is a very small place. It doesn't take much for someone to overhear something they shouldn't and then spread it around. But we can get to all that in good time, after we relax a bit."

Dickie turned back to the view. The sun was starting to lower through the sky, heading toward a distant range of hills, a hazy afternoon, casting the town in a melancholy glow. As it turned out, he was glad now that there had been a mix-up when they arrived at the restaurant, it had worked in his favor, had actually made a good impression on Selby, though Dickie was aware that it could have appeared quite differently. Earlier in the day, Dickie had called the owner of the place, Dom DiBenedetto, whom Dickie had known since they played basketball together in high school, and reserved this end table next to the windows, as well as the tables around it, telling DiBenedetto that he'd pay the extra charges for them, to keep the tables unoccupied while Dickie and his business associate were there for drinks. But when he and Selby arrived, there was a young couple, holding hands and looking dreamily into each other's eyes, sitting at one of the adjacent tables. Dickie told DiBenedetto that he wanted the couple moved.

"Dickie, I know what you said on the phone. But they're such nice young people and they wanted a table by the window. I was sure you wouldn't mind, those two are so wrapped up in each other you won't even know they're there."

Dickie excused himself from Selby and took DiBenedetto by the elbow and escorted him a few steps away. "I want the couple moved," Dickie said under his breath.

DiBenedetto looked at him, trying to laugh, trying to ease the situation. "Dickie, I really don't think they'll cause you any trouble. . . ."

"You're not hearing me, Dom," Dickie said, his voice regretful but tinged with a deadly calm. "I wouldn't be asking you if it wasn't important. Now, you can either move the couple, or we can talk about some other things, such as your ongoing problems with health code violations, or that loan you're going to need me to cosign in a few months. Me, I'd move the couple."

DiBenedetto was about to say something, then looked at Dickie again and thought better of it and went with the waitress to move the couple.

"Impressive," Selby said as Dickie rejoined him. "And I didn't see any money exchange hands. Must have been some other form of inducement."

Dickie decided to let the remark pass, allowing Selby's imagination to fill in the details, figuring they would be more colorful than anything he might say. Now, across the room, as Dickie and Selby sat there, the young man of the couple glowered at Dickie, sulking, offended and angry. Dickie considered going over and asking him if he wanted to take it outside, but decided that might be pushing matters with Selby; manipulating the owner of a restaurant was one thing, initiating a parking lot brawl was another. Besides, if the guy was serious about his grievance, he'd probably follow Dickie outside when they left, which would come to the same thing. The way Dickie was feeling at the moment, he'd welcome the chance at him, not because he had anything against this particular young man—He's probably a nice kid, I don't blame him for hating my guts, if somebody tried to bump me from a table when I was with Pamela I wouldn't move, they'd have to drag me away—but because he wanted to take a swing at someone, anyone—why? He didn't know. I guess I should be a little careful, I'm not as young as I used to be, a young guy like him might clean my clock. Wouldn't look good to a client. . . .

He thought briefly of Pamela, of seeing her earlier today at the Racquet Club. . . . I said I'll call you and she said I'd like that and I said I missed you and she said Dickie Sutcliff, you never missed anyone in your life. And there was another memory too, flitting in and out of recognition, something else from this afternoon that the incident with the table and the young couple brought to mind, though he couldn't grab hold of it. Is she right? Is that the kind of person I am?

Selby was finished eating; the picked-over remains of the antipasto looked as though someone had dropped the platter on the floor and hastily tried to assemble it again. After the waitress cleared the table and brought another round of drinks, the two men settled back in their chairs. Selby offered him a cigar, which Dickie declined, before lighting one himself, enveloping that side of the table periodically in a blue cloud.

"I got your memo about preserving and renovating some of the older buildings," Selby said after a few moments. "You sure it's a good idea?"

"I was dubious about it myself at first. But I had a consultant look into it, and I'm convinced it's the way to go. It'll give some much-needed character to the development, some identity. What we lose in revenue from the scrap, we'll more than make up for in marketability. We're going to need everything we can in order to promote this site."

"Have you talked to the architects? You may have some opposition there. You're sort of stepping on their toes, you know. That's the kind of idea we're paying them to come up with."

"I was prepared to use that very argument, if they started to get pissy about it. But I talked to Blake and he seemed excited about it—said he had begun to think along the same lines but didn't know if he should propose it. Whether that's true or not I have no idea, he may be trying to save face for his firm. But regardless, he says he supports the idea. He's coming out next week to go over it."

"Well, whatever you think best," Selby said, looking out at the late afternoon, the lengthening shadows of the town and the partly demolished mill. "We're lucky to have you looking out for our interests. I'm not just saying that, the subject has come up a number of times in senior-level meetings."

"I'm glad for the vote of confidence." Dickie looked at his hands for a moment, fingertips lightly touching his rocks glass. It seemed fortuitous, the perfect lead-in to what he wanted to talk to Selby about. "I doubt that your corporation had any idea what it was getting into with a project like this."

"I'll be blunt, Dickie. It's been a real drain. We have to do it, of course. With the changes that are going on in the steel industry, there was no way we could maintain an older mill like this one. There were no capital improvements made here in decades, it's a real shame. It was also a miscalculation that the entire industry was guilty of, and now it's come back to haunt us. Add to that all the union problems. . . ." Selby, his hands resting on the table, turned them over, as if the remainder of the statement were written on his empty palms.

"I doubt if there was anyone in the industry who was prepared for the changes of the past five years."

"It caught us flat-footed. We're good at making steel, not closing down steel mills. For me personally, it's been a very sad business."

Dickie nodded, looking appropriately sympathetic. "Unfortunately, I'm afraid it's only the beginning, as far as Furnass Landing is concerned."

"Those are not words I'm happy to hear."

"Nevertheless, I think it's my job to tell you. It's going to be a very long and arduous process to market this property, much less to get the buildings razed and the site itself in any condition to start new construction. We haven't even begun to deal with all the hazardous waste. Buchanan was dumping and burying by-products for over a hundred years, and the same was true of the old Keystone Steam Works on the property. We've got thousands of leaky oil drums filled with who knows what and acres of polluted landfill, not to mention all the asbestos that has to be dealt with. And the government is coming up with new regulations for brownfields every day."

"I shudder to think."

"The bottom line is that your corporation wants to close out the books on the Allehela Works, and you've found yourself tangled up in a business you know or care very little about. It's going to be a continual drain on your resources for some time to come."

Selby twirled the stem of his martini glass slowly back and forth between his fingertips; he studied Dickie a moment, then took a sip. "Where are you going with this?"

Dickie smiled and leaned forward, his forearms resting on the table, shoulders hunched confidentially, warming to his subject. "I have an idea, an arrangement that will benefit the interests of both our companies. Here's my thinking: Buchanan Steel and Sutcliff Realty form a limited partnership, with Sutcliff Realty as the general partner, and your corporation as the limited partner. If the project becomes profitable—no, *when* the project becomes profitable—I will guarantee you two points above prime, say a fifteen percent return annually. Meanwhile, I assume complete control of the project. You—that is, Buchanan Steel—no longer have to concern yourself with either the demolition of the mill or the development of Furnass Landing. And as for you personally, you get out from under a project that you particularly dislike, while at the same time you get credit for orchestrating a deal that not only eliminates a large corporate headache, but turns a project that has been a thorn in Buchanan's side into a potential revenue stream. I'm sure that wouldn't go unnoticed in Buchanan's hallowed boardroom."

"In order to get that hallowed boardroom to buy an idea like you've described, you'd have to put up a significant chunk of money."

"I'm aware of that, and I'm working on a deal that will cover it. I should secure my financing within a few weeks."

Selby thought a minute, watching his drink swirl gently as he tilted the stemmed glass one way and then another. "It sounds interesting, and it would certainly solve a lot of our problems. A lot of my problems. Tell you what: talk to your attorney and draw up some preliminary papers. I'll make sure they get before the board."

"In this case, I don't think I trust my attorney enough to handle something this important."

"A man who doesn't trust his own attorney! I like that." Selby laughed. "Would you be willing to trust ours?"

"Normally no, for obvious reasons. But I would if you pave the way with your legal department. If you let them know you're behind this."

Selby continued to watch his martini in the glass. Then he took a drink and looked at Dickie.

"You're good, you know that."

"Yes, I know that."

"Or, if not good, at least thorough."

Selby smiled a little and took out his pen and wrote a name and number on the edge of a cocktail napkin. "This is the man to talk to. Wait to call until after nine-thirty tomorrow morning, I'll have spoken to him by that time. In fact I'll probably call him tonight as soon as I get back to Pittsburgh."

Dickie took the napkin, folded it, and put it in his pocket for safekeeping. "That was easy. I was ready to spend the next couple of hours trying to convince you."

"No need. If it gets the job done, if it gets this monkey off our backs, I'm for it one hundred percent. Though I'll admit I'm not sure why you're so anxious to take on a project like this."

"It's property. Buying and selling. It's what I do."

"Maybe so. But you've never done anything this size before, have you?"

"No, and maybe that's part of the answer right there."

"I can't imagine you doing it as a public service. I know you care about this town, but I doubt if you want to destroy yourself for it. Yes, if Furnass Landing is successful and you are in fact able to attract new industry here, you'll undoubtedly make yourself a lot of money. But the risks are astronomical for a small player."

"Let's put it this way. I am a small player, as far as a corporation your size is concerned. But Furnass Landing is the biggest development project this valley has ever seen. And I want to be the one who does it."

"Yea, even though I walk through the Valley of the Son-of-a-Bitch, I will be the biggest son-of-a-bitch in the valley," Selby intoned, then laughed at his own theatrics. "I like the way you think, Dickie."

Dickie started to demur but Selby interrupted him, growing serious again. "That wasn't idle flattery. I meant it, or I wouldn't even begin to entertain what you're proposing. You and I are very much alike, that's probably what I like about you. Take a look around this restaurant and you'll see what I mean. You and I are the only ones in this room who are killers. That's what you have to be if you're going to make it in business these days."

Dickie did look around the restaurant. He expected to see the young man of the couple he displaced to be still watching him; but sometime during his talk with Selby the couple had left, they were nowhere to be seen. Too bad, Dickie thought, I was going to pick up their bar tab and buy them dinner for their trouble. Oh well, add two more to the list in this town who think I'm a bastard. A son-of-a-bitch. As he thought about what Selby said, he supposed the man was right; in ways that Selby would never know or appreciate, he was a killer.

And he remembered now the other thing that kept flitting in and out of his memory earlier, something else he remembered from seeing Pamela today but couldn't quite put his finger on. Until now . . . Pamela said What would you have done if I had been there at the Club with another guy, and I said I would have probably run him over with my car, and she said That's what I'd expect from Dickie Sutcliff. The sad part was, he supposed, that, unlike how the world would say he was supposed to feel, it didn't seem to bother him. He could live with it. Is she right? Is that the kind of person I am? Is that all? He had already lived with the town thinking that way about him for so long now, cast in the role where his father left off. He didn't think it always suited him, but he seemed to wear it well enough. As long as people in town didn't think that he was a prick just to be like his father, as long as they knew he was a prick all his own, thank you very much.

He looked back at Selby, hooking his finger over the ridge of his jaw. "It's a deal, then."

10

Instead of lying down as his mother suggested—for the very reason that his mother *did* suggest it, even he was aware of that— Harry Todd in a fit of renewed energy spent the afternoon carrying suitcases and cardboard boxes and duffel bags from his car in the garage up the three floors—twenty-three trips up the twenty-nine steps including the one into the back door—to his room in the attic. Then, for sure, he was tuckered out, as his mother had put it, and he wanted to lie down except he had covered the bed with stuff. It took him another hour or so to arrange the boxes and cases in a pile in the center of the room so he could get at things while still being able to move about. Sweating, worn-out, he went over to the windows open in the tower and stood in the slight cross breeze, the gauze curtains stirring around him.

Feeling, in every muscle in his arms and legs, shoulders and back, and places he didn't know he had muscles, very much a soon-to-be-fifty-year-old man who was out of shape. And running out of time. Running out of options.

From this height, the tower windows—the windows themselves weren't curved, the flat-planed windows were set at angles to follow the curve of the tower—formed a diorama of the town and the valley. His old desk sat under the windows; when he was younger, a teenager, he would climb up on the desk and sit, his knees drawn up under his chin, looking out the windows. Sitting there for hours. Thinking about how he wanted his life to be. His life, obviously, had turned out quite differently from what he imagined then. He had assumed, as it was assumed for him, that he would go into his father's firm, Sutcliff Realty, after graduating from high school and college. The only questions that filled his life at that age were what kind of car he would have when he grew up, a Jaguar or a Porsche. Would he live in this house or build a new one for himself? Would his wife look like Marilyn Monroe or Elizabeth Taylor? Questions that occupied his thoughts for hours at a time, days.

On a whim, he pushed aside his shaving kit and the underwear he had unpacked but not yet put away and climbed—awkwardly, it wasn't nearly as easy to do now as it was then—up on the desk. He found, among other things, that his knees no longer fit comfortably drawn up under his chin, and that he had to shift around and sit on a couple of his folded T-shirts to accommodate his hip bones. *Oof,* I've got pains in places I never knew existed, the problem's not that I'm a middle-aged man, it's that I'm getting to be an old man, an old duffer. Lord, I never thought I'd have to say that, got to remember it's better than the alternative— but once he got himself settled the effect was the same as when he was a kid, like being the figurehead of a ship, or riding high above in the crow's nest, slung out over the edge of the bluff, hanging suspended above his hometown.

Below, the S-curve of the river wound between the fluffy tree-covered hills, defining the limits of the town; the rows of peaked roofs bit through the billowy green of the tree-lined streets like the cogs of so many gear trains. Down in the valley, the valley so low-oo-oo, he found he was singing to himself, I lost my true love, for courting so slow-oo-oo . . . Now, where do you suppose that came from? When he first arrived in the Bay Area to go to the University of California at Berkeley, the thing that struck him, disturbed him in some way, was the lack of trees, the uninterrupted planes of the rooflines—houses, garages, neighborhood stores—against the blue-white sky. It had taken some getting used to, that and the hills were brown instead of green, until the new landscape had begun to feel like his own. In the evenings during his first months in Berkeley, he went for long solitary walks in the neighborhood where he was living near Shattuck and Ashby, along the streets of small stucco bungalows, marveling at the differences to be discovered in the world—marveling at the views at twilight down the long sloping streets, views unimpeded by trees, of the darkening waters of the Bay, the distant lights coming on in San Francisco, and, beyond the latticework of the Golden Gate Bridge, the last sliver of the sun sinking into the Pacific.

It was on one of these walks that his life had changed. One evening after he had been living in Berkeley close to a year, he went out late for a loaf of bread. Around the corner from his apartment was a little shopping district, a Lucky Market and a hardware store, the local five-and-dime and the Elbow Room—and one storefront that had always been a mystery to him. At times he had seen lights inside, or heard someone banging around, but the large front windows were painted over and the double doors were always closed. This evening, however, the doors were standing open, and he could see some kind of work going on inside. As Harry Todd leaned in the doorway for a better look, a girl's voice said, "Come on in, if you want to."

It was dark right inside the door and he couldn't see who spoke to him, but he stepped in. She was sitting on a stool off to one side in the shadows, a girl a few years younger than himself, dressed in black toreador pants and an oversized paint-splattered sweater; she had one leg pulled up so her chin rested on her knee, giving him a dark view of her crotch.

"What is this?"

"This is art," she said serenely.

As he looked around, he realized it was a painters' studio. Canvases and framing materials were stacked against the walls; under the rows of overhead lights and a number of portable spotlights, several painters his age were at work in different areas of the large open space. Somewhere in the back, a phonograph was playing Charlie Parker. He felt awkward standing there and left after a few minutes. But the next night he went back and found the doors standing open again. The girl was again sitting in the shadows, her leg pulled up. When he walked in the door, she tilted her head to rest her cheek on her knee and smiled.

"I thought you'd be back."

"Why'd you think that?"

"I don't know. But you came back, didn't you?"

Her name was Laurel. She was still in high school—her father was a Nobel Prize–winning physicist who taught at the university—but she was friends with several of the painters and occasionally modeled for them. The studio belonged to one of the professors in the art department who let his students use it if they needed studio space. Harry Todd began going there in the evenings, talking with Laurel and getting to know the other students. In another context—say, if he had been there with the guys he grew up with on Orchard Hill—he would have mocked the goings-on, these shabbily dressed, long-haired young people splattering paint on canvases and then sitting around till all hours of the night drinking wine and discussing aesthetics and the ills of society; but as it was he found he felt comfortable at the studio; he enjoyed the company of people he would have otherwise thought were weirdos. And he enjoyed the introduction to things he wouldn't have otherwise thought to try: at first it was the cheap Red Mountain wine they bought in glass jugs, then the strong beers, Colt 45 and Rainier Ale. When they got to know him better, it was grass, hashish, mescaline. Over the months he began to let his hair grow, found an army field jacket at an army-navy store, combat boots.

The studio was an open door to a new way of life for Harry Todd. Whenever they had the chance, he and his new friends piled into Laurel's Citroën and traveled across the Bay Bridge to San Francisco; in North Beach the beatniks had pretty much passed their zenith, but there were still remnants of the original scene at Vesuvio's and the Co-Existence Bagel Shop and Le Trieste. He heard the followers of Ferlinghetti and Kerouac and Rexroth read at the Coffee Gallery; he sat in the basement of City Lights bookstore to read the latest art journals; he heard Miles Davis at the Blackhawk and Gerry Mulligan at the Jazz Workshop, and flamenco at La Bodega. Harry Todd never figured out if Laurel was sleeping with any of the other painters at the studio, but she began sleeping with him, staying over at his backyard cottage on Prince Street and leaving from there in the mornings for her classes at Berkeley High. After he graduated, he and Laurel set up housekeeping together, for a while in North Beach in San Francisco, then in Marin County, at first near Muir Beach, then farther north in the tall forests of Lagunitas, Harry Todd trying his hand at opening several shops catering to the counter-culture people they lived among—natural foodstuffs, drug paraphernalia, huaraches he brought up from Mexico—as well artworks, especially Laurel's paintings, for the weekend tourists who wanted to dip into the hippie lifestyle.

Mr. Todd's. Todd's Odds and Ends. Odd Todd's. I think there was another name in there too. What do you suppose got me thinking about all this? I was lucky to have stumbled into that other way of life, Laurel opened up so many things for me. Even if the drinking and the drugs did get the better of me eventually, I'm still drying out, I was lucky to have gone to California, Jennifer was right about that, otherwise I would have been buried here in Furnass, I never would have known what all was out there. But I guess it wasn't luck that got me there in the first place, was it? What did Father say to me? I'm setting you free. I'm giving you back your life. You have the opportunity to return the unused portion and get double your money back. Someday you'll thank me for this. Yes, Father, sure, thanks a lot.

*

When Harry Todd came in that evening the summer after he graduated from high school, his mother, busy cleaning out cabinets in the kitchen, said his father wanted to see him. At the time he thought it a bit odd, his mother working in the kitchen at that hour, but he didn't dwell on it; it was late, after eleven-thirty, and he wanted to go to bed. He had spent the evening as he did most evenings that summer, cruising the main street in his mother's car with his girlfriend Donna, her legs curled up on the seat, tucked in close beside him; later, after he dropped her off because she had to go to work the next day, he continued to make the circuit through town, listening to the radio, Porky Chedwick from Pittsburgh or Sill the Pill up on the Hill from Beaver Falls, then drove out to Shine's Pizza near Indian Camp for his usual, two cuts of pepperoni with anchovies and a glass of milk, before returning to town and calling it a night. As he stood at the sink drinking a glass of water, he watched his mother on the step stool, dressed incongruously in a pair of lederhosen, taking a peek at her pretty legs, before continuing through the downstairs. He left his mother's car keys on the monk's table in the front hall, and went on into the living room where his father was watching television.

He thought he knew what his father wanted to talk to him about; it undoubtedly had something to do with his school year coming up, the arrangements for his first year at the University of Pittsburgh. His father was sitting in his favorite overstuffed chair, one leg hooked up over the chair arm, watching a late-night Western; he had been drinking, there was the smell of alcohol about him, but that was nothing out of the ordinary, he usually smelled that way these days. Harry Todd stood beside his father's chair, but his father didn't acknowledge his presence. All the lights were on in the room, the chandelier of crystal teardrops, the sconces of electric candles above the fireplace, the table lamps his mother had made out of metal statues of early explorers and conquistadors. On the screen a group of good guys in white hats chased a band of bad guys in black hats through the mesquite; because of the age of the film, the outdated technology, everyone's motions were a little too quick. After a few moments when his father still hadn't said anything, Harry Todd turned to leave.

"Don't go away," his father said, still looking at the screen. "There'll be a commercial in a few minutes."

Harry Todd was getting impatient; he was sure whatever it was could wait till morning. Fortunately, in another minute, a commercial for a veggie chopper came on and his father turned toward him.

"Did you see Donna this evening?"

"Yeah," Harry Todd said, a little surprised. Donna wasn't usually a topic of conversation between him and his father. He wasn't so confident now that he knew what this was about.

"Did she say anything to you?"

"Anything . . . about what?"

"Anything that might be of interest to me."

"No. Why would she say anything that would interest you?"

His father shook his head, as if to say No reason. "And did you two have a nice time?"

"Yes. . . . Look, what's this all about?"

"Well, I'm glad you had a nice time. I'm afraid that's the last time you'll be seeing her."

"I know you don't like Donna because you think her family's not good enough or some bullshit reason. But I love her and I'm going to keep on seeing her as much as I want to and there's nothing you or anybody else can do to stop me . . . What?"

His father, unlike during their previous discussions about Donna—yelling bouts that had sent either father or son storming from the room—continued to sit there calmly, looking at him, as if studying him, a slight smile on his face, as if regarding the changing prices on a tally board.

"As a matter of fact, her family seem like very nice people. I didn't know if Donna said anything to you about it or not, or if she even knew. Though I'm sure she knows by now. I spent most of today talking to her father and mother. Yes, nice people. Very reasonable. Considering my son knocked up their daughter."

"Knocked up?" Harry Todd felt something give way inside him.

"She's having a baby. Presumably yours. And thank you for letting me know about it ahead of time. So I could be prepared for it."

"I didn't know. Her period was late this month and she went to the doctor but the tests aren't back yet. She didn't seem worried about it, so I wasn't either."

"The tests are back, all right. Dr. Neely called me yesterday, as soon as he got them. He thought I'd want to know, and he was right. And of course Donna wouldn't be worried. She assumes if she is pregnant that you'll be marrying her, which is what she wanted in the first place."

"You mean the doctor told you before he told Donna?"

"George Neely is an old friend. He knew there would be some arrangements to be made."

Harry Todd turned and started to leave the room. His mother was standing in the doorway to the hall, her arms folded around the straps of her lederhosen, as if holding herself in lieu of something else.

"Where do you think you're going?" his father said.

"Down to see Donna. I should be with her. . . ."

"Kitty," his father said.

His mother looked at Harry Todd regretfully. Then she went past him and placed her car keys in her husband's outstretched hand. His father held them up like a dead mouse by the tail, to make sure Harry Todd saw them, before sticking them in his pocket.

"Big deal," Harry Todd said. "So I'll walk downtown. It's not that far."

"And if you try it, I'll have the police pick you up."

"You think the police work for you?"

"Try me."

"Harry Todd, honey-lover, listen to your father," his mother said. "It'll be for your own good."

"What do you expect me to do? Just forget about Donna?"

"More or less, yes," his father said, looking at his nails for a moment, then back at Harry Todd. "It was one of the conditions I worked out today with Mr. and Mrs. Bruno. They don't want you to have anything to do with their daughter any more than your mother and I do. It seems you're not one of their favorite people, which is understandable, given the circumstances. This isn't what they hoped for their daughter, any more than it is what I hoped for my son."

"But what about the baby?"

"That's all been taken care of. George Neely found a nice place in Ohio for young girls in Donna's condition. They'll take good care of her, she can have the baby there, and afterwards they'll find a good home for it."

"All very neat and tidy. Out of sight, out of mind," Harry Todd said.

"That's right. Because I'm willing to pay to make it neat and tidy. Mr. and Mrs. Bruno agreed to let the matter drop as long as I was willing to take care of the financial end of things, and as long as I would guarantee that you wouldn't be seeing Donna anymore. I've even agreed to help Donna when she comes back to town, I said I'd give her a job at Sutcliff Realty. I don't have anything against the girl, actually I rather like her. I just don't like her with you."

"And what about me? How are you going to keep me from seeing her?"

"You, young man, are on your way to California. That was the other arrangement that needed to be made. It took some doing, some favors of friends of friends, but I got you enrolled at the University of California in Berkeley for the fall term. You'll be leaving in about a week, so you can find a place to live and get yourself settled before classes start."

"Suppose I don't want to go to California."

"It's not open to discussion. You have no choice."

"You'd have to tie me up and put me on the plane to get me away from here."

His father looked at him, as if measuring him, and smiled sadly. "Kitty, leave us."

"Harry," she said.

"I said leave us."

His mother looked at the two of them for a moment, then left the room, going upstairs. Slowly his father unwound himself from the chair. He was a big man, at one time athletic, though swollen now from too much alcohol, too much of everything.

"I'm not afraid of you," Harry Todd said, slighter in build than his father though in better shape, thinking he could take him.

His father grinned, deadly. "Do you think I'm going to fight you? Don't be ridiculous. I'm just standing up because I'm stiff from sitting too long."

He hobbled a few steps, as if to get his circulation moving again in his legs, though Harry Todd still didn't trust him.

"You can't do this. People aren't pieces of property that you can buy and sell at your convenience."

"That's pretty good," his father said. "You probably read it somewhere but that doesn't matter. It shows you know how to apply what you read. I know you're not used to working hard in school, your classes here never gave you much of a challenge. When you were younger I thought of sending you to a private school; I probably should have, but your mother wanted you at home. But no matter. Berkeley's a good school, you'll have to work your tail off out there, you won't be able to get by so easily. Actually, things are turning out better this way, you'll get yourself a better education than if you had gone to Pitt, though this isn't the way I would have gone about it."

"You can't make me go there. You can't make me forget Donna. I love her—"

"Don't talk like an idiot," his father said, and something in the way he said it stopped Harry Todd from going further.

His father stood in the middle of the room, to one side of the chandelier, the light washing down over him, accenting his scalp through his silver-white brush-cut hair, his flushed complexion, the broken blood vessels webbing his cheeks and nose. He looked down at the picture on the TV for a moment—the Western was starting again—his hands in his pockets, before looking at Harry

Todd again. He wasn't gruff now, he wasn't angry or threatening; his voice had a quiet intensity that was even more chilling.

"Forget all that talk about loving her, I know it isn't true and so do you. You're like me, whether you want to admit it or not. You like your piece of tail, the same way I do, you can't get enough of it. So tell me this: Are you ready to give up all those other girls because you now have a wife and kid? Because that's what's going to happen. Once you're a married man with a child, most girls are going to stay away from you. Are you really ready to limit your chances of finding a truly special girl? Are you really ready to give up having all the girls you want? And when you have a wife and family, are you ready to devote yourself to Sutcliff Realty? Because you're going to need all the money you can get to live the way you want to, the way you're used to living, and nobody else but me would be foolish enough to pay the kind of money you'll want. And forget about going to college because you're going to be too busy earning a living and changing diapers and taking the baby down to see Donna's folks. Are you really ready for those kinds of sacrifices? I doubt it."

His father let himself down easily, back into the chair again, hooking his leg again over the chair arm, like a kid who refuses to sit up straight. "I'm the best friend you've got right now, and you can't even see it: I'm getting you free of that girl. And I know you want to get away from her, even if you can't admit that either. She's wrapped herself so tightly around your ankles you can't move, and you don't know how to get loose and you're too bullheaded to admit you've made a mistake. You're tired of her and you think there's something wrong with you because you feel that way and you only know to go forward, to push and push and push, to insist that you're right with the hope that somehow you'll be able to drown out that part of you that knows you're wrong. And because you need something to push against you've made me the enemy because you can't stand the thought that she is. But the truth is she *is* the enemy, of everything you might want to do and everything you're capable of doing with your life. Her only goal in life is to have you sitting there beside her for the next forty or fifty years, keeping her company until you both wither away and die. Well, I'm setting you free, I'm giving you back your life. You have the opportunity to return the unused portion and get double your money back. What a deal."

"What makes you think you know so much?" Harry Todd said, his voice cracking, but still unable to give in, still unable to admit his father might know him this well. "What gives you the right?"

His father laid his head back in the crease of the chair, against the plump wing back, and closed his eyes. "Because I've been there. I'm there right now. I've been married to your mother for nearly twenty years, haven't I? The goddamnest longest war I've ever been in. I know what it's like, believe me."

Harry Todd's knees felt watery—no, it was more than that, he felt as if he were sinking through the floor, as if he were dropping into some endless space within himself, the known world gone forever, left far behind. Because his father was right, apparently he did know his son. Harry Todd must be more like him than he ever imagined. He was tired of Donna and had wanted to get away from her but he had been unable to say it, either to himself or to the world. Hearing it from his father was like having his innermost thoughts ripped from his heart and laid out in front of him. He felt vulnerable and shaky, and yet cleansed in some way. He turned and left the room in a daze, heading upstairs, up the dark staircase that led to the second floor and his room in the attic.

Later, in the months and years to come, as he grew increasingly embedded in his new life in California, as he grew increasingly distant and estranged from his family and the life he'd known growing up in Furnass—as he realized that the things he thought as a child would comprise his life as an adult, primarily taking over Sutcliff Realty and his father's position in the town, would never happen now, especially with the rise of his younger brother in his father's favor, now living the life Harry Todd thought he was supposed to, thought he was entitled to—Harry Todd came to see his sojourn in California as an exile, a maneuver of his father to get his oldest son out of the way in favor of the younger, for whatever reason, a trick of his father that his mother allowed to happen, raising no objection to prevent or stop it; but this night climbing up to his room at the top of the tower, the lights of the little mill town and the furnaces of the mill along the river filling the night, Harry Todd listened to another inner voice, one of wonder and apprehension—California. Wow, I'm going to California.

*

The late afternoon sky had grown hazy and the light yellowish, not buttery or golden, but ocherous, heavy, the hot murky melancholy light of southwestern Pennsylvania in summer, like no other he had experienced across the country. He thought about what his mother had told him during lunch. That she didn't know what Kathleen's death certificate said, or if there was an autopsy or not, because his father would never talk to her about such things. That she had no more idea of how Kathleen died than he did. He decided it was a good thing she didn't find an article on toenail fungus or alien death rays, she would have had Kathleen dying from one of those instead of a coronary thrombosis. And there's Julian Lyle again. What's he got to do with all this? I wonder if this is something I should know more about, I wonder if any of this is something I could use. . . .

A red-tailed hawk was making slow effortless circles over the hillside, riding the unseen currents of air, watching for darting movements below. From somewhere came the sound of crows. After a few more minutes, Harry Todd climbed down from the desk and, staggering a bit, easing his weight from one leg to the other until the sponginess went away, until his knees stopped aching and felt strong enough to support him, walked around the pile of boxes and suitcases in the middle of the room—if I'm going to be living with this monster for a while I should give it a name— and went over to the bed. His mother was right about one thing: he was totally exhausted, as if someone had pulled a plug and all his energy had drained out. He lay down and closed his eyes, listening to the sounds of the old house settling as the day began to cool, the occasional ticking of the woodwork, the creak of the joints, almost as if someone were moving about, almost as if someone were trying to move carefully on a staircase hidden in the walls. . . .

. . . and afternoon turns to evening, and evening to night in Furnass (pronounced by most people the way it looks, "Fur-nass," or even "Fern-ass," though there are those of the more proper sort who pronounce it "Furnace," following some inner dictum to set themselves apart from the harshness of the western Pennsylvania accent and the vaguely suggestive nature of the more common pronunciation, unaware that Furnace was supposed to be the name of the town in the first place except that the early citizen who made the first road sign to direct drovers with their wagons of firewood and coal and iron ore to the place couldn't spell and the misspelling stuck), which, now that the mills are closed, without the flames of the furnaces and the coke batteries, without the lights tracing the outlines of the mill buildings and the spotlights on the cranes and those in the switching yards and where the barges used to unload along the river, without the bustle of traffic in town from the change of shifts, daylight to swing, swing to graveyard, graveyard to daylight, a seemingly endless cycle of hundreds of cars and pickups coming and going through the narrow streets at three in the afternoon and eleven at night and seven

Some Rise

in the morning, some of the cars stopping at Isaly's and the 13th Street Dairy and Mikey's All-Niter, at the Triangle Tavern and the Reo Grill, the D&G and Smitty's Service, places that stayed open late and opened early to match the flow of traffic (a seemingly endless cycle, "seemingly" being the operative word because it did end), is more than an emptying of light, the darkness in the town is a palpable thing, a presence of its own, as if night is the natural world, broken only by an occasional pocket of light from a streetlight, the stoplights on the main street flashing warnings to themselves, a solitary porch light left burning late awaiting someone's return, and the world of daylight is an absence . . . as at Onagona Memorial Hospital, nurse Pamela DiCello leaves the nurses' station and squeaks down the hallway in her ridge-soled shoes to the Records Room, which she knows is unoccupied at this hour, and closes the door behind her and dials her home number to see if there are any messages on her answering machine, specifically, if there are any messages from Jack, but the only message is from Dickie Sutcliff saying that he'd like to take her up on her offer to see her townhouse, that he'd like to see her tomorrow morning if that is okay and asking her to call him at his office if she gets this message early enough, otherwise she can expect him a little after ten or so, as soon as he can make an important call and shake himself free from the office, and she hangs up the phone and looks around the darkened room crammed floor to ceiling with medical records, records of traumas and sorrows all listed neatly in the right boxes on the right forms, thinking It's always so easy to file somebody away and then call them out again when you need them, isn't it? thinking that nevertheless she'll see Dickie in the morning, that it's too late to call him now, he's home by this time, home with his wife, curious as to why he's decided to pay attention to her again but glad that he is, glad that somebody is . . . as in Highland Hills, the expensive suburb in the rolling hills beyond the town, Dickie Sutcliff sits alone in the darkened family room on the lower level of his sprawling split-level home, drinking the one tumbler of Johnnie Walker Black that he allows himself at home each night, the one tumbler on top of whatever other drinking he's done during the day or evening, his effort to keep his drinking under control so he doesn't end up sitting here drinking half the night, so he doesn't end up like his father—that bloated, blustery man, his face at the end of his life inflamed and cauliflowered and webbed with broken blood vessels, whose presence still haunts Dickie's life—sitting alone staring at the blanked-out television screen, putting off going upstairs as long as possible, putting off climbing into bed beside Tinker in case she's still awake, wondering if Pamela got his message this evening and if it's okay to see her tomorrow morning, deciding that even if she calls and says no he'll go out to see her anyway with the hope of convincing her otherwise—he wants to see her, to be with her, that badly—and remembers what she said today about Harry Todd, asking if he thought his brother had come back to claim a share of the business, and Dickie wonders if it's true, though he lacks the bravado he felt when he assured Pamela that he wasn't concerned, remembers when they were growing up that Harry Todd always got everything he wanted, the best toys and the best clothes and the best girls, and Dickie got what was available—he flashes briefly on the day he watched from the top of the stairs as Kathleen wearing only a towel after her shower went downstairs and on her way back up Harry Todd sitting in the living room reached out and pulled the towel from her body and they ended up rolling on the floor and Dickie ran back to his room and put what he witnessed away in a recess of his mind reserved for special hurts and mysteries and scores to settle— because everyone thought such things weren't important to Dickie, everyone said Dickie was so much easier to please than his fussy, demanding older brother, and he thinks Well, I guess everyone is in for a surprise, because guess what, I do want

*things, and I'm going to make sure I get them . . . as in her room
at the other end of the house, his daughter Jennifer sits crosslegged on her bed in her bra and panties listening to the Grateful
Dead's* Workingman's Dead *as she goes over the site plans for
the Furnass Landing development spread out over her coverlet,
making mental notes to herself on which buildings she thinks important to save now that her father told her this evening that he's
willing to consider saving some of them, ranking the buildings in
importance in her mind for her presentation to him tomorrow so
she can bargain with him if she has to, Okay, I can see where
you need that parcel of land where the old Riveting and Punching
Shop is, even though it's a wonderful example of a Fink truss roof
system, but that means you've got to save the Brass Foundry,
humming along with the Dead as they sing "Uncle John's Band,"
and thinks of her own uncle, making up new lyrics to sing along
with the chorus,*

> *Come hear Uncle Harry Todd's band,*
> *Playing for the dance.*
> *Got some things to talk about*
> *As he tries to get in my pants . . .*

*and smiles to herself, is flattered actually that he's interested, and
she has little doubt that he's interested, it's written all over him,
he might as well have a lump in his pants every time he looks at
her and for all she knows he does, and thinks Well, maybe so,
that would certainly be something out of the ordinary, wouldn't
it? and considers that even though he's an old guy by some
standards, an older guy—she can hear the girls she knew in college going "Ewww" at the idea—he's not that bad-looking for all
that, I'll bet he was a fox when he was younger, and he's undoubtedly seen and done a lot of things with a lot of different women,
considers that she might be able to learn something from him—*

Is it incest if you do it with your uncle?—as she unrolls another sheaf of drawings looking for the soil engineer's report . . . as in the big house on the edge of the bluff on Orchard Hill, Kitty wanders through the downstairs humming a 1930s show tune to herself, doing a few half-hearted glissades and pirouettes through the darkened rooms, watched by Merry Anne who lies on a Persian throw rug in the entryway between the living room and dining room, the cat barely lifting her head as Kitty glides past and Kitty stops and looks down at her and says, "It's coming back, isn't it, dear?" and the cat looks up at her and doesn't say anything and Kitty says, "Let's wait a little longer, to see if maybe it goes away again," and Merry Anne starts to get up and then appears too tired to move and puts her head back on the floor again and Kitty says, "That's okay, sweetheart, you rest now, I'll stop moving around so much," as she steps over her carefully and goes on into the dining room, goes to the shoebox-sized imitation treasure chest sitting on the end of the table and opens it and takes out the last group of photographs she laid out on the table, the ones she whisked away before Harry Todd had his lunch, hoping that he had a chance to see them, stands there as she shuffles them around in her hand a bit, trying different arrangements and groupings, then gathers them up with one swift motion like a blackjack dealer and puts them back into the chest, sifts through other pictures and papers inside until she finds what she's looking for, first a photograph of her husband Harry lifting her in his arms, holding her like a newly married husband about to carry his bride across the threshold though he actually never did that, cradling her that way however in the photograph, standing in the tiny backyard at his mother and father's house, a proud grin on his face, more in defiance to his mother's camera and her eye to the viewfinder than from any actual pride in his young wife, though Kitty will take even that semblance of pride now as she did then, lingering over the photograph longer than she means to before she lays it on the table and takes out a few more items from the chest, a set of two photographs, one of herself and one of Harry, from approximately the same period as the first photo, along with a letter that she takes from a sheaf of letters, the first letter in the stack that she slides out without undoing the bow because she knows it so well, a letter she wrote to Harry while he was away on one of his early business trips when he was setting up Sutcliff Realty, opening the letter to the third page and laying it out on the table with the photos, standing back to view this latest display as she says to herself Oh Harry Todd, maybe this will get you thinking, maybe this will help you see that love and hate are never as easy as they look . . . as on the third floor of the house Harry Todd is dead to the world from when he fell asleep on the bed earlier this afternoon, lying on his back until he is startled awake by a loud Crash!—Is it in his dream?—from the other end of the room: the room in darkness, there is only an oblong patch of light on the ceiling, the light coming in one of the tower windows from the solitary streetlight at the end of the dead-end street, and he looks around straining to determine what could have caused the noise—Did something fall? Is there someone there?—or if there was a noise at all, the collection of boxes and suitcases in the middle of the room like a dark cubist fantasy apparently still in place, nothing out of place that he can see—Is someone crouching behind it? Is somebody there? Don't be ridiculous—and he vaguely makes out the row of armoires lined against the wall of the dark room, the last armoire in the row that he would swear he left open before he went to sleep, which is closed now, and thinks It must have been Merry Anne again, the cat must have been fooling around and somehow slammed the door shut, but then realizes that the door to his tower bedroom is closed, that unless the cat is still here in the room with him it must have been something else that closed the door to the armoire, if something indeed closed the door to the armoire, and he switches on the light and sits up and calls, "Here, kitty-kitty-kitty," with a growing sense of uneasiness as it becomes apparent that there is no cat to be found in the room. . . .

11

Tuna salad, tuna salad, tuna salad. The words rang through Harry Todd's thoughts like a litany, the most beautiful words in the language. Or if not the most beautiful, the most satisfying, the words of his dreams. At least for the moment.

It had started, the litany, the craving, soon after he woke from his nap, put into motion by his remembering what his mother told him earlier, that there was some tuna salad in the refrigerator, the first echoes of the words in his mind, and then other words along with them . . . Made the way you like it with celery and onions—some good rye bread too—good for a sandwich a sandwich a sandwich . . . and continued, growing stronger by the minute, supplanting even the things his mother had told him during lunch, things that at the time sent his thoughts reeling . . . Oh no, dear, I don't know how Kathleen died, I only guessed it was a coronary thrombosis. Your father would never let me know about things like that, poor man . . . gaining momentum and intensity as he putzied around his room, made a half-hearted attempt to unpack his clothes and put them away in the dresser and armoires. When it was close to one o'clock in the morning, after he heard his mother finally come upstairs and turn off the light in her bedroom, Harry Todd tiptoed as quietly as he could—the old house creaked with his every step as he made his way down the stairs and through the second-floor hall, his movements telegraphed through the old woodwork, setting off chain reactions of crackling joints and creaking floorboards in distant rooms—Good grief, it's enough to wake the dead, that's not funny—downstairs to the kitchen and fixed himself the much anticipated tuna salad sandwich. On his way back through the darkened rooms of the first floor, sandwich in hand, carrying it back to his room in the attic so he could savor it without the threat of his mother interrupting him—Oh what he'd give now for a beer to go with it!—he noticed what appeared to be some new photographs laid out on the dining table. He turned on the lights, the grimy chandelier over the table, for a better look. I wonder what she's up to? Why is she laying them out this way? Is she just playing around? Or is she trying to get at something? Must be for me. But why?

There were three photographs and a letter. The first photo showed his father as a young man lifting his young wife in his arms. It was startling to see them in such an intimate pose, looking like lovers; Harry Todd had never thought of them this way, as being young and in love, though it seemed typical in a way, his father showing off, his mother playing the coquette. Of the two remaining pictures, one was of his father, a tall trim young man in his early twenties, dressed in what was probably a new suit, perhaps the first suit of his new business career, standing on a country road, somewhere in the hills beyond Furnass; the matching photograph was of Kitty also dressed to the nines, a laughing pretty young woman in a tailored fitted suit, the skirt short enough to show a sampling of her perfect legs, and a cloche hat with a half veil. Both photographs were taken at the same angle and distance to the camera, the figures standing in identical poses, though his mother appeared to be standing on a different country road, or a different section of the same road, than his father. A young couple, out for a Sunday drive, taking turns with the camera, delighted with themselves and who they were.

The letter was opened to the final page:

> . . . and today your mother and Doctor played with little Harry Todd while I took care of Kathleen. Her

earache or whatever was bothering her seems much better after Doctor gave her the medicine.

Now I'm up here in our room lying on my tummy on our bed. All I've got on is your old white pajama top and my legs are waving in the air and I'm thinking of you. I hope you get home soon and not just because you abandoned me to your parents—actually your mother is nicer to me when you're not here, and Doctor is Doctor.

Dearest as your letter today said—it takes you and me together for either of us to be happy and content and I'm hoping we'll be together in a few days. Things just aren't right when you're away. But oh we have grand times together, don't we lover?

I do love you so,

Kitty—Your Miss Pussy

Why on earth would she want to show me these? Yes, Harry and Kitty undoubtedly had a life together when they were first married, I never doubted that. Or did I? I guess I never did really consider their life together before. I guess they must have had one. . . .

He put the letter back in its place, slightly uncomfortable, as if he had witnessed something between his mother and father that he shouldn't have. For several minutes he studied the photographs, saddened for these faces frozen in time, wondering what happens to people, what happens to the love they start out with, where does love go? But such thoughts were depressing him—I don't suppose I did any better in my life, but at least I didn't have any children to let down in the process. It's probably a good thing I didn't have children, as far as that goes, there's every chance I wouldn't have done any better. I never thought of that before. He turned out the light again, stood in the darkness of the house—Woo, things sure do get dark when you turn out the lights, a bit of profundity there—waiting until his eyes adjusted, and, with shuffling steps, afraid of tripping over or stepping on the cat wherever she might be—Sorry, Mother, I squashed your cat—made his way out to the hall.

There was a woman in white sitting in the straight-backed rocking chair in the living room. He saw her out of the corner of his eye, only for a second; his first thought was that it was his mother, he was about to say I thought you were in bed, but she was gone, the chair was empty, it had never happened. Kathleen? He laughed to himself, he was really seeing things lately, buckets of blood, vaporous women, but his laugh carried little conviction. He must be having drug flashbacks, what else could it be, brought about by the stress of being home again, the stress of the uncertainties in his life. After checking one more time to make sure the chair was empty—it was, there was nobody there, never had been—he went on upstairs, sandwich in hand. On the second floor, the light from the single streetlight outside cast a dim glow in the windows of Kathleen's old bedroom, creating patches of vague leafy shadows on the walls. No question, a dark house. From the end of the corridor, at the front of the house, behind his mother's partly opened door, came the whir of the air conditioner in her room, the sound of her deep labored breathing. He had a momentary urge to peek in at her, but good sense prevailed. Oops, sorry, oh no, I didn't want anything, just wondered what my mother looked like in bed, that's all, ha ha. He went on around the corner and up the narrow stairs to the third floor.

He was halfway up the stairs when, at the periphery of his vision, a white shape crossed the hall in front of him, as if it had been looking in the door to his room, on the edge of light spilling out into the dark corridor, and heard him coming, flitting away down the side hallway. He hurried up the last few steps and peered after it, beyond the doors to the storerooms, into the total darkness at the end of the narrow hall. For the briefest instant he thought he saw the dim figure of a woman in white gossamer sliding away from him along the wall, fading, evaporating into nothing. He wondered if it could be the light from a car passing on the street. That's got to be it. No, it's a dead-end street, idiot. Maybe a car turning around? He realized he had squeezed his sandwich into a bread-and-tuna-salad wad.

Normally, he would have gone down the hallway to the bath-room, to get a towel to wipe off his hand. But tonight, all things considered, he thought he could live with a little mess on his fingers, he thought he would just go on into his room. Wishing that the door opened inward so he could wedge a chair against it.

PART TWO

12

When you're down just click your heels,
You'll be surprised how good it feels . . .

How did that go? One two three and one, kick, kick, backstep,
backstep, kick. . . .

Kitty stood at the sink in the kitchen, eating a banana, going
over some of her old dance routines in her mind as she listened
to Harry Todd move around on the second floor. He was trying
to be quiet but the creaking floorboards of the old house betrayed
him as he tiptoed along the hall, moving toward the front of the
house, making a survey from the doorways of the various rooms.
Now he must be in the doorway to Kathleen's old room, in the
middle of the house. Go on inside, dear, sit down on her bed,
touch some of her things. Maybe it will help. He hesitated—the
threshold to Kathleen's room creaked once as he leaned farther
in—then retreated, continuing back down the hallway to the
bathroom. The sound of his stream of urine hitting the water in
the toilet bowl was as strong as if he aimed at her head.

Lying on the floor near her food bowls across the room, Merry
Anne looked up at the ceiling where the sound was coming from.

"It's only Harry Todd, dear," Kitty said to the cat between
bites of banana. "Did you think it was spooks?"

Merry Anne lowered her head again and gave a slight whim-
per. Kitty could tell the cat was in pain, but the sound of Kitty's
voice seemed to soothe her so she kept talking.

"He was that way as a baby too. Always trying to be secretive
about everything, but as transparent as could be. Poor baby. Half
the time he wouldn't know himself what he wanted, he only knew
that he wanted something. The one who was genuinely secretive
was Dickie, though in a different way from how Harry Todd tried
to be. Dickie would not only know exactly what he wanted, but

he'd sit there watching you, confident that it would either come his way eventually or that he'd get up and go after it himself."

Merry Anne's eyes were closed, though the end of her tail flicked slightly like a blind worm seeking a direction.

As Harry Todd finished in the bathroom and tiptoed back down the hall toward the stairs, Kitty whispered to Merry Anne, "I wonder if he's trying to avoid being seen, or trying to avoid seeing me?"

The cat kept her own counsel.

Kitty looked around to make sure she hadn't left any telltale signs, then tiptoed herself, still carrying the half of banana, into the shadows of the walk-through china cupboard, a shortcut that led from the kitchen to the dining room. It's dark in here, he probably won't come this way, as jumpy as he is about being in the house in the first place, he'll probably go through the dining room. If he does come this way, he'll run into me in the dark, scare him to death. Think he's seen a ghost. She tiptoed on through the doglegged closet to the other doorway—she imagined herself mimicking him step for step, the mirror image, he on the upper floor, she on the lower—to where she could look across the hall to the dining room. This way I can see what he thinks of the things I left for him.

She could hear him coming down the stairs, trying to ease himself from one tread to the next, though the old house creaked and groaned like a ship under sail. He really is trying to sneak out without seeing me. The poor dear. He'd make far less noise, seem less obvious, if he'd walk normal. Peeking around the door-frame, keeping in the shadows of the china cupboard, she watched him step into the front hall and look around, checking to see if anyone was about, and continue to tiptoe into the dining room. On the table were the items she had left out for him yesterday, the pictures of her and Harry when they were first married and the letter where she talked about lying on the bed in nothing but

Harry's shirt. Harry Todd glanced at the display on the table and kept moving through the dining room. Well, so much for that. Kitty tiptoed, smiling sadly to herself at the absurdity of the little game, back through the darkness of the cupboard to where she could see him come into the kitchen.

After looking around and evidently deciding that she was gone from the house, Harry Todd relaxed; he went to the refrigerator, drinking some orange juice from the half-gallon container. Your children grow up, and they don't grow up. Merry Anne was watching him, still lying stretched out on the floor, her tail beating slightly as if to some unheard song.

"Hello, cat," Harry Todd said, carefully stepping over her on the way to the sink. "If she asks, say you didn't see me, okay?"

If I answer in a little cat voice, Okay, Harry Todd, he's liable to die on the spot.

From the bowl of fruit on the drainboard, Harry Todd took an apple and two bananas. He looked around guiltily and hurried out the back door.

My son, my son, what have I done?

After he left, she went on into the kitchen, standing back from the sink so he wouldn't see her, watching as he headed down the back walk. Before he got to the garage, he stopped and considered something; he looked back at the house a moment before heading off across the grass, circling toward the front of the house. Kitty hurried through the downstairs to the living room, where she could watch from the angled windows of the tower as he walked briskly across the front yard. He was on his way to the wooden stairs at the edge of the bluff when he stopped and looked back at the house.

What? What is it he sees, or thinks he sees? What is he looking for?

Then he was gone, down the stairs, into the woods.

She realized she still had the banana in her hand, holding it in front of her like a small torch. She peeled it the rest of the way and ate it as she continued to stand at the windows, looking out at the rolling contours of the front yard, the robins listening for the sounds of scrapings in the earth, a grinnie sitting at the base of the sycamore tree biting at a flea. Then she closed the drapes in the room for the day and, carrying the peel like a limp rag, went back to the dining room, humming to herself,

> When you're blue go tap, tap, tap,
> Take a bow and tip your hat . . .

Merry Anne had tried to follow her through the house but had given up; she lay in her favorite spot on the scatter rug, on her side, legs curled as if falling through space forever.

"That's a good place for you, dear. You rest now. If it's not better by tomorrow, we'll go to the vet's."

The cat flapped her tail once in acknowledgment as she appeared to doze.

Kitty closed the drapes in the dining room as well, then regarded in the half-light the display on the table.

"Either he saw it already in the middle of the night sometime, or it didn't make much of an impression on him. Either way, I guess I'll try laying out another. At this point, knowing the way he feels about me, what else can I do?"

Merry Anne opened her eyes and looked at Kitty, blinked, her face like a strange flower among the tendril patterns of the rug.

13

There were the morning songs of robins and the intricate trills of finches, the whistle of cardinals and the rasping of jays, the chirping of sparrows and Lord knew what all from the mimicky starlings; from the eaves of the house came the cooing of pigeons, from a nearby branch of a sycamore came the plaint of a mourning dove—a pigeon in tweeds to Harry Todd's mind—from the woods came the drumming of a woodpecker, and crows, of course, always somewhere the crows . . . the collective twitter-warble-squawk of the birds of summer, sounds Harry Todd wasn't used to hearing having lived within earshot of one California freeway or another for the past twenty years, sounds that he wasn't even sure he remembered from when he grew up here. God, what an unholy racket at this hour of the morning. No wonder everybody's slightly screwy around here, all these birds are enough to drive you batty. . . .

As he crossed the front lawn, clipping through the dew-soaked grass, heading toward the steps that would take him down the bluff, he could see glimpses of the remains of the mill through breaks in the trees, trucks and heavy equipment moving about like ants working on a carcass. He wondered if Jennifer was there, clomping around in her work boots and hardhat, her long metallic-auburn hair down her back, slobbered over by every workman who saw her . . . Don't start this, don't start thinking about her all the time, wondering what she's doing and what she meant by what she said and if she ever thinks of you because she doesn't, you go through this every time a pretty girl even looks at you. . . . He stopped at the top of the steps and looked back at the house.

The sun was to the right of the tower, setting the orange-brick facade in shadow, the shadow of the house elongated out across the lawn. In the angled windows of the living room he thought he saw his mother, just a glimpse of her, before she disappeared again, back into the shadows of the interior. A moment earlier, on his way to the garage before he decided to walk downtown instead of taking his car, he thought he saw her at the kitchen window too. When he came downstairs this morning she wasn't around and he assumed she must be out somewhere; either she was playing hide-and-seek with him or he was still seeing things. Great. Now I'm seeing ghosts of people who aren't even dead. Afraid to look at the house again for fear of seeing someone or something else, he plunged down the wooden steps.

There were a hundred steps to get away from home. One hundred exactly, broken up into sets of twenty, with a small wood platform at each level, that led from the edge of Orchard Hill down to the main part of town. He knew this number for a fact, having walked the steps every morning for the better part of five years, on his way to junior high school and the first years of senior high. Not to mention the years as a child when he played on this hillside, scrambling over the bluffs and running up and down these stairs all day long. What he hadn't considered when he thought of walking downtown was that he was younger then. *That means there are a hundred steps to get back home too. If the old adage is true: what goes down must come back up. It's not even the heat of the day yet either, and I'm already wearing out. I may live to regret this, if I live through it at all. I can see the headline: "Prodigal Son Succumbs to Steps." Willow, weep for me? My mistake, madam, you're a red oak.*

At the bottom of the steps he stopped and leaned against the wood railing to catch his breath and ease the pain in his ankles and calves—*The girls in Furnass should have the best-developed legs in the world*—before continuing, out across the brick-paved street along the base of the bluffs. Away from the woods on the hillside, the covering trees and the heights of Orchard Hill, he felt exposed, vulnerable, in foreign territory. He wondered if he had felt this way when he was growing up here but never realized it at the time, thinking it was the way things were supposed to be. He looked up at the top of the bluffs but he couldn't see his family's house from this angle. Screwing up his courage, he continued along the narrow streets—*I've got to go through with it, if I'm going to find out anything about what happened to*

Kathleen. Why would anyone be afraid of a place called home? Why would anyone in their right mind not be?—the sidewalks lumpy from tree roots pushing up through the cement and paving brick, toward the main part of town. Feeling as if he were taking the first steps on a journey of a thousand miles.

14

As soon as she was nineteen years old and had graduated from high school, Kitty Sutcliff, who was then Kitty Todd, the star of Miss Abigail's School of Dance in Rome, New York, boarded a train for New York City to realize her dream of becoming a Rockette.

Two years earlier, in the spring of 1933, Kitty's father, a well-to-do shoe manufacturer in Rome, took the family down to Manhattan to see why everyone was talking about the new Radio City Music Hall. Kitty, who was seventeen at the time, already knew she wanted to be a dancer and had studied with Miss Abigail since she was seven. But she hadn't known what kind of dancer she wanted to be until she saw the Rockettes in the live show that followed the feature, *King Kong*. The precision dancing, the gorgeous costumes, the opulence of the stage itself shaped like a golden sunset—it seemed like the chance to live the life of a Busby Berkeley movie. Besides, everyone said she had the legs for it. From that day forward, she had her heart set on being a Rockette, and nothing else would satisfy her.

When she arrived in New York City, she found out that there were a few things that Miss Abigail hadn't taught her. Kitty realized this at her first Music Hall audition, where she discovered that there were a lot of young girls with the same dream as her own—a lot of young girls who were better dancers. Still, the Rockettes thought she had promise—there was still the matter of her great pair of legs—and told her to come back when she had a little more training. For the next year she took every dance class she could find between waitressing jobs, and at her next audition the Rockettes welcomed her into the fold. Soon she was onstage two and three times a day, pretending to be locked in the near-touch embrace of the girl on either side of her, kicking her legs in the trademark eye-high kick with the long row of girls, proud of her position in life as the tenth girl from the left.

Kitty had the misfortune of learning early in life about the emptiness that often occurs when your dreams come true. She loved being a Rockette—she loved the camaraderie with the other girls, she loved being a part of something so exciting and grand, she loved being in the spotlight while among the safety of numbers. The question was: Okay, now what? Having attained her goal, it now seemed rather shallow (she also had the misfortune of being intelligent). She saw what happened to dancers in New York when they got older and she didn't want to end up like that, struggling against the ravages of age and loss of muscle tone. Being a chorus girl was one thing, but being an ex–chorus girl was quite another.

As the years danced on, her disillusionment grew. "Don't worry, Kitty," the other girls said, "someday some guy will come along and sweep you off your feet." That seemed unlikely, given the way her life was going. Sure, a lot of the girls met nice men—nice *rich* men—and quit the stage to get married, but those were the girls who went out after the shows and spent a lot of time in clubs. Kitty wasn't much of a party girl, as it turned out; she liked to have a good time as much as the next girl, but the fact was she was becoming rather bookish. She found she would much rather curl up in a corner with a good book than spend her time away from the Music Hall meeting businessmen from Saint Louis and would-be producers from LA. Her future wasn't looking very promising.

Then one night as she was leaving the Music Hall, a young man came toward her. There were always men waiting in the alley outside the stage door after the shows—along with the families of starry-eyed little girls like she had once been—but Kitty had given up long ago any idea that these male admirers were there to see her. This young man, however, seemed intent on speaking to her. He walked right up to her, a broad smile on his broad handsome face, a dozen roses in his hands, and said, "You're the tenth girl from the left."

His name was Harry Sutcliff. She had to admit that she was a little disappointed that he wasn't a financier or movie mogul—he was a college student a few years younger than herself from a small mill town in western Pennsylvania—but he was good-looking and had a certain air of confidence and bluntness about him that she found appealing. He told her that he had been in school at a college in his hometown when he got fed up with it and left to come to New York, both to see the sights and to sort out what he wanted to do with his life. He had been in town about a week; the first night he was there he had seen her in the show, and he'd been back every night since to see her again. He figured he had to speak to her tonight if he was ever going to; his money had about run out, he wouldn't be able to come to any more shows. As it was, he had spent several days' room money on the roses.

The other girls oohed and aahed over him appreciatively when he was standing in the alley again the next night, and Kitty's roommates took to him like a younger brother. Harry was tall and muscular with a blunt face, melancholy blue eyes, and short blond hair that covered the top of his head like peach fuzz. Besides being self-confident, he knew how to use his charm. When Kitty's roommates learned of his quickly dwindling funds, they invited him to stay with the four of them in their little apartment, extending his money so he could remain in New York a few weeks longer. Kitty was aware that a couple of the girls were hoping he might become interested in them instead of her, but Harry had eyes for only Kitty. And his feelings toward her were more than brotherly.

*

In the time that Harry was in New York, he had come up with a plan. He told Kitty that being in New York had broadened his perspective, that he had become aware of what was going on in the world at large. It was 1937. Germany had violated the Treaty of Versailles and instituted military conscription; its troops had occupied the Rhineland and were looking threateningly at Poland; moreover, Hitler had placed the Gestapo above the law, stripped the Jews of their rights, and was said to have a plan to invade the whole of Europe to provide the right environment for his master race. At the same time, Italy under Mussolini had invaded Ethiopia, and Japan was ravaging the Chinese mainland. Harry's newfound interest in current affairs—acquired strictly from reading the newspapers in coffee shops—convinced him that it was only a matter of time before there would be a new world war. Which meant that the United States would inevitably be drawn into it . . . which meant a need for more steel. The steel mills in his hometown of Furnass and around Pittsburgh had started to recover from the recession that followed the Depression and orders were flowing from Europe for arms and war supplies; Harry reasoned that it could only get better. Which meant the mills would be hiring more workers . . . which meant more workers would be moving to the area . . . which meant that these new workers would be looking for places to live. . . .

Harry's idea was to go back to Furnass and open a real estate agency. His father was a respected doctor in town, and Harry was sure he could use his good name to get financing from the local banks. His idea was to buy up and remodel as many houses as he could get his hands on, dividing them into two- and three- and four-family dwellings. If anyone wanted inexpensive housing in Furnass, they would have to come to Sutcliff Realty.

It was an ambitious plan. One that Kitty questioned in terms of its morality, for one thing. "Won't you be taking advantage of people? Won't you be making money from their desperation for a place to live?"

"Let me get this straight. You get up onstage twice a day and kick your legs to show off your crotch, and you're questioning my morals?"

She had to remind herself that his bluntness was one of the things she liked about him. He had all the graciousness of a constipated bull, but his certainty and sureness of himself were refreshing—he didn't so much sweep her off her feet as swept her along in his wake for a few weeks. There was never any question about Harry as to what he liked or disliked. Or what he wanted.

Then he was gone, back to Furnass to start his business, leaving Kitty to her life again. When in a few weeks she went to the doctor and found out she was pregnant, she wasn't really surprised; she had never been pregnant before but she guessed this was what it must feel like. She wrote to Harry right away to tell him, and to tell him what she planned to do about it; one of her roommates knew a doctor who took care of such things. Kitty didn't actually come out and ask him for money, and she wasn't particularly disappointed when she didn't hear from him. She wasn't asking anything from him, she didn't want anything from him; their time together had been a pleasant interlude, but it was over now, that was that. She went on ahead and made the arrangements with the doctor on her own. Then the night before she was to have the procedure, she came out of the theater and found him standing among the crowd at the stage door. He walked up to her with the same certainty he had the first time, a smile on his handsome face, a dozen roses in his hand, and said, "You're the tenth girl from the left. Will you marry me?"

It didn't promise to be the way she always imagined her married life would be, and he wasn't the type of man she always imagined herself married to. But here he was, almost as if he had planned it all from the beginning, ready to take her back to Furnass, ready to give her a life more of his choosing than of hers. But she decided to take it. She had not only been singled out from a line of girls, she was wanted enough to come back for; she didn't expect that would happen many times in her life. Within a few days they were on a train heading west.

Harry had talked a lot about his home—the mills, the smoke, the chains of little towns tucked away among the valleys—so she thought she knew what to expect. But nothing he said could have prepared her for what she found. Approaching Pittsburgh at midday, they were plunged into darkness as heavy as night, a world where all the lights were on at noontime and thick sulfurous smoke drifted through the narrow streets of the little towns along the right-of-way, a world where the day flickered variously orange and yellow and red from the false sun of the furnaces and coke ovens beating against the heavy air before turning into false night. As the train wound along the Monongahela River, past towns with names like Monessen and Donora, Rankin and Homestead, past the mills with names like Clairton and Duquesne and Edgar Thomson that muscled in close to the tracks and the river, Harry leaned over, looking past her out the Pullman window at the fiery scene, and said with something like affection in his voice, "Someone once called it *Hell with the lid off.*"

Kitty studied the side of his face for a moment, then turned back to the smudgy window. She would agree with the part about Hell, all right; her concern was that the lid seemed very much in place.

15

Naked except for the white terry cloth towel draped over his groin, Dickie sat on the living room floor of the townhouse, one leg folded under him, one leg stretched out beside the tray of coffee and toast and pickled herring. Pamela came back from the kitchen, a sheet wrapped around her toga-style, with a pair of long-handled forks.

"This always seemed to me the height of elegance. Or maybe the depths of depravity." She folded her legs and dropped straight down, effortlessly, the sheet billowing out with air. "Pickled herring in the morning. Yum."

"The 'elegance' part would probably mean more to me if you had a little more furniture in here."

"Hmm," she said, her mouth full of toast, looking around. The room was empty except for the white wall-to-wall carpeting and a cardboard packing box, with the word *Mayflower* on the side and the stylized logo of a sailing ship, on which she had placed a black-shaded Stiffel lamp and the phone. Pamela put down her coffee cup and leaned over to reach a catalog on the makeshift coffee table. "Let me show you what I'm going to get."

As she stretched to reach the catalog, the sheet pulled open to expose her upper thighs. "Looks to me what I already got," Dickie said.

She swatted at him as she sat upright again. "Animal." She held up the catalog so he could see the cover—*Ethan Allen*—opened it to a well-thumbed page, and held it up again to show him a picture of a sofa. It was a full-sized, overstuffed sofa with rounded arms, taupe-colored, covered with a fabric not really rough but with occasional tutfs and snags for added texture.

"Isn't it handsome? That will be my first purchase for the living room. Then there's an overstuffed chair and an ottoman to go with it."

Dickie decided he didn't like pickled herring in the morning, especially without a stiff drink to wash it down—he could feel the heartburn starting already—but he speared another piece from the jar, waiting for the liquid to drain off before he popped it into his mouth.

"Let me get it for you."

"What?"

"The couch. Let me get it for you. It'll be a housewarming present."

"First of all, it's not a couch, it's a sofa. And second of all, thanks but no thanks." Pamela looked at the picture one last time, then snapped the catalog closed and laid it on her lap. "I'll get it myself. I've got it all figured out. I've only got a few more payments to the anesthesiologist for my dad's operation, then I'm in the clear."

"I don't see why you should have to wait for it if you want it. I'm the guy who can get it for you right now. It would be no big deal for me."

"That's the point: It *is* a big deal for me. That's why I want to do it myself. Sometimes things are even more special because you have to wait for them," Pamela said, patting the cover once for emphasis. As she skated the catalog back across the carpet in the general direction of the cardboard coffee table, the sheet draped over her shoulder became undone, slipping down.

Dickie leaned over, took his index finger and moved aside a curl of black hair from her neck, then brushed his lips along the line of her fine broad shoulder, her soft soft olive skin. "You know me, I don't like to wait for anything."

She pulled back to look at him and gave him a coy, questioning smile. He moved closer, moved against her and she lay back on the floor, unwrapping the sheet to welcome him, spreading it wide to wrap them together, cocoon-like.

"Yes, I know you," she giggled as he came inside her again. "Mr. Appetite."

16

"So, you finally decided to come back home," Julian Lyle said, sitting at his desk, leaning back in his high-backed leather chair and folding his hands in front of him, pointing the tips of his index fingers against each other and tucking the rest of his fingers underneath themselves, like the old children's game, Here is the church, and here is the steeple. . . , peering at him across the reach of his stately old walnut desk. "How long has it been? Twenty years? Twenty-five?"

"Something like that," Harry Todd said.

"And to what do we owe this great honor?" Lyle said, chuckling to himself, as if pleased with his own cleverness, as if pleased beforehand at what he was about to say. "To what auspicious occasion do we credit our good fortune?"

"You haven't changed a bit, Julian."

Harry Todd sat across from the desk, in one of the cushionless curved wooden office chairs, trying to make his unruly hip bones conform to the molded seat, the bumps of his spine fit between the slats of the arcing back. The initial good feeling he experienced at seeing an old childhood friend—Julian was Dickie's age, a few years younger than Harry Todd, more of Dickie's friend than Harry Todd's, though all the kids from Orchard Hill hung out together at one time or another—bringing back a flood of pleasant memories, quickly dissipated as he remembered the traits that made him dislike Julian at an earlier age. The smugness, pedantry, pretentiousness. In a teenager those traits had made Julian Lyle an eccentric, offbeat, one of the gang but not a close friend—how did Bryce, Lyle's next-door neighbor, ever put up with him all those years?—someone you could tolerate as long as it was in small doses. In a man approaching his fifties, however, those traits seemed merely smug, pedantic, pretentious. Foolish.

Lyle's office was dark, with only a wedge of midmorning sunlight spilling across the carpet from a tall bare window, having fought its way down between the rear of the other buildings along the alley. The office had all the trappings of a successful and established law firm—the heavy walnut furniture, the glass-door barrister bookcases, the green-shaded desk lamp. The problem was that the office was located inside the old Alhambra movie theater, at the end of an arcade of small boarded-up shops and boutiques, the cutout plywood storefronts painted to look like the stalls of a Middle Eastern marketplace, Lyle's failed attempt to convert the interior of the building into a mini-mall, a shoppers' bazaar. On the wall behind Lyle was a large rendering of the Keystone Steam Works during its heyday at the turn of the century, the company Lyle's great-grandfather had started in town, the company Lyle's father had steered into bankruptcy. It reminded Harry Todd of where the furniture came from: it was part of the few things that Lyle's father had managed to salvage when the company went under; Harry Todd had seen it squeezed into the Lyles' tiny house when he was a kid.

"Those were the days, weren't they?" Lyle said from the gloom beyond the desk lamp. In the glow of the lamp, Lyle turned his hands over, revealing his spiky interlaced fingers . . . Open the door and see all the people. "We had some good times, growing up on Orchard Hill, didn't we?"

"Yes, I guess we did."

"I think about those days a lot. There was something special about growing up on the Hill, you know? Maybe it was the presence of the college, and the fact we had kids from families from all walks of life. I don't know. I've never been able to put my finger on it. But the result was a very special time."

Of course you'd think a lot about those times. They were undoubtedly the highlight of your life, you had a ready-made audience for all your crackpot ideas because we didn't know any better, we were stuck with you as a friend because you lived among us, we thought that's the way the world was, you've probably never had anyone since who would pay any attention to you.

"Do you remember," Lyle went on, "those wars we used to have with the kids from downtown? Everybody scrambling over the bluffs below your house winging crabapples at each other. It's a wonder somebody wasn't seriously hurt. Those things could have put out an eye."

"It's a wonder anyone ever lives through childhood," Harry Todd said, thinking It's a wonder anyone ever lives it down.

"You were always getting into something," Lyle said. "You and your family's cars. You certainly did your best to sow your wild oats."

"And you did your best to talk us to death. You found the perfect career for yourself, as a lawyer."

"Yes, I did, didn't I? Interesting, where life's little vicissitudes take us."

Harry Todd ignored the sarcasm of the remark, the veiled or maybe not-so-veiled put-down, remembering something else from the time they were kids: the folded, well-worn sheets of notebook paper, the story Julian had read somewhere and copied out in his meticulous handwriting to pass around, the story of a teenage brother and sister home alone one hot summer afternoon while the girl is taking a shower and comes out of the bathroom wearing only a towel and happens to look in her brother's room and sees him lying naked on his bed, his penis flopped up on his stomach and she goes in and sits on the edge of the bed and says Hi, and he says Hi, and she says What are you doing? and he says Nothing, and she says Were you playing with yourself? and her brother blushes and says Yeah, I was going to, and she says Can I do it for you? and takes his penis in her hand and it grows suddenly firm and erect but instead of stroking it she bends down and starts to lick it. . . ; he remembered the guys passing around the story in study hall and even giving it to some of the girls, but when they passed it to him and he started to read it he couldn't finish it, it seemed too dirty, and he quickly passed it on, but then a week or so later Kathleen asked him if he had read it, someone had passed it around in their study hall too, and Harry

Todd asked her what she thought of it but Kathleen only giggled and blushed and wouldn't say anything more about it, though for a few days afterward she kept watching him funny. . . .

Lyle seemed to be musing about something, as if he hadn't yet determined what he wanted to say, or found the way to say it.

"I see your mother around town now and then. She seems to be getting along very well."

"She's strong as an ox. She'll probably bury us all."

"Yes. Hmm." Julian folded his hands judiciously under his chin, looking either learned or coy. "And your brother has certainly put on the mantle of power in this town left by your father, hasn't he? It seems to suit him well, I might add."

So that's what this is about. Just had to get a dig in about my brother. Rub my nose in how successful Dickie is. Well, I'm not going to play.

"I took a tour of Furnass Landing. It's quite a project."

"Yes, your brother should do very well for himself with that one," Lyle said, examining his nails.

Don't let him get to you. That's what he wants. Just ignore him.

"There are some great old buildings down there. Some real architectural gems. I was surprised."

Lyle was obviously thinking about something else. Harry Todd went on, trying to make small talk; he thought he'd put in a good word about Jennifer's ideas, he liked to think he could help her in some way, though he was unsure how much influence Lyle had with Dickie.

"Too bad they can't save more of the historic buildings while they're at it. A lot of the old Keystone Steam Works buildings are still down there too, aren't they?"

"Hmm," Lyle allowed.

"Maybe they should turn the whole place into an industrial museum. I would think there would be more money in tourists paying to see something like that than in any new business you could bring to town. You could probably get government grants to help finance it."

"You think so? Do you think that many people would be interested?"

"Sure. It's a shame to see all that history go to waste. It happens all the time in California, developers come along and destroy the very buildings that give an area its character. And like it or not, that mill is what defined this town, it exemplifies an entire way of life. If you made the place into an industrial museum, people would flock to it. You'd attract the same crowds that visit Colonial Williamsburg to see college kids on their summer breaks go through the motions of making candles and cobbling shoes."

Harry Todd was proud of himself: it sounded like a great idea, it had come to him all of a sudden. He'd have to remember to tell Jennifer about it, something for her to propose to her father. Lyle had swiveled in his chair to an oblique angle; he studied Harry Todd, looking around the side of his hands folded in front of him as if peering around a corner.

"Who gave you your tour of the place? I'll bet it wasn't Dickie."

Just can't let it go, can you, Julian? You just have to dig. "As a matter of fact it was Jennifer."

Lyle nodded, swiveling back and forth a couple of times. "Jennifer. Of course. Attractive girl, isn't she? Though I always get the feeling that if you say the wrong thing to her, she'll slug you." He consulted his folded hands a moment, propped up in front of his chin as if on two legs of a tripod. "Did you happen to see my secretary when you came in?"

"No, there was nobody out there."

"That's too bad," Lyle smiled to himself, as if he knew a secret. "She'd probably interest you."

They just won't let you forget, will they? They just won't let you put things behind you. Small-town life, small-town minds. He thinks girls are still the only thing I think about.

Lyle surprised him by standing up abruptly, signifying that, at least from his point of view, the conversation was over. Is he right? Are girls still the only thing I think about? Harry Todd stood, but there was still the subject that brought him here.

"There's something I wanted to ask you."

"Certainly. What can I do for you?" Lyle said, coming around the desk and putting his hand on Harry Todd's shoulder, walking with him, guiding him in the direction of the door, to make sure Harry Todd knew he was on his way out.

"I was hoping you could tell me what my sister died of."

Lyle had been leaning toward him, head inclined, as they walked together, as if to concentrate on whatever Harry Todd had to say, patrician; now Lyle stopped and stiffened, looking at Harry Todd head-on. Lyle took his hand from Harry Todd's shoulder.

"Why would you ask me?"

"I understand you were involved with some of the details after she died. That your office handled them."

"Well, yes. I was your father's attorney at the time. Just as I'm supposed to be Dickie's now. Your father and mother were understandably upset and didn't want to have to deal with such issues. As the family's—or at least the business's—attorney, I was able to help make sure all the documents were in order and went through the proper channels. I like to think I eased their burden somewhat."

He's defensive, backpedaling already, and all I did was ask him a simple question.

"It may sound odd but I never heard the exact cause of death. Mother and I were talking about it yesterday, but she doesn't seem to know for sure either. She says she never saw the death certificate. And I was out there in California at the time. Over the years I guess I assumed some things about what I thought must have caused it, but now I'm not so sure."

"What did you assume she died of?"

"I thought it must have had something to do with her asthma. That seemed the logical thing. Then yesterday Mother told me Kathleen died of a coronary thrombosis, but it turned out she only thought that because she read something in a magazine. It seems incredible that she doesn't know for sure how Kathleen died."

"It's more common than you think. Very few people ever learn the exact cause of death when someone close to them dies. As for Kathleen, it could have been any number of things."

"What's that supposed to mean?"

Lyle sighed and closed his eyes momentarily, as if trying to summon his patience. "The death certificate said she died of natural causes. The exact term used in the autopsy report was *cardiac arrhythmia.*"

"So there was an autopsy."

"Who said there wasn't?"

"Nobody. Mother wasn't sure whether there was or not."

"Yes, there was an autopsy. . . ."

"So Mother was right in a way."

"What about?"

"You said cardiac arrhythmia, so Kathleen did die of a heart attack. It just wasn't a coronary thrombosis."

"Not necessarily," Lyle said, apparently feeling on firmer ground again, cracking a smile at Harry Todd's naïveté. "I'm afraid *cardiac arrhythmia* is a term pathologists use when they can't find any other reason for the cause of death. It's sort of a catchall phrase, I've run across it a number of times in these instances."

You just can't resist showing off, can you, Julian? Even about something like this. "How can they do that?"

"Well, most of the time no one questions the findings. And if they are questioned about it later, whoever signs the death certificate says, 'Well, I did this before I got the results back from the laboratory, sorry.' And there's no way to disprove it. . . ."

"No, I mean how could they not find the reason why she died?"

"Oh . . . well, your sister wasn't very strong, and eventually one system or another must have failed. I remember Dr. Neely saying that your sister wasn't a very stable piece of protoplasm—his words. A bit cold and detached, I agree, but probably accurate from a pathological point of view. More than likely, she died from a combination of things, and they were never able to pinpoint any particular one." Lyle wagged his head, regretful of Harry Todd's lack of understanding, as he tried to continue to move him toward the door. "Unfortunately, things aren't always as clear-cut in this world as we would like them to be."

"Thank you, Counselor. I never knew that before," Harry Todd said, not budging.

"If I were you, I would let the dead stay buried at this point."

I wish I could. Somebody tell that to Kathleen. A nervous smile passed over Harry Todd's face at his unfunny private joke.

Lyle walked on, through the door into the outer office, leading Harry Todd by example, looking around his secretary's office.

"So, you didn't see my secretary when you came in."

"You asked me that."

"Yes, yes, that's right." Lyle smiled, palming the top of his salt-and-pepper crew cut, patting it like a man ringing for someone to come carry his bags.

Christ, Julian, let it go. I can see you're a big important man in town who even has a secretary.

"Fine, fine," Lyle went on absently, thinking about something else for a moment. Then he offered his hand. "Well, thanks for stopping by. You're looking good, looks like you're staying ahead of the ravages of time. Are you a runner?"

"Not really."

"Even so, you look in good shape. Why don't the two of us go running sometime?"

"Oh no you don't, Julian, I know you."

Lyle blinked once, apparently surprised. But Harry Todd went on. "You'd get me out there and try to run the legs off me, to show off what good shape you're in. You probably run a couple miles a day, don't you?"

"It's more like six or seven. But I'd slow up and wait for you, if I got too far ahead."

"Like I said, you haven't changed a bit."

Lyle looked pleased, as if he had received a compliment. He gave a little wave and headed back into his office. "Keep in touch. And hey, thanks for the idea about the industrial museum."

17

They had moved into the bedroom when the phone rang.

"Leave it," Dickie said, Pamela resting in his arms. He could feel her already starting to move away.

"It could be the hospital," she said, and was gone, bounding naked out of the bed and across the room, out to the living room.

Dickie sighed and undid his arm from under the sheet to look at his watch: it wasn't even noon yet. He smiled to himself contentedly, thinking about what he'd normally be doing at this time of the morning, what he should be doing, sitting at his desk in his office or in the trailer at Furnass Landing, shuffling papers, making phone calls, talking the talk. This is great. . . . Through the wall behind his head he could hear a distant TV, what sounded like a game show, not disturbing but present. He lay there trying to remember the drawings for these units, the specifications, whether they had done anything special to block out noise from adjoining townhouses, to beef up the shared walls. We've got to do that next time, people deserve their privacy, especially from noisy fuckers like me. . . .

In a few moments Pamela came back to the room. He pulled back the sheet for her but she rummaged through her clothes scattered around on the floor and started to pull on her panties and jeans.

"What's up? Where're you going?"

"I have to leave for a while."

"Why? Was that the hospital?"

She fastened the jeans, sighed, and looked at him, bare breasted. Her nipples were aimed at him like twin headlights.

"I have to go see a friend of mine."

"What kind of friend?"

"He's an old friend, he's—"

"'He?'"

"It's Jack."

"That construction worker? The guy from the Towers?"

She stopped to collect her thoughts. "I don't expect you to understand this. You're welcome to stay here until I get back, or you can come back later. But he's an old friend, something's come up and I'm going to go see him. I'm sorry, I wish it were different, I wish this hadn't happened today, but it did, I can't change that, and that's the way it is."

Dickie, never one who responded well to ultimatums, got up and, without a word, his jaw clamped tight, started putting on his clothes.

18

He thanked me for the idea of an industrial museum, Harry Todd mused as he left Lyle's office. Sure, old friend, you're welcome, it's all yours. Run with it.

The long passageway through the abandoned shoppers' bazaar was dark, winding back through the depths of the old theater to the outer lobby, lit by only a few small oyster-shaped sconces splaying dim light up the walls, the arcade full of shadows. Spooky. He laughed to himself, thinking, What's the matter? You afraid you're going to start seeing ghosts and goblins everywhere you go? Then something moved in the shadows.

"Harry Todd," a female voice hissed to him.

Kathleen? Harry Todd froze, his heart pounding. He stared into the shadows so hard his eyes hurt.

"Over here. Come over here."

There was someone standing in the doorway to what had been Apple & Spice & Everything Nice. He went a few steps closer. In the shadows, he could see she was older now, but he recognized the girl he had once known, Donna Bruno, in the woman standing in front of him.

"Oh my goodness, how are you?" he said, delighted, starting to reach to hug her, but she shushed him and brushed his arms aside, looking past him, back down the dark corridor.

"I heard you talking to Julian," she said, glancing at Harry Todd furtively, then away, as if unable or unwilling to look at him for any length of time.

"What are you doing here?"

"Don't you know? I work for Julian. I have . . . for a while."

Now Lyle's repeated questioning as to whether or not Harry Todd had seen his secretary made sense. You bastard, Julian.

"I can't talk here. I don't want him to see me talking to you," Donna said, continuing to avoid looking at him for very long, tilting her head and looking off into the distance again, as if watching something move away from her, or move toward her, in the darkness across the floor. "Meet me at the Furnass Grill in fifteen minutes. I'll tell him I forgot something and have to go back out again."

"What are you so secretive about?" Harry Todd smiled, trying to put her at ease, surprised at how genuinely glad he was to see her.

"I heard what he was saying to you when I came in. About the autopsy? He's lying to you. That's not at all what the report said about Kathleen's death."

"How do you know?"

"Meet me there," she said, looking at him intensely now, for a brief moment gazing up into his eyes; then she touched his arm before slipping past him and hurrying on down the corridor, into the darkness, her high heels clicking on the wood floor, a dark silhouette against the light at the end of the passageway, the dim glow coming from Lyle's office.

19

The two men watched the ball arc high down the fairway, their right hands shielding the light from their eyes as if in a flat-hand salute. The ball landed twenty yards or so beyond Harvey McMillan's, close to the rough but with a clear shot to the green; Harvey McMillan's had landed among the trees.

"Nice shot," Harvey McMillan said.

"I was thinking of slicing into the woods," Dickie said. "To keep you company."

"I'm glad you didn't. Then I would have known this wasn't just a friendly game between a Realtor and a local banker."

"Harvey. How could you say such a thing? You wound me." Dickie put his hand to his chest, pretending to be aggrieved.

"You should wound so easy. I can say such a thing because I know you."

"Well, as a matter of fact, there is one thing. . . ."

"That's more like it. God's in His heaven, Dickie Sutcliff has an angle, and all's right with the world."

"We'll let the caddie bring the cart. Let's walk."

They handed their clubs to the caddie and headed off down the fairway. Harvey McMillan was a large plumpish man, whose golfing clothes, purple with white trim, displayed his many bulges and soft spots; his impeccably polished white shoes made his feet, which were already considerable, appear many times larger than they were, so that he seemed mounted on movable platforms. He gazed around at the trees, the graying sky, a mourning dove that squeaked off into the tall grass.

"Lord, what a beautiful day," Harvey McMillan said, the smile on his face more of a grimace from the bright haze. "Regardless of your motives, I'm glad you called. It's good to be away from the office for a while. Must be nice to get a tee time whenever you want."

Dickie kept his eyes ahead of him. As the day grew hotter and more humid, the sky was slowly turning the color of a worn dime, though without losing any of its radiance; the haze over the hills was beginning to blur the edges of the landscape. Poor Harvey, Dickie was thinking, if this is a beautiful day to him, he really needs to get out more. What Dickie was trying not to think about was the other thing on his mind, other than why he was occupying himself chasing a little white ball over these hills for Harvey McMillan's benefit, the thing that would have taken over all his thoughts if he let it . . . She said I'm going to go see this guy, whether you like it or not. That's just the way it is. Don't start thinking about this, old friend, it'll eat you alive. You've got business to attend to. . . .

"I understand Furnass Towers is about to be sold off at a sheriff's sale."

Harvey McMillan glanced at him as they continued along the fairway. "These things usually take longer—sometimes they can drag on for years, as you well know. But with Sycamore Savings & Loan going under, I think they wanted to get it over with as soon as possible so they could forget it ever happened."

"Let me run a scenario by you," Dickie went on. "Suppose I were to purchase Furnass Towers, and then some friendly person—a banker, say—reappraised the Towers at a higher value than what I paid for it. Which wouldn't be hard to do, incidentally, because I expect to pay very little for Lyle's misadventure."

"I'm not sure I see where this is headed."

"Well, with Furnass Towers reappraised at a higher amount, I could then use it as collateral for a loan to purchase Furnass Landing. Or at least my share of it: Buchanan has said they would be interested in forming a limited partnership with me, with themselves as silent partner."

"No one could ever accuse you of not being ambitious. And I knew Buchanan was unhappy with the situation as it is. The question that comes to mind is: How do you propose to get the money to purchase Furnass Towers?"

"Well, I guess I'd have to borrow it."

"Um-hm. Okay, now I see where we're headed. But I'll continue to play the straight man for you. What would you put up as collateral? With a project as shaky as the Towers, I can't imagine you'd want to risk any of your prime holdings."

"No, you're right about that. I'm not like Julian, who put up everything he had, including his own house, to try to do that building. That's the difference between an amateur and a pro."

"No one would ever mistake you for an amateur, Dickie. Believe me."

Dickie nodded acknowledgment. "I suppose, in order to swing a deal like the one I'm talking about, I would have to hope that the right party heard about it and liked the prospects and came up with an idea for some inventive financing."

"You're going to make me say it, aren't you?"

"Harvey, you know it's always better to accept a proposition than to make one. That's good business."

"And no one would ever accuse you of not being good at business either."

"I'll take that as a compliment. But I'm afraid that still doesn't solve my dilemma. I still haven't heard any inventive ideas on how I could finance these projects."

"Well, suppose a bank such as First City became interested in cross-collateralizing the loans?"

"Hey, now there's an idea. Why didn't I think of that?"

"We would be interested, as I say, but don't get me wrong. I'm not doing this out of friendship or anything like that. This is strictly a business deal—and a pretty good one if I do say so myself. If you default—and to tell you the truth I don't see how you'll be able to avoid it, given the circumstances, but that's your problem—as I said, if you default, the bank will end up with two major pieces of property, at less than what you were paying for them."

"Don't get your hopes up, Harv. I've never defaulted yet on a piece of property that I cared about. But thanks for your interest in the deal."

"No thanks necessary, as I say."

Along the edge of the fairway a cloud of midges danced in the heavy air. Dickie supposed he should be happy about Harvey McMillan's interest in working with him on the loans, and he was happy to an extent, but his other thoughts were weighing down his spirits . . . She said I don't expect you to understand this. No, I don't understand it, she left me to go see another guy. What's to understand? And some older potbellied construction guy at that. What am I, chopped liver? The two men were getting closer to the green; behind them came the hum of the electric golf cart as the caddie caught up to them.

"I think your ball went into the trees somewhere along here," Dickie said. "You want me to help you find it?"

"No, if it's not an easy shot in plain sight, I'm not going to spend any time hacking away at it. I'll take the stroke."

"Cut your losses and move on. You're a good businessman yourself."

"Go on ahead, I'll meet you at the green."

Dickie walked a few steps, then stopped. "You knew I was going to propose a deal to you today, didn't you?"

Harvey McMillan snorted, stopping at the treeline to look at him. "It wasn't too hard to figure out, Dickie. The only time you ever ask me golfing, or anywhere else for that matter, is when you've got a deal going."

Dickie smiled and gave a little wave and walked on down the fairway, thinking I suppose he's right, I wouldn't ask Harvey or anybody else to accompany me someplace if it wasn't for business. That's sort of sad, I guess, except why would I? I can't stand most people, the same way that most people can't stomach me. The only reason most people want anything to do with me is because they want something. Just like I want something from them. That's the way the world is. Isn't it? He thought of Pamela, of how things were different with her, how much he liked to be with her. How much he hoped she liked to be with him.

She said That's the way it is. I don't expect you to understand. Is there more to understand about why she left? I certainly didn't wait around to find out. . . .

Ahead he saw his ball near the edge of the rough, sitting in the grass like a white egg, as if it had fallen from a nest in a nearby tree. As he stopped to wait for the caddie to bring his clubs, Harvey McMillan's shot came blasting out of the treeline— a second or so before he yelled, "Fore!"—missing Dickie's head by less than a foot. Dickie ducked even though the ball had passed, then straightened up cautiously, looking around, lest something else came zinging his way.

Nice try, Harv. But I guess that's par for the course. Next time aim lower.

20

"Do you remember when we used to come here when we were in high school?" Donna said, settling herself in the booth across from him. "You used to meet me here every night after school, after I got out of cheerleader practice."

Harry Todd smiled and nodded at the memory. "We probably spent enough money in here to be part owners of the place."

"And after I graduated and you were still in school, I'd meet you here after I got off work. That's when I was working at Stall's insurance agency, my first job. We'd meet here, and then we'd drive around the rest of the afternoon and evening in your mother's car, up and down the main street. Except when we'd go and park somewhere."

Don't let her get started on anything. "They used to have great burgers here. And milk shakes."

"They still do." She glanced at him and looked away again, smiling to herself, as if she had read his mind, as if she knew what he was trying to do, to stay away from certain subjects, and it amused her.

The booth was large enough for six people, eight if they crowded in, along the side of the restaurant, next to the large windows, looking out at the narrow side street, slanting down the hill toward the river; from where he was sitting, Harry Todd could see, farther up the main street in the middle of the next block, the skeleton of the half-finished ten-story Furnass Towers, a stack of empty concrete floors above the smaller buildings around it, Julian Lyle's abandoned project that Harry Todd's mother had written to him about, sent him clippings about from the papers.

Donna continued to look at him only for brief instants, the same as she had outside Lyle's office, up under her eyebrows or quick glances from the side, her gestures nervous, furtive, secretive. *She isn't afraid of me, is she? Is she afraid of something?* Away from the shadows in the old theater, her face showed more of the differences, more of the changes, from when he knew her thirty years earlier, though he was sure he would have recognized her anywhere. She had the same squarish features he remembered, more attractive than pretty, but her deep brown hair was streaked with gray now and much shorter, close-cropped, as short as if it had grown back from having been shaved to mark a collaborator; in the harsh light from the windows, the noontime sunlight in shards across the table, her face in places seemed sunken, pushed in, as if crushed by a vise, and her brown eyes, whenever he had the chance to see them, ringed with dark circles, seemed sadder, as if she had just finished crying or was about to begin, even when she smiled. When the waitress left after bringing them their coffees, Harry Todd leaned across the table and said under his breath, "Isn't she the same waitress who used to wait on us back then?"

Donna giggled, and the joke seemed to have the effect he wanted, to put her more at ease, though she still wouldn't look at him for any length of time.

"You're looking well," he said, then added quickly, "and good."

"Well and good. There's an expression like that, isn't there? 'It's all well and good.' I guess you could definitely say that about me. How long are you home for?"

"I haven't decided. Leaving it open."

Donna nodded, looked at him and looked away again, out the window, reflective. "I see your mother around town now and then, but she doesn't speak. When I first came back to town she was nice to me, your whole family was. Then after Kathleen died, everything changed. Everything."

He was wary—Be careful, don't let her get started on something—but she changed the subject herself right away, again as if she were aware of what he was thinking, as if she were afraid she might say the wrong thing and scare him off.

"How does the town look to you now?" she asked gaily, becoming animated again. "I'll bet it feels weird."

"Yes, a little. It also feels the same too, and that's even weirder."

"It's a lot different than San Francisco."

Harry Todd looked at her quizzically.

"You're wondering what I would know about San Francisco."

"No . . . I was—"

"Yes, you were," Donna said and took a sip of coffee. "As a matter of fact I've been to San Francisco . . . oh, I guess about a dozen times now. Every couple years or so I try to save enough money and go there for a week."

"Why do you do that?"

"Just to be there. Just to see what it's like. I love it. I walk all around and go to the museums and galleries, I eat at Tadich's and have a drink at the Buena Vista, all those San Francisco things. One year I saved enough money to stay at the Fairmont, it was wonderful."

It was spooky, somehow, to think of her there. He hadn't lived in the city for years, but she wouldn't know that, the Bay Area was San Francisco to her, and he continued to go into the city over the years; it was unsettling to think of running into her on the street, coming across her in a restaurant.

"You're looking at my hand, aren't you? To see if I'm wearing a ring." She smiled and held up her left hand, the back toward him, waving her fingers like grass blown by the wind. "No, I never married. And I still live in the same house, in case you want to come looking for me. That was a joke. I lived with my mom and dad until they died, and then I decided to keep the house, it's not too big for one person and I'm comfortable there. You were married for a while."

"Yes. . . ."

"But I guess it didn't work out."

"An understatement."

She smiled. "And you never remarried. But I'll bet you've lived with women since then."

Watch out! What was she getting at? The idea that she might carry a torch for him was touching and, he had to admit, flattering. But he tried to think of something else to talk to her about, he had almost forgotten why he had agreed to meet her here.

"How long have you worked for Julian? The last thing I heard you were working for Sutcliff Realty."

"Did you ask about me since you've been back? No, I guess not, or you would have known where I was now."

It was a sudden flare-up of petulance, recrimination, even anger, that subsided just as quickly. She reached in her purse for something, rummaging around for a moment, then put the purse on the seat beside her again, not so much as if she couldn't find what she was looking for, but as if she wasn't sure what she was looking for in the first place. She smiled at him briefly, like turning on and off a small lamp, and continued, looking at her hands, out the window, anything but him.

"Let's see . . . I've worked for Julian for almost thirteen years now. Actually, your brother arranged it. I don't think Julian was too keen about it at first, about the idea of me working for him, but Dickie had a talk with him and had his way. Dickie usually has his way with things, doesn't he?"

"So it seems. I guess he always did."

"Well, I owe him my job. And now I've been with Julian so long, he can't do without me. For one thing, he'd lose what little income he has coming in. He's no good at collecting for his services, he'll represent someone and if they don't want to pay him afterwards, he won't press the issue. If it was up to him, he'd wind up doing half his jobs for free, because he doesn't like to ask for the money. That's where I come in: I'm his bill collector, among other things. I don't have any trouble asking people for the money they owe us. I figure it's my money too."

"That sounds like Julian."

"When I first went to work for him, I thought the reason he didn't like to ask for his money was that he thought he was too good or something, that he thought it was beneath him. But then I realized he's just backward about some things."

Harry Todd laughed. "When Julian was a kid, he used to have a paper route. And he really liked delivering papers, walking around with the stack of papers strapped to his chest and folding them as he walked along and winging them onto people's porches. The problem was, he hated to collect the money at the end of the week. If he didn't like the people in a certain house or if they made him uncomfortable in some way, he wouldn't collect from them—he'd keep on delivering their paper but he wouldn't stop and ring their doorbell to get the money they owed him. There were some people on his route who got their paper free for years."

As he talked he realized Donna was watching him steadily, for the first time, sideways, out of the corner of her eye, her face turned slightly down and away from him, watching him intently. Maybe she's starting to feel more at ease talking to me, he thought. This is actually very nice. Having a nice conversation with her about old times. There's no reason why we can't be friends, what happened was a long time ago. He motioned the waitress over for more coffee, still smiling from his story, the memory of Julian.

Donna, however, wasn't smiling. She continued to stare at him, after the waitress had filled their cups and left again, looking at him, it occurred to Harry Todd, as if there were something amiss, almost as if there were something caught in his teeth or stuck on his chin. He touched his face self-consciously, feeling awkward. Donna looked away petulantly, her mouth set, seemingly fed up with him, before addressing him again.

"Aren't you going to ask me about Kathleen's death? That's the only reason you agreed to meet me here, isn't it?"

"No, that isn't the only reason," he said, taken aback by her sudden change of mood.

Donna looked away again, laughing a little, derisive, under her breath, looking out the window at a truck going by, as if Harry Todd were trying her gullibility.

"Well, I'll tell you about it anyway, if you're not going to ask, because it's something you should know. It's what I told you outside of Julian's office. He was lying to you. The death certificate said natural causes, all right. But that other term he told you, *cardiac arrhythmia*, that wasn't in the autopsy report."

"How do you know?"

"Because I saw both the death certificate and the autopsy report." She nodded, giving him again her *Surprise!* face.

"What did the autopsy report say?"

"There were a lot of medical terms I didn't understand. And then your father came back before I finished reading all of it. . . ."

"Came back? Where did you see it? At Julian's office?"

"No, silly. I was still working for your father then." Donna folded her hands in her lap, looking somewhat prissy. "I saw it a few days after Kathleen died, before her funeral. I thought we should have kept the office closed, everyone was very upset, we all loved her. But your father insisted on keeping the office open. I don't think he knew what else to do."

"Why would he close the office simply because his daughter died?" Harry Todd said sarcastically.

Donna ignored him. "Dr. Neely called your father and said he had to talk to him about the autopsy and he brought the report over to the office. Then Dickie got involved and the three of them had a long talk about it, I could hear your father in his office. He was real upset but they had the door closed so I couldn't hear exactly what they were saying. Then they must have called Julian because he came over and all four of them had a long talk. When your father finally came out, he was as white as a sheet. He gave me the report and said to destroy it, that he never wanted to see it again, he told me to run it through the shredder and he left and that's when I had a chance to look at it. But then he must have had second thoughts about it because he came back in a few minutes and asked if I had destroyed it yet and I said I was just going to—I don't think he saw me reading it. He took the report and said he'd take care of it himself. He looked at it again while I was sitting there and then he tore it into pieces and ran the pieces through the shredder and that was that. That's when he told me I must never mention anything about Kathleen's death or the autopsy report or anything else about it ever again, and then he left and went to the hospital to talk to somebody there. I don't know what happened after that. I only know your brother and Julian and Dr. Neely talked some more for a long time and when Dickie came out of his office he told me that Julian was taking care of all the arrangements about Kathleen's death, that I was to tell people I didn't know anything about it and if there were any questions I was to direct them to Julian. He also told me to forget that I had ever seen him and Julian and Dr. Neely talking about it, and that I didn't know anything about the autopsy. So here I am, thirteen years later, telling you."

"Did my father say anything about it after that?"

"I wouldn't know. Right after the funeral your father decided he didn't want me around anymore." Donna looked down at her hands for a moment, a wrenched expression on her face as if she were discussing something internally with herself, before she went on. "Dickie told me later that your father got rid of me because I reminded him too much of Kathleen, our being friends and all. That's when Dickie got me my job with Julian, he was real nice to help me. Your father was a changed man after Kathleen died, I think especially so after he found out the results of the autopsy, that's my opinion. He was never himself again afterwards, that's when Dickie started to take over more of the business. Your father sort of wasted away."

Donna was watching him again, a catlike smile on her face. "Don't you want to know what the autopsy said was the cause of death?"

"You saw what it said? I thought you said you didn't have time to read it."

"Not all of it, but I read the important part, all right." She leaned forward against the edge of the table, denting her breasts; with her hands in her lap it appeared as though she had no arms. When Harry Todd didn't say anything, Donna cocked her head and said in a stage whisper, "The report said she died of a barbiturate overdose."

Harry Todd stared at her. Donna nodded once and sat back in the booth again.

"Just like Marilyn Monroe."

"What?" Harry Todd said.

"Well, maybe not *just* like Marilyn Monroe. They poisoned her with barbiturate suppositories or maybe even an enema. Can you imagine, somebody sticking all those things up your bottom? They must have held her down or got her drunk beforehand, it must have been awful. I don't think anything like that happened to Kathleen—"

"What are you talking about? What does any of this have to do with my sister?"

"You don't believe me, do you? You think I'm making all this up, don't you? You never did believe me, about anything." Donna pulled her purse onto her lap, apparently getting ready to go, then thought of something else. "Were you going to look me up while you were here? Or were you going to go back to California without seeing me?"

Harry Todd was still in a state of shock from what she had told him about Kathleen. "I've only been here a couple of days. . . ."

"Long enough to be poking around about Kathleen's death." Donna suddenly leaned forward and placed her hand on top of Harry Todd's resting on the table. She gazed intently into his eyes, her voice full of unexpected passion. "Every night after work I go to Holy Innocents and pray for you, pray for us. I have every night since I came back to Furnass, after your father sent me to that home to have our baby. What do you think of that?"

Harry Todd was dumbfounded by what all she was saying. When he continued to stare at her, Donna sat back again and gathered her things and started to slide out of the booth. "Well, so much for that. I have to get back to work. No, don't get up, I can get back to the office on my own, thank you very much. I've been getting by on my own for a good many years without your help."

She's upset, I can't let her go like this. "Donna," he said, reaching for her hand, touching her, but she pulled away quickly from him, as if his touch burned.

"Look at you. So that's the reason you wanted to see me today. It's written all over your face. You want me to do that for you again, don't you? You think that would be fun again. Fun for you."

Harry Todd was at a loss as to what to say, afraid that she was about to make a scene, afraid of what she might say next.

She stood up and looked around, then leaned down close to him, whispering in his ear.

"If I did that for you again, how do you know I wouldn't bite it off? That's what you deserve. You and your brother. All you Sutcliffs."

She straightened up and looked at him again, wide-eyed, as if mocking his surprise, pretending to be scandalized; she opened her mouth wide and snapped her teeth together once, *Chomp!* Then she smiled at him, pleased with herself, and, with her head held high, clicked away on her high heels, up the aisle and out the front door.

As he watched her through the large window cross the intersection and continue up the street, heading back to Lyle's office, flouncing along, never once looking back, he felt drained, empty. And more confused than ever . . . Barbiturate overdose? Poison enemas? She must be out of her tree. He wondered whom he could tell about what just happened. The only person who came to mind was Jennifer.

21

I guess I shouldn't have left the way I did. I guess I should have given her a chance to explain. Even though she already knew I wouldn't wait around for an explanation anyway. Because she knew that's not the kind of guy I am. . . .

As Dickie drove, faster than he knew he should, along Seneca Road, heading back to town from the country club, he was still thinking of Pamela, as much as he tried not to, still thinking of the call she received when he was with her and how quickly she left her townhouse to go see the guy who called her. He knew she had had some kind of relationship with this guy Jack, but Dickie thought it was over. And he had never understood the relationship to begin with—an older, potbellied construction worker? Okay, construction superintendent, but still. . . . Obviously the guy must still mean something to her. Dickie knew he could make no exclusive claims on Pamela, they had never had that kind of relationship, they had only been sometime friends, somebody he'd run into at a bar and have a drink with, once in a while racquetball partners, who over a few months had started sleeping together occasionally—Dickie Sutcliff, you never missed anyone in your life—he told himself she had no way of knowing that he was thinking now of something more between them. I know you, Mr. Appetite. He kept remembering her lying beside him, holding her naked in his arms, remembering the way her body fit into his, her softness; he tried not to imagine her lying in the arms of some other guy.

He could imagine her lying naked in the arms of some other guy. An older, potbellied construction worker's arms.

What made him think of Harry Todd and Kathleen? Well, he knew the answer to that too. At the time all that happened between his older brother and sister, he had no idea what couples did together, he had only vague suspicions, he only knew that whatever Harry Todd and Kathleen did together that way it didn't include him. He remembered, after the time he saw them from the top of the stairs starting to roll together on the living room floor, he spied on them for months afterward, trying to catch them again, trying to see more of what went on, to see what it was they did together, but Harry Todd and Kathleen spent less time together after that day; he remembered spying on her, peeking through keyholes and cracks of doors, hiding on the attic stairs, to see her without her clothes in the bathroom or in her room. Over the course of his life, he had had plenty of women, and he would sometimes say they were beautiful, each in her own way, but he had never been awestruck with a woman—the wonder of her, finding beauty in the turn of her leg or the line of her jaw that in anyone else would have elicited nothing—the way he had been with Kathleen. Until now, until Pamela.

Dickie turned on the radio, turned it off again. He turned the fan for the air conditioner a notch higher, then turned it back to where it was because it blew too cold on him. He punched in the cigarette lighter, waiting for it to pop out, even though he had given up smoking some time ago. There were other memories too, flitting in and out of his consciousness . . . of the day he was upstairs in the house . . . he was married by that time and he and Tinker had a place of their own but he had gone over to the big house for some reason or other . . . and was walking down the second-floor hall when Kathleen came out of her room naked and stood in the doorway, a grown woman now, just stood there . . . but he didn't allow that image to stay around.

The big car floated over the asphalt, up and down the rolling hills. I'm going to go see him. I'm sorry, I wish it were different, I wish this hadn't happened today, but it did, I can't change that. . . . In the rearview mirror he met the pair of eyes looking back at him, superimposed on the road in front of him, like a floating mask, bandit eyes. So. What are you going to do about it, old friend? He turned on the radio again, turned it off again.

22

When Kitty Todd first came to Furnass—she was still Kitty Todd at the time, she and Harry weren't married until after they arrived in town; that was part of the problem with his family right there—they lived for several years with Harry's parents in their house at the upper end of the business district on Seventh Avenue, on the edge of what was known as *upstreet* or *downtown*, depending upon the frame of reference. The house was a little strange to Kitty's tastes, though it was nice enough once you were inside; it was dirty orange brick, the same dirty orange brick used to build most of the buildings along the main drag, with the first floor flat-faced against the sidewalk and the upper stories set back and looking more like a traditional house. Later on, after his parents died and Harry sold the property, someone opened a barbershop in the lower part—the place next door, built exactly the same, eventually became a bar—but when Kitty arrived the first floor was Dr. Sutcliff's office. Doctor, as everyone called him.

If Kitty had had her wits about her when she arrived—she would have been the first to admit that she didn't have her wits then, what with being several months pregnant and plopped down here in the middle of this smoke-and-soot-filled town, beholden as it were to a man a few years younger than herself whom she barely knew except in bed, and to this young man's parents— she would have realized how things were going to be with his family when she found out that Mother Sutcliff—that's what she wanted Kitty to call her—Mother Sutcliff sat downstairs each day in Doctor's waiting room during his office hours, crocheting doilies for the Red Cross—Kitty never did determine why the woman thought disaster victims or the starving children of Armenia needed doilies—giving advice to his patients regarding their ailments as well as her opinion as to whether or not their conditions were serious enough to be taking up her husband's valuable time. That Doctor's practice survived despite his wife was testament to his skill as a physician and how much the town thought of him.

Doctor was a stout, expansive man who always wore a waistcoat with his brown worsted suits—and always wore a brown worsted suit, summer or winter—along with board-like detachable collars on his shirts, long after such collars were out of fashion. Similarly, Mother Sutcliff seemed to be the last of the Victorian ladies. The times being what they were, she couldn't very well wear floor-length skirts and a bustle, but she did the best she could, favoring severely tailored clothes that fit snug on her snug figure—there wasn't an ounce of fat, or, to Kitty's thinking, an ounce of softness, to the woman—and collars buttoned tight to the neck. Traditionally, men in the Sutcliff family had three choices when it came to what they could do with their lives: a Sutcliff male could be a farmer, a preacher, or a doctor. When young Harry Sutcliff broke with tradition and announced that he didn't know what he wanted to do in life but he knew it wasn't farming, preaching, or doctoring, things were certainly bad enough. But when he went to New York to find himself and came back, not only with the idea to sell real estate, but, into this staunch Scotch-Irish Presbyterian atmosphere, brought a dancer, a Rockette—unwed, and carrying his baby to boot—the attitude in the Sutcliff household was that, if it wasn't the end of the world, at least the Day of Judgment was close at hand.

Later, even though she knew they had had some good times together, even though she thought there were times when they were very much in love, there was something in Kitty that never let her quite forgive Harry for getting her into this. *This* meaning, essentially, Furnass, and everything associated with it. Particularly after she got to know him better, got to know the way his mind worked.

Kitty was quick to grasp that she was never going to get out from under the Sutcliff family's and the town's preconception of her. The preconception that she was a New York showgirl, meaning: a floozy, a tramp, a gold digger. But Kitty was a fighter; she decided she wasn't going to just lie there under the weight of their collective disapproval. Her answer was to become as outlandish, outrageous—in another situation, she would have said that she was only being colorful, showy—as everyone already considered her to be. The most obvious manifestation was her wardrobe. When she came to Furnass, she fully expected to take on the role of housewife, wearing cotton print dresses and low-heeled pumps as she worked around the house, the same as her mother and the housewives of Rome, New York, had done when she was growing up. Instead, she decked herself out in white satin peignoirs and pom-pom mules—her models were actresses like Jean Harlow and Katharine Hepburn whom she'd seen in the movies at Radio City Music Hall between her Rockette numbers—no matter that her outfits quickly became dirty and spotted with the soot floating in the air as she cooked and washed clothes and changed diapers, she simply changed her ensembles as they became soiled, sometimes two and three times a day. Eventually, when Harry's business grew successful and they moved out of Doctor and Mother Sutcliff's into a home of their own, Kitty gave up the peignoirs in favor of more practical, though no less provocative, outfits, ranging from kimonos and Indian saris over bright colored jerseys to Amish-like jumpers and Peruvian serapes. But her clothes by that time were incidental; Kitty would have been considered a town character—meaning: an outsider, a misfit, a handful—no matter what she wore.

"Mother actually said something nice about your clothes today," Harry told her one evening after dinner, when they were in their own house, two blocks away from his parents, after Harry had stopped and made one of his rare visits to his parents' house. "She said considering the kind of woman you are, she thinks it fortunate that you wear any clothes at all around the house."

"And you think that was nice? Did she say what kind of woman she thinks I am?"

"I think we both know the answer to that," Harry laughed.

Kitty, with one-year-old Kathleen crooked on her hip as she spoon-fed two-year-old Harry Todd in his high chair, looked at him. It was good to know Mother Sutcliff was holding up her end of the war; if the woman had begun to actually like the way Kitty dressed it would have taken half the fun out of it. But she was curious.

"So, what did you say to defend me?"

"What could I say?" Harry said, disappearing again behind his newspaper. "You know Mother."

Yes, she did know Mother Sutcliff; it was the woman's only son whom Kitty had begun to question. Harry had certainly fought to bring her here, battling both his family's and the town's disapproval. But as time went on and Harry appeared to retreat somewhat in his feelings toward her—as he began to act toward her, if not as an enemy, at least as a neutral; as he spent more and more time away from her and told her less and less of what he was doing—she began to wonder if there were treaties and alliances of which she wasn't aware. Began to wonder why he brought her here in the first place.

Doctor was her sanctuary in those days, her refuge, her friend; he seemed removed from the goings-on in the town, engaged but distant, even within his own household, a country unto himself. Years before Kitty arrived, Mother Sutcliff had decreed that there would be no smoking in her house. Not wishing to dispute such territorial claims—he told Kitty later that he had realized that even if he fought his wife and won the right to smoke in the house, he would still lose, worse than ever, because then he would be forced to be with her not only during the day when she sat in his waiting room but in the evenings as well—Doctor found it easier to simply withdraw. In wintertime after supper, he would return downstairs to his office, where he would smoke to his heart's content as he worked his way through the list of Great Books of Clifton Fadiman's *Lifetime Reading Plan*; in the summertime, while his wife would be crocheting on the front porch overlooking the main street, Doctor would do his smoking and reading on the porch in back, overlooking their tiny enclosed yard and the rear of the police station across the alley.

Kitty didn't smoke, but while she lived at the house she took to joining Doctor in the evenings during his smoky, self-imposed exile, either in his office or on the back porch; after she and Harry moved to a house of their own, she continued the visits whenever she could—given the fact that Harry was rarely home in the evenings now, that proved to be fairly often—stopping by as she took the children for an evening stroll. Some nights she and Doctor talked, some nights she would join him reading, tagging along behind him on the reading list; when she brought the children, Doctor would play with them to give Kitty the chance to pick up where she left off in *The Meditations of Marcus Aurelius* or *Paradise Lost*. The subject of Harry rarely came up during their talks, except in passing, though one evening Doctor said, "What does your husband say about you coming over here so often?"

"I'm not sure he even knows. He's busy working most nights."

"Working," Doctor repeated, letting out a cloud of blue haze as he rocked slowly back and forth in the straight-backed rocking chair he kept in his office for his nightly sessions, the same straight-backed rocking chair that later sat in Kitty's living room. He brushed a few ashes from the front of his waistcoat and looked at Kitty.

"He works late," Kitty said, feeling surprisingly defensive under his gaze. "He's either at the office or he's out showing properties. The business is doing very well."

Doctor thought about something for a moment, then stopped rocking and leaned forward, watching the children, two-year-old Harry Todd and one-year-old Kathleen, playing with some wooden cars at his feet. "The business must be doing very well, if it means he doesn't have more time to spend with beautiful children such as these." Then he looked at her again. "Or a wife as pretty as you."

Kitty felt herself blush, though it wasn't from the compliment; she knew already it was something else. "Harry has a plan. About how he wants the business to develop over the next few years. . . ."

"Ah yes. I'm sure Harry has a plan. He always did. For everything." The portly, elderly man sat back in the rocker again and started rocking again, slowly back and forth, taking another long, meditative drag on his cigarette, issuing in time another blue cloud.

When he said it Kitty wasn't sure what he meant, but she was sure he meant something, the way he said it, the way he wouldn't say any more. But later, when she began to admit to herself what she had suspected for a while, that Harry wasn't spending all his late-night hours with his work—when what was going on became so blatant that she couldn't avoid the truth any longer—what Doctor said, or wouldn't say, made more sense to her.

There had been inklings of Harry's extramarital activities, of course, if she had chosen to acknowledge them—telephone calls at strange hours that always rang off if she answered; the smell of perfume on his clothes that he attributed to the women he was showing properties to; even the fact that he no longer tried to hide his drinking from her, that he came home most nights if not drunk—she learned he had a voracious capacity for alcohol, as he did for anything that affected his senses—then at least tipsy, in another state of consciousness, a different Harry from the one she had ever known before. Then the two images, the Harry she had known and the Harry he had become, merged, like the two ghostly figures coming together in a camera's rangefinder, suddenly snapping into focus.

She watched as the tall muscular young man who had courted and won her grew stout, developed the paunch of his father except that it was never kept in place with a waistcoat, his expanse of tummy descending from his chest and surging out over his pants tops, not a roll but a swell; she watched as his short blond hair, which had once covered his head like fuzz, turned prematurely white and grew into a flattop, as if to square off at least the top of his face, which had become increasingly puffy and jowly; she watched as his complexion became incessantly enflamed, and his once melancholy blue eyes turned rheumy and webbed with blood vessels, like small watery nets intent on keeping his eyeballs in their sockets. The images of her husband as he once was and her husband as he was now converged in the same time frame as she found a handkerchief stuffed into one of his jacket pockets with the unmistakable stains of sex; as she found a receipt for a room at the Colonel Berry Hotel in town, a room for two, after an evening he said he had to drive to Harrisburg; as she heard for herself on the extension, one of the rare evenings when he stayed home, his whispering the obscenities of love, of what all he intended to do with the woman on the other end of the line, the next time they were in bed together, the next time he could get away from, in the words he used for Kitty on the phone, his "cuckoo clock," his "nutcase."

*

"You said once that you thought he had a plan."

"Take off your coat, Kitty. Sit down. Where are the children?"

"I think I'll keep my coat on, thank you, I'm chilled to the bone, and I don't want to sit down. I left the children with Harry—or rather I told them to go see their father and tell him to get off the phone and take care of them, that Mummy was going out. You said once that you thought he always had a plan. I take it that means he had a plan that involved me as well."

"I suspect he did. I always considered he did. Even as a little boy he—"

"So what's so wrong with him having a plan? He wanted me to be his wife, so he came to New York to get me, to bring me back here."

"I don't think bringing you back here, or making you his wife, was his primary plan. I don't think it was even the initial step of another plan. I think it was the second step in a secondary plan."

"What was the first step?"

"He wanted a wife from New York. He picked you because you suited what he was looking for. Then after he found you, he had to find a way to make it work."

"If getting such a wife was only his secondary plan, what was his primary plan?"

"To find a way of life that would support her, that would make him worthy enough to have such a wife. A way of life that was different than anything his mother and I would want for him, in the same way that such a wife was different than anyone we would want for him."

"But why would he feel that he had to go to New York for a wife?"

"Because he wanted the prettiest girl he could find."

"That's very flattering but there are pretty girls in Furnass, or in the other towns around here. In Pittsburgh."

"No, they weren't pretty enough. Or to put it another way: they weren't prize enough. And besides, none of the good-looking girls around here would have married him. They already knew him too well, because he had already known most of them, in the biblical sense. They had already been used by him, or knew he wasn't the marrying kind, only the kind to have fun with."

"And?"

"And what?"

"And what else is there that you don't want to tell me?"

"And because with a local girl, even if he had found one who would marry him, even if there was one, say, who took it as a challenge because she thought she could be the one who could change him—this is all speculation on my part, of course, but remember I've known him since I pulled him with my own two hands kicking and screaming from his mother's womb—it would have been too easy for a local girl to leave him once she found out she couldn't change him, once she found out he was still running around. A girl from New York would not only carry the aura and glamour of the Big City, she would be more dependent on him once he got her here. More without resources, more compliant."

"Do you think I'm more compliant?"

"No, and neither does Harry now, though it's come as something of a shock to him. In some ways it's made it harder for him, in some ways it's made it easier. Because you are as strong as you are, he found he can leave you alone more because he knows you'll get along okay without him. And because you're so defiant, because you've found your own ways to throw back in our faces the who and what we are in this town, he can use that as an excuse to want to get away from you. He can blame you for driving him away, even though he was out the door to start with."

"Those are things that make it easier for him. How do I make it harder?"

"Because he didn't expect to respect you as much as he does. He didn't expect to like you. Admire you."

"He has a funny way of showing it."

"I doubt if he could ever show such a thing. He's only good at making people do what he wants them to, not at showing any positive feeling toward them. Maybe that was something his mother and I should have taught him. Maybe he wasn't born with the capacity to learn it. He's very strong in some ways, but I often think it's a damaged strength."

"And the children? They were to help tie me to him? Tie me down here?"

"Partly. And there was the army."

"Oh."

"He needed children to stay out of the service. The draft hadn't started yet but there was talk it was going to be, and he didn't want to take any chances. Not because he was afraid of fighting, I think, or because he didn't want to serve his country, but because he saw an opportunity if he could stay here to make a success of his idea for a real estate business. And he wanted that more than anything. I guess we instilled that in him, at least. He wanted to go against his mother and me so badly, wanted to make his own name in his own way in this town, that he was willing to do anything to get it. Or use anybody."

"That's why he needed two children. To make sure the army wouldn't take him. That's why Kathleen came along so soon after Harry Todd. And I thought it was because he couldn't keep his hands off me. Silly me. Stupid me."

"That's what makes this whole thing so difficult. Because the fact was he couldn't. Keep his hands off you."

"You think he should want to keep his hands off me?"

"No, but the fact that he couldn't keep his hands off you makes it less easy for me to blame him for the rest of the way he's acted toward you. Because I think that's the one thing that really disrupted his plans. When he came back from New York he became physically ill. I didn't know what was the matter with him, he wouldn't eat, he couldn't sleep, all he did was lie around the house all day. Finally I took him to another doctor here in town, an old friend of mine, and asked him to take a look at Harry. And he told me what it was: 'It's a girl, Bruce,' he said, 'the boy's in love. I don't know what's standing in his way to be with her, but whatever it is he's heartsick over her.' That, incidentally, is why his mother will never forgive you. She could have tolerated it if you were only to be the bearer of his children, the keeper of his house, his bedmate for procreation. But that he might actually love you, that he might already love you more than her, was unforgivable. Though up to that point in time his mother was still ahead of the game, because she was here and you weren't. Once he was back here after being in New York, he made up his mind not to go after you. The one thing he hadn't figured on was falling in love with you, and the power that gave you to upset his plans for himself and what he wanted to do with his life. To keep to his plans he was just going to forget you, or try to; he fully intended to ride out the illness until his body had grown used to the idea of living without you. Then when he found out you were pregnant it changed things. That you were pregnant was the reason, or the excuse, he was looking for to be able to go back after you, to bring you here."

"If you knew all this, or even suspected it, why did you let him do it?"

"How could I stop him? I had already tried to set his life in certain directions, which had guaranteed that he would go in some other direction entirely. What could I possibly say to him that would change what he was going to do?"

"Then maybe my question is this: How could you let me? How could you let me get into this?"

"I didn't know you. I didn't know that maybe you wanted what he was offering, no matter what the price."

"But after you knew me, why didn't you try to warn me? Why did you let me stay? I thought you liked me."

"I like you, all right. I like you too much. Your coming down here with me in the evenings, or sitting with me out on the back porch, has become very special to me. I've grown to live for these times with you."

"What you're telling me is that you let me stay here in Furnass because you want me here too, as much as Harry does. You're in love with me too."

"It happens to old men, as well as young. It happens that men fall in love with their daughters, their son's wives. People think love is pretty, but it isn't. It's usually ugly on some level, because it means one person wants another person's mind or soul or body for his or her own purposes. Love is one person trying to devour another in some way."

"That's not love. That's selfishness."

"You show me any other kind of love in this world, and no matter what flowery, exalted claims people make for it, I'll show you indifference."

"That's disgusting."

"I would agree. It is also very sad, and not at all admirable. But most people don't seem to be able to live without it."

*

After her discussion with Doctor that evening, Kitty went back to the house, but she never looked at Harry or her marriage in the same light. She decided that, if that was the way of the world in which she found herself—if that was the way love was, at least for Harry, at least for the Sutcliff family—she would need to have certain things in order to survive. Not compensations or amenities necessarily, though they might appear that way to some, but foundations on which to build her own world within the world of Furnass—fortifications, ramparts and bastions and redoubts, in which to entrench her forces and protect her citadel. She had known, for instance, that the old Buchanan House on the bluff of Orchard Hill was for sale—Sutcliff Realty, in fact was showing the property—though she had never considered it for herself and her family. Until now. The next day, while the sound of her husband whispering obscenities to his lady friend on the phone was still fresh in her ears, and while the sound of her clicking off on the extension was still fresh in his, she told Harry she wanted the house.

"You're crazy," he laughed.

"You only hope so," she smiled.

"What would we—you—do with a big old house like that?"

"Live in it. Make it a home. It would be a great place to raise the children, all that yard."

"Well, you can forget about it," he said, getting up from the breakfast table and putting on his suit coat.

"No, I won't forget about it. I said I want you to buy that house. Today."

Harry stopped and looked at her, not angry, really, though a brief wave of anger coursed across his face, the fact that she had talked back to him in that manner, the first time she had ever done so, but mainly puzzled, bewildered, wondering what she was up to this time, cautious. "The business is doing well, but it's not doing that well."

"Oh yes it is. You've brought your statements home and I've looked at them. It will be a stretch, particularly to furnish it the way I want, but we can do it."

"Who are you to be dictating to me this way? Telling me how to spend my money?"

"I'm telling you how to spend *our* money. And I'm doing it because I'm your wife and the mother of your children and the only woman you will ever find to put up with you for more than the two minutes it takes you to take care of your business in bed. And because if you don't buy it, I'm going to telegraph my father today for the fare and the children and I will be on the first train out of here, back to Rome. For good. And if you doubt that I'll do it, you don't know me."

Harry stared at her for a moment; then he couldn't help but smile. As if in admiration. "Yes, I do know you."

It softened her a bit, she was prepared for a real fight; and she had to admit she did love him—as they used to say in the movies at Radio City—the big lug.

"Besides, you want that house as much as I do, if you stop and think about it. It's the only house that everybody in this entire town can see no matter where they are. It's the only house that will not only show the people of this town what you've made of yourself, it will throw it in their faces."

Harry smiled again. "And yes, you do know me."

To fortify her position even further, aware that it was going to be a long siege, she decided to have one more child, before sealing herself off from Harry, at least sexually, once and for all. Dickie was to be both her front line of defense and her reinforcement. Harry Todd would always be her first-born, her first love,she supposed, as far as the children were concerned, but

Dickie, being the last of her children, would always be foremost in her heart, the child who most reminded her of who she was now, a mother, and of what she had given of herself, the commitment to live in a constant state of war, to continue to be.

The bond that held all the divergent forces of the family together was Kathleen. She was their common ground, the love that each member of the family felt for her, their common focal point. But though each member of the family had reason to lay claim to Kathleen's affections, the bond was strongest between father and daughter, Kathleen and Harry. Kitty saw it, she later came to realize, even when Kathleen was a baby. Kathleen would be in her crib and refuse to settle down until her father would come to her, then lie there with her large liquid blue eyes fixed on him, a coy happy smile on her face, watching every move he made, flirting with her father before she could even walk.

"That come-hither look," Harry said, looking up from the baby and laughing to Kitty, both intrigued and unsettled. "You females are born with it, aren't you?"

At the time, before she knew too much of the makeup of this man, her husband, Kitty was flattered, thinking she was his point of reference. It was years later, when Kathleen was older and Harry, the more she got to know him, had become a complete stranger to her, that Kitty remembered the remark. And shuddered.

. . . as in the intensive care ward at Onagona County Memorial Hospital, Pamela stands beside the bed of a sleeping patient, the man who was once a construction superintendent on the project across the alley from her old apartment who in time became her friend and lover, his heavy frame a rotund mound beneath the white sheet, stands beside his bed to check the monitors and the IVs in his arms, when the man, as if he senses her presence, opens his eyes and smiles and says faintly, "Hey," "Hey yourself,"

*Pamela says taking his hand, "How are you feeling?" "Like shit,"
and Pamela smiles as she says, "You had a heart attack," "That's
what I figured it was," "You shouldn't have risked driving all the
way here, there were closer hospitals," "I figured my chances
might be better where I knew somebody," he grins, not saying
what they both know, and Pamela says, "I told you, Jack, no
matter what happens, I'll always be here for you, all you have to
do is call," "And I called," "And I'm here," and Jack smiles and
gives her hand a little squeeze but he's already drifting into sleep
again and Pamela bends down and kisses his hand and lays it on
the bed and continues to stand there to make sure he's resting
comfortably before going to find a chair so she can keep
watch . . . as in his office on the main street of town, in the
building that is known for lack of a better name as the Sutcliff
Building, Dickie barely gets seated at his desk before he picks up
the phone and calls his secretary and tells her to get him in touch
with the nearest Ethan Allen, "I'm going to buy a couch, correc-
tion, make that a sofa," "For your office?" Mrs. Jansen says and
Dickie says, "Never mind where it's for, and get me someone who
can authorize immediate delivery, I want it delivered tomorrow
morning," and Mrs. Jansen says, "I doubt if they can do that
kind of rush order. . . ," and Dickie says, "Don't talk to me about
can't, talk to me about how," and rings off before she can say
anything else, thinking That's one more thing my father taught
me, everything and everybody has a price, and a cost . . . as in
the darkened dining room of the big house with the tower on the
edge of Orchard Hill, witnessed by hundreds of eyes of the figu-
rines and knickknacks that crowd every flat surface of the room—
a knobby giraffe that can be bent into impossible positions and a
porcelain elephant, the wood carvings of a moose and a cow and
a bear, half a dozen black ceramic panthers elongated in mid-
stride, figures of angelic but naughty little boys and dozens of
mugs in the shape of disembodied heads including a Beefeater*

and Ebenezer Scrooge and Winston Churchill—Kitty Sutcliff reaches in her mock treasure chest and pulls out the next three photographs she has decided to lay out for Harry Todd, the first a picture of herself standing on the front porch of the first house she and Harry owned, a typical young housewife except that she is dressed in a gypsy outfit; the second of Harry at the time that Sutcliff Realty was coming into its own and sewing up the real estate market not only in Furnass but in the entire area, standing in front of the three-story building with a glass front on the main street that he recently had built for his offices; and the third a picture of Harry's father and herself sitting side by side in a speedboat moored at a dock, herself in a sunback dress and straw hat, Doctor as always buttoned up in his suit and vest even though the family was on an outing to Conneaut Lake, the two of them looking totally incongruous and perfectly comfortable together, thinking, There's a story here, my son, if you'll only put the pieces together . . . as a short while later Harry Todd, back from his trip downtown to see Julian Lyle, and then his surprise run-in with Donna Bruno, enters the silent house from the garage and makes his way through the kitchen and into the dining room, in turn looks at the three photographs he finds laid out on the table, the first one of his mother standing on the porch of an unfamiliar house, a typical young housewife except that she's dressed in a harem outfit with flimsy pantaloons and a bare midriff, holding a mop and bucket, and Harry Todd thinks Good Lord, did she really dress like that to clean house? No wonder Father got a little potty; the second photo of his father in his mid- or late thirties, in a rumpled ill-fitting gabardine suit, his muscular build starting to go soft and pudgy, sporting one of the high-crowned gray felt hats he ordered specially from Pittsburgh, and Harry Todd thinks He's standing there on the main street with his legs apart like the Colossus of Rhodes, confronting the camera the way he did everything and everyone else, head-on; and the third photo of his

*mother and his grandfather in what appears to be a speedboat,
only it's tied at a dock and not going anywhere, the two of them
looking as though they're totally enjoying each other's company
and Harry Todd thinks That's the only picture I ever saw of my
grandfather where he's smiling, what's Mother getting at, that she
and Grandfather were in the same boat? and turns away from the
table and goes into the hall, thinking again (or perhaps still) of
the things Donna told him at the restaurant about Kathleen, wondering how much he should believe, and how much he should tell
his mother, thinking again as he looks at the straight-backed rocking chair in the living room of the day when Kathleen came downstairs after her shower and he tried to make a joke by pulling the
towel from her and they ended up rolling on the floor, he was on
top of her naked body, and like he'd seen in the movies he got his
pants down and started to enter her and she gasped which to him
sounded like a scream and before he knew what was happening he
had exploded all over her stomach and there was semen dripping
everywhere and all he knew was that he had to get out of there,
got to his feet pulling on his pants as she was crying behind him,
"Harry Todd, what's wrong, don't leave me," as he ran from the
house and got in his mother's car and drove downtown, the start
of the afternoons and evenings he drove endlessly up and down
the main street when he wasn't dating every girl he could get his
hands on and put his hands on them he did, going through dozens
of girls in the back seat of his mother's car until he started to
date Donna and the idea of dating a cheerleader from the class
ahead of him fed his interest in her long after his actual attraction
to her had dwindled away, on the track to marriage and babyland
until his father stepped in and sent him away to school, thinking
That's how it all got started with Donna, wasn't it, it started with
me trying to get away from Kathleen, because I was afraid to be
in the house alone with her again, and stands in the doorway of
the living room looking down at the place on the living room floor*

where it happened, remembering that for months after it happened he continually checked for a bloodstain on the carpet, at the time he thought it must have blended into the pattern and it was a red rug, though later after being with other girls and experiencing what it felt like to be inside them he realized he was never inside Kathleen that day, probably wasn't even close, thinking regardless that after he ran from the house that day Kathleen had to clean up the mess by herself because he was too afraid or embarrassed or something to stay around her, thinking I wonder what was going through her mind then, I wonder if she knew it was me I was running away from, not her. . . .

23

As he rounded the landing to the second floor, there was thumping, the sound of something moving about behind the closed door to what had been Kathleen's room. Okay. This is ridiculous. That's got to be Mother doing something, another one of her projects, maybe she's decided to add another room onto the house, I don't know, take out a bearing wall or something. That's all it is. . . . He tried the door but it only opened six inches or so, something was against it, blocking it from opening further. The room had become one of several storerooms where his mother dumped anything and everything that she didn't know what else to do with, crowded almost to the ceiling with cardboard boxes, plastic storage containers, green garbage bags, piles of clothes, stacks of picture frames, books, magazines, with pathways leading to the bed, the closet on the opposite side of the room, the window. He pushed on the door to try to open it further, but it pushed back. His mother's disembodied head canted around the edge of the door, looking at him quizzically, then smiling.

"Oh, it's you," she said.

Wonder who else she thought it might be. "Everything okay? I thought I heard something fall. . . ."

"No, everything's fine. Just starting to go through some of these things. I think it's about time, don't you?" As she moved away from behind the door and it opened a few inches further, he watched as she dug into a box and pulled out a long-eared rabbit. The rabbit had definitely seen better days, its fur was moth-eaten, patches of its cloth body visible, and the stuffing had shifted and clumped so the body hung limp and disjointed, the head flopping around, its single eye rolling suggestively. His mother held it up for Harry Todd to see, then regarded it sadly and waggled it at her son again. "I guess we certainly don't need her anymore, do we?"

She put the rabbit back in the box and closed it up. Looked at him and shrugged. "Did you see anyone you know downtown?"

And how did she know I went downtown? I didn't tell her where I was going. It pissed him off that she was butting into his business, keeping track of where he was going. He was almost fifty, for Christ's sake. He'd show her. "As a matter of fact I did see someone. A couple of people. Julian Lyle for one."

"I thought you might go see Julian. After our little talk."

Which pissed him off even further. "He said there actually was an autopsy after Kathleen died."

"Yes dear, I know."

Wait a minute. "I thought you said you didn't know if there was one."

"I don't know where you got that idea. Of course there was an autopsy, because the way Kathleen died was so sudden. Mysterious. I never saw it though."

Harry Todd was confused; he raked his hand back through his hair. In the crack of the door his mother moved out of sight for a moment, then moved back into view, a collection of purses dangling on her wrist. She waved her arm so the purses swung to and fro in a little dance.

"And then I ran into Donna when I was leaving Julian's office. She seemed to know more about the autopsy than Julian did."

"I'm not surprised to hear that about Julian. He seems to have lived in a fog most of his life. How is Donna?"

"She looks good. I was surprised." He knew he shouldn't say it, he knew it even as he said it. "She said the autopsy said that Kathleen died of a barbiturate overdose."

His mother looked at him for a moment, then took the purses off her wrist, one by one, put them back into a plastic container. "I know there was talk of something of the sort at the time. But I assumed it must be just that: talk. People say a lot of things when a tragedy happens, trying to make sense of it all, when the truth is there may be no sense to it, no easy answer. For one thing, how would your sister get barbiturates? It's not as if they're lying around, and Kathleen certainly wasn't a drug addict, not with her asthma. But as I said, your father would never let me know about such a thing, if that was the cause of death. He was always trying to shield me, poor man. And you have to be careful about anything Donna says. She was sleeping with Dickie around that time, so she's probably not the most reliable source of information."

Wait. "Donna was sleeping with Dickie?"

"You needn't look so surprised. You slept with her first, if you recall. Now, let's talk about something else, instead of all this sordid business. Do you have any use for this baseball glove? Anybody around to play catch with?"

Harry Todd's thoughts were reeling. He backed away from the door and went on upstairs to his room on the third floor. Thinking Barbiturates? Dickie and Donna? And Mother knew about all this? What kind of animal is Dickie? And I thought I was supposed to be the bad one. I know, little brother, that you always wanted to do everything I did, but still. And he must know about the barbiturates too. What the hell is going on here. . . ?

24

After Harry Todd went upstairs to the third floor, Kitty continued to work in the room, going through the boxes and piles of things, reminding herself of what all exactly was in the room, the things themselves reminding her of people and events, the reasons why she kept the things in the first place, their importance in the history of the family—all of the children's artwork from grade school, Kathleen definitely the artist of the three; the clothes still on their hangers from Harry Todd's and Dickie's closets that they left behind when they moved on with their lives, and the clothes from Kathleen's closet after she died; boxes of family photographs she always meant to put into albums but never got around to; things that she saved simply because she didn't know what else to do with them, that seemed sacrilegious somehow to throw away, as if in doing so she was throwing her children, her husband, away, their lives together as a family—until she heard the sound of the riding mower from outside and realized what time it was getting to be. She looked around the room once more, then turned off the overhead light, squeezed through the opening of the door, and went downstairs.

In the dining room she pulled back the heavy drapes from the windows, flooding the room with grayish, dirty light, singing to herself Doctor's favorite song:

> Beautiful dreamer, wake unto me,
> Starlight and dewdrops are waiting for thee. . . .

The downstairs of the house, most of the summer, would remain cool as long as she kept it dark during the heat of the day, as long as she tended religiously the business of keeping the drapes and windows closed on the sun-filled side of the house, opening the drapes and windows on the side away from the sun. But on humid days like this, the heat permeated the house, as if seeping through the walls, no matter what she did. And it seemed to be getting more humid as the afternoon became evening. She finished opening the drapes and then the windows, hoping to get a breeze started in the house, as well as to keep an eye on Jennifer.

. . . Sounds of the rude world heard in the day,
Lulled by the moonlight have all passed away. . . .

From the bay window, Kitty could see her granddaughter on the riding mower as Jennifer bumped back and forth across this end of the backyard. Kitty thought it was too hot for the girl to be cutting the grass, but she knew there was no telling that to Jennifer. Her granddaughter was like herself in that regard: to tell her not to do something was to guarantee that she'd do it. Unlike Kathleen, who had always been so eager to please, who would never go against anything that was told to her. Though Kathleen was more dangerous in a way because of her secret side, her wants and desires that she tried to keep from view.

Kitty sat down on the window seat in the bay window, listening to the sound of the mower, watching Merry Anne asleep on the rug, the cat's paws quivering slightly.

She must be dreaming, maybe she thinks she's a kitten again, chasing a moth or a ball of yarn, I hope she's happy, we chase our dreams to the very end, if we're lucky. . . .

She loved Jennifer deeply, but there were times her granddaughter was like a living recrimination to her. She had watched Jennifer grow from a precocious butterball into a mature, intelligent, capable, and lovely young woman. Whereas Kathleen's journey into adulthood had been quite different. Kathleen had been a beautiful blond-haired, blue-eyed baby—she and Harry Todd were often mistaken for twins then—a willowy and bright and bouncy child, who, starting in her midteens, became increasingly sickly and plain, a pale and beaky girl with limp hair and touches of acne. She remembered the day, after she had been to see Dr. Neely, that she went to Harry's office to talk to him about Kathleen, to tell him what the doctor said. It had been a while since she had been to her husband's office, and this was a convenient excuse; she liked to visit now and then, to see what all was going on. To make sure everyone there knew who she was, to make sure she knew everyone who was there.

"So that's your new secretary," she said, standing in Harry's office near the doorway, standing where she could see the plumpish redhead, in gold lamé mules and tight skirt and a white blouse ruffled in tiers like a flower in bloom, who was filing in the outer office. "Janice, is it?"

"Janet. As you very well know."

"That's right, Janet. What happened to Suzanne? Or shouldn't I ask?"

Harry, sitting at his desk, was doing his best to appear absorbed with some reports. "Suzanne moved on," he said without looking at her.

"I'll bet she did. With a push, no doubt. I'm surprised at this one though, I would have thought she's a little too roly-poly for you. I guess she's good for a change."

Harry continued to busy himself with his papers.

"On the other hand I can see where Suzanne would wear thin after a while," Kitty said. "Was she starting to question when you were going to divorce me and marry her? Which one was that . . . Ruth, I think it was. . . ."

Harry, exasperated, put down the report and took off his metal-framed glasses, but before he could say anything Kitty hurried on.

"Guess who I saw on the street a few minutes before I came in here? Harry Todd and Kathleen, they were walking downtown after school, but not together. Kathleen was across the street, watching her brother with another girl. It was a little strange, not to see them together."

"They're in high school. You can't expect them to be together all their lives. It's good that the boy's getting out, seeing other girls. I was beginning to think it was unhealthy, the way the two of them were together all the time."

"That's what the doctor said, too."

"What's that?"

"He thinks Kathleen's too attached to her brother. He thinks it may be creating an emotional situation that's making the asthma worse. I'm not sure I agree, I think she's always looked to Harry Todd as her protector more than anything else."

"I don't know where George Neely comes up with that stuff. Emotional situation, indeed. And why would Kathleen need a protector? There's nothing wrong with the girl."

No, in your eyes there wouldn't be.

"Still, it was sad to see Kathleen that way. She was obviously upset about Harry Todd being with somebody else. I think she was following them, to see what they were up to. I have the car today, so I guess Harry Todd can't be up to very much. Though Sutcliff men seem to find ways to get what they want from girls, don't they? The same way girls find ways to get what they want from Sutcliff men." She looked again through the doorway at Janet, then back to Harry.

"What is it, Kitty? What do you want?"

Kitty demurred and wagged her head. "I was downtown and thought I'd stop in and say hello and tell you what Dr. Neely said. . . ."

"No, Kitty, not that." He stood up behind the desk, a big man in his shirtsleeves, his face showing increasingly the signs of his age and his drinking, perpetually enflamed, though he was still an impressive if not handsome man. "I'm not talking about today, all this small talk and innuendo. I mean the big picture, the bottom line. I really want to know. What do you want? What do you want from me?"

To stay away from Kathleen.

But she didn't say anything. She didn't answer him, she only smiled, a bit apologetically, feeling suddenly dishonest about being there, as if she had played a game too far, feeling almost sorry for the man in all his ignorance, and left his office. She knew that if there was a problem with Kathleen and Harry Todd, it was only a peripheral one; and she knew her husband could never accept what the real problem was because he could never accept such a thing was possible. Not only that, she knew it was more her responsibility than his to keep Kathleen and her father away from each other. It was her responsibility because she knew more than the doctor about Kathleen's attractions and vulnerabilities. She had known for years, she had even tried to take Kathleen away from here, once Kitty finally admitted to herself the kind of man she married, once she knew things between herself and Harry were never going to get better, and things between Harry and Kathleen could only get worse. She took Kathleen away—and then brought her back again because of her own attractions and vulnerabilities. It was her responsibility because, by bringing Kathleen back to Furnass, Kitty knew she was putting them all in harm's way. It was a responsibility she had chosen to live with, because she found it was the price she was willing to pay to have something to live for.

The sound of the mower had grown distant; Jennifer had moved on to the yard behind the house, down by the tennis courts. Kitty patted her thighs through the cotton housedress—C'mon, old girl, get on with it—and finished opening the windows and drapes in the room. In the grayish light, she went to the dining room table and laid out the next three photographs from the treasure chest that she had selected to put out for Harry Todd. The first showed her husband as a young married man, his shirtsleeves rolled up, with Kathleen when she was only a year or so old; he held the baby by the scruff of her dress, ready to airplane her about as he did every evening when he got home from work, Kathleen in her bonnet laughing and laughing. The next showed Harry Todd on the front porch when he was five, proud in a new white sailor suit, his arms clasped behind his back; he stood with his chest puffed out so far that his arms looked chopped off at his sides. The third photo showed the children playing in the yard with the cardboard box the new refrigerator had come in; their father looked on from the porch as Harry Todd and Dickie tried to camouflage the box with boughs from trees of heaven, Kathleen peeking out from a window cut in the side.

Put her in a pumpkin shell, and there we kept her very well. . . .

Kitty continued through the downstairs, opening the drapes and windows as she went, sashaying from room to room trying, unsuccessfully, to stir up a breeze for herself. Trying, unsuccessfully, to boost her spirits. Then she stood at the front door, looking out at the lawn and the front steps, the trees at the end of the property and a glimpse of the town below in the valley. She rested her forehead against the screen; it was probably filthy, she could smell the caked-on soot, the rusted metal, the years of weather, but she didn't care. She felt she had failed so badly, so badly. She thought about what she'd remembered earlier, that she had once taken Kathleen away from here, to the safety of her parents' home in Rome, New York, fed up with Harry's duplicity, afraid of where it might lead, only to return to Furnass a few months later, having discovered the duplicity of herself. She remembered the morning they returned, descending from the Pullman car; she helped Kathleen down the metal steps, thinking at the time it was as if she were helping the eleven-year-old step carefully into quicksand, the kindness of a prison guard to the condemned. Coming down the station platform were the two boys towing their father; the greetings were a blur to her. But through the confusion of hugs and steam billowing from underneath the train and hurried hellos, she saw briefly, standing by himself at the end of the platform, unknown to the others, Dr. Sutcliff. He met her gaze with a mixture of sadness and knowing, before turning and walking away.

As soon as she could get away that evening, as soon as the children were safely in bed and Harry had left on one of his late-night rambles—nothing had changed, nothing—she left their big house on the bluff above the town, walked out into the flaming night air of the mill town and drove down into the town, parking in the alley across from the police station and let herself in the back door of Doctor's office, the door she knew he'd leave unlocked for her, joining the older man in his smoke-filled office as he rocked slowly back and forth in the wood rocker, Kitty sitting across from him in a straight-backed chair.

"So, you came back."

"Yes, I came back. And here we are again."

"This is crazy. This is against the natural order. . . ."

"I know, you told me that. But it doesn't matter. I'll redefine the natural order. Or I'll learn to live in the unnatural one."

"But what can come of it?"

"Nothing. And everything. . . ."

There was a tapping, the hum of tiny wings. Kitty straightened up away from the screen, away from the dent she put in it with her forehead. On the outside, a ladybug was crawling up the mesh, unshelling its wings and beating its head periodically against the unyielding net before walking on to try somewhere else. Kitty flicked her finger against the screen and set the insect flying. Ladybug, ladybug, fly away home. Your house is on fire, your children will burn. What a curious rhyme to teach children. Believe me, bug, you don't want in here. It's buggy enough as it is.

25

Harry Todd woke to the sound of the mower ebbing and flowing across the lawn. He looked at his watch. A little after seven-thirty. Gradually it came to him that it was seven-thirty in the evening. From the bed he could see into a section of the circular tower, the edge of his desk under the windows and the wooden chair; the windows were gray with dusk, pearly, but no light seemed to enter the room, as if it refused to come inside, not wishing to become involved. He lay on his back for a while, staring up into the planes and angles of the attic ceiling, the geometry created by the underside of the hips and valleys of the roof. The heat weighed on him like a presence, holding him down; he was sticky with sweat. He thought he should get up, he wasn't really hungry but he should eat something, but decided to lie there a little longer.

After a while—he had no idea how long he lay there—he rolled his head to the side on the pillow. The figure of a young girl came into the room and slid across the wall, heading toward the tower. . . . This is no reflection from a passing car, this is not from a car turning around in the street. As Harry Todd watched, the girl sat down in the wooden desk chair, the bars of the carved back visible through her as if he were peering through a mist. He was surprised that she didn't look more like Kathleen, she didn't look like anyone he recognized. She got herself comfortable, arranging her cobweb-like dress around her, then looked at him, not smiling, not anything at all, totally blank, the eye sockets empty. Harry Todd sat bolt upright on the bed. The girl was gone.

He was no longer sweaty. A chill washed over him like a breeze, as if something were passing through the room . . . I must have been dreaming. But she seemed so real. Don't start thinking like that. . . . Stiffly, he got up and went over into the tower. He kept an eye on the chair, half expecting to see the girl still sitting there. Across the room, the fan on the floor continued to push the hot muggy air back and forth; from outside came the sound of the mower. Harry Todd leaned his weight on his knuckles, simian-like, on the desktop and peered down from on high.

Below, Jennifer was piloting the riding mower back and forth across the lawn at the rear of the house. For several minutes he watched the foreshortened figure of the girl, dressed in shorts and halter, her not-quite-red hair under her Stetson pulled into a ponytail, bumping along, making parallel patterns with the freshly cut grass. A wise man at this point would know to stay up here. A wise man would know better than to go down there and talk to her. After several minutes more, as she was close to finishing— Lord, I wish I was a wise man—he straightened up and headed downstairs, slowly, taking his time, or trying to, so he didn't appear too anxious, either to himself or to his mother if she happened to be around, to catch Jennifer before she left.

He strolled out across the lawn—That's right, look around, a guy out for a breath of air, enjoying the evening—as Jennifer was finishing her last pass, along the edge of the yard close to the trees. Harry Todd angled across the grass to intercept her. He grinned and gave a little wave as she approached; she reset the straw Stetson on her head in acknowledgment, and bumped right on by him, leaving him standing there with his arm half-raised, tilting her head at him and mugging wide-eyed as if she were being carried away by a force beyond her control. Well, what did you expect? That she'd stop everything she was doing for the chance to talk to you? Yeah, I guess, kinda. . . . When she finished the swath, she lifted the cutting blades of the mower, shifted into another gear, and putt-putted back to him. She stopped beside him, the engine idling, and leaned on the steering wheel, looking up at him from under the brim of the hat with her unreadable smile, waiting for him to say whatever it was he had to say. In the evening glow, her thighs glistened with a slight sheen. Don't let her catch you looking. . . .

"I've been wondering who cut the grass now," Harry Todd said, talking loudly to be heard over the engine. "Your father and I did it with gasoline push mowers. It would take forever, and by the time we got it done it was time to do it again."

"The way Grandmother tells it," Jennifer said, leaning toward him, "she tried to get you and Dad to do it, but you always made such a mess of it that she had to hire a gardener."

"That's probably closer to the truth."

He smiled awkwardly, realizing he had nothing else to say to the girl . . . Why did I think I wanted to see her? I'm standing here like an idiot. He expected her to put the mower back into gear and drive away, but she turned off the engine and tipped her hat back on her head as if to get a better look at him. The sudden silence was even more unnerving than the sound of the engine. Look at the way she's looking at me, batting her big green eyes, like she's got me all sized up, classified and wriggling on a pin. She's at the age when she thinks being difficult is asserting herself, being coy is an inalienable right, she's young.

"How's the visit going?"

"It's okay. A little weird. More than a little. I took your suggestion and talked to Julian Lyle. And I think I found out that Kathleen died of a barbiturate overdose."

"You think you found out? Is that what Lyle said?"

"Not exactly. But yes, indirectly—it's complicated," Harry Todd said, being evasive, not wanting to mention talking to Donna Bruno. "You sound as if you don't consider Julian Lyle a reliable source of information."

"Lyle likes to think he represents the interests of Sutcliff Realty and my dad. But Dad only gives him menial things to do, things that he doesn't consider important or that require the services of a good attorney. It was the same way with my grandfather too. Granddad kept him around because he knew he had Julian under his thumb."

"That's not very complimentary to Julian."

"It's not meant to be. It's the truth."

"Speaking of: there seems to have been some attempt to keep quiet that barbiturates were involved in Kathleen's death. Your father apparently knew what happened and was part of keeping the lid on it. That's probably why he told you not to bring up the subject." Harry Todd thought a moment. "If barbiturates were involved, I guess it means she committed suicide."

Jennifer climbed off the mower, stretching first one leg and then the other while reaching up inside the leg of her shorts to adjust the elastic of her panties—For my benefit?—and walked a short distance away along the treeline. The valley had sunk to afterglow. As she thought about something, Jennifer reached down and pulled up a few tall blades of grass the mower had missed. What's this about, is she trying to show me her ass? It's very nice. . . . Then she came back. Something was bothering her; in the growing darkness her face looked troubled.

"I wasn't going to say anything, but as long as you've found out this much I guess it can't hurt. After I found Kathleen that morning and Grandmother and Grandfather got her back up onto the bed, I saw Grandmother find a pill bottle in the bedclothes and try to hide it in a pocket of her robe. Grandfather saw her do it too. But he didn't say anything about it so I thought it must be okay."

"That would mean Mother's known all along that pills were involved. So why did she tell me it was a coronary thrombosis and pretend she didn't know anything about the results of the autopsy?"

"Probably for the same reason she hid the bottle when she found it. She didn't want anyone to know it was suicide. That's not the nicest thing to know about somebody you love. If it was suicide."

"If?"

"You don't know that for sure. I mean, yes, that's probably what happened. I'm just saying. People do take too many pills by accident."

"But what was she doing with barbiturates at all? I mean, wouldn't you have to be careful with medicines like that with her asthma? I never heard that Kathleen had a prescription for them or anything."

"How would you? You were never here."

Harry Todd ignored the comment and its implications. He shook his head in amazement. "My mother's continued headlong flight from reality."

"What are you going to do?"

"I don't know what there is to do. There's a part of me that wants to confront her with it. But there's another part of me that wonders if there isn't more to it. The trouble is, the way Mother's acted so far I doubt that she'd tell me what it is. I'd like to find out more about what happened, but I don't know who else would know about it."

"Maybe you need to forget about it for a while. Relax a little, not think about things so much."

"Yeah, maybe," Harry Todd said absently.

Jennifer got on the mower and was about to turn on the ignition when she looked at him again. "Maybe you need to have some fun. After I put this mower away, I'm going to take my bike out to the old strip mines near Mingo Junction and go skinny-dipping. Want to come?"

It took Harry Todd a moment to realize what she was offering. She grinned at him a little sideways, her head tilted, her eyes dark and playful, almost hidden under the brim of the hat. Well, here it is. What you wanted. What are you going to do about it? He studied her a moment in the afterglow.

"You know, I'd really like to. But I think I'll pass."

"Whatever." She gave a little shrug and started the engine. "Bye, Uncle Harry Todd. Don't think too much."

Her smile had returned to unreadable as she put the mower into gear and lurched forward across the dark grass, heading toward the storage shed in the backyard. She probably thinks I'm a wuss. Maybe I am. I turned down a really pretty girl. Got any ideas why? Maybe it's because I'm getting old. Maybe it's because she's my niece. Hard to believe I'm developing scruples at this age. As he headed back up the lawn, a trail of lights came on in the downstairs of the dark house, one after another, marking his mother's progress through the rooms. Not knowing what to say to her at this point, he sat on the porch swing, waiting until she moved off to another part of the house. After a while, Jennifer roared down the driveway on her motorcycle, in the half-light the beam of the headlight picking out individual trees on the other side of the street, before she rode away into the evening. Bye, pretty girl. I wish things were different. I wish I was. In more ways than one. . . .

26

Dickie was at his office late, after hours, finishing up the day's business when the phone rang. It was Harvey McMillan from First City Bank, though at the moment Harvey was calling from home.

"That was quick," Dickie said, trying to sound jovial, to mask his concern that something had gone wrong already with the deal Dickie proposed to him today at the golf course. "You said you'd get back to me but I didn't expect anything this soon."

"Actually, I'm calling about something else, though it's related to what we discussed today. Julian Lyle called a little while ago."

"And what was on Julian's mind?"

"Yes, Julian, well, he asked my opinion on the idea of turning the Allehela Works into an industrial museum."

Dickie felt his anger well up, but he kept it in check, laughing a little. "He's a bit late, don't you think? Or has he forgotten about a certain project that's already under way called Furnass Landing?"

"No, he hasn't forgotten about it. I'm afraid he's considering the possibilities of trying to stop any further development of the site with a court order."

"That's crazy. You know he has no basis for an injunction."

"I'm assuming he doesn't. But I'm afraid I don't know that for a fact. The courts are handing down some crazy decisions these days, what with all these environmental concerns and all."

"Even so, Harvey. . . ."

"You understand, don't you, Dickie, that if there is any danger of Lyle going through with something like that, if he tries to get a court order—or worse, if he mentions this museum idea to the papers and gets some public support behind it—I would be in no position to pursue the kind of financial arrangement we discussed."

Dickie's anger swept over him now in waves, like the chills accompanying a fever—That fool, that goddamn fool—though he continued to keep his voice under control, sounding even more reasonable, more conciliatory and good-natured than before.

"Of course, I completely understand. But I'm sure there's been some misconception on Julian's part. I'll have a talk with him tomorrow and get the whole thing straightened out."

"You might also want to have a talk with your brother."

"Harry Todd? What's he got to do with it?"

"I'm not sure. But it seems from what Lyle said that Harry Todd was the one who gave him the idea."

Dickie forced a chuckle. "It was probably Harry Todd's idea of a joke, and that fool Julian took him seriously. Don't worry, Harv, I'll take care of it." He ended the conversation as quickly as possible.

For a few moments, Dickie continued to sit there at his desk, waiting until he got his anger under control before he considered what to do next. *What's your game, Harry Todd? Was Pamela right, are you here to try to get a piece of the business? Or is it to weasel your way back into the family, maybe take over the big house and milk Mother for everything you can get out of her? Whatever, it all adds up to the same thing. Well, we'll see about that, brother of mine, we'll see.* Through the open door he had a view of the outer office, the gray melancholy light of dusk slanting over the empty desks, everyone else gone home to their families. To loved ones. He calmed himself with the thought that tomorrow morning he'd drive out to see Pamela again, to make sure the couch—er, sofa—had been delivered as promised. It better be. He could imagine her surprise, the smile on her face. Maybe they'd even christen it then, spreading a sheet on it first so they didn't stain it, she'd insist on that. He smiled to himself, rubbed his hand across the blade of his chin. When he was sure he was in control of himself again, he picked up the phone and called Donna Bruno.

. . . as in Furnass Heights, on the rim of the hills above the town, Julian Lyle, in a pair of well-worn New Balance track shoes, tank top with the number 32 printed on it from a race he ran several years ago, and running shorts cut a little too high and showing a little too much leg to be quite in good taste, runs in the growing darkness along the berm of Seneca Road, then turns down steep Downie Hill Road Extension, hauling back against the windy

*quarter-mile grade lest the forces of gravity get the better of him
while at the same time letting those same forces pull him along,
at the bottom continuing along Berry's Run Road, his nightly six-
mile run though he's a little later than usual this evening after
calling Harvey McMillan at home, keeping a marathoner's pace,
the easy strides of a long-distance runner, staying far over on the
shoulder whenever he sees the headlights of an occasional car
coming toward him in the afterglow, and thinks of the visit he had
today from Harry Todd Sutcliff, thinks about how Dickie must be
taking it with his older brother back on the scene—No wonder he
was testy the other day when I talked to him about taking over
the Towers project, that explains why he said those things to me—
thinks about the questions Harry Todd asked regarding his sister's
death, about Dickie's reaction when he finds out Harry Todd is
trying to exhume that old business, and thinks about the expression on Dickie's face when he finds out that, not only is Julian
starting proceedings to turn the old Allehela Works into an industrial museum before Dickie can destroy any more of it, but
Dickie's own brother was the one who gave him the idea—Dickie
likes to jerk people around, well, let's see how he likes being the
jerkee for once—smiles to himself as he runs on through the heat
and the twilight on the seldom-traveled road, the only sounds the
chirr of cicadas in the woods and the steady pace of his footfalls
in the gravel and the whumpa-whumpa-whumpa of his heart,
imagining the scene if Harry Todd would take him up on the idea
to come running with him some evening, imagining the two of
them running side by side for a while, before Julian begins gradually to pull away, drawing farther and farther ahead, Harry Todd
obviously in no shape to keep up with him on a run like this,
imagines looking back over his shoulder and seeing the conster-
nation and strain and grudging admiration on Harry Todd's face,
Julian eventually leaving him far behind in the nightfall, in this
imagining the only time he ever got the better of a Sutcliff in his*

*life . . . as in downtown Furnass at Holy Innocents Church,
Donna Bruno kneels at the railing of a side altar, before a statue
of the Virgin Mary holding the infant Jesus, reciting her twenty-
fifth or maybe it's her twenty-sixth rosary of the evening, when
on the other side of the large empty church Father Mulroy comes
from the sacristy and sees her and shakes his head a little, comes
across the sanctuary, stopping to genuflect in recognition of the
host residing in the tabernacle on the main altar, and proceeds
down the steps and across the church to the niche decorated to
look like a grotto and says softly, "It's time, Donna," and she
looks at him with what if he didn't know better could be called a
beatific smile and says, "So soon?" and Father Mulroy nods and
says, "I gave you an extra hour as it is, it's almost eight o'clock,
I have to lock up now," and Donna looks up at the Virgin who
smiles to her and she thinks maybe, just maybe she sees the infant
Jesus wave His little fingers at her and Donna smiles and makes
the sign of the cross and says, "You're right, Father, I shouldn't
keep you any longer," and gets up and genuflects in the direction
of the main altar and clicks on her high heels up the aisle past
the rows of empty pews toward the front doors, followed by Father
Mulroy who says, trying to make small talk, "It feels like it's
getting warmer outside," and Donna stops at the large birdbath-
sized font of holy water in the foyer and says, "It's the humidity,"
and the priest looks at her in the dim light and says, "Are you
okay, Donna? Because, you know, if you need some help, there
are agencies up in Pittsburgh. . . ," and she smiles again beatifi-
cally and says, "I know, Father, you've told me before, but I'm
fine, really. Good night," and takes a few drops of holy water on
her fingertips and blesses herself and he says, "Good night, I
won't be here tomorrow evening, so Father Campion will be lock-
ing up," and she says, "I'll be here," as she leans her weight
against one of the oversized front doors and pushes out into the
warm summer evening, content, fulfilled, having thanked the*

Virgin for bringing her love home to her again, for giving her one more chance to show how much she loves him, the years of penance and sacrifice and prayer answered, at peace with herself, knowing she is a child of God . . . as at the nurses' station in the intensive care ward of Onagona Memorial Hospital, Pamela checks the chart for the latest update on a certain patient, then goes on down the aisle, her shoes squeaking softly on the polished floor, and steps within the curtained area to check for the umpteenth time on the sleeping figure, checks the monitors and the IVs in his arms, when the man, as if sensing her presence again, opens his eyes and smiles faintly: "You still here?" and Pamela says, "I was about to ask you the same question," and he says, "The other reason why . . . I wanted to come here is . . . I thought if I lived through this . . . and started to get better . . . maybe you'd climb into bed with me. . . ," and Pamela says, "Stranger things have happened," and he says, "We did have . . . some good times . . . didn't we?" and Pamela says, "Remember when you used to tell me that we only get screwed in this world by our friends, because we never let our enemies get close enough? Well, you get healthy, mister, and I'll screw you, all right, and you'll know I'm your best friend," and Jack smiles but is already gone again and Pamela continues to stand there for a while, reluctant to leave, thinking Dickie would never understand this, why I still feel the way I do about this guy, and yet the two of them are very similar, the two men of my life, two sides of the same coin, both hard-ass bastards who will die with my name engraved on their hearts, only Dickie still thinks it's our enemies who screw us and he can't figure out how I fit into the mix . . . as still in his office at this late hour Dickie picks up the phone and dials Donna's number again, so surprised when she actually picks up the phone that it takes him a moment before he can say anything:

"Hello, Donna, it's Dickie Sutcliff."

Some Rise

"I know who you are, Dickie Sutcliff," she says, sounding a bit impudent and flirty. "I thought you might be calling me."

"And why would you think that?"

"Because Harry Todd's back in town and I thought you might become suddenly interested in me again."

Dickie laughs, to brush aside the implications. Careful. "You know I'm always interested in you, Donna. In fact that's why I'm calling now. I need you to do me a favor."

When Donna doesn't say anything, he goes on.

"I need to have a look at Julian's financial records for the past few years, tax returns, bank statements, loan agreements, anything you have."

"Dickie, what makes you think I would do something like that?"

"Because it's payback time, Donna. Pure and simple."

"But you know I can't let you see that kind of confidential information."

"I know you shouldn't, but I also know you will. Because when I got you that job with Lyle I told you there might be occasions like this. And you know that you'll never find another job in this town that would pay half of what you're making there. You know that because you also know I've been footing the bill for at least half of your salary since you started with Lyle. And you know something else too: you know that if somebody doesn't stop Lyle and his crazy property-investment, get-rich-quick schemes he'll run himself and his little practice right into the ground, if he hasn't already, and this town will lose the only attorney, however mediocre, it has, and you won't have a job regardless. And you know that I'm the one person who can stop him once and for all, if I decide to, and I've decided to. So make your copies and get them over to my office as soon as you can in the morning, and by that I mean before nine a.m. I'll be expecting you" . . . as in the hills beyond Mingo Junction and Indian Camp, in the wilder *more isolated part of the county, a dozen or so young people, of college age and after, sit around in the darkness on the craggy outcroppings of an abandoned strip mine, old friends who have been coming here since high school and have continued to gather here on hot summer evenings, all of them naked, including Jennifer who lies on a blanket, propped up on one elbow as she drinks an Iron City and watches those who are swimming—nearby a couple is fucking, giggling about something as they slowly rock back and forth; Jennifer watches them disinterestedly for a moment, then turns back to the swimmers—and thinks I was crazy to even think about balling Harry Todd, he's not interested in me, he's still in love with his dead sister, whether he knows it or not, and for that matter if I'm going to mess around with an uncle I might as well just fuck my dad and be done with it, at least it would be more honest . . . as in the big house on Orchard Hill memories live on in the rooms, coming alive in the darkness of evening as if certain scenes are played out here forever, as if stepping into a room is like stepping into a memory in progress, scenes that live on at times beyond the lives that lived them . . . of Dickie as a boy, after he saw Harry Todd and Kathleen lying naked on the living room floor, himself lying naked with his older sister in her bed . . . of Kathleen as a young woman home at midday from her job at Sutcliff Realty, still dressed in the clothes she wore to work as she sits on the edge of her bed, gasping for breath, lighting the mound of asthma cure and starting to inhale the smoke, the house once again filling up with smoke . . . of Kitty standing in the doorway watching her daughter, filled with her own betrayals and sorrows this particular day, and is unable to give any more, she turns away and leaves the house, leaves her daughter in the house alone, and gets in her car and drives . . . of her husband Harry who later that same day sits on the edge of their bed in his undershorts and in the late afternoon shadows amid the remaining wisps of smoke drifting through the house*

from his daughter's asthma cure sees the vision of a young woman
standing naked in front of him . . . though these scenes are years
in the past, the house is still this evening as Kitty, an old woman,
climbs the stairs to her bedroom, which used to be their bedroom,
hers and Harry's, turns on the lamp at the base of which is the
figure of a ballerina in the costume and birdlike position from
Swan Lake, *and climbs into bed with the latest issue of* Cosmo-
politan *though she doesn't feel like reading at the moment, she*
lays there looking into the deep shadows of the room, the bed
placed in the center of the circular tower like a lighted display in
an alcove, thinking about how even after she found out he was
seeing other women that she and Harry had continued to have
their good times together—How could I blame him when I was so
deserving of blame, in many ways I was more shameful than he
was because with Harry it was only his body that sometimes went
to someone else and with me it was my heart—at least in the
early years when they first moved into the house, she would drive
the children to Sunday school and then hurry back to meet Harry
here in this room and they would romp naked through the upstairs
before she had to get ready for church, the children upset and
bewildered as to why she was always late, waiting for her outside
on the sidewalk until she got there and the four of them hurrying
into the church, the service already started as she herded them
down the aisle and into the family pew, standing there during the
singing of the doxology, able to name three women in the choir
in the loft behind Reverend Lorimer whom she knew Harry had
been with, while she could still feel him inside her, feel the rem-
nant of their combined juices trickle down her leg—If I felt any
trickles now it would be incontinence—and she would look over
at the end of the pew and Doctor would be there, in his brown
worsted suit as always, tall and rather pear-shaped in profile, his
full head of dark wavy hair framed against the stained-glass win-
dow of Christ carrying a lamb, looking at her as he sang his

praises to the Lord, and she would know what was meant by the phrase separate lives, *was living the concept of parallel universes . . . as Harry Todd pulls his Honda Civic into the three-stall garage beside his mother's Cadillac and closes the door, back from a late-night dinner at Shine's Pizza (it wasn't as good as he remembered, the crust was burned and the pepperoni greasy and the place gave him the feeling that it hadn't been cleaned the whole time he was gone), and stands for a moment in the driveway looking at the night, the black sycamores against the starless sky, the sky the color of stone, tinged with reddish-purple along the horizon from the lights of Pittsburgh in the distance, heavy and close with the overcast, the heat and humidity still oppressive at this hour, the back of the dark house looming over him—If it isn't haunted it sure looks like it should be. And I want to go in there? Maybe I could sleep out on the lawn tonight like I used to as a kid, no, I used to be scared out here too—and resigns himself and goes in the back door and through the downstairs turning off the lights his mother has left on for him, checks the dining room table but the photos laid out there are the same ones he saw earlier, and turns off the dining room lights as well, goes into the front hall and sees the phone on the stand and considers again calling Emily in Walnut Creek but reminds himself why that's not a good idea, thinks of Jennifer and her offer to him earlier this evening and marvels all over again that he turned her down, realizing, if he's honest with himself, that he wasn't really attracted to her in the first place despite the fact that she's an attractive girl, that it was the idea of her that he was attracted to more than to the girl herself, though the pain and yearning for her was real enough—It's like the pain and yearning exists on its own inside me and I just find the young girls to embody it—and unable to consider where that line of reasoning might take him, turns out the last of the lights and stands for a moment in the total darkness of the downstairs, unable to see a thing, and feels suddenly a*

*slight breeze on his face as if touched by an insubstantial hand—
I guess if I was ever going to see a ghost now would be the perfect
time, ha ha—stands rooted to the spot until his eyes finally begin
to adjust and then starts up the dark stairs, imagining what it
would be like to actually see a ghost now, sees in his mind's eye
the vaporous figure of the young woman he thought he saw earlier
in the chair in the attic preceding him up the steps, gliding ahead
of him as if to show him the way, can almost see it though there's
no question it's in his mind's eye only, then it disappears at the
top of the staircase into the shadows of the second floor, he
imagines it gone as quickly as it came—Alas, poor ghost, whither
will thou lead me? At least I have the good sense not to be haunted
by my father's visage, in the words of the poet, though I'd make
a lousy Hamlet anyway, all my ghosts are pretty young things,
Ophelias—hears his mother snoring softly in her bedroom at the
front of the hall and is ready to turn up the narrow stairs to the
attic when out of the corner of his eye in the doorway to Kathleen's old room he sees what he thinks is someone standing there,
just outside of his line of vision, a figure, motionless, watching
him, not a shadow, lighter, a wisp, a young woman, regarding
him almost as a challenge—Look at her, just turn your head and
look at her, if she's really there she wants you to—but he goes
on, up the narrow staircase to the attic to his room and closes
the door, turns on the light and sits down on the bed until he
stops shaking, knowing that he had been afraid almost as much
that she wasn't there as that she was. . . .*

27

He woke to find the lights on in his room and Dickie standing at
the foot of the bed, looking down at him. Harry Todd jumped,
then squinted against the light, shielding his eyes with his hand.

"What time is it?"

Dickie looked at his watch, a gold and silver Rolex the size of two watches. "A little after midnight."

"What are you doing here?"

"I decided to stop by and ask you the same question."

"I was trying to get some sleep," Harry Todd said, struggling to put his thoughts together . . . It's like a visit from the local Mafia boss. Gestapo in the night. Something must be really bothering him. He sat up a little, propping his shoulders against the headboard. As strange as it was to see Dickie here at this hour, it was also a bit of a relief, given his recent experiences in the house; there was no question that his brother was real, not an apparition.

"Let me rephrase my last statement," Dickie said. "I've heard all about what you're doing. All your shabby goings-on behind everybody's back. And I came to put a stop to it."

"In the middle of the night?" It's got to be about Jennifer, he must have found out she asked me to go skinny-dipping and thinks I tried to hit on her. "You can relax, Dickie. Nothing's going to happen."

"You're right, nothing's going to happen. I'm here to make sure of it."

Dickie paced a few steps along the foot of the bed and back, keeping an eye on Harry Todd. He was dressed in a dark blue double-breasted suit, elegantly tailored with a European or Italian flair, as if he were still dressed for the office. Dickie had changed quite a bit since the last time Harry Todd saw him; he was still trim and muscular, he looked like he worked out, but he had aged noticeably. Harry Todd thought his brother appeared older than he did, something in his bearing, the weight of the world he carried, the lines etched in his face. I guess if I had a daughter like Jennifer I'd be worried too. Dickie was obviously agitated, and Harry Todd found the circumstances somewhat amusing.

"Maybe I should be flattered that you think I'm worthy of so much attention," Harry Todd smiled.

"You needn't be. I consider you on the same level as a cancer with a road map."

"Hey, wait a minute. . . ."

"No, you wait a minute. I didn't say anything when you first came back because it seemed to make Mother happy, Lord knows why. But now you're starting to poke around in things that are none of your business. And I want it stopped."

He's not talking about Jennifer after all. This must be about Kathleen. "All I did was ask a few simple questions. . . ."

"I said it's none of your business and I mean it."

Harry Todd lifted the sheet and let it fall again, watching it re-drape itself over his legs. "I'm not surprised you're upset about me asking around. From what I hear you were very much involved with—what shall we call them—the arrangements?"

"I don't know what 'arrangements' you're talking about. But I've worked very hard on this project, and I'm not going to sit by and see you ruin it."

Project? Covering over the facts of his sister's death is a project? "As long as you're here, let me ask you. What's your version of the results of the autopsy? There seem to be several."

"Autopsy? What autopsy? What are you talking about?"

"You don't have to put on an act for my benefit. I know there was an autopsy. What concerns me is that I'm told there's a difference between the cause of death listed on Kathleen's death certificate and what the autopsy report said. I'm also told she died of a barbiturate overdose, and that you were involved with covering it up with Dr. Neely. I'd like to know what really happened."

Dickie was visibly taken aback. He stared at Harry Todd for a long moment, the color drained from his face; then his eyes locked onto Harry Todd's, his voice deadly. "I think it's time you packed your bags and got out of here. I want you out of here. Now."

He even looks like Father, that's what it is, the same voice, the same gestures. "I don't have any intention of going anywhere. Not till I find out what this is all about."

"Why would you want to hurt Mother by stirring this up again?"

"How would it hurt Mother? From what I'm hearing she's known all along how Kathleen died, even though she pretends not to. Whatever that's about."

Dickie regarded Harry Todd curiously. Why is he looking at me that way? What don't I know about? For a moment Dickie seemed almost relieved.

"Is it money? Is that what you're after?" Dickie dug in his pants pocket, took out a money clip and began peeling off one-hundred-dollar bills. "Here, take this. It's enough to get you back to California. I'll send you some more later. Just get out of here and leave this whole thing alone."

Harry Todd was pop-eyed: Dickie had tossed down close to a thousand dollars on the bed. "If it wasn't Kathleen, what were you talking about before?"

"Furnass Landing. About you putting a bug in Julian's ear about developing an industrial museum. But the reason why doesn't matter. It's time for you to be gone. Go back to where you came from."

"You must really want me out of here if you're willing to pay this much."

"This is nothing. I'll get you more later. I'll get you whatever you need to get situated somewhere. As long as it's as far away from here as possible."

Harry Todd mused; he felt as if he had gained the upper hand, though he wasn't sure how. "That's the way Father always solved a problem: throw money at it. You learned your lessons well. Was that part of the package deal in taking over the firm?"

Dickie studied him. After a moment he said, almost a whisper, "You really are a bastard, aren't you? You really are a son-of-a-bitch."

"I'd say it runs in the family."

Dickie turned and started to leave, then came back and gathered up the money on the sheet.

"You sure you don't want to leave it? In case I want to take you up on your offer later?"

Dickie smiled, a changed man, in control of himself and the situation again. "No, it doesn't matter whether you go or stay. And it doesn't matter what your intentions are either—whatever it is you think you're up to. I know you, Harry Todd, I had forgotten momentarily, but it all comes back to me in living color. I know you firsthand for what you are. And you're nothing. A non-entity. Zero. No more than an annoyance. Whatever you do, whatever you try to pull, I'll take care of it. I'll cover it over or send it away or do whatever else needs to be done, just like Father always did, just like I have continued to do for what's left of this family. You're a gamester who no longer has a game, a trickster who lost all his tricks. Your rabbits no longer come out of the hats, you literally have nothing up your sleeve. Enjoy your stay here, Harry Todd. I pity you."

Dickie started to put the money back in his pocket, then took one of the hundred-dollar bills and tossed it back on the bed. He cocked his head at Harry Todd, as if to say You'll probably need this, and left the room.

Harry Todd sat forward on the bed to make sure he was gone; through the open door all he could see was the gaping darkness of the attic hallway. Everybody and their brother thinks they can walk in on me. . . . Muttering to himself—trying to make a joke out of it, trying to make himself feel better that he had nothing to say in the face of Dickie's disdain before he left—Harry Todd got up and closed the door. I should have asked him about what Mother said, that he had slept with Donna, though that could have been another one of her flights of fancy. Even so, that she would have reason to even think such a thing, talk about shabby goings-on. He's the one with something to be ashamed of. And why is he so determined to keep me from finding out how Kathleen died? He never did answer my questions, I don't know anything more than I did. Now I'm really curious. I'm going to have to think of some other way. . . . Before climbing back in, he took the hundred-dollar bill from the bed. He thought of several grand gestures to do with it—burn it; put it in an envelope, maybe tear it into pieces first, and mail it back to Dickie; donate it to a charity—but he ended up folding it and sticking it into his wallet. Dickie was right, he might need it before too long.

PART THREE

28

There were crowds along the narrow main street, standing around as if waiting for a parade. Except the crowds were only on the side of the street toward the river; everyone was standing in the intersections, not along the sidewalks, with their backs turned. What's going on? Do they do everything backward in this town? Harry Todd grinned to himself. Obviously they were watching something that was going on farther down the hill. When he passed Thirteenth Street he pulled into the first parking space he came to and walked back.

It was a gray morning, a gray day, the heat and humidity all the more oppressive from the lack of sunlight, the color drained from the sky; the air was like a physical presence that had to be moved aside to get through. At the intersection, the crowd stood five and six deep, with more people scattered on down the steep side street; in the blocks farther down the hill were more crowds, ribbons of people across the intersections. They were all looking in the direction of the mill, but Harry Todd couldn't make out what held their interest. If anything there seemed to be less activity than usual around the abandoned buildings; there were no dump trucks trundling back and forth, the bulldozers and cranes sat idle, there were no flashes of cutting torches from the carcass of the BOP Shop. The only thing out of the ordinary, as far as he could tell, was a large banner across the towering black cylinders of the blast furnace that read, GOOD-BYE BIG BETTY.

Standing next to him was a guy in a Steelers T-shirt who seemed vaguely familiar, someone Harry Todd might have gone to school with. Sal something or other, he thought. "Who's Big Betty?" Harry Todd said pleasantly.

"It's the name everybody used for Betty Six."

"Okay, who's Betty Six?"

The guy looked at him as if he couldn't decide whether Harry Todd was kidding or not, and depending on the answer, whether he was going to hit him. Finally the guy moved away. The other people nearby were watching Harry Todd suspiciously. Whoever Big Betty is, she's got a lot of friends in this town . . . don't mess with Big Betty.

A honking siren from somewhere near the river drew everyone's attention down the hill. Big Betty must be sailing away . . . on a barge like Cleopatra? . . . some local ethnic festival? . . . maybe a Polish feast day . . . farewell to Big Betty for another year. . . . The crowd stirred. Somebody yelled, "There she goes!" Where? Where? At the base of the towering blast furnace appeared several puffs of smoke, followed by the sounds of detonations. Firecrackers? Too big . . . no, wait a minute. . . . A series of larger explosions followed. As Harry Todd watched, the steel columns supporting the tall black cylinders buckled and the entire structure toppled forward suddenly as if sinking to its knees—Wait! Wait!—then the furnace crumpled in upon itself, falling rapidly now—Oh my God!—disappearing into a billowing cloud of dust and smoke that rose triumphantly over the valley— It's gone!—the rumble of the destruction becoming lost in the cheers of the crowd standing on the hill. They think it's a party. Their lives just changed irreparably and they're dancing in the streets. Good thing it wasn't the apocalypse, they would be having an orgy. What am I missing here? Harry Todd slowly turned away, surprised at how shocked he was to see the familiar landmark gone—apparently the only one in town bothered by it— feeling more lost and alone and out of step with the world than ever.

29

He thought he might feel better if he ate something. He left his car parked where it was and continued down the street to the Furnass Grill, taking a small booth at the rear against the wall; when the waitress came, he ordered coffee and the breakfast special. The coffee shop was busy, as it always seemed to be no matter what hour of the day or night he was there—young families with two or three kids, the parents looking as if they could barely afford to put clothes on their children's backs much less afford a meal out; older retired couples who got dressed up to come here, apparently any chance to eat out an occasion, moving slowly and cautiously, aware that a simple fall could mean disaster; as well as a few of the local merchants and office workers. More people came in after he was seated, everyone chattering and making jokes about the blast furnace coming down.

In a large booth across from him was a group of businessmen, men his own age and younger, in dark polyester suits, from a local insurance agency perhaps, or an accounting firm. Or Sutcliff Realty, for that matter. He wondered if they knew who he was; if things had worked out differently he might have been the big man in Furnass instead of Dickie, they might have been working for him. Whether they recognized him or not, they were watching him, and he sensed from their glances that they generally disapproved of what they saw. If nothing else he was a stranger in town, someone who didn't belong. For something to do, he asked the waitress if he could borrow a pen and began to doodle on a napkin, a crude sketch of interlocking squares building first in one direction then another, slowly filling the space of the napkin. When his breakfast came he continued to work on the sketch while eating.

"How is it? Your breakfast?" the waitress asked.

"Oh. It's good. Very good."

"I had them do it special for you. The breakfast special only goes to ten-thirty, we're not supposed to take orders for it after that, but I told the cook this was a special case."

"Well, thanks. I appreciate it."

"That's okay," she said, and padded away on her soft shoes. When he was through eating, he moved his plate aside and went back to his drawing.

"Oh, I get it."

The waitress was back again, standing beside him looking over his shoulder. She was in her mid- or late thirties, flat chested almost to the point of being concave, though not an unattractive woman, her mustard-yellow hair in a Dutch boy. Her bottom lip was straight, with her upper lip arched noticeably over it, duck lips. The tag on her uniform said *Shari*. She spoke with a slight lisp and her laugh was like a series of staccato coughs; she laughed a lot, either at the beginning of what she said or at the end.

"It's sort of like a maze, except there's no way to get into it, much less find a way out."

He stopped and looked at the drawing. "Yeah, I guess it could be. I was just filling up time."

Shari laughed, ready for a joke if there was one. "You're Harry Todd Sutcliff, aren't you?"

My fame has spread to the waitresses of Furnass.

"I recognized you, you've been in a couple times lately," Shari went on, finishing clearing the table and wiping the surface with a cloth. She leaned over him close enough to nearly tickle the end of his nose with her name tag. "You were in the other day with Donna Bruno. I asked who you were then. You're Dickie's brother."

Dickie's brother. I guess I better get used to that here.

"You know Dickie?"

"Oh sure, he comes in sometimes. Though he prefers fancier places most of the time, like the Blue Boar. The Furnass Grill isn't his kind of place."

"Well, it's fancy enough for me." It's also cheap enough for me. "Dickie's the rich brother, and I'm the smart one," he said, trying to make a joke on himself, but he was afraid it came out sounding flat.

Shari had stacked his dirty dishes on the tray, but she left the tray sitting on the edge of the table; she rested one knee on the seat across from him and leaned against the back, ready to stay a while.

"I've heard about you. Your mother comes in sometimes and I wait on her. She talks about you all the time. You're the one out in California. It's sort of nice meeting you after hearing about you."

Mother talks about me. Donna said that too. Maybe Mother is proud of me after all. Strange to consider. What is there possibly to be proud of? One failed venture after another. My son Harry Todd was just fired from being a manager at a Denny's, isn't that wonderful? "Well, it's nice to meet you too, Shari."

"I've known all your family, since I worked here. Your father used to come in all the time, he wasn't stuck-up like Dickie, excuse my French. Your dad was great because he always tipped a lot. I didn't mean that so you'll tip me that way too. I only said it because it was true."

"I'll bet Dickie doesn't tip well."

"Oh sure, he tips good too. Real good. At least he did for a while. That was when he had a sometime thing going on with Joann, that waitress over there. He used to tip us a lot so we'd keep quiet about it," she giggled. "His wife's flower shop is right down the street, Tinker's Flowers. He didn't want her to know what was going on."

"That sounds like Dickie."

"He wanted us to be nice to Tinker too, that's what he told Joann. He didn't want anyone to make fun of her or think badly of her, because he was seeing Joann and all. I thought that was kinda sweet of him, if you ask me. Because to tell you the truth I don't think it mattered to Tinker one way or the other, if Dickie was seeing Joann or not, or anyone else for that matter. And we're nice to Tinker anyway, because we like her. But we took Dickie's money all the same, as long as he was dishing it out."

One of her other customers was motioning for his check and she was off again, bouncing on the balls of her feet as if she were spring-loaded. Dickie was certainly upholding his father's reputation in town, the way it sounded. Our father, who screwed in Furnass, hollow be thy name. . . . He wondered if Dickie had slept with Shari; he wondered if Shari was coming on to him. He hoped she wasn't, at this point he didn't feel like going to bed with anyone, much less to be compared with his brother; he didn't know how he'd get out of it without embarrassing himself, not living up to the family name, at least as far as Sutcliff males were concerned. He tried to bury himself in his doodling. But in a few minutes Shari was back, braced on one knee on the seat across from him.

"Yeah, I've known all your family. I used to know Kathleen when she came in too."

"When she was working for my father?"

"Oh sure. She used to come in with Donna Bruno all the time. I knew Donna real well too."

She tucked her lower lip under her upper, as if she remembered something, and looked away. Harry Todd wondered if Shari knew of his relationship with Donna, knew that Donna had once been sent away from town on account of him, if that's what occurred to her. But if Shari thought she said something she shouldn't, she didn't let it deter her; she giggled and chattered on.

"It was nice for Donna with Kathleen around. Before, I think Donna was lonely. They got along well together, except when your dad was around."

"What was different when my father was around?"

"Oh, it wasn't like they argued or anything like that. But they had this thing between them, like they were both trying to get

your dad's attention all the time. It was sort of funny. They used
to flirt with him, and your father would flirt back."

"With Donna?"

"With Kathleen too. It was something, boy. They used to get
pretty foul-mouthed too, if you know what I mean. Talking dirty
about this and that. They were funny," Shari giggled. "But that
was before your dad got sick and all and didn't feel very good.
Then he toned it down a lot."

"I thought he got sick after Kathleen died."

"No, he was sick before that too. I don't think I ever heard
what the matter was, but you could tell, he wasn't himself. He
was worn-out all the time, his face was sort of drawn-looking, you
know? And I think he was starting to have a lot of pain. I think
whatever finally got him in the end was already starting to get
at him back then. I have to go."

She was off again, and apparently forgot about him, she didn't
come back. Despite himself, Harry Todd felt a little slighted.
*Kathleen used to talk dirty. And with Father. That's hard to
believe, I don't think I ever heard Kathleen say a dirty word in
her life, maybe it was Donna who got her started. . . .* He stopped
his doodling as he remembered the photograph his mother had
left for him on the dining room table this morning.

There had been only one photo this time, a grainy enlargement
of a snapshot taken on the front porch, three young women sitting on the porch swing, all of them dressed in their Sunday best
as if showing off their new Easter outfits, with Kathleen at one
end of the swing and Donna on the other and in the middle
Dickie's wife, Tinker. At the time he was surprised to see the
three of them together, though he didn't dwell on it; but the fact
that he was thinking about it now indicated that it made more
of an impression than he first thought. *What was Donna doing
at our house?* He was also curious at the time why there was only
the single photograph, but he hadn't pursued that line of thinking

either. Now he wondered if there was only one because she was running out of pictures to show him, or because it was so important that she didn't want to mitigate its effect.

Why would the three girls together be important? Other than the idea that I would never think of the three of them together. Particularly not at the house. But then I never considered that Kathleen and Donna might have been friends. Weird thought. I guess I could go talk to Tinker. Maybe she knows the link between them. . . .

He busied himself with the doodle for a while, still hoping Shari might come back and talk to him some more. But he was running out of room on the napkin; he scribbled over the doodle and paid his bill and left.

30

Dickie Sutcliff was a happy man. He was on his way to see Pamela, driving too fast as usual out Seneca Road, to see that the sofa he had ordered had been delivered this morning as promised. Though he had little doubt that it wouldn't be. At first the store manager, a Mrs. Garver, had been insistent that they could never make the delivery on such short notice, just as Dickie's secretary had predicted, but Dickie was able to convince Mrs. Garver otherwise. Dickie considered himself a master at overcoming other people's reluctances.

"I'm afraid you don't understand, Mr. Sutcliff. We're simply not set up to deal with this kind of rush order. The sofa is at our warehouse, not here at the store, and the order would have to be processed and. . . ."

"I do understand all that, Mrs. Garver. What you need to tell me is how much money we're talking about in order to make this happen."

Dickie felt he was on a roll, things were definitely going his way.

So far it had been a successful morning. The demolition of the blast furnace had gone well, the structure had come down without a problem. And rather than an occasion of sadness or regret, a public outcry about a landmark gone—or, for that matter, outrage at the manifestation that their jobs were gone forever, that steel was gone from the valley once and for all—the town seemed to treat the demolition of the furnace as if it were a kind of celebration; there was a party atmosphere before and after it came down, he was told there were even cheers when it fell. Thank goodness for the common man's self-destructive tendencies, that people left to their own devices would much rather have the thrill of seeing something they prized destroyed rather than confront the implications of their own thoughts. Two TV stations from Pittsburgh had covered the story, it was sure to be featured on the six o'clock news tonight—it was the kind of publicity that the project and the town needed if the transformation to a new economic base was going to succeed. Down with the old, up with the new. Now if Julian or someone else pursued the idea of an industrial museum or some such retrograde nonsense, it was a moot point. He would take care of Julian himself later on, to make sure the man didn't get any more bright ideas that could lead to lawsuits or court injunctions. Yes, Dickie was a happy man. Despite the heat of the gray morning, he turned off the air-conditioning and rolled down his window, letting his open palm rebuff the warm, oncoming wind, riding the unseen waves.

His good mood changed, however, as soon as he pulled into a parking space in front of Pamela's townhouse. There, sitting on the small lawn in front of her door, under a stick-like sapling, was the taupe-colored sofa he ordered, still wrapped in its plastic covering for shipping. A few children played nearby; one little girl sat on the grass holding her doll, crooning to it, staring at the sofa in its translucent shroud as if she were seeing a vision.

Dickie slammed the car door and started up the walk, searching through his pockets for the store manager's number, when Pamela opened the front door.

"Look, I'm really sorry about this. It was meant to be a surprise. What the hell kind of deliverymen would go away and leave it on the lawn like that? But don't worry. Let me use your phone and I'll get this straightened out in no time. . . ."

"Dickie, I told the deliverymen to leave it there."

"You what? How are you going to get it in the house?"

"I'm not. That's the point."

Dickie wasn't understanding this at all. She was wearing a halter and shorts; he reached to touch her bare shoulder but she shied away, her arms wrapped around herself as if she were cold.

"Isn't that the sofa you showed me in the catalog?"

"Yes, that's the sofa. But I don't want it from you. I don't want it this way."

Dickie laughed, relieved. Then there hadn't been a screw-up in the order. If this was all that was bothering her, he could deal with it.

"I know, I know, you said you wanted to get it yourself. But it seems a shame for you not to have it now, when you want it so much. And I decided as long as I was doing it, I'd get you the matching chair and ottoman too. They're coming later, they weren't in stock, in fact they had to get this from a warehouse in—"

Pamela was shaking her head, becoming more emphatic. "No, Dickie. You don't understand. I want to get the sofa and the other pieces myself. It's important to me to do it on my own."

"Well, then how about if we say it's a loan? You can pay me back whenever you have it, it doesn't have to be right away. You can take your time. . . ."

She rubbed the flat of her hand up and down the muscle of his arm. "I know you mean well. And I really do appreciate you trying to please me. But this isn't the way to do it. This isn't the way."

She looked at him sadly, but before he could say anything else she closed the door.

Dickie stalked back to his car, trying to think of whom he could call, whom he could yell at, to make this right.

31

Sitting in the waiting area, Kitty crossed her still-pretty legs, trying to get comfortable on the molded plastic chair, thinking, Too much of the bad news of the world, the news that changes our lives forever, is given to us in doctors' offices.

She remembered sitting in Dr. Sutcliff's office a few years after she arrived in Furnass, the evenings she would join Doctor during his exile from his wife, keeping him company as he smoked, talking about the great books and the latest gossip; she remembered it was in that office one evening where she first learned that Harry's bringing her to Furnass was only the result of a secondary plan for himself, a plan to have a compliant, needy wife along with a baby to keep him out of the coming war. She remembered it was in that office where Doctor confirmed his son's many affairs around town. Where she learned that Doctor was in love with her, more so than her husband . . . he said Love is one person trying to devour another, it's ugly and sad on some level, but most people can't live without it. She remembered it was in another doctor's office where she first learned that Harry had cancer and later that he had only a few months to live, where she learned that Kathleen had asthma and emotional problems that were thought to be centered on her older brother. She remembered, too, a later visit to the doctor's, where she learned her worst fears for Kathleen were true.

*

"I have to ask you this," George Neely said, coming from around his desk and sitting in the chair beside Kitty while Kathleen was in the examination room getting dressed. "Have you ever suspected anything . . . improper, I guess would be the polite word for it . . . between Kathleen and her father?"

"Why would you ask that? Did you find something, did Kathleen say. . . ?"

"No, no, nothing like that," George Neely said. He was Harry's age—they had grown up together in town, gone to school together—short and stocky, barrel-shaped, his frame swelling out the stiff white lab coat; if he wasn't wearing a toupee, his barber had done him a grave disservice. He sat stiff and erect, turned slightly toward her so his bulk would fit between the arms, filling the chair as if he were a tree stump. He thought for a moment before he went on.

"I've come to realize that I misjudged the situation when Kathleen was younger, thinking that her emotional problems stemmed from her relationship with her older brother."

"You think it has something to do with her father?"

"Well, I certainly have to wonder. It's quite evident talking to her that her world revolves him. And it's only going to get worse. She's graduated from college, but she's still living at home and starting to work at Sutcliff Realty. She's going to be with him day in and day out. His influence over her can only get stronger."

"Thank you, George, but you're not the only one who's known Harry Sutcliff a long time. And I can assure you there's nothing improper, as you describe it, going on between my husband and his daughter."

Kitty looked at her hands, started to unclasp her purse in her lap, then closed it again, forgetting what she thought she was looking for. She was trying her best to mask her feelings, her own concerns in regard to what George Neely was saying, aware that she wasn't doing a very good job of it. Remembering all too well

Kathleen fussing in her crib until her father would come to her, her large liquid blue eyes fixed on him. That come-hither look Harry said, pleased, you females are born with it, aren't you?

George Neely sighed, his stubby hands folded in his lap, on the stiff white lab coat, as if he'd like to pray. "I think Kathleen should go away. I think she should be thinking about a place like Colorado or Arizona, someplace that would be better for her asthma."

"Do you think her condition is getting worse?"

"No . . . not necessarily. . . . Her asthma doesn't seem to be life-threatening, at least not at this stage. But it definitely takes its toll on the rest of her system. It's just that I think there would be other places that . . . would be healthier for her."

"Do you think burning the asthma-cure powder helps her?"

"Frankly, I don't see how it could. Smoke and dust are among her main problems as it is. She gets enough of those living here in this mill town. More smoke certainly can't be any good for her."

"I've tried to tell her that and get her to stop using it, but she's convinced the smoke helps her. I think she wants it to help her so badly that she's ready to believe anything. Believe in anything. And every time I try to talk to her about it, her father says to leave the girl alone, if she thinks it helps her that's good enough for him. It's the same with trying to get her to go someplace else where the air would be better for her. We tried that, if you recall, her first year at college. We sent her to Slippery Rock, but she seemed to get sicker being away from home than she was when she was here. I don't know what else to do."

"And did Harry have the same attitude about her going away as he does about her burning the asthma powder?"

"Yes. And whenever a subject like this comes up, Kathleen gets so upset that I end up going along with her and her father so I don't look like the bad guy. And then I'm the one who has to continue to pacify her about it, long after her father has forgotten the entire discussion, so it ends up looking like I'm the one who's telling Kathleen that she should burn the asthma-cure powder and that she doesn't need to go away from home."

"I think that's what I was getting at when I said it would be healthier for her, healthier for all of you, if she could get away. She needs to get out on her own. She needs to get away from Furnass and all these influences and find herself, find out who she is. She needs some breathing room, literally."

"And suppose she won't go?" Kitty remembered the scene a few years earlier when Harry Todd came home from California and wanted to help her move away from Furnass. This is my home, my home, why would you think I would ever want to leave here? Kathleen had cried hysterically at her brother as she buried her head in Kitty's lap. Across the room, her father beamed.

George Neely patted his thighs twice as if a signal to himself and stood up. When Kitty got to her feet, he looked at her intently, the two of them almost touching. "You know what I'm afraid of, don't you? You know where I'm afraid this will lead?"

He was barely taller than she was, looking into her eyes at eye level. And for the briefest second she remembered another doctor's office, lying on the examination table waiting for her yearly examination, waiting for the loose gown to be lifted up over her breasts, her legs spread in the stirrups as the shy probing finger entered her. Without knowing she was going to do so, she embraced George Neely. Her arms fit around him, his own arms caught against his sides, as if she were hugging a tree. He smelled of antiseptic and talcum powder, like a baby.

"Yes. I know. I know very well."

*

Behind the counter, the vet came from the examining room in the rear of the office, carefully carrying with two hands the wicker basket that Kitty used to transport Merry Anne.

"Mrs. Sutcliff. . . ?"

32

I know you mean well. But this isn't the way to do it. . . . As Dickie pulled out of the driveway from Pamela's townhouse complex onto the county road, the big Town Car fishtailed on the asphalt paving, slick with oil from the heat. This isn't the way. What the hell does she mean this isn't the way? Dickie decided he better slow down before he did something stupid. Before he did something else stupid. I don't need this. I don't have to put up with it. Somebody laying down conditions to me, somebody telling me what to do and what not to do. I'm going to go see this guy, she told me, whether you like it or not. This isn't the way to treat me. Well, it's not the way to treat me either. I've had it. Dickie rolled up the car window, turned on the air conditioner again, the cool unnatural air blowing in his face until he reset the vents. This isn't the way to do it. Then what the hell is the way? It's the only way I know.

The sky was the color of dirty sheets, an unmade bed; the heat and humidity of the gray day were palpable even inside the controlled environment of the car. Dickie realized he was holding on to the wheel with two hands as if trying to snap it off the steering column; he relaxed his grip, slouching down into his usual one-handed style, propping his elbow on the armrest, bracing his chin on his upturned fist. He decided he had wasted enough time thinking about Pamela, he'd concentrate more on his work, on Furnass Landing, Lord knew there was enough there to keep him occupied. This was what he got for letting himself get distracted, for letting himself get led around by his cock. You'd think he'd have learned by now. Never mind his own experiences, if nothing else he had seen what it did in the long run to his father. Scary thought. A man brought low by his own excesses. A man who couldn't control not only his cock but his heart as well.

Beyond the Seneca Towne Centre Mall, he passed the Racquet Club. Dickie Sutcliff, you never missed anyone in your life. Was it only the day before yesterday I saw her there? She seemed really happy to see me that day, the way she smiled . . . Forget about it. Forget about her. He thought of stopping at the club for a quick game or two to work off his anger, but he was afraid she might come there herself. I'll just beat up some of my office staff this afternoon, that'll take care of it, isn't that what a big-time executive is supposed to do? Oh sure. . . . At the crossroads beyond the mall he passed the cement block building where his father had once considered opening a branch office. Once considered opening an office for Kathleen.

"I'm thinking of something," his father had said. "I want your take on it."

"Okay," Dickie said. His father was groggy, slurring his words, with long pauses between phrases. He sat leaning back in the chair at his desk as if talking in his sleep or drunk, ready to doze off, but Dickie knew it was only the medication the doctor had given him since he started to have some health problems. Dickie chose to sit on the edge of the credenza rather than in one of the wing-backed chairs, aware that the chairs always made him feel either as if he were being grilled or too much at ease, neither one of which he wanted to feel at the moment.

"I'm thinking of opening a branch office out in Seneca."

"That's a good idea. There's a lot of growth out there, and there'll undoubtedly be more in the future, if you're thinking—"

His father cut him off, as if he weren't listening, or as if he were running out of time to say what he wanted to. "I'm not thinking of a big office. Only one person, just to have a presence out there. I want to keep our main operations here in town."

"I see," Dickie said, wondering what his father was getting at, where this was going.

"I was thinking of putting Kathleen out there. As the person to staff it."

"Do you think she's ready for that?"

"No, but I think we can make her ready. And you can spend some time there with her."

"I was wondering if you were thinking of moving me out there. . . ."

"Of course not. You need to be here, at the main office, where the important things are happening. I was only thinking of you checking up on her once in a while."

"I guess I don't understand what your goal is, then. It doesn't really sound like this is a business decision. . . ."

"I think it would be a good idea to get Kathleen away from this office."

"If you're concerned about the thing with me and Donna," Dickie said, shifting his weight in his half-sitting position, "that was over a while ago."

His father grinned, lazy-eyed. "It has nothing to do with you and Donna. Or you and anyone or anything else. I think Kathleen needs to get out on her own. Start to have a life of her own."

"That's not the way you used to think about Kathleen."

"No, it's not. I know that. And I've learned I was wrong. Very wrong. It's made her too dependent on me. . . ," his father said, waving his hand vaguely, his voice trailing off.

The admission seemed to take something out of his father. Dickie waited while his father sat there with his eyes closed for a few minutes, gathering himself before going on.

"I hope you understand. About me putting her out there instead of you. Why I'm starting up another office for her, not for you."

"I understand completely," Dickie said, smiling his business smile, a smile he knew his father would recognize and appreciate. "And why would I object? It'll be good for business, to have the name out there. Besides, eventually it's all going to be mine anyway."

It was bluster on his part and Dickie knew it, but it served its purpose, it put his father's mind at ease for the time being, his father assured that it was the same old Dickie, molded he thought in his own graven image.

The big car barreled over the hazy rolling hills, the tires hissing in the heat. Dickie turned on the radio, turned it off again, punched in the cigarette lighter but never heard it pop. Ahead the road was covered with blood, fragments of internal organs, the torn and twisted carcass of a deer lying on the shoulder; farther on was the head. Crows stood along the berm, waiting for him to pass so they could get back to their meal. He turned the radio on and off again.

That day, talking to his father, had been a landmark for Dickie. It was the day he learned that his father realized his palling around with Kathleen and Donna wasn't good for Kathleen, that Donna wasn't good for Kathleen, that Kathleen was in trouble and something needed to be done. That perhaps the office flirting and playing around and innuendo had gone too far in her presence. Was that why his father couldn't sleep, couldn't eat, was wasting away, as if eating himself alive? Regardless, it was also the day Dickie failed to help his father. Held back from doing so by his own embarrassment. Maybe he could have said something that would have helped ease his father's burden about her. Dickie should have told his father examples of her emotional troubles that started long before she was around Donna or the office chatter, his own experiences with Kathleen. . . .

It was hot that day too, he remembered, hot inside the house; it happened before his mother bought the window air conditioners for the bedrooms, the smells of oil and sulfur and coke and slag from the mills drifting through the house from the open windows, the soot in the air clotting the mesh of the window screens. Dickie stood in the doorway of Kathleen's room. She sat on the bed, the dirty bedclothes twisted about her, sitting with her legs folded under her, a *Saturday Evening Post* draped across her lap. Even from across the room he could hear the whistle in her breath. She smiled when she noticed him in the doorway.

"Hi," she said between gulps of air. When she noticed the whistle, she gave a couple sharp intakes to make it whistle more. They both laughed.

"Maybe you'll get good enough to play a tune," Dickie said.

"I'm sure getting . . . plenty of practice . . . I could go on *Ed Sullivan* . . . 'Whistling Hope'. . . . "

He waited a moment, until he built up his courage.

"Can I ask you something?"

"Yes."

"When Harry Todd did that thing with you a couple weeks ago, did he hurt you?"

She looked at him quizzically. "Did you see us?"

"Yes, I was at the top of the stairs. I heard you cry out. Then I couldn't watch anymore."

Kathleen thought a moment. Then she wiped her blond hair behind her ear and looked at him again. "No, he didn't hurt me. He surprised me more than anything. When his stuff came all over me. But I guess he was afraid he hurt me. He hurt me more when he ran away. Now he won't even talk to me."

"Why won't he?"

"I don't know. I guess he doesn't like me anymore." Through her troubled breaths, Kathleen looked as if she might cry. Dickie felt panicky.

"I'll talk to you."

"You're very sweet, Dickie." She patted the bed beside her. Dickie went over and sat on the edge. Kathleen scooted over to make more room, and he pulled up his legs. He could smell her, warm and sweaty; dark odors too, girl smells.

"Is Harry Todd home?"

Dickie shook his head. "He took Mother's car and went driving. And Mother took Father to the office in his car so she could go to one of her women's club meetings. Nobody's here."

Kathleen tossed the magazine aside. "I was getting ready to take a nap before you came in."

"I guess I better go." Dickie started to get up but she grabbed at him, holding on to his arm, hurting him, her face suddenly pleading.

"No, please, don't go . . . please stay with me. Everybody always runs . . . away from me."

"I wasn't trying to run away. . . ."

"Just stay with me. . . ."

It occurred to him to lie down with her, but he was afraid to, somehow that didn't seem right. But after she arranged her pillow and stretched out, she tugged on his arm to pull him down beside her.

"Take off your shoes," she whispered. Her whistly breath tickled the hair over his ear.

He kicked off his tennis shoes and snuggled in against her; she put her arm around him, held him close to her. He didn't usually take naps—he was twelve, naps were for little kids—but he loved lying there beside her. He could feel her body through her light cotton pajamas, feel her breasts resting against his arm, her thighs against his thighs.

"Don't move," she said. "Just hold me, just hold me. . . ."

He remembered that day as one of the special moments of his life, the beauty of her, the feel of her body, her body against him. He remembered hoping the next day that they would be alone together in the house again, he remembered hoping over a period of the next couple of years that she would get sick again, so she would be in her room and he could go in and lie with her again. . . . What kind of guy thinks things like that about his sister? But the opportunity never came, there was always some-one around, and in time he forgot about it, forgot those feelings and desires about Kathleen, forgot about a number of things, until Harry Todd came home and brought them back.

I was over at the big house for something after I was married and I didn't think anyone was there, I was walking down the hallway on the second floor on my way to the bathroom and then Kathleen came out of her room and stood in the doorway naked, just stood there looking at me, as if to make sure I got a good look at her. . . .

At the top of Downie Hill Road, Dickie turned and began the long descent back into Furnass. Under the gray sky, saggy as a net over the valley, through the green of the trees of summer, he caught glimpses of the town and the remains of the old mill along the curving river. As if he didn't have enough to be concerned about, he thought, his brother was down there someplace, run-ning around buttonholing everyone he could think of to ask ques-tions about the family.

So you found out that Kathleen committed suicide. Well, I guess that isn't so terrible in and of itself, the fact is you should know what happened to her, she was your sister. The danger is that you'll find one of these little fragments of information and confront Mother with it. I know you, brother, you'll think you've found some great dark secret, the Rosetta Stone that exemplifies everything you consider wrong with the family, that typifies all the wrongs you think Father and Mother did to you, without knowing that whatever was wrong with this family, it was the sum of a long list of wrongs, the entries in a ledger where each and every one of us made our additions and subtractions.

At the bottom of the long grade, as he passed through the culvert under the railroad tracks and one-handed through the curves past Smitty's Service, he wiped his other hand down over his face like lowering a visor or a mask, entering the back streets of Furnass, getting himself ready to take care of the next thing that needed taking care of.

33

Tinker's Flowers was down the street, a block and a half from the Furnass Grill on the other side of the street, toward the end of the main street and the hill that led to the lower end of town, a storefront in a flat-faced building Harry Todd remembered as a hardware store, situated in the dogleg of the main street, the unexplained hitch in the main drag, facing the length of the shopping district so that, although the shop itself didn't have a particularly good location, it had an unobstructed view of the shops that did. The front display windows were crowded with arrangements of potted plants and silk flowers, a jumble of colors— apparently Tinker favored assortments of tall spiky blossoms and clashing hues, at least in this season—with ceramic figures of trolls and gnomes and cute forest animals tucked in among the leaves.

Inside, the shop was surprisingly busy. Several customers were ahead of him, scheduling delivery times and discussing bouquets, waited on by a staff of eager, earnest middle-aged women each wearing a green smock with the name *Tinker's Flowers*. But there was no Tinker in sight. While he waited Harry Todd studied the fresh arrangements in the display cabinets—Who buys all these flowers in Furnass? Are there this many funerals?—the posters of ready-made arrangements available to wire across the country. For a moment he had the urge to send flowers to somebody, imagined the surprised look on her face when they arrived, when she read the card. Then he remembered there was no *her*, no *she*, in his life at the moment. No one that he would want to send flowers to. Or that would be particularly happy to receive them from him. Emily, the waitress he had been living with in Walnut

Creek, would think he was crazy. A sentimental waste of money. She would prefer he chip in on the rent. When one of the saleswomen finally got to him and he asked if Tinker was around, she directed him through a curtain made of heavy plastic strips to the rear of the shop.

The workshop was as chill as a garage, with the same conflicting sensations of emptiness and clutter, though instead of engine parts scattered around and the smell of motor oil, there were trash bins of cuttings and a sweet sickly odor, a mixture of perfume and decaying plant life. The tools of the trade were hanging on a pegboard on the wall—clippers and scissors and pruning shears. Under a bank of lights on a large metal-topped worktable, beside a pair of heavy rubber gloves and a lethal-looking knife, were several clusters of long-stemmed flowers wrapped like babies in green paper swaddling; Harry Todd thought the place had the cold efficiency of an operating room, a morgue. An abattoir for plant life. At first he didn't see anyone; then in the dim light at the back of the room, he saw Tinker sitting on a stool at a slanting table mounted against the wall. She was smoking a cigarette, the smoke curling around her head, watching him, a bemused expression on her face.

"There's something you don't see every day."

"It's nice to see you too, Tinker. You haven't changed a bit."

"Of course I have. But I guess it's nice of you to say so. C'mon and have some coffee."

"I just had some, with breakfast."

"Then be polite and have some more while I have some."

She slid off the stool and led the way to a kitchen area beside the walk-in refrigerated units for the flowers. Tinker was Dickie's age, in her mid-forties, though she appeared to be very much the same tomboy, only a bit taller, still wiry, whom Dickie used to pal around with all through school, whom Dickie was dating when Harry Todd last visited here. Her complexion was as moon-white as Jennifer's, though there was a reddish cast to it from her freckles, and her short auburn hair was styled into a wavy cap. The name Tinker was short for Tinker Bell, a junior high school nickname that stuck, given to her in honor of her bottom, which at the time seemed, to pubescent boys, as perky and high-set as that of the Disney cartoon character. In the long green smock she was wearing over her jeans, Harry Todd couldn't tell if she had retained that characteristic or not.

As she poured their coffee, then started to make a fresh pot, Harry Todd said, "I hope I'm not interrupting something. . . ."

"Of course you're interrupting something. But it's okay, I was only making some notes for my flower orders for the next couple of days. The truth is, I like to hide back here and let the other girls take care of the customers. That's one thing I didn't count on when I started this shop. I thought I'd be dealing with flowers, and I like flowers. But if you're going to sell flowers you have to deal with people, and I found I don't like people. So I try to do as many things as I can back here. But I'm okay with being interrupted, even if it's only you."

She raised her eyebrows at him, handed him a mug, and led the way back into the work area. He thought she was kidding with her last remark, though with Tinker it was often hard to tell; he remembered she tended to play rough, she and Dickie perfect for each other in that regard, their relationship, from what he knew of it, based on a long-standing contest of who could outlast the other, in anything. . . . Tough lady. I can see where Jennifer gets a lot of it. He followed her back to the large worktable in the center of the room, the two of them taking up positions on either side of a corner.

"Jennifer told me that she had seen you a couple of times. She also told me this morning that she asked you to go skinny-dipping."

"Why would she tell you something like that?"

"To shock me, I suppose. To see how I would react. I probably disappointed her. I told her if she was fool enough to ask you, she'd get what she deserved."

"Did she also tell you that I turned down the invitation?"

"Yes, as a matter of fact she did. Which shocked me more than her asking you in the first place. Not at all what I would expect from a Sutcliff. Though I think it's a good thing you did. She would probably eat you alive. Don't take it personally."

"I don't," Harry Todd said, though he felt his masculinity definitely had been called into question. That's just Tinker being Tinker. Why did Dickie ever marry her? Was a ball-breaker the only kind of woman he could relate to? I guess I solved it by never settling down for any length of time with any woman. I wonder if that's true.

Tinker was studying him over the rim of her coffee mug. Finally she said, "So, why are you back in town?"

"I figured after twenty-five years of being away, it was high time for a visit."

"Of course you did," Tinker said, a smile on her face that said she didn't believe him in the least. "Dickie thinks the only reason you're here is to stir up as much trouble as you can. Just for the hell of it. Which may not be that far off."

"He said that?"

"Not in so many words. We don't talk much these days. But I know the man. That's probably what's in the back of his mind. Or maybe up front."

"Well, that's not the reason," he said, thinking, So that's what Dickie thinks of me. That explains a lot. . . . A pair of clippers lay on the metal-top table; Harry Todd idly gave them a whirl, like playing a game of spin the bottle. The clippers pointed to the blank wall.

"Jennifer said you were asking a lot of questions about Kathleen. I figured you came back because of a guilty conscience."

"That's not the reason either." Why would she say that? There's no reason for me to have a guilty conscience. Is there?

"You wouldn't tell me if that were the reason. But it doesn't matter. I decided if you were really interested in Kathleen, that sooner or later you'd get around to me."

"I saw a photo of you and Kathleen and Donna Bruno, sitting together on the front porch of the big house. You know the story about Donna and me, don't you? I mean, that when I was in high school—"

"You mean, do I know that Donna once had your baby? That your father paid to send Donna away to have it? Yes, I know about that. Everybody in town knows about that."

Harry Todd winced. He spun the clippers again; this time they pointed at him. "Then what was she doing there at the house? Was she there very often?"

Tinker nodded.

"Didn't that seem a little bizarre to you, given the circumstances?"

"It seemed more than a little bizarre. It seemed downright sick, if you asked me, though obviously nobody asked me. For a while your father and mother were calling Donna 'our third daughter,' meaning, I guess, that they took me for the second one. I put the kibosh on that idea real quick. The last thing on earth I wanted to be was a daughter in your family, no thank you."

Harry Todd started to spin the clippers again, but Tinker reached over and took them away from him, putting them on the other side of her.

"Whose idea was it to have her over to the house?"

"I'm not sure if it was your father's or Kathleen's, but I know why she was there. It was because she was Kathleen's friend. You knew about that, didn't you? That Kathleen and Donna became good friends when Kathleen started working at Sutcliff Realty?"

"I didn't know until a little while ago. I was talking to one of the waitresses at the Furnass Grill and she told me that Kathleen and Donna used to go in there all the time. A lot of the time with my father."

"Ah yes, the jolly threesome." Tinker seemed ready to say something else, then thought differently of it. She gave a laugh that was partly a sigh. "I guess Kathleen knew Donna from high school, when Donna was your girlfriend, even though Kathleen was younger. Then after she was away to have the baby, Donna came back to town and took advantage of your father's offer of a job as part of the arrangement. The problem was, when Kathleen started working in the office she expected to be the center of attention, especially her father's attention, and she found Donna, another young attractive woman, already in place. So for a while there was a kind of competition between them. Then Kathleen found out that Donna had had your baby. She took it pretty hard."

"She didn't know before that?"

"Evidently not. She must have been the only person in town who didn't. You never told her?"

"Well, no. . . ."

Tinker shrugged. "There you are. I guess nobody else ever got around to it either. So it upset her badly when she finally found out. She had a really bad asthma attack, she was off work for a couple of weeks."

"Who told her about the baby?"

"Probably Donna. The weird thing was, after Kathleen went back to work, she started treating Donna like her long-lost sister, that's when Donna started going over to the house all the time. Your father went along with it for a while, both because he wanted Kathleen to be happy, and because he enjoyed having as many young women around as he could get—you know how he was. Then he backed off a little. More than a little. I think it got too complicated for your father when Dickie started sleeping with Donna."

"You knew about that?"

"Damn, I was trying to shock you with that little tidbit of information."

"I wouldn't say I was shocked when I heard it. But it certainly does seem rather sordid. Were you shocked by it?"

"Remember, I've known Dickie and your family a long time. It would take quite a bit to shock me. Disappointed perhaps, that he would be so predictable. On the other hand, with Dickie boffing Donna, it took a lot of the pressure off me, didn't it? Besides, all sorts of interesting things were starting to go on around here about that time," Tinker said and headed back to her desk.

Harry Todd stared after her for a moment. What did she mean by that? As he followed her, he decided he needed to change his tack.

"At least I'm glad to hear my father was decent to Donna, that he honored his promise to give her a job and all when she came back to town. It's a wonder, considering all the trouble there was when he first heard she was pregnant."

Tinker, after wiggling back onto her stool, looked at him for a moment, as if trying to gauge whether he was serious or not. "Your father. . . ," Tinker started to say, then gave a little shake of her head. She sipped her coffee before going on.

"Your father was also the one who fired Donna right after Kathleen died. Not just fired her, but turned on her, out of nowhere, the day after Kathleen's funeral. Donna was sitting at her desk and your father, for no apparent reason, came out of his office and started screaming at her to get out, in front of everybody, he didn't even let her pack up her things."

"I didn't know that. Donna only said he let her go. . . ."

"Being fired that way really hurt her," Tinker went on. "Have you seen Donna since you've been back?"

"I ran into her the other day. We had coffee together. . . ."

"Then you know that Donna's not the most stable creature on God's good green earth. Whatever else was going on at the time, she and Kathleen were friends before Kathleen died, the only friend each other had, except for me. Donna was trying to piece together a life for herself in this town when she came back, I give her credit for that. Here's something else you probably didn't know: The reason she came back, the only reason as far as I know, was that her mother and father were ill and needed someone to look after them. They died shortly after she got here, within a month or so of each other, that's undoubtedly one reason why she accepted Kathleen's offer to start going over to the house. So when your father fired her that way, she not only got turned out of her job, she lost what she thought was her surrogate family. That wonderful family of yours."

She cocked her head and raised her eyebrows at him, as if to say, What do you make of all that? Harry Todd didn't know what to make of it. He sensed that Tinker had her own agenda, her own scores to settle, her own list of family wrongs against her. Maybe she was bothered by Dickie's sleeping around more than she knew or could readily admit, and it came out as anger against his family, against his father. Whatever, he was surprised to find that he felt defensive about his family, surprised to find himself thinking that if his father fired Donna in such a manner there must have been a good reason for it.

"Knowing that Dickie and Donna were once lovers, it makes more sense why he was so generous in getting her a job with Lyle after Father fired her," Harry Todd said. "He was taking care of one of his old girlfriends."

"Maybe. But with Dickie there are usually several reasons for anything he does. Besides, by that time things were more complicated than you could ever imagine."

Harry Todd was thinking about something else. As he stood beside her desk, he picked up a pen from the tray and began to play with it on the desktop.

"The thing that bothers me is that nobody seems to know for sure how Kathleen died. Or if they know they won't tell me."

"I know. She died of a barbiturate overdose."

"That's what Donna said it was."

"Damn again. That's the second time I failed to shock you. You're not much fun."

"I didn't know whether to believe Donna or not when she said it."

"On that you can believe her." Tinker grabbed the pen from him before he could twirl it again and put it back in the tray. "I know because Dickie told me."

"How did Kathleen get hold of barbiturates? Did she have a prescription?"

"Didn't Donna tell you? No, I guess she wouldn't know about that. She was out of the family circle by that time."

"She told me some crazy ideas about Marilyn Monroe and poisoned enemas."

"Maybe Donna knows more than I give her credit for."

"What are you talking about?"

"Your mother gave the barbiturates to Kathleen. At least that's what your father thought. He blamed your mother for giving Kathleen the pills that killed her. He said your mother gave her pills knowing full well what Kathleen was going to do with them. I think he had the idea that your mom even encouraged Kathleen to commit suicide. Well, surprise, surprise. Looks like I finally found something to shock you with after all."

"My father thought my mother helped Kathleen kill herself?"

Tinker scrunched her shoulders, pulled a face.

Across the room one of the saleswomen from the front of the shop had come through the curtain with a question for Tinker. Tinker grinned at Harry Todd.

"Saved by the bell. What is it, Nancy? My friend here was just leaving. It seems he came looking for a flower, and ended up with a handful of thorns."

. . . in his office in the Sutcliff Realty Building on the main street Dickie sits at his desk looking over the photocopies of Julian's records that Donna delivered to him this morning, tsk-tsking to himself as he sees a financial picture develop of the man—not a pretty sight—confirming everything he suspected, staring at the numbers in Julian's past until his eyes glaze over and he's seen enough, he closes the file folder and puts it back in his locked drawer and turns his thoughts to the myriad of details regarding the everyday affairs of the office that were waiting for him when he came back from Pamela's this morning, that Wendy the receptionist wants her vacation at the same time as Jeannette, the secretary who usually covers the phone for her, that the lease on his car is up next month and he'll have to arrange for the dealership to send over a new one, that Mrs. Wysnuski in one of his rental properties needs her air conditioner fixed, to say nothing of the stack of papers waiting for his attention regarding Furnass Landing, the contracts and change orders and submittals that need to be reviewed, his thoughts however with thoughts of their own, the memory that earlier started knocking at the edges of his mind on the drive back to the office crowding now into his consciousness, the day he was over at the big house for something a short time after he was married and he didn't think anyone was there, he was walking down the hallway on the second floor on his way to the bathroom when Kathleen came out of her room and stood in the doorway naked, her hands inverted to each other

shielding her tiny breasts, one hand up one hand down, fingertips touching like a half-formed yin-yang symbol, as if she held something very delicate between them, stood there looking at him, as if asking him something—and he shakes his head violently, refusing to think of it anymore, refusing to think of the implications of that day to the events that happened either before or after, reaching instead for the telephone to call Pamela to tell her about the silly thing he did this morning about ordering a sofa until he catches himself and realizes that's not going to work either—This isn't the way to do it, Dickie—and he dials his secretary instead and tells her to come in and bring her pad as he starts to dig into the stack of change orders for Furnass Landing, burying himself and any wayward thoughts under the weight of blessed paperwork . . . as at Grandview Cemetery on a ridge overlooking the town and the valley, Kitty parks her car on the side of the narrow gravel lane and gets out, takes off the jacket of her pink brocade suit and the veiled hat and lays them on the back seat and from the front seat takes the wicker picnic hamper she uses to transport Merry Anne and starts up the gentle slope, grasshoppers and flying insects arcing away from her with every footstep in the recently cut grass—a cloud of midges dances before her eyes; she holds her breath and closes her eyes as she steps through—tottering a bit in her spectator pumps with the uneven footing, past the relatively unweathered and fresh-from-the-showroom-looking gravestones in this newer part of the cemetery, toward the tall black marble monument, actually a slab on end, with the name Sutcliff, sitting on the crest of the hill, setting down the basket with Merry Anne on the grass and taking a moment to catch her breath as she surveys the condition of the monument—she understands now why more people didn't choose polished black marble: rain leaves splotch marks, dulling the surface and showing the dirt, and bird shit stands out like bullet holes; around the base are two evergreen bushes that were meant to be trimmed into low rounded shapes but as they grew she found she liked the unkempt, scraggy effect among the otherwise well-tended graves and has let the bushes go wild until they threaten to hide the monument, hide the name; she notes the geraniums and the border of marigolds she planted a few weeks ago on Memorial Day have died, thinking Come on, Harry old love, you're not doing your part, you're sup- posed to be fertilizing these things to help them grow. But I guess helping things grow was never your strong suit, was it, honey- lover? Helping things be themselves. You were always best at helping yourself, at being yourself. But that was only right—then sits down on the grass beside Merry Anne, crossing her ankles and folding her hands in her lap, uncaring that she's probably getting grass stains on her skirt—How many times in my life will I wear this suit again anyway?—looking at the world around her, the afternoon hot and hazy, the sharp edges of everyday reality softened with the heat so that things seem more distant than they actually are, the view of the town in the valley, the colors muted— exposed on the gentle slope, with no trees around her, the disk of the veiled sun seemingly too close, the gray sky too encompassing—sitting among the graves themselves before the monument, on one side the headstone flat on the ground that reads

HENRY "HARRY" BRUCE SUTCLIFF
1919–1978

Husband, lover, friend—Too bad you never figured out how to be all three at any one time—and on the other side, closer to the center of the plot, the other headstone,

KATHLEEN MARY SUTCLIFF
1939–1975

thinking about how when Kathleen died she and Harry picked out this plot for the family; Harry had envisioned where he thought they would all lie when the time came, with Kitty and himself directly in front of the monument, and Kathleen close beside him on the right, and they placed Kathleen accordingly, but when Harry died three years later Kitty had him placed where he was now, to the left of where she would eventually lie, which put him off-center as if on the periphery of the family, another example to some of her craziness or perhaps some vindictiveness on her part according to the talk around town, her putting him on the fringe of the family to get back at him in death for all his carousing and running around in life, or for any of a dozen reasons people came up with, the town thinking they knew enough about the family to guess what the reason might be, though Kitty didn't care, she never felt the need to explain her reasoning to anyone, until today, addressing Merry Anne inside the wicker hamper, "I wanted you to see it, I wanted you to know what I was talking about all these years, because after trying to keep Harry and Kathleen apart for so long I couldn't very well let her lie beside him in death, could I? Harry deserved his rest after all he'd been through. And burying him with me between them this way seemed better than digging her up and moving her before we buried him. I considered that too, you know. Though that certainly would have had the people in town talking, wouldn't it? That almost would have made it worthwhile. . . ," sitting there for a time taking in the day before she struggles to her feet again—accomplishing it in stages, first rolling over onto her hands and knees, then up on one knee, then to her feet, tottering in the soft footing until she regains her balance and her head stops swimming—and carries the wicker hamper farther on into the older part of the cemetery, setting it down again in front of a traditional stone marker shaped like a small headboard, and takes a seat herself on the grass halfway down the length of this particular grave, shifting around to

*make herself comfortable almost as if she were sitting on the chest
of the inhabitant underneath, and says to the hamper, "And now,
sweetheart, I want you to meet a very special person in my life.
That's right, this is the man I've told you about. This is Doctor" . . . as in the big house on Orchard Hill, Harry Todd, having
returned from downtown, stands at the dining room table looking
at the two latest photographs that his mother laid out for him, the
first taken when he is perhaps five and Kathleen four, on the front
porch on a warm summer's day, just the two of them, Dickie only
a baby and probably inside taking a nap, Kathleen sitting in her
little wooden chair dressed in a long granny skirt and bonnet
holding her Raggedy Ann doll, Harry Todd standing beside her
dressed in a white sailor's outfit with short pants, bending down
to kiss his sister, a cute picture unless you consider the fervor
with which Kathleen is turned in her chair, every muscle of her
little body straining upward as she stretches to meet his lips, the
two children even then looking for all the world like lovers, though
in the second photo Kathleen is older, perhaps ten or eleven, on
the threshold of puberty, again on the front porch but this time
standing beside her father who sits on the top step, the man laughing as he holds on to her leg, to him it's all a big joke, his hand
up under the edge of her short skirt, holding her thigh as he might
a post except this is his daughter, her head turned away, looking
off to the side into the shadows of the porch where Harry Todd
stands holding Dickie by the hand, the two brothers watching what
is going on between father and daughter like spectators at a show,
Kathleen with one finger shyly touching her lips, though it is uncertain whether she is being demure and coy or if she is saying
"Shhh," her shoulders scrunched, the expression on her face one
of sheer happiness and something else too, peace, and Harry Todd
turns away from the table more confused than ever, his thoughts
reeling with some of the things Tinker told him at her shop—
Your father thought your mother murdered Kathleen, that she*

gave Kathleen the pills on purpose . . . Your father turned on Donna the day after Kathleen was buried, threw her out of the office . . . with Dickie there's usually several reasons for everything he does—though all his thoughts return to one question, Why would Kathleen kill herself, whether Mother helped her or not? What would make her that despondent to do such a thing? and moving on through the dark downstairs of the house Harry Todd taps one of the strings of his mother's collection of bells dangling in the doorway to the living room, the velvet rope with Shiva dancing on a handmade bell from India and the several elephant bells, a Buddhist prayer bell and a camel bell made from a tin can, sending a ripple of tintinnabulation through the silent house, and he stands in the shadows of the front hall as the silence settles once more around him, wondering what the ringing bells might have summoned, listening for the sound of movement upstairs, watching for the glimpse of a ghostly figure slipping just out of his line of sight, but there is nothing, the dark house remains still, there is only the sound of the grandfather clock tocking sonorously beside the stairs to the second floor, the dull pattern of the transom window over the front door spilling across the ceiling and down the wall from the gray afternoon light outside, and Harry Todd nods to himself and purses his lips, confident that he's on the trail to understanding the tragedies of his family, revealing the same traits and failures of character that allowed them to turn him out when he was younger, ignoring any message much less self-revelation that might be contained in the photos his mother left for him in favor of his own solution, his wedging together the few pieces he has of the puzzle to fit the picture he wants to create, convinced in his heart of hearts that whatever bad things happened in the family before his father's death, the tradition of perdition and sordidness is being carried on by his conniving, opportunistic younger brother. . . .

34

Harry Todd was ready to head upstairs to his room and take a nap when he heard a car pull into the driveway; he peeked out the front screen door in time to see the tail fins of his mother's Cadillac glide by on the way to the garage. His first inclination was to run, hide, hurry upstairs to his room so she wouldn't see him—What do you suppose that's about?—but he knew what he should do; he should go and greet her, see if she needed help carrying groceries or whatever. Taking a deep breath—I'm probably going to regret this—he retraced his steps through the house and out the back door.

By the time he got to the garage, his mother had pulled the car inside and was unloading something from the passenger's side.

"Here, I can help you with that," Harry Todd said cheerily.

"Thank you, dear. That would be a help."

He expected the wicker hamper to be heavy, full of plates and dishes, the glassware from a covered-dish luncheon at her church or woman's club, but the basket was surprisingly light, it seemed to pop up from the seat when he lifted it.

"Where were you, on a picnic? Any goodies left over?"

His mother ignored his attempts at good humor. "That's Merry Anne's carrier. That's what I use to take her to the vet's."

"You mean ol' Merry Anne's in here? Hi kitty, how you doing?" He lifted the hamper to eye level and tried to peer inside the cracks between the wicker. He shifted it back and forth, bobbed it up and down. "She's awful light. And doesn't seem to move around much."

"She's dead, dear. Please be careful with her."

His mother walked past him and disappeared around the side of the garage. Harry Todd stood holding the hamper for a moment, looking from it to where she had gone and back again, before following after her, carrying it by its handles, trying to keep it away from his body as if something inside might reach through the wicker and get him. His mother was in the tool shed, fumbling around in the darkness.

"What happened to her?"

"She died, dear," his mother said, her back to him as she shifted some bags of fertilizer, sorted through a collection of long-handled tools. "I knew it would have to be done, sooner or later. I kept her as long as I could, but the doctor said the pain she was in would only get worse. It seemed a kindness to take it from her and I had her put to sleep. But it's hard to know what's right about these things, life itself is so precious. Don't you think?"

She emerged from the gloom at the rear of the shed carrying a spade. She smiled at him sadly and went on across the back-yard, heading toward the tennis courts. Harry Todd followed.

"What are you going to do?"

"I'm going to bury her. That's what you do with a dead cat, dear."

Midway down the gentle slope she paused, then wandered back and forth across the grass a few times, tottering in her spec-tator pumps, as if measuring the feel of the place, before she de-cided on a spot.

"This will be nice. It will get lots of sun. Merry Anne always loved the sun. Sometimes when she was younger she'd come out here and sit in the grass, watching the birds and the bugs and enjoying the day. And I've always wanted to have a little garden out here."

She took the basket from Harry Todd and gently set it down. Then she took the spade and tried to break the surface of the earth; the earth didn't budge. She smiled at Harry Todd and reset the tip of the spade in the grass, this time placing her foot on the top edge of the blade for added push, but the tool still couldn't get a bite. Then she mounted it, standing on it with both feet like a pogo stick. For a moment the tool and his mother remained upright, quivering slightly, suspended in time and space, before slowly tipping over to one side, his mother stepping clear at the last second.

These things are but sent to try us. And they're doing a very good job, I might add. . . .

"Here, Mother, let me." He took the spade, thinking it wouldn't be that hard to dig a hole the size of a cat—Digging a hole is a man's job—he'd be in the house and taking a nap in no time. But he found the earth after several weeks without rain was rock-hard; his first bite with the pointed shovel brought up only a fist-sized clod of grass, a few dingleberries of dirt clinging to the matted roots, and what appeared to be half a dried earthworm. His mother headed back toward the garage.

What? She's giving up on me already? She never did think I could do anything right. . . .

He attacked digging the hole with more determination— Maybe she's gone to call Dickie, I'm sure my little brother could dig a hole that would please her—enlarging the first bite of grass until, after a few minutes of furious activity, he had cleared a two-foot-square area of sod. He stood bent over, braced on the handle of the spade, already out of breath and his back hurting. I'm in trouble here. As he wiped the sweat off his face with his handkerchief, the head of a pickax sailed past his ear and embedded itself in the exposed earth.

"Oops," his mother said behind him.

"Mother!"

"That's right, I remember now. This pick is broken." She looked at the handle in her hand. "I was swinging it to see how heavy it was. Good thing I missed you."

If I live through this trip it'll be a wonder. . . .

"I think I'll stick with the spade. Why don't you go get something to put Merry Anne in. It doesn't seem right to just put her in the ground."

"That's a nice idea, Harry Todd. I'll be right back."

He watched his mother wobble in her low heels across the grass, making her way back up the slope to the house, and started in again. She must be used to this by now, burying those around her, first her daughter, then her husband, now her cat. Grandfather and Grandmother must have been in there too, somewhere along the line. Mother's an old hand at this, she's getting good at it. That's unkind but probably true. . . .

The dry earth did not give easily but he worked away at it, making progress chunk by chunk. He was glad that at least the hot sun wasn't beating down on him, though the heat and humidity had settled over the afternoon like plasma, a presence of its own; the light had turned yellowish-gray under a yellow-gray sky. His vision of a nice square hole was compromised when he encountered several large rocks sticking out from the sides, along with tangles of tree roots, he supposed from the sycamores, extending all the way from behind the house, their underground feeder system reaching for sustenance through the darkness of the earth—at the moment nothing seemed more insidious to Harry Todd, and more human-like in its dark entanglements, than a tree. As the hole descended farther it became more cone-shaped but it seemed an impossible task to change it. She's going to think I can't even dig a hole. She'll be right. His sweat had soaked through his shirt, his hands were starting to blister.

By the time his mother returned, he had decided a cone-shaped hole would do fine. She was carrying a plastic sweater box into which she had placed an old flannel shirt, a ball, a sock-shaped toy, and an old brown shoelace.

"These were Merry Anne's favorite things. I thought they should go with her."

"Of course."

"I never understood those pharaohs and Chinese kings, being buried with their servants and food and sometimes even their wives and children. But now it's beginning to make more sense."

Just keep quiet, don't say a word. . . .

She placed the box on the grass. Then she hiked up the skirt
of her pink brocade suit—Mother!—knelt down on one knee and
opened the lid of the hamper. Inside was a ball of black and brown
fur curled into itself, barely recognizable as once a cat, once a
living thing. His mother lifted it out and placed it on the flannel
shirt in the plastic box, arranging the toys around it, talking
softly to it. "Here you are, dear. You'll be comfortable in here,
and nothing can hurt you now, it's all over now. . . ." Harry Todd
felt a catch in his throat. He moved a few feet away, feeling that
he was intruding.

She really loved that skinny old cat. I guess I never realized
how much it meant to her. Why do we allow ourselves to feel for
animals those things that we can never feel for the people around
us? Probably because there are none of those other feelings that
get involved as soon as other people are involved, the endless
little disappointments and betrayals from those we love or want
to love us that drain us like a thousand pricks of a knife. Or
maybe it's simply that she loved the cat, no more, no less. What
control do we have over who and what we love? None at all, as
far as I can see. . . .

In a few minutes his mother placed the lid on the box and
stood up and brought it over to the hole.

She's ready now. I'm ready now."

She handed the box to Harry Todd. The box with the cat
curled inside looked like the reliquary of some ancient religion . . .
Centuries from now someone's going to unearth this and think
they've found an artifact of some esoteric cult, the Tomb of the
Unknown Kitty. He placed it carefully in the hole.

"Any last words? I guess that sounds silly."

"No, not at all. It's touching, actually, that you'd think of it.
But I guess when it comes down to it, the only thing one can say
is . . . Rest in peace, little one."

In his mind he heard himself echo, Rest in peace, little one. He took the first spadeful of dirt and looked at his mother; she nodded to go ahead. He tried to lower the dirt onto the box so it wouldn't make any noise but some of it spilled, sprinkling down, drumming on the lid. He had one last clear image of the box, glowing dully at the bottom of the hole surrounded by the dark earth, before he scraped in the pile of dirt and filled the hole quickly, tamping it flat.

"That's all right, Harry Todd. Leave it as it is."

"Don't you want me to put the grass back over it?"

"No, I think I'll plant some flowers here. Why don't you go on in the house now. I can take care of it from here."

"I'd be glad to help. . . ."

"I'd like to be alone, dear."

She smiled at him pointedly, a smile that was no smile at all. Feeling very much unwanted and in the way, he gathered up the spade and broken pick and carried them back to the shed. Then he went on into the house.

In the kitchen he washed his hands, running hot water over them until they burned. Me, blisters. My friends in California would never believe it. He let the cold water run for a drink, but it never got cooler than tepid and tasted metallic. Feeling at loose ends, he went through the open-ended china cupboard into the front hall. The house seemed empty and more forlorn than usual. He realized he missed the cat lying there, watching him from her usual spot on the hall carpet. If I'm feeling that way, imagine what it will be like for Mother. . . .

He went upstairs to the second floor. Now he was really tired, he wanted to lie down more than ever, but he stood in the up-stairs hall for a moment and listened: nothing. Was Kathleen in the house now? The idea didn't seem spooky to him, just lonely . . . Now I suppose there will be a cat-ghost running around too. He went down the hall toward the back of the house to Dickie's old room. The air was stuffy and smelled of old clothes, old books, dust. Hanging from the ceiling were some of the model planes Dickie had made as a boy, a P-51 Mustang, a MiG-15, an F-86 Sabre jet; on the shelves were more of his models, the battleship *Missouri*, an LST, a Sherman tank. I said to her Your father was always good at building things, and Jennifer said You don't have to try to be nice. The grayness of the day barely seeped in through the windows, the leaves of the sycamores outside were as still as a photograph. He knelt at the window, to see if he could see his mother through the trees, remembering that Dickie used to kneel here as a child to watch Kathleen and himself down at the tennis court.

Was he here watching that day, the day Kathleen won and we raced to the house and I stayed downstairs while she took her shower because I guess I knew what would happen if I went upstairs and I guess I must have wanted it to happen too, but then she came downstairs anyway after her shower and walked past me on the way to the laundry and I tried to pretend I wasn't watching her wrapped in the towel and then when she came back again I thought it would be a great joke and as she passed the door to the living room I reached over and pulled the towel off her expecting her to scream or laugh or get mad or something but when she held on to it I ended up pulling her over on top of me and we tumbled onto the floor and we were rolling on the floor and before I knew what was happening but that's a lie I knew very well what was happening I had my pants down and I tried to put it in her and she made a noise and I thought Oh my God this is wrong this is so wrong and I ran out of the house, if Dickie was in the house he must have heard us, maybe he even saw us, he knew what happened, I never thought of that before, maybe that's what's been eating at Dickie all these years about me. Mother said You never realized how close Dickie and

Kathleen were. No wonder the son-of-a-bitch hates me, I'd hate me too. Maybe I do. . . .

Below, in the backyard beyond the garage, his mother knelt in the grass, rounding the corners of the filled-in hole with a hand trowel to make a circle; beside her were several trays of flowers, pansies and chrysanthemums. *I was too harsh on her, about all the practice she's had in burying her dead.* He thought of going on upstairs for his nap, but it seemed more important to stay here at the window and watch. To bear witness, somehow be part of it.

35

For perhaps the dozenth time since he got back to the office, Dickie reached for the telephone to call Pamela, and stopped himself again. *I'm like a goddamn love-sick teenager,* he thought, except that he had never felt this way in high school, he had never felt this way before in his life that he could remember. This dull ache, this hunger he felt was about to consume him. Women, girls, had never been a concern for him, in high school or college or after, there were always plenty who were interested in him, his only problem deciding which ones to choose; they were the ones who ached for him, not the other way around. And of course there was always Tinker, he couldn't remember a time when Tinker wasn't there. Dickie reached for the phone again, and stopped himself again.

No, he had to accept that the thing with Pamela was over, it didn't work out, he blew it, he pushed too hard or whatever he did wrong, she was mad at him, she didn't want to see him again. *This isn't the way to do it, Dickie.* He had made a mistake, he had to move on, forget about her, it wasn't worth it. He rested his elbows on the contract in front of him, washed his hands down over his face. He thought what his father would say about Dickie's fretting about Pamela: *Go get yourself another girl,* when it comes to Sutcliff men it's not as if it's a seller's market out there. Dickie smiled to himself. His father always had a way with words. And principles to live by—other people to live by. But he knew his father had a point. That was the thing about his father, he was wrong so much of the time, in the way he handled people, in the way he bullied and cajoled and pushed too hard, overbearing in all his dealings, but he was usually right too, right in what he was trying to achieve at least. It made it hard to condemn the man. For Dickie it would be like condemning himself, because he was aware his father had schooled him in business, schooled him in life. For better or for worse.

He sat back in his chair, leaned back, turned at an angle from his desk, swiveling back and forth restlessly like a radar dish seeking hidden blips. Through the open door he could see the outer office, the rows of empty desks, everyone else having left for the day promptly at five, the dull light coming in the front windows overlooking the main street. The afternoon was getting darker, it looked like it could rain. Across the room was a large painting of his father, illuminated in his dark office by a small light above the frame, painted from a photograph taken in middle age. He remembered when he first showed it to his father, up at the big house. His father was no longer strong enough to get out of bed by that time; the last operation had taken his left arm and shoulder and half of his right leg. They rented a hospital bed for him and placed it in the tower area of the living room so he could look out the windows, propped up on pillows, wedged into a sitting position to help his breathing, looking like a pajama-clad astronaut ready for zero gravity. His father and mother filled their days watching television together, *Jeopardy!* and *The Price Is Right*, reruns of *20,000 Leagues Under the Sea* and *Bonanza*, and *The Merv Griffin Show*. His mother sat beside the bed knitting a scarf she said he'd need to keep him warm when he got better—they both knew he was never going to get better, they both knew he was dying, there was hardly anything left of him at that point, and yet whatever had happened between them in the past, they seemed to get closer again during his last days, they held hands and looked forward to watching their shows together and to being with each other; was it the presence of death that did that, or was it feelings deeper than those that had driven them apart all those years?—his father fading in and out of consciousness. It was Halloween; when Dickie stopped by the house he found a little party in progress. His mother had made herself a witch's costume and his father had directed her on how to wrap him like a mummy; they joked that Dickie had come dressed as a businessman. After they had some cider—even his father took a few sips through a straw before nodding off—Dickie brought in the portrait and propped it on a chair across the room. He and his mother waited a few moments, until his father drifted awake again and rolled his head to the side to see it. He smiled faintly.

"Good-looking devil . . . wasn't he?" he rasped.

"He still is," his wife said, looking at Dickie and nodding for him to agree.

"Hell of a man," was all Dickie could think to say.

His father turned away, as if he didn't have time for such sentiments, already drifting off again. "Amazing what you can do . . . with a little paint."

The trick-or-treaters started to arrive then, and his mother left the room to answer the doorbell. Dickie sat in her chair beside the bed, watching his father sleep. After several minutes his father opened his eyes and looked at Dickie again.

"I have to tell you something."

"It can wait, Dad. Don't tire yourself out."

"No, it can't wait. I want you to know. I never . . . fucked her . . . I never laid a hand on her . . . if that's what you thought."

"Dad, you don't have to. . . ."

His father closed his eyes and waved feebly for Dickie to be quiet. "Yes, I do have to. I want you to know. I never . . . I wouldn't. . . ."

"Nobody ever thought you did, Dad."

"Your mother did. Thought I did. . . ."

"It's okay, Dad. Now get some rest."

"There was always that smell of smoke, wasn't there?"

"I guess so," Dickie shrugged, not knowing what he was referring to.

"Fire and brimstone . . . something burning . . . always the smell of smoke. . . ."

"You mean in town? Well, sure, that's Furnass."

His father lifted his hand slightly, as if he wanted to say something more, or said it somewhere in his mind, and drifted away again.

Dickie was touched that his father wanted to tell him that nothing had happened between him and Donna, but it wasn't necessary. Dickie's own affair with Donna had been casual at best, she was one of several women he had been seeing off and on at the time. It had started soon after she came back to town with Dickie taking her out for a drink a few times after work, and developed into Dickie stopping down at her house once a week to spend a couple of hours in bed. Neither one was at all serious about the other, it was only a matter of convenience, for both Dickie and Donna, something available close at hand; but after Kathleen started working at the office, and then his father started hanging around with the two girls, going out to lunch together and occasional drinks together, Dickie broke it off with Donna— a relief, actually—thinking things were getting too chummy for his tastes, too many chances for someone to say too much about his business. But over the years he and Donna had remained, if not friends, at least friendly. Dickie had learned that from his father too: one never knew when an old girlfriend might come in handy.

His father's efforts to set the books straight about Donna was another example of the concern that Dickie felt his father had always shown toward him. Concern that Dickie was prepared for the things he might face in the future. Concern that Dickie had the advantage of learning from his father's mistakes. As his father slept that day, Dickie reached out and took his hand, the only time outside of a handshake that he could ever remember holding the man's hand. It was waxy and cold, but Dickie wouldn't have traded the experience for anything. Sitting now in his office—his father's office, in the building his father built—he wondered if his father knew how grateful he was to him. Wondered if his father knew that Dickie—there was no other word for it—loved him. He hoped so, though it seemed unlikely, Dickie had never consciously thought it himself before today. Dickie certainly never told his father while he was alive. Something he regretted now.

You have to tell people that. If you have the chance. If you can say the words.

It was time to go; he gathered up his car keys, locked his desk drawers and file cabinets, put on his suit coat. But before he left the office he sat down at his desk again and reached for the phone. This time he dialed Pamela's number, letting it ring till he got her answering machine, and left her a message he hoped she'd get after work:

"Okay, so maybe I was wrong about the sofa. But at least give me credit for not calling the damn thing a couch."

36

Unfortunately, as soon as the door swung closed behind him, he was in total darkness. Shit. Show me thy light, oh Lord, before I bump into something. He walked forward tentatively, into what felt like the edge of a round table. *Oof!* He reached out his hand, into a puddle of water. Must be holy water. In a font large enough to drown in. He traced around the edge to what he thought was a hundred and eighty degrees and headed forward again, arms outstretched like a sleepwalker's, until he found a row of doors but no handles. Emblematic of a church, I suppose. After feeling around for a minute or so, it occurred to him to push; the door opened. Push and it will open unto you. Seek but be careful of what you find.

The inside of the church was lighter than the foyer but not by much. The stained-glass windows glowed dully with little illumination, backlit by the gray light from outside. On the wall between the windows were half-life-sized friezes of the Stations of the Cross, as if Christ's struggles to drag the cross through the streets were seeping out of the plaster. Flanking the sanctuary were grottos and niches displaying holy statues; confessionals lined the rear of the church like a row of guardhouses. Or wood porta-potties. Banks of small votive candles flickered at the railing in front of the main altar. The church was empty except for one lone figure kneeling in front of a grotto with a statue of the Virgin holding the infant Jesus. Harry Todd sidestepped through the empty pews to the side aisle and approached her, taking a seat nearby. It was several minutes before Donna lifted her head and looked at him. She smiled, a dreamy, almost beatific expression on her face, as if she weren't at all surprised to see him, almost as if she were expecting him. Harry Todd smiled in return.

I'll bet I'm going to wish I had waited outside. . . .

Donna motioned for him to come over to her. Harry Todd shook his head. Donna smiled sympathetically.

"It's okay," she said out loud. "I won't bite. And neither will she, will you, Mary?" She looked at the statue as if she expected it to answer, or at least nod.

She talks to statues. Uh-oh. . . .

Slowly, Harry Todd got up and went over to her. She nodded
for him to kneel beside her at the railing. Standing there, he felt
awkward and exposed; it seemed less conspicuous to join her. But
I'm not folding my hands like I'm praying. . . .

"This is where I come every day after work."

"I know. That's why I'm here. You told me."

"Isn't she beautiful? And such a healthy, happy baby. They're
together always."

"Is there someplace we can go to talk?'

"We can talk here. Father Mulroy is a friend of mine. He won't
say anything. And you don't have to whisper. Nobody ever comes
here at this hour."

From outside came the sound of a sudden wind, pushing
against the windows, against the one side of the building; the
church creaked as if it moved a few inches leeward. There followed a rapid ticking against the glass, the roof, the first drops
of a hard rain, with more heavy gusts. Harry Todd looked around.
I was kidding about the end of the world, you know. . . . The
church seemed darker and emptier than it had before. He looked
again at Donna.

"I guess I know what you want to talk to me about," she said,
looking a little sad. "You must have thought of some more questions about Kathleen."

"Well, sort of. . . ."

It seemed awkward and unfeeling to simply plunge into such
a topic, but now that she brought it up he decided to go ahead.
He took a deep breath.

"Mother told me that you and Dickie were. . . ." He hesitated
again; he didn't know if it was appropriate to say such a word in
a church.

"Lovers?" she asked, then nodded in reply. "I guess you could
say I've been sort of a family affair, haven't I?"

Maybe that's the real reason she comes here to pray every afternoon. Because she feels guilty. Life's been rough on her. . . .

"I was wondering if Kathleen knew about it."

"About me and your brother?" Donna looked at her hands folded on top of the marble railing, smiling to herself as if she could guess where this was going. "Yes, she did, as a matter of fact."

"How did she find out?"

"I told her."

"Why did . . ." you do that? he started to ask her, then thought better of it. The sound of the rain outside had become a steady din, thunder far in the distance. He shifted his weight on the kneeler. She must have knees like hubcaps to be able to do this every day. "Was she upset about it, do you know?"

"I suppose, but I don't why she thought it was such a big deal. Besides, it was over between me and Dickie a year or so earlier. Just what is it that you're trying to find out, Harry Todd?"

"I'm trying to understand why Kathleen might have killed herself. What drove her to do such a thing."

"Who said that she did? Kill herself?"

"You said she died from a barbiturate overdose. That has to mean she either took them on purpose or by accident."

"And you think the reason she might take them on purpose is because Kathleen was depressed at the idea that Dickie and me were lovers?" Donna pursed her lips, trying to contain her smile, though she was obviously pleased. "That's really very sweet."

"I figured that's why Father fired you so abruptly after Kathleen died. He found out that you told Kathleen and he blamed you for upsetting her."

Donna's mood changed; she became pensive, looking past him into the shadows of the church as if staring at scenes from an earlier time. "Your father blamed me, but it wasn't for telling her that." Donna turned away; then she was happy and animated again, gazing up at the Virgin. "Look at the way she holds the baby. Sometimes the baby smiles at me. Oh, I know he doesn't really, but sometimes it seems like he does."

Donna fluttered her fingers at the infant Jesus. Outside the rain had shifted, now it was starting to drum on the opposite wall of the church as it passed over. Harry Todd stared in front of him, dazed. Is she completely out of her tree? You have to be careful about anything Donna tells you Mother said, she's not the most reliable source of information. . . . Out of the corner of his eye he thought he saw the statue of the Virgin move, shift her stance slightly. Kathleen? Don't tell me I'm seeing ghosts here too. . . . Donna put her hand on top of his as it rested on the railing; her hand was cooler than the marble.

"I hoped that you'd come here to see me, because I have something else to tell you. I told you that I pray every day for us. Well, I also pray every day for our little boy."

"Our what?" He had forgotten—or rather, he had never thought about—that there was actually a child somewhere, a child with his and Donna's genes.

"Our baby," Donna said, squeezing his hand, peering into his eyes as if trying to see the back of his skull. "And you've come home at just the right time. I've been trying to locate our little boy for years. When they place a child, the adoption agencies work real hard to keep the name and the location of the new parents a secret. But that's one of the advantages of working for an attorney. I can get access to records that I couldn't otherwise. And I think I've finally found him. He was adopted by a dentist and his wife from Dayton. Their name is Sullivan, and his name is Alex. Alex Sullivan. But we can have that changed back to his real name. Right now he's a student at the University of Ohio in Columbus. I want us to go there together. I don't even have to talk to him, at least not the first visit. I just want to see him with you. That's what I've prayed for all these years, and here you are, you've come home to me."

Run! Run for your life! Out of the corner of his eye, he saw Kathleen on the pedestal holding the baby as if she had it in a chokehold. He looked up but it was the stone Virgin again. I'm losing it. . . . Donna's hand had turned into a claw, her nails biting into his flesh. When he started to get up, she pulled him back down beside her again.

"You can't get away from me. I'll always be with you."

Scary thought. "Donna, let go of me."

"You'll never find anyone who loves you like I do."

Too true. Harry Todd pulled away from her and hurried back up the aisle. Poor woman . . . but get me out of here! The back of his hand was marked with five fingernail-shaped scratches. On his way through the dark foyer he thought of dunking his hand in the font to help stop the burning but was afraid of infection. It may be holy but it sure ain't sanitary. He pushed on the heavy oak door, expecting to step out into the rain. But the rain had stopped as quickly as it started. The clouds overhead had turned silvery, the darkness that roiled across the sky earlier only a memory above the distant hills. The streets were wet, water ran in the gutters, it was dripping from the eaves and branches; there was the smell of ozone in the air. Otherwise, it was as if the rain never happened.

37

Kitty lifted her eyeglasses from where they dangled around her neck, holding them like a lorgnette to look at the photograph in her hand. It was a picture of Kathleen taken when she was three or four, a pretty little girl dressed all in white, sitting on the top step of the front porch holding her doll, waiting as she did every afternoon for years, in rain or snow or sunlight, for her father to return from the office. We thought it was cute and endearing, we thought it was something to smile about, or at least I did. It wasn't until a few years later that I realized how serious she was about it. How serious she was about her father. What did you think, Harry, old love? It's not what we know of another person that destroys love, it's the slow and painful discovery of how much we don't know, will never know about the other, that ruins us, that ultimately defines the limits of our love. Kitty looked at the photo for a few more minutes, then put it back in the imitation treasure chest, letting her glasses drop into place again around her neck, down the front of her floor-length denim jumper. She had thought to leave the photo for Harry Todd to look at, but she realized it would mean nothing to him, it would only look like a picture of a sweet little girl sitting on the front steps holding her doll.

She closed the lid and carried the box back to the chest of drawers across the room. The box fit into its place amid the clutter on top of the bureau like the missing piece of a puzzle, nestled among the swell of orphaned white gloves and used Kleenex and magazine clippings and candy dishes and bills to be paid and receipts from the drugstore. If Harry Todd didn't understand by now what she had been trying to show him with the pictures, he never would. Which she had decided was probably the case regardless. Harry Todd's newfound interest in the family seemed to diminish somewhat after he found out that Dickie had slept with Donna. She had tried to tell him with the photos she laid out that there was more to it than that; but she knew her oldest son well, he had undoubtedly decided that the fact his younger brother was mixed up in it somehow was enough for him. It fit too cozily into Harry Todd's need for singular villains in the world, a single source for treachery wherever it was found, along with the conviction that had grown over the years in both of her sons that each one had a brother whose sole purpose in life was to cause him as much grief as humanly possible.

It was getting dark in the house, darker than usual, though it was only late afternoon; the drapes in the bay window were blowing. She opened the drapes in the center window and looked out. The gray sky had lifted somewhat, but now it was in layers over the valley, striations of gray, with black clouds over the distant hills; a breeze had come up, there was the smell of rain in the air, but the wind was hot, sultry. She pulled back the drapes in the side panels of the bay window, then went through the downstairs, opening the windows in every room, letting the gray light fill the house as if the house existed underwater, letting the warm air blow from one end to the other as if the walls weren't there. In the rooms, the eyes of dozens of porcelain figures followed her progress.

Merry Anne lay curled in her favorite spot on the carpet in the hallway. No, it was only Kitty's imagination, her expectation. Or perhaps a spirit cat, gone in the blink of an eye. It didn't surprise her, nor did it disturb her; in fact the possibility made her smile. A lot of things seemed real to her these days that turned out not to be; it was encouraging to think the opposite might be true as well, that some of the imagined things might turn out to be real. She stood at the foot of the steps, her hand resting on the dome of the newel-post, and listened. Was someone stirring in a far corner of the house? She was sure Harry Todd was out somewhere. Which one of her wandering spirits could it be? From outside came the distant sound of the bells at the college ringing the hour—a sure sign of rain, it was the only time the sound carried this far. She looked around for Merry Anne again, remembered again.

What was it she had started to do? It was terrible, her mind was beginning to slip away; one moment she would be thinking of something, then it would be gone, only a memory of a thought. Oh yes, now she remembered. . . .

She had been thinking of Harry Todd and his rush to judg-
ments. In the living room, the chairs held only stillness; the cush-
ions on the arched-back sofa seemed collapsed under their own
weight; the windows glowed mother-of-pearl. Looking into the
room from across the hall, she remembered the scene during
Harry Todd's last trip home when he tried to help Kathleen get
away from Furnass, his plan to help her go to graduate school in
Arizona, and she turned away from him, turned on him in front
of his parents, accused him of trying to make her do something
she didn't want to do. Dear child. She wanted it so badly, and
yet she couldn't do it, she couldn't go against her heart, nobody
held her back, it was her inability to rise above her own feelings
that kept her here. But Harry Todd would never understand that,
or forget what happened. Forgive. In his universe he is prosecu-
tor, judge, and jury, and in his court of law his sister committed
the cardinal offense, the ultimate betrayal: Kathleen had had
thoughts and desires that were different from and didn't coincide
with Harry Todd's, something he could barely accept in others
and found intolerable in his own sister, especially when it made
him appear foolish in the eyes of his father who had become his
ultimate nemesis by that time. Harry Todd could never forgive
her for that. Though it turned out Kathleen had a number of
thoughts beyond those that anyone knew or could influence.
There's no way to forgive any of those now either. She patted the
top of the newel-post as if it were an old friend and continued on
through the darkling breeze-filled house to the kitchen.

She went to the cupboard and surveyed the shelves: What was
she going to do with 163 cans of Little Friskies cat food? The
accumulation of buying each week more cans than Merry Anne
could eat. Little Friskies meat loaf? Fried up with a package of
frozen vegetables, it might not be too bad. She decided to keep
them for an emergency, along with the packages of Jell-O and
vanilla pudding, jars of bouillon cubes and stacks of baking cups

and tins of cocoa, not one of which was less than twenty years old. If Armageddon ever arrived, or even a good power shortage, she could rest assured she was ready.

From the window over the sink, she watched the effect of the approaching rain on the backyard. Away from the view of the valley, without the panorama of the clouds rolling across the gray and layered sky, the approaching rain mainly took the form of a growing darkness under the trees, the wind gusting through the branches, blowing the leaves. She had been standing here that day at noontime listening to Paul Harvey on the radio when she heard a car in the driveway and saw Kathleen pull into the garage and then come running to the house. She burst through the back door and looked at her mother, the girl's face racked with crying and the effort to catch her breath, and ran on, through the house and upstairs.

Kitty hurried after her, drying her hands on her apron and throwing it in a corner as she went, through the house at midday—it was the same time of year, she remembered, though the day was sunny—the downstairs rooms full of dark and dappled sunlight, following the sounds of the crackling joints of the wood on the staircase and the creaky floorboards along the upstairs hall as Kathleen fled whatever she thought was chasing her. Kitty caught up to Kathleen in her room. The girl lay on the bed, curled into herself, clutching the pillows to her stomach as if to stop her innards from spilling out.

"Kathleen, what is it? What is it, sweetheart?" Kitty said, sitting on the edge of the bed and reaching for her.

Kathleen cringed, turning away from her and trying to crawl to the far side of the bed. Kitty grabbed her and dragged her back.

"What is it, Kathleen? Tell me, tell your mother. . . ."

Well, she asked for it, she supposed. Kathleen told her how she and Donna had been talking in the office, about nothing, really, and Donna said—as if it were a slip of the tongue though Kathleen was sure it was nothing of the kind, she was sure Donna said it on purpose to hurt her—that she and Dickie had been lovers. Kitty rubbed her hand slowly up and down Kathleen's back, as much trying to soothe herself as to comfort her daughter. Well, what did she expect? Was Kitty surprised? No. Both her sons had followed their father's lead, of course the sons would be as sexually opportunistic as their father. She hated to see Kathleen like this, in such pain, she wanted to be sympathetic to her, but the fact was she was tired, tired of all the betrayals and lies whenever the men of her family were involved. Tired of what her husband's appetites had done to the family. Tired of Kathleen idolizing a man who followed the whims of his cock and had obviously passed along his predilections to his sons. After several moments of watching her daughter crying, she couldn't hold off any longer.

"You shouldn't be surprised, sweetheart. You know how your brothers are, and if you didn't by now, you should know how your father is too. . . ."

Kathleen rolled over on her side, her face streaked with tears, looking up at her mother. "But why? Why are men like that? We're like hunks of meat to them, hanging on hooks waiting to be picked out. Why do they have to be so mean about it?"

That was the question, wasn't it? She wanted to tell her daughter that it was what women had wondered for millennia, but Kathleen's crying took on another tone. She raised up on her elbow, staring at her mother.

"What's wrong with me? What's the matter with me? Why do they go after girls like Donna?"

She wanted to tell her because girls like Donna were cheap and easy, they got what they deserved from men, and just like what happened with her sons, once they were through with a girl like Donna they tossed her aside. But Kathleen seemed in no condition to hear such things, she had buried her head again in her arms and was sobbing harder than ever. Kitty continued to sit with her for a half hour or so, until the girl had cried herself out, then helped her stretch out on the bed, covered her with a blanket, and left her to go to sleep.

She recognized later that she should have stayed in the house, if not in the room with the girl at least somewhere close at hand in case Kathleen woke up and needed something. Recognized that she made a fatal mistake. But at the time she was weary of the whole affair. She put on her favorite cape and pillbox hat and drove downtown to run some errands, looked at shoes at Markson's, bought a couple pairs of hose at Benson's, stopped at Kroger's and bought bread and eggs even though she knew they really didn't need them, she only wanted to stay away from the house as long as she could, wanted to be out in the world around other people. Most of all she wanted to talk to Doctor. After she had exhausted every other excuse to stay away from the house, she parked on upper Seventh Avenue across the street from Doctor and Mother Sutcliff's old house. Though Doctor's office on the street level was now a barbershop, the red Insulbrick house above looked much the same, except for the canvas chairs and child's Big Wheel on the front porch. But nothing was the same now, Doctor dead for five years now, Mother Sutcliff a few months behind him, the surprise that she apparently couldn't live without her husband any more than she could live with him. Love is one person trying to devour another in some way, Doctor said. It's sad and not admirable, but most people can't live without it. Was that true for her too? If she knew that, why make such a big deal now, learning of another of her son's indiscretions, another instance of like father, like son. She put the car in gear and reentered the traffic heading up through town toward Orchard Hill.

Why had she come here to the kitchen? She wasn't hungry . . . oh yes, the cat food. But now there was no cat to feed. The rain of the fast-moving shower began to thrash through the trees, the bursts of wind turning the leaves upside down, the rain pelting the glass in front of her. She turned away from the window, making her way slowly through the open-ended china cupboard, into the dining room. Suddenly she felt very very tired, as if the accumulated loss she had carried for so long had become unbearable under the added weight of a lifeless ball of brown and black fur. She sat at the dining room table, folding her arms on the tabletop and resting her head on them for a moment, like a schoolgirl taking a nap at her desk. How could I blame Kathleen for what happened when I got back to the house that day after running those errands, after staying away from the house as long as I could, when I was the one who placed her in the situation years before by bringing her back to Furnass from New York. When I was the one who understood the danger of the situation. When I was the one who knew what it was to love a father. . . .

She lay on the examining table in the loose gown, listening for his footsteps coming down the hall, the gentle knock on the door and his voice asking her if it was all right to come in. But it was apparent from the moment he entered that something was wrong. Terribly wrong. She hadn't seen Doctor for several weeks, he had always been too busy with something else whenever she looked in on the house or his office, and he had failed to stop by for a morning cup of coffee as he often did when he was out making his house calls—it was only then, lying there on the strip of paper that ran the length of the leather-topped table, that she began to wonder if he had been purposefully avoiding her, apprehensive of this moment when he would have to confront her—but in that short time he seemed to have aged, his face was hollow, as if something inside was starting to give way, the flesh hanging loose, ready to slough off. He stood across the room from her, near the door, afraid to come farther into the room, afraid to get too close.

"What's wrong? Are you okay?"

He managed a brief sad smile. "I'm the one who's supposed to ask questions like that. Put your clothes back on, Kitty."

"Why? What is it?" She was sitting up now. "Tell me what's wrong."

"This. Everything. It's wrong, it always has been. I'm not the one who should be examining you, not today, not ever. It breaks every code of ethics imaginable."

"But what did I do?"

"You didn't do anything. It was all me. From the very start. I don't know what I was thinking . . . No, that's wrong too, I know very well what I was thinking. But I can't let it go on any longer, I can't stand to touch. . . . From now on Dr. Neely will be your physician. I spoke to him already. He should have been your physician all along with the rest of the family."

He turned away, miserable with himself, put his hand on the doorknob as if he were about to leave, about to leave it there.

"Wait."

She got up from the table and slipped the gown off her shoulders and stood in front of him naked, truly offering herself to him. He looked at her for a moment, the tears welling in his eyes, before he walked quietly from the room. It was a week or so afterward that she gathered up Kathleen and took the child with her to Kitty's parents' home in upstate New York, intending to leave Harry once and for all, only to return to Furnass again a few months later.

What was I thinking of? A young woman offering herself to an elderly man like that, no wonder he started to cry, I might as well have just clubbed him, showing him all the things he couldn't have, all the things he missed in his life and would never have then. I hope he thought I was pretty. . . .

She sat up again, refusing to dwell on such unpleasant thoughts, though determined to carry the weight of her memories, knowing they were always there, knowing she had to bear the weight if she was going to go on, just as she had all this time. She smoothed the tablecloth in front of her, chasing the wrinkles away, working her hands as if clearing the film from the surface of a pond, remembering that this was the table and chairs from Doctor's house, Kitty took them after Doctor died and they had moved Mother Sutcliff to the nursing home. And for a moment it is Sunday dinner again at Doctor's house, they are all sitting around the table as they used to after church, Doctor at the head of the table of course, and young Dickie in a high chair beside him, grandfather and grandchild equally charmed and charming with each other.

"A fine boy you have here, Harry, a fine lad."

"Thank you, Father."

The compliment to his younger brother makes Harry Todd squirm in his seat. He leans over and says something to his sister beside him and Kathleen giggles and slaps at him and he slaps back and they begin paddling at each other until Mother Sutcliff speaks up.

"Harry, say something to your children."

"'Something to your children,'" Harry says and winks at Kathleen who beams with delight, but the children know that they have drawn the attention of their father and they settle down. Dickie responds to the shift of attention by dropping his spoon over the side of the high chair, leaning over to watch it fall.

"I'll get it," Kitty says and gets up from the table, moving around the side of the high chair next to Doctor.

"But then how could he fail to be a fine lad, when he has a mother like this?" Doctor says, and as Kitty straightens up again and replaces Dickie's spoon with her own, Doctor reaches out and puts his hand on her waist, a kind of hug.

"Oh you," she says, and leans down as if to kiss him on the cheek, but instead rests her cheek against his, and for the brief moment that they touch all time stands still for Kitty, her cheek against his, the smell of him all smoky from his cigarettes, the tang of the witch hazel he uses for aftershave, his face with the slightest hint of stubble, a roughness that holds her softness to him, flesh against flesh, his hand still on her waist, securing her heart forever.

38

Loose gravel pinged up against the undercarriage, the car lurched violently, for a split second out of control riding off the edge of the pavement, as Dickie pulled into the turnout and skidded to a stop, the pickup truck that had been tailgating him for the past few miles speeding on down Berry's Run Road, horn blaring.

"Fool," Dickie said out loud, "asshole," referring to himself as much as to anyone else, upset with himself for letting the other driver get to him. He sat for a moment until the quiet settled around him again, until the wave of anger had passed—I should go after that son of a bitch and ride his tailgate, see how he likes it, I should force him off the road and pull the guy from the cab and beat him beat him—and he was calm again. After a few moments he got out of the car and stood, leaning the small of his back against the curve of the fender.

Dusk had settled in the hollow, darkness filled the craggy, tree-covered hills, though the sky was still the color of old nickels and dimes, a pocketful of change, and the heat was still as close after the brief hard shower. Crickets chirred in the spike-grass and underbrush, birds sang their evening songs from the hillsides, crows called from the woods; otherwise the only sound came from his car ticking cool. The surface of the turnout was hardly damp, the rain earlier hadn't been enough to turn it to mud, though there were a few standing puddles on the hard earth where the water

hadn't sunk through, and twigs and small branches were everywhere; nevertheless, Dickie had only stepped from his car and the
sides of the soles of his carefully polished shoes bore a muddy
stain. Dickie sighed. The things we do for the things we love. . . .
In the distance the road curved dimly into view from the direction
of Berry's Run Park, but the road was empty, no one else was in
sight. He was in no hurry.

He was thinking about what all he had found out about Julian
Lyle's affairs this afternoon, from the copies Donna brought him
of Julian's financial records. A sorry mess. Curious that he had
never delved into them before, though it was probably a good
thing, if he had known Julian's affairs were this bad—had been
for quite some time—he would have been inclined to stay completely away from him, or tempted to take advantage of him more
than he had already. And he was thinking of all the things he
had yet to do in regard to the deal for Furnass Landing; he needed
to check in with Selby to let him know the financing was nearly
in line, and he needed to call Harvey McMillan at the bank to
tell him that Julian no longer posed a problem with his idea for
an industrial museum, that it was a dead issue, or soon would be.
So much to do, so many details to take care of. He loved it, he
knew that—the taking care of business, the making of a deal—
and he knew he was good at it, that he had a talent for it, the
art of negotiation and gaining advantage and closure; though he
also was aware of the persistent feeling that if he didn't take care
of all the things in the world that needed taking care of, who
would?

You seem to forget, I've been cleaning up your family's dirty
little messes for years, Julian told him a few days ago in the
trailer. Don't make me laugh, Counselor.

"Get Julian Lyle," he remembered calling Donna on the inter-
com, it was while she still worked at Sutcliff Realty, "and tell
him that if he wants to keep his retainer I want him here in this

office in fifteen minutes." He hung up the phone and looked at his father and Dr. Neely. "Who authorized the autopsy?"

"I did," his father said, sitting collapsed in his chair behind his desk, staring vacantly in front of him. He was under his medication, as he usually was these days, but it wasn't that he was groggy now; since the morning Kathleen died his father had borne the dazed expression of a man who had traveled several stops beyond his destination, and had learned that there was no return trip home. Ever.

For a moment, Dickie ignored the implications of his father having ordered the autopsy as he tried to sort out what was going on, what had been discussed in the conversation before his father called him into it.

"There were barbiturates in her system? What are we talking about, two, three tablets? That doesn't necessarily mean she—"

"There was evidence of twenty to thirty capsules in her stomach and large intestine," Dr. Neely said, standing beside his father's desk. "The exact number is hard to say because many of the capsules were in stages of decomposition. I appreciate your reluctance to accept what I'm telling you. But there is no question: Kathleen died of a barbiturate overdose, and the number of pills leaves no mistake that it was intentional."

"Suicide," his father said hollowly.

Dickie looked at him. "You must have suspected something of the sort. If you authorized an autopsy."

"Yes. I suspected it. Among other things."

"But why? Mother keeps saying it must have been a heart attack or stroke or something."

"Your mother. . . ," his father started to say, then waved his hand as if to wave the thought away.

"You don't have to talk about this now, Harry, if you don't feel up to it," Dr. Neely said.

"Yes, he does have to talk about it now," Dickie said. "Whether he feels up to it or not. I have to know what's going on, I need all the information I can get if I'm going to deal with this."

His father looked at him, and in that instant they both realized the truth of what Dickie had just said, that he would be the one from now on to deal with the difficult situations, that he would be the one to make the decisions. At that moment the reins of power changed in the business, and in the family, and Dickie had controlled them ever since.

It seems a little funny, to hear Dickie Sutcliff talk to me about morality, Julian said to him. We'll see about that, Counselor, we'll see. . . .

Down the road as it straightened out of the curve, at first like a shadow appearing out of the dusk, a figure was coming along the shoulder, a man in track shorts and a tank top with the number 32 printed on it, running steadily, evenly, the practiced, methodical strides of someone used to covering long distances. Dickie remained leaning against the fender of his car as the figure approached; when Julian recognized him, he slowed to a walk, hands resting on his hips, and came over to him.

"Enjoying the night air?" Julian said, breathing regularly, without effort, as if he had been interrupted merely on an evening stroll. "You should come running with me sometime. We could find out what kind of shape you're in."

"Thanks, but I already know what kind of shape I'm in, Julian. Besides, running was never my game."

"I asked your brother if he wanted to join me, but he turned me down too. I guess the Sutcliff boys were always into other pursuits."

"As a matter of fact, Harry Todd has something to do with why I'm here. . . ."

"I thought he might."

He's giving me that smug look of his, he thinks he holds all the cards. Fool. Dickie took a moment to keep his emotions in check, get his thoughts in order, before proceeding. "I want you to stop all this talk about turning Furnass Landing into an industrial museum, or whatever the hell your idea is for it."

"You know it was your brother who gave me the idea."

"Yes, I know that. I don't know what he was thinking when he talked to you. But I'm reasonably confidant Harry Todd won't be passing along any more of his bright ideas to you in the future."

For the first time since the conversation started, Julian looked questioning as to his position.

"Why do you think your asking me would be enough to stop me from pursuing the idea? It's actually a pretty good one."

"Just do what I ask, Julian. Don't make me take this any farther."

"Who do you think you are? What makes you think you can order people around any way you want to? The world isn't like that, Dickie. People aren't like that."

Dickie looked away, at the dark scraggy hills, the shallow valley filling with night; it was strange to think they were on the back side of the Allehela Valley, only a couple miles or so from Furnass as the crow flies, the place seemed so secluded here. How many of these hollows and glens were there in the area? Hundreds, probably. Strange to think there was this much wilderness so close to a metropolitan area. Undervalued, unused land. In any other part of the country, this close to a major city like Pittsburgh, this would be prime property for luxury commuter homes, hillside views, "Your little touch of wilderness only a half hour from downtown." Western Pennsylvanians are funny people, he thought, they don't build on hillsides unless they have to. Unless there's no way around it. Unless they run out of space on the flat. And if they do build there it's never for the view in and of itself.

Probably some innate fear they might see too far, too much. They'd rather see the limits that surround them, and fantasize about what lies on the other side of the hill, than build on the heights and get a good look at what's on their side of the hill, the everyday world they find themselves in. After a long moment he turned back and regarded Julian in the half-light.

"Julian, let's not fool around here. I know how you were juggling the books on Furnass Towers. Using the construction loan to pay off the real estate loan. I know all about it."

"There was nothing illegal about what I did with Furnass Towers."

"Maybe, maybe not. That's something the courts will have to decide, if it gets that far. But even if it wasn't illegal, it was certainly ill-advised. And all of it is bound to come out. Good God, Julian, what were you thinking?"

"How do you know so much about my affairs? Wait a minute. Is Donna telling you things?"

"Did you really think all this time that my putting Donna in your office was simply an act of charity on my part? Because I felt sorry for her? You underestimate me, Counselor."

Dickie was angry at himself for saying such a thing, for taking such an attitude. For casting himself in such a light. He had wanted this to be friendly, if it could. The Kickers and the Kickees. Julian can no more not be kicked than I can resist kicking him. Dumb bastard. Poor dumb people. Julian appeared ready to start running again.

"I'm not going to listen to any more of this," Julian said, clasping first one foot behind his leg and then the other, loosening up. "Nice to have seen you, Dickie. If you ever want to take me up on the offer to come running, let me know."

As Julian took the first few strides away, Dickie called after him, "Before you run off I thought you might want to hear about the new situation with your mortgages."

Julian took a few additional steps, then stopped and stood there for a moment, looking down at his feet. Then he turned and came back slowly, his footsteps crunching in the gravel and fallen twigs. "What about my mortgages?"

"I also know that your assets have been frozen since Sycamore Savings & Loan shut down. You haven't been able to make the mortgage payments on either your house or the old Alhambra Theater, both of which you used as collateral for Furnass Towers, and both of which are being held by First City Bank. Both of which are about to be foreclosed."

In the twilight Julian waited for Dickie to continue, as if he knew there would be more. *I can't blame him for hating me. Dad was hated this way too. Guess we were born strong enough to take it.*

"Here's the way it's going to be," Dickie went on. "I spoke to Harvey McMillan at the bank this afternoon and I've arranged to take over the payments on both your mortgages. I'll have to sell him a piece of property he's wanted for a long time in order to do it, but so be it. You'll sign both titles over to me for the sake of formalities. That seems a better way to do it than having the bank take them over and then me buying them from the bank. For one thing, it will keep your name out of the paper, which would discredit you even further in this town. For the time being, things will stay as they are. When the Furnass Landing project is complete or well on its way, I'll shift ownership of your house back to you. By that time, we'll hope your legal problems with Sycamore Savings & Loan are straightened out and you're getting back on your feet again. And if things don't turn out in your favor, you won't have anything in your name for the courts to come after. As for the Alhambra, we'll discuss what to do with it contingent upon the ruling given on Furnass Towers. The important thing is that you and your family will be able to stay in your home."

"In other words, you own me."

"I don't blame you for seeing it that way. But for what's it worth, that's not the way I see it. If for no other reason than, if you lose your practice, this town won't have an attorney."

"And what do I have to do for you in return?"

"Not a thing. Our business relationship will continue as it has. I'll continue to pay the retainer. Of course, I expect you to say nothing about this to Donna. You can't blame her for doing what I asked her to do. She had some debts of gratitude to pay back of her own."

"Debts you established . . . what? Ten years ago?"

"What can I tell you?" Dickie shrugged. "It pays to plan ahead." He started to leave, to get back in his car, then turned again, almost as an afterthought. "Oh yes, and one more thing: I don't want to hear any more talk about making Furnass Landing into an industrial museum or historical site or anything of the sort. I don't want to hear of such ideas coming from you, and if anyone else should happen to bring them up, I expect you to be the leader in stanching them and positing the economic value to this town of having Furnass Landing as an industrial park. Such support will sound better coming from a disinterested party, such as yourself."

Julian stared at him in the gloom. Dickie stood beside his car door, waiting to see if the man had anything else to say. In the twilight, the number 32 on Julian's tank top glowed like a branding.

"I don't know how you look at yourself in the mirror," Julian said finally.

"Counselor, strange as it may seem, I don't have any trouble at all."

*

As Dickie piloted the big car up the steep windy curves of Downie Hill Road Extension, heading back toward Furnass Heights, he thought again of the western Pennsylvania peculiarity of not building on hillsides to take advantage of the view. I guess when you're born in a valley, and start out at the bottom of the social spectrum, your comfort zone tends to be one of looking up, not down. There will always be people who are more comfortable sitting in a hole than climbing out of it. He was sad, disgruntled, unhappy with himself, after talking to Julian. He felt sorry for the man despite himself, despite thinking the man was a fool. Perhaps because he did think the man a fool. He felt like someone who just had his dog put to sleep, even though he knew what he had done for Julian was the best thing, for all of them, that it would save Julian and his family from ruin. I've cleaned up your family's dirty little secrets for years. Alone in the car, slouched at the wheel, his chin resting on his fist, speeding one-handed through the growing night, Dickie thought of something else too, of the memory that had been breaking in and out of his consciousness all day, giving over to it at last. The time shortly after he was married that he encountered Kathleen upstairs in the big house. . . .

She stood in the doorway to her room naked, her hands inverted to each other across her chest partly shielding her tiny breasts, one hand up, one hand down, fingertips touching like a half-formed yin-yang symbol, as if she held something very delicate between them, stood there looking at him, as if asking him something, and he took her in his arms and walked her backward back across her room and sat her down on the edge of her bed and she looked up at him, already crying, and said "What's the matter with me? Why aren't I pretty like other girls?" and he said "You are pretty like other girls. You're pretty in your own way" and she said "Then why don't guys want me like they want other girls? Why do they run away from me?" she said, crying harder, falling over sideways onto the bed and sobbing and Dickie looked at her a moment longer and had to leave, afraid of what he might feel, walked back out of her room and down the hall and down the stairs, out to his car and drove away struggling to get his thoughts in order, his anger under control, thinking of the day as a child he saw his older brother and sister rolling on the floor of the downstairs hall, thinking he had a pretty good idea who she was referring to when she talked about someone running away from her. . . .

As he crested the top of the valley and headed down Downie Hill Road on his way back to Furnass, night upon the valley now, the lights of the town below moving through the dark trees like searchers with flashlights, a posse on a manhunt, the torches of an angry mob, it occurred to him that he should have realized at the time just how disturbed an individual his sister was, how dangerous, that the greatest threat to all his efforts to keep the family safe and secure came from within the family itself, from the one he thought needed all of their protection the most.

39

In the darkness at the end of the street, the big house sitting on the terrace seemed exposed, startled, in the sudden glare of his headlights as he turned into the drive; the wash of light swept along the slope of the terrace and the bushes and the trunks of the sycamores, along the edge of the dark lawn, coming to rest on the closed doors of the garage. Harry Todd decided to leave the car in the drive, rather than put it away; after talking to his mother, after confronting her with all the things he had learned about Kathleen and the family, he had a feeling he would want to go out again, for a long drive in the country to clear his head, or to the nearest bar. He turned off the headlights and the engine and opened the door; he was starting to get out, one foot on the asphalt, when a voice in the darkness said, "Harry Todd."

He froze. In the dim light coming from the car's interior, Dickie was standing a few feet away.

"Didn't mean to scare you," Dickie said, and laughed.

Harry Todd went ahead and climbed out and closed the car door, straightened up, smiled, and took a swing at Dickie's face. Dickie ducked and juked to the side so that the blow glanced off his shoulder.

"Don't do anything stupid, Harry Todd."

"You're a fine one to tell me not to do anything stupid. After all the things you've done."

"What are you talking about—?"

Before Dickie could finish Harry Todd swung at him again, though this time Dickie was ready and blocked it easily with his forearm. When Harry Todd swung a third time, Dickie blocked that one as well, and countered with a blow to Harry Todd's solar plexus that doubled him over and sent him sprawling backward onto the driveway.

"Son-of-a-bitch."

"I told you not to do anything stupid."

"You hit me," Harry Todd said, sitting up and holding his stomach, knowing as he said it that he sounded ridiculous.

Dickie laughed as he stood over him. "Well, you were trying to hit me. You okay?"

Dickie extended his hand to help him up; Harry Todd took the hand and let his brother pull him to his feet, then kept going, head down, right into Dickie's midsection, wrapping his arms around Dickie and propelling him backward into one of the garage doors. Dickie let out a loud *Oof!* as they slammed into the door and the air went out of him. Harry Todd hit him in the stomach and got a good punch to the side of his brother's head before Dickie recovered and let loose with a series of quick blows to the face, another solid left to the stomach, and a right to the nose that put Harry Todd back on the ground again.

Harry Todd didn't lose consciousness, but it took a few moments for his head to clear. Dickie was leaning against Harry Todd's car, shaking his right hand, stretching his fingers.

"You going to stop now?"

"Yes, I'm going to stop now," Harry Todd said, raising his head a little, but unable as yet to sit up.

Dickie continued to work his fingers. "Goddamn it. Feels like I broke something."

"You're lucky I didn't really hurt you."

"Hurt me?"

"Yeah. Slamming my face into your fist that way. I could really have done you some damage."

They looked at each other in the darkness for a moment, one brother leaning against the car, the other flat on his back, and started to laugh a little, a mild progression of snorts and snickers and chuckles.

"You sure it's over?" Dickie said, coming over to help him up again.

"Oh yes, I'm sure it's over," Harry Todd said, holding his bleeding nose as Dickie pulled him to his feet a second time. The sound of Harry Todd's nasal twang got them grinning all over again.

Harry Todd was having trouble standing upright, the world had a definite case of the spins. Dickie draped his brother's arm across his shoulders and helped him over to the side of the house where there was a water spigot. Light from the kitchen windows spilled out over them as they stood among the bushes. There were some spots of blood on the front of Dickie's white shirt from Harry Todd's nose. Dickie took off his suit coat and draped it over a bush, took off his white shirt and tore it in half, and gave one half to Harry Todd. They took turns wetting the cloths under the spigot and cleaning themselves up.

"What was that all about, anyway?" Dickie said after a few minutes.

"Because I felt like it. Because I thought you had it coming. Because I thought it was time somebody did that."

"Thanks a lot."

"You're welcome." Harry Todd took a piece of cloth, wet it, and held it clamped on his nose as he leaned back to stop his nose from bleeding. "You really did sleep with Donna, didn't you? After she came back to town."

"Ah," Dickie said. "So that's what this is about."

"How could you do that? Take advantage of someone like that, when she was so vulnerable?"

Dickie was looking at him in the darkness, an ironic smile growing on his face.

"What?" Harry Todd said.

"Well, for one thing, you and I have very different perceptions of Donna's vulnerability. You obviously aren't aware just how strong and conniving Donna is, for all the neurotic behavior. Nobody ever took advantage of Donna unless she wanted them to, because she saw some way to gain from it. But no matter—what's really funny is that you'd be concerned about Donna at all. You certainly forgot about her quickly enough when you were on the other side of the country smoking your marijuana dreams."

Dickie wrung out his cloth, standing with his legs apart so he wouldn't splash his shoes. It crossed Harry Todd's mind to take another swing at him, but realized he'd only end up in worse shape than he was. He leaned back, his knees slightly flexed, his head held to the black sky. "Well then, what about all this cover-up business about Kathleen's death?"

"Where did you hear anything about a cover-up regarding Kathleen's—oh right, of course. Donna again."

As Harry Todd straightened forward, testing his nose to make sure the bleeding had stopped, Dickie tore off another piece of cloth, rinsed it under the spigot, and held Harry Todd's face with one hand as he cleaned off a streak of blood that had run down his cheek to his neck. "As far as that goes, I'm the one who should be taking a swing at you, for coming back here and stirring up all this business about Kathleen."

"Yeah, the idea that Father thought Mother gave Kathleen the pills that killed her. I would think that's something you'd want to keep under wraps. It wouldn't do to have the Sutcliff name soiled in town, would it? Not good for business."

Dickie held Harry Todd's chin in his hand, firm as a vise, turning his brother's head first one direction and then the other to check his cleanup. Then he let go of his brother's face just as decidedly, like dropping it from a height. "God, that woman must hate us. The Sutcliff men, all screwing her."

"You mean Donna? Actually, I heard that about Mother and the pills from Tinker—wait! All the Sutcliff men? Did Father screw Donna too? Oh my God. I heard he was flirting with her hot and heavy when he would take her out to lunch but. . . ."

Dickie was shaking his head. "No, I'm sure he didn't, at least not in that sense of screwing her. Though he probably thought about it, knowing Dad. . . . It's strange, one of the last conversations I ever had with him, there at the house before he died, he insisted on telling me that he hadn't slept with someone but he never actually said who that someone was. He said, 'I never laid a hand on her, I wouldn't.' I figured he meant Donna, he knew I had been involved with her and wanted to make sure I didn't think he had slept with her too, but his mind wandered off again before I could ask him, he was in and out of consciousness at that time. Either that, or there was actually some woman in town he didn't fuck and he was proud of it. No, I'm sure he meant Donna."

"Which avoids the question: Why did Father think Mother had something to do with Kathleen's death?"

Dickie sighed and looked out across the dark lawn for a moment before speaking.

"For some reason he thought Mother gave the pills to Kathleen. Gave them to her on purpose knowing what Kathleen was going to do with them."

"Why would he think that?"

"I have no idea. I know something happened to make him think that, but he wouldn't talk about it. And I wouldn't ask him."

"That's how you and I are different."

"Don't kid yourself. There are a lot of differences. Look, I don't blame you for wanting to find out about Kathleen's death, but all you're doing is stirring up a lot of bad feelings. Kathleen's gone, there's nothing any of us can do to bring her back, and that should be the end of it. And in particular, I don't want you to do anything that will upset Mother. That's why I came over here this evening. I wanted to ask you not to say anything more about this to her."

"Mother's the one who got me started on all this."

Dickie looked at him questioningly.

"She's been laying out photographs and letters for me to look at, like she's leaving a trail for me to follow. Like she wants me to know what happened, or find out more about it."

Dickie thought a moment, searching Harry Todd's face, for signs of either blood or truth. "Cut the crap now, Harry Todd. Once and for all. What are you doing back here? What do you want?"

Harry Todd thought he saw an opening. "What's the matter, Dickie? You afraid I came back to claim my part of the business? Afraid I might horn in on your little empire?"

Dickie laughed. "Not hardly. At one time I wondered if you had some such cockadoodle idea. But I also know you could no more hold your own in my affairs than fly. The people I deal with in my business would laugh you out of town in one week."

Harry Todd looked away, into the darkness at the dark trees and space where the glow of the mills used to be. "Yeah, I suppose you're right. I know you're right. I thought about it at one time but. . . ." He looked back at his brother. "The truth is, I came back because I don't have anywhere else to go. You said yourself the other night, I'm all out of options. Tricks, you called them. I'm broke, nobody's ever going to hire me at this age, not with my track record, and everything I own in the world fits in the back of my car. There was nowhere else to go except here. Believe me, brother, if there was anyplace else I could think of—"

A shadow passed across the light coming from the kitchen windows above them. Harry Todd and Dickie ducked down and hid in the bushes close to the house. Their mother's shadow came to the window and peered out, her silhouette in the oblong of light stretching out over the dark grass. After taking a look around, she moved away from the window and left the kitchen, and Harry Todd and Dickie came back out of the bushes. There was an awkwardness between them now that wasn't there a few minutes earlier, as if they were each embarrassed about something.

"So. What are you going to do?" Dickie asked.

"I'm going to go in the house and talk to Mother." Dickie had a strange look on his face. "What?"

"I was thinking more in terms of what are you going to do with your life."

Harry Todd ignored what he took for sarcasm. "For some reason, she apparently wanted me to find out something to do with Kathleen's death, so I'll tell her what I learned. Maybe she'll tell me why she wanted me to find out, and maybe she won't. Why don't you come inside with me while I talk to her? We can ask her about it together."

"I don't think so," Dickie said, looking off into the darkness again. "She wanted you to do the investigating, not me. If you're going to talk to her about this, you do it on your own."

"Then I'll call you afterwards. Let you know how it turns out. . . ."

"That's okay. Don't bother."

Harry Todd looked at his brother in the dim light washing down from the windows. "We're not going to be friends after this, are we?"

"I don't see any reason why we should be."

"I just thought . . . after we've talked and all. . . ."

Dickie looked at him. "I still consider you a first-class prick. That hasn't changed."

"And you're still a son-of-a-bitch."

"There you have it. Just because we're brothers doesn't mean we have to like each other. It's enough that we're brothers. Take care of yourself."

The way Dickie said it, it sounded like a caution, a threat. Dickie cocked his head and looked him in the eyes, holding his gaze there for a moment longer than he needed to, before collecting his suit coat from the bush and draping it over his arm. As Harry Todd watched him cross the lawn, his white undershirt glowing in the darkness, gradually fading into the night, Harry Todd thought, Take care yourself, little brother. It sounds like you and I aren't finished with each other. Not by a long shot.

. . . the downstairs of the house is blinding with light, the way a stage can be blinding when the spotlights are on, every light on the first floor blazing away though there is no one here—Now where did she get to? Harry Todd thinks, she was here when Dickie and I saw her in the window, now she's disappeared again, spookiest house ever—as he wanders through the dining room and into the living room, thinking about the encounter with Dickie, of

what all his brother told him, that Dickie confirmed what he had heard from Tinker, that his father thought his mother was instrumental in Kathleen's death by giving her the pills, though he still didn't know why his father would think such a thing of his wife, thinking of all that he's learned of his sister since he started asking questions and how much he still doesn't know—in some ways it's more unnerving, to have the house this bright at this time of night than it is to have it filled with darkness and shadows the way she keeps it during the day, everything about the place turned topsy-turvy—thinking even if his mother gave Kathleen the barbiturates that killed her, where would she get the pills—Kitty pulls up to the street corner in the lower end of Furnass and rolls down the window of her big white Cadillac and calls to the guy standing there in his platform soles and a gunslinger's Stetson, "Hey dude . . ."; well, maybe not—remembers something that Shari at the Furnass Grill said about his father, that his father was sick before Kathleen died, his face drawn and that he was worn-out all the time, you could tell he was in a lot of pain, and Harry Todd wonders if the good Doc Neely gave his old friend something for it, something to help him sleep—wait: Harry Todd is in the living room when it occurs to him and he leaves the room and goes back to the dining room, even from the doorway his eyes falling on the row of prescription bottles lined up across the mantel, twenty or more, and he goes over and sorts through them at eye level until he finds the one he is afraid he'd find, the one with a yellowed label for Nembutal made out to his father and the date, June 1975, One a day at bedtime or when needed for pain or anxiety, *and he opens the bottle: empty: and thinks* After all these years, after what these pills did to her daughter, she kept the bottle, she couldn't bring herself to throw it away, it's a wonder she didn't have it bronzed to go along with Kathleen's baby shoes, *as he returns the bottle to its place on the mantel and goes back to the hall and hears the sound of creaking floorboards coming from the second floor, Kathleen's bedroom, goes over and cups the top of the newel-post and starts slowly, heavily up the stairs, thinking he should go see what she's up to now, make sure she's not in trouble . . . and as Harry Todd's footsteps climb the stairs, they are met by the sounds of clothes hangers clicking against one another and the rustle of a plastic bag as Kitty in the second-floor bedroom continues sorting through Kathleen's clothes, the old house aware of the two people, embraces them in a way within the protection of its walls, a kind of alertness to mother and son on a course toward each other, embodiments as it were of* quantum entanglement *or* spooky action at a distance, *the idea of nonlocality in the universe where two physically separated but entangled particles can have correlated properties, can act in consort with each other, can in fact affect each other's behaviors and reactions even though separated by what we think of as space until space and distance themselves don't exist, the idea that it's only an illusion that events happen in any one absolute location, the house funneling these two people, mother and son, in what appears to be a collision course but which may be altered as in quantum mechanics by the act of being observed as our story progresses . . . while outside the wind comes up again as it did in the afternoon bringing another shower rolling down the valley in the darkness, the big house on the bluffs withdrawing into itself as the branches of the sycamores in the yard begin to sway against its eaves, drawing up into itself as the wind presses against its walls, suffering the ignominy of leaves and loose twigs and candy wrappers and old newspapers hurled against it, aware on some level of existence of the two people within its walls in the same way it is aware of other lives who seek its protection or refuge or comfort, the two pigeons who wriggle down further into their nest in the crook of the drainpipe, the squirrel who lives in the space between the roof and the attic ceiling, the pill bug on the cellar stairs and the silverfish skittering out of the basement-floor drain*

*and the nest of wasps in the woodwork below the bathroom win-
dow, the thousands of creepy-crawlies within its structure and the
millions of life-forms too small to see churning in the matrix of
being . . . the house is keeper and guardian of all these living
things, just as it keeps and holds the memory of the afternoon
Kathleen as a young woman having spent the last few hours crying
until she is cried out stands in her underwear before the full-
length mirror in her bedroom, gasping for breath as she studies
the image of this thin but ripe young woman in the glass before
her, bewildered beyond comprehension that no one seems to appreciate her, that other girls are chosen to love and be loved but
not her, never her, the one time in her life she did experience
such attention he ran from her as if she were diseased and
wouldn't even be friends afterward, asking herself "Why? What's
wrong with me? Aren't I pretty? Aren't I pretty enough?" when
she hears someone on the stairs and reaches for her robe to cover
herself until she hears him cough as he passes her door and goes
on down the hall and, desperate now, beyond consolation, feeling
that if she can't find that the world holds something for her she
can't bear to go on, unfastens her bra and slips out of her panties
and opens her bedroom door and steps out into the hall . . . the
house will always carry the memory of the day Harry Sutcliff is
home early from the office to change his clothes for a Rotary Club
dinner, the afternoon he sits on the edge of his bed to take off his
pants, thinking about the smell of smoke in the house, the acrid
smell throughout the upstairs of the house from his daughter
Kathleen's asthma-cure powder, gets his pants off and sits for a
moment in his boxer shorts, leaning on his knees wondering what
to do about the girl, frustrated that he doesn't know how to help
her, he's tried to include her in the life of the office, open her up
to the playing and joking around that goes on between people
during the workday, to try to get her out of her shell and discover
the fun that can be had if she'll only participate, has done*

everything short of directing one of his young Realtors to take
her out on a date, concerned that despite his efforts she's still too
emotional and sick all the time and frankly isn't doing a good job
at the office, ashamed for thinking that he's tired of her stinking
up the house all the time burning that god-awful-smelling powder,
looks around the room and swears he can see wisps of smoke still
lingering in the corners, starts to turn his head away when he
catches a glimpse of something moving and thinks for an instant
he's having a vision of a naked young woman coming out of the
shadows toward him, but it's Kathleen who comes around the bed
and stands naked in front of him, "Kathleen, you shouldn't be
here, not like that," and she says between gasps for breath,
"What's wrong with me, Daddy, what's the matter with me?" and
he wants to touch her to comfort her but he doesn't dare, knows
that wouldn't be right, "Oh sweetheart," his heart breaking for
her, and she starts to walk forward between his legs for a hug
when she looks up suddenly and Harry looks over his shoulder to
where she's looking and there is Kitty standing in the doorway
and knows already from the look on his wife's face that he'll never
be able to explain this situation to her, knows already that from
this point forward none of their lives will ever be the same. . . .

40

The only light on the second floor came from Kathleen's old
room. Harry Todd peeked in the door. His mother had emptied
the contents of the closet on the bed, draping Kathleen's clothes
over the clutter that was already piled high under a protective
sheet. Against the wall was a stack of light metal storage lockers,
shaped long and low to slip underneath a bed; his mother had
shifted a number of them about and left them standing open, the
lids up like a display of small flat coffins. The access lanes she
usually maintained in the room among the cardboard boxes and
piles of junk were clogged now with open cartons and half-filled

large plastic garbage bags. In one of the few open areas left in the room, his mother was standing in front of a full-length mirror, humming to herself, holding up one of his sister's old dresses against her to see how it looked. She noticed Harry Todd in the mirror and whirled around, curtsied to show off the garment.

"Kathleen had some of the nicest clothes. She always prided herself in looking very professional for the office."

"I don't think it will fit you."

"On me? Goodness no, I wouldn't think of it." She held the dress at arm's length to look at it again, wiggling it in the air to see it dance, then balled it up and stuffed it into one of the plastic garbage bags. "You may think I'm a crazy old woman, but I don't think I'm that far gone to start wearing my deceased daughter's clothing."

Harry Todd felt guilty; that was exactly what he had been thinking . . . How does she do that? Read my mind? "Whatcha up to?"

"I decided to get rid of Kathleen's clothes. I've kept them long enough. Maybe somebody else can get some wear out of them. Though I suspect they're out of fashion by now."

"The way things go around, they're liable to be back in fashion pretty soon."

She held up another outfit, blue bell-bottom trousers and a short, light yellow jacket with a floral pattern. "That's very true, my son. And if a person didn't have anything, these clothes might look pretty good." She stopped and looked at him over the top of her glasses. "You don't object to me getting rid of them, do you?"

"Not at all. I would think it's time."

"Yes. That's what I thought. It's time."

She held the short quilted jacket under its arms in front of her as if it still contained the person who once wore it, then added it to the bag of clothes. She started singing again under her breath; at first Harry Todd thought it must be the bye-lo lullaby, then he recognized another one of the songs she used to sing to herself as she worked around the house:

Oh dear, what can the matter be;
Oh dear, what can the matter be;
Oh dear, what can the matter be;
Johnny's so long at the fair. . . .

Harry Todd could go only so far into the room; the path he had chosen dead-ended with a low stack of boxes. In the box open at his feet were a dozen baby dolls, jumbled over themselves like in a mass grave. One of the dolls lay with her head twisted to the side, her bright blue eyes staring up at him, her mouth half-open as if there was something she wanted to say; her short pink dress was pulled up to reveal her white cotton crotch.

"Like boxes of family secrets," he said.

"We've certainly got enough of those around here," his mother said absently, judging a red knit sweater and assigning it to a garbage bag.

"Boxes or secrets?"

His mother smiled.

"So, do you want to tell me why you've been laying out those photographs and other things about the family? I have to assume you meant them for me."

His mother shrugged, continuing to rummage through the old clothes. "I know that over the years you've blamed your father and me for a lot of bad things that went on with the family. I thought now that you've come back and are older, you might be interested to learn more about this family of yours. The background and the . . . contributing factors, let's call them."

"Well, I learned that Father thought you helped Kathleen kill herself." He said it to shock her out of what he took as her complacency, then felt bad as soon as he said it. Why did I do that? Try to hurt her? But his mother didn't seem fazed by it.

"I was afraid that's what he thought, though he would never say anything to me about it. I suppose one of the things I hoped you'd find out is why he thought that. Though I have a good idea."

"I was told he saw you find the pill bottle in her covers and then put it in your pocket. I guess he figured you were trying to hide it because you had something to do with why she had the pills. Gave them to her on purpose, knowing what she intended to do with them. But I don't know why he would think such a thing."

Kitty looked at him, one of Kathleen's coats half-folded in her arms, a sad, noncommittal look on her face. Harry Todd felt a sudden wave of compassion for her, for what she must have gone through living with the man all those years, the load she must have carried. "You know Father, the way he was. He'd have to blame somebody. Father had to control everything. I'm sure the idea that something could happen without his having a say in it, even something like Kathleen's death, would drive him crazy. . . ."

"No, he was right to blame me."

Wait. "You mean you did help her . . . kill herself?"

He stood at the end of the blocked pathway into the room; his mother was across the room, separated from him by the seemingly insurmountable clutter, as if the piles of boxes and junk had grown back around her as she moved deeper into the room, closing her off. She looked around, as if realizing there was no place to turn, no place to go; she pushed aside the clothes and boxes on the edge of the bed and sat down, looking at her hands folded in the lap of her denim jumper.

"I didn't give her the pills, if that's what you mean. But yes, I hid the bottle when I found it in the sheets because I didn't know what had happened, what caused her collapse, and I didn't want that implication if pills had nothing to do with it. Kathleen must have gotten the pills herself, Lord knows they were easy enough to find, sitting there on the mantelpiece all that time. But I've always felt responsible for her death in other ways, I might as well have killed her."

Harry Todd didn't know what to say, thought it best not to say anything, waiting for her to go on.

"I never should have left her alone that day. She came home from work, all fussed up because she just found out that Dickie had slept with Donna, I guess Donna told her for whatever reason Donna does anything. And I was weary of it. Everything to do with this family, your father's and your brother's indiscretions—and too, all the Sutcliff males, like living in a pen of over-sexed. . . ." She brushed away something on her lap, picked at something else before continuing. "But that's neither here nor there. I probably knew if I thought about it that her father was coming home that afternoon to change his clothes, he probably told me about it and I forgot or didn't care enough to pay attention. I just wanted to get out of the house for a while, to get away from the whole mess, have some time for myself. So there it was, I spent all those years trying to protect her father from Kathleen, and the one time that counted most I didn't do it."

Wait. "Don't you mean protect Kathleen from her father? But why would you even think that, you don't think Father ever. . . ."

His mother was shaking her head. "No, I mean protect her father from Kathleen. I knew what the man was like. I also knew that your father would never initiate anything to harm Kathleen. He loved her very much, that was one of the problems, he probably loved her too much, he always thought of her as his little girl. But I also knew what Kathleen was like, she didn't just love him, she adored him, the same way she adored you, the two men in her life she cared about, and then after she lost you—yes, after she lost you, you needn't act surprised, I never knew what happened between the two of you there in high school, but whatever it was she felt you abandoned her, wouldn't have anything to do with her, and I know she blamed herself for whatever it was. One time I sat with her when she was so sick, she called herself an 'evil, evil girl' and said you were right about her. But that's something you'll have to work out for yourself, my son, I can't help you there. Whatever the reason was, after she felt she lost you, all those feelings that were divided between the two of you before became focused on her father, there wasn't anything she wouldn't do for her father's attention, she was frantic for it. And presented with a situation, I wasn't sure how your father would handle it. I knew he wouldn't do anything, but even if it occurred to him he'd never forgive himself. I had known I needed to keep her away from him even as a little girl so he wouldn't be tempted. And then it happened just like I was afraid it would. . . ."

Wait. "Wait. . . ."

"When I came back that afternoon, I found Kathleen naked with your father."

Wait. "What? You mean he was . . . in bed. . . . ?"

"No, no, nothing like that. Your father was seated on the bed, without his pants, he must have been changing his clothes when she came in on him, and Kathleen was standing in front of him, naked. She was reaching for him when they saw me."

"You think he was . . . going to. . . ."

"No, I knew he wouldn't. But your father was probably afraid I'd think the worst. We didn't have time to talk about it that evening, I helped Kathleen back to her bedroom and sat with her for several hours, she was extremely upset, she had an asthma attack to start with that day, and now she could barely breathe at all. By the time I got her settled down and she went to sleep, your father was gone from the house. That's another thing I blame myself for, I probably should have stayed with Kathleen, to keep an eye on her, she must have gotten the pills sometime in the night, if she didn't have them already. But I went to bed, and was asleep when your father got back."

"But how could he think you could ever do such a thing? Your own daughter?"

"He knew how unhappy Kathleen was, how very desperate. Poor girl, at some point she must have felt her life was over, there was never going to be anything to hope for. Maybe he thought I would try to ease her pain. And your father didn't know how desperate I was. He didn't know my state of mind, what I would do after seeing them that way."

"And you never talked to him about it?"

"No, it wasn't something you could bring up. And then with time, it receded into the background, something that was there, of course, but we had learned to live with. I knew your father would carry the guilt of it to his grave. And I knew that if he thought I did have something to do with her death, he'd do everything in the world to protect me. To keep anyone else from finding out. That's why there was so much mystery about the autopsy and the death certificate. The poor man, considering everything that had gone on that day, he must have been out of his mind with guilt and blame and heartbreak."

"So you each held the secret of the other one."

She smiled, thinking of something. "As he got sicker, we learned to be kind to each other again. As you'll learn, my son, at the end you find you can overlook a lot of things simply because it is the end."

His mother patted her leg once and stood up slowly. She came around the bed, finding her way among the clutter, as if the boxes and piles of old clothes parted for her, made pathways for her that weren't there before. In the time they had been talking, his mother seemed to have aged; Harry Todd realized for the first time since he had been home that his mother was an old woman. She stopped at the corner of the bed, leaning one hand on the footboard for support.

"You need to be forgiving of your father about all this. It's a terrible thing, when a daughter loves a father. Loves him too much."

"I guess so."

"No, you have no idea. People say it's because the daughter is jealous or in competition with the mother, but that's a bunch of hooey. It's because he's an older man who's strong and knows how to protect you. It's because he's settled in his life and has seen enough of the world to know what makes you unique and special. It's because he sees you and appreciates you for who you are, not what he wants you to be."

She looked at Harry Todd, and he realized she was crying. Before he was aware that he was going to do it, he stepped forward and opened his arms and embraced her. She laughed a little with surprise, almost a burp of emotion, then held on to him as if she were afraid he might fly away.

"I didn't think anyone would ever hold me again," she said, into his chest.

Harry Todd couldn't think of anything to say. Her hair under his chin smelled of shampoo and sweat, old woman smells. After a moment she patted his chest and stepped back again, laughing at her foolishness, wiping her eyes with a Kleenex she took from her pocket, adjusting the bangs over her forehead.

"Thank you," she said, rather formally, laughing a little nervously and looking around, looking away from him. "I'll bet this visit home has been a surprise to you in a lot of ways, hasn't it?"

Harry Todd nodded, feeling equally shy and awkward now. "I guess I better be getting to bed."

"Yes. I'll be going to bed soon myself."

He looked around, wondering if there was something else he should say, but couldn't think what it could be. Giving a little shrug, he smiled tight-lipped and left the room, scuffling down the dark hall toward the stairs. He was about to start up the narrow staircase when his mother called, "Harry Todd."

He turned and looked back down the hallway. She stood in the wedge of light coming from Kathleen's room, her hands holding each other in front of her. "I mean it. Thank you. I needed to tell somebody about Kathleen. I needed to tell you."

"I think Dickie wonders why you haven't talked to him about it."

She thought a moment. "Because Dickie has always accepted things as they are. Despite his brusqueness, he's actually a nicer person than you are."

"Thanks a lot."

"I don't mean it unkindly. But it's true. You were always harder. More judgmental. That's why I had to tell you. I needed your judgment before I could get absolution."

Harry Todd considered what she said. Then he grinned slightly, raised his hand and made a haphazard sign of the cross, though it ended up looking more like an *X*. "Go, my child. Peace be with you."

"Oh go to bed, silly," his mother said, waving her hand at him as if to dismiss him, and walked back into the light.

As he turned to go up the stairs, a movement caught his eye, beyond where his mother had been standing, the vague shape of a girl, but when he stopped and looked again there was nothing there, the hall was empty. My imagination. It's been a long day. Harry Todd shook his head at himself and climbed the dark narrow stairs to his room.

41

The clouds in the distance flickered in the night, outlining the distant hills, the shapes of the young trees along the curb of the parking lot, the saplings spaced across the continuous lawn in front of the row of townhouses; beyond the hills came the sound of faraway thunder, a low rumble like that of cities at war, tectonic plates grinding against one another, worlds in collision. The wind was starting to come up. A paper cup from Burger King skittered across the parking lot, caught in a sudden gust, rattling across the asphalt until it came full stop against the tire of his granite-gray Lincoln. Behind him came the insistent tinkle of wind chimes from one of the balconies.

They always seem like such a nice idea, don't they? So homey and peaceful . . . wind chimes . . . like water trickling over crystal goblets . . . then the damn things won't shut up . . . you end up wishing there was an off switch or mute button or something. . . .

Dickie sat on the sofa on the lawn in front of Pamela's townhouse, one arm stretched across the back, the warm wind blowing up the sleeve of his suit coat and across his T-shirt underneath, watching the play of light and shadow across the dark grass as the saplings shifted this way and that in front of the streetlights. The heavy plastic covering that had been on the sofa this morning was nowhere to be seen, victim he suspected of the neighborhood children. As he waited for Pamela to get home from work, he had time to think, among other things about his run-in with Harry Todd earlier in the evening . . . He got a couple good ones in on me there. He touched his face gingerly where Harry Todd had hit him. He was actually rather proud of his brother; he didn't think Harry Todd had it in him. . . .

Harry Todd said We're not going to be friends after this are we? and I said I still consider you a first-class prick and he said And you're still a real son-of-a-bitch and I told him Well, there you are.

And he thought about what else Harry Todd had told him, that it was their mother who got him started poking around about the family. She's been laying out photos and letters for me to look at, it's like she's leaving clues for me to follow. Like she wants me to find out what happened. So his mother had waited all this time, until Harry Todd came home for a visit, to ask Harry Todd to find out for her the details of Kathleen's death. Rather than to ask Dickie, the one person who knew the most about it. Well, he couldn't say he was surprised, but he was saddened nonetheless. Disappointed. Maybe she knew that his father had enlisted Dickie to cover up the suicide . . . no, he was only kidding himself if he thought that was the reason. He knew the reason well enough.

As he mulled things over in his mind, something occurred to him, a memory he had long forgotten: he was very young, probably only eight or nine, and he and his father and older brother were down at the Pennsylvania Railroad station, at the lower end of Furnass; his mother and Kathleen were arriving, they had gone to Rome, New York, to visit his grandparents, his mother's mother and father, and he and Harry Todd and Father were there to meet them. What made that come to mind all of a sudden? He couldn't recall thinking about it before in his life, yet now he could see it vividly in his mind's eye. He remembered standing on the platform, the three of them, as the train rounded the curve into view, the engine rolling past them and coming to a stop beyond the semaphore tower. Smoke and steam engulfed the platform, and there were people bustling everywhere, the railway express wagons trundling by; for a time he couldn't see a thing, then out of the crowd and the mist, like a vision, there she was, his mother, holding Kathleen by the hand, hurrying toward them. He remembered for a moment his heart sang with joy at the sight of her, he was so happy, and he and Harry Todd left their father behind and ran toward her as she broke into smiles to see them, to see him. . . .

The wind was starting to come stronger, the tops of the trees all leaning toward the east, bowing in unison with the stronger gusts as if in agreement; it was only a matter of time now before the rain started. Several houses down, a woman stood in her front door, framed in the light coming from the interior behind her, yelling at her pre-teenage son, Jamie, to hurry as the boy ran out across the common lawn to retrieve his bicycle left lying in the grass. From another unit came the sound of upstairs windows being closed. As he watched, Pamela's Corvette turned off Seneca Road into the lane and pulled into the parking space in front of her townhouse. She stared at him for a moment through the windshield, as if letting it sink in that yes, he was in fact sitting there on a sofa on her front lawn, before turning off the engine. As she got out of the car and came toward him, the wind tousled her black hair; her white nurse's uniform glowed in the darkness. He hadn't been sure how she'd take seeing him again, the memory of her walking away from him this morning when he was here, the ease and finality with which she did it, all too fresh in his mind; but she seemed not unfriendly as she came across the grass.

"What's this about?" she said.

"I figured I'd sit here and watch the rain. Always liked rain, there's something comforting about it, don't you think? Nice of you to leave this out here so I'd be comfortable."

"No, I mean what's with the suit and T-shirt routine? You going for the Hollywood look?"

"Oh, that." Dickie adjusted the lapels of his suit coat. "It's a long story."

"Does it have something to do with why you've got a fat lip and what looks like the beginnings of a black eye?"

"It could very easily."

Pamela sat down on the other end of the sofa and crossed her legs. "Then you're in luck. That's why I left this out here, so I could be comfortable during long stories. Or a summer rain, whichever came along first."

She's really good at that, coming back at me . . . that's why I love her. No, it's more than that. Much more.

"It's probably not *that* long a story. I had a little talk with my brother. . . ."

"Dickie. . . ."

He raised his hand for her to hold on. "No, it was okay. It got off to a . . . shaky start, but I think we got some things straightened out. I think we understand each other a little better now."

"What does he look like?"

"He's got a bloody nose."

"And the shirt?"

"We needed something to clean up with."

Pamela nodded as if it all made sense to her, but she seemed relieved too, that it wasn't more serious. She was worried about me but doesn't want to show it. There's hope for this yet. After a moment or so, she said, "So. Maybe some good came out of it."

"Maybe." He thought about what he wanted to say, and how he wanted to say it. Apologies, concessions, didn't come easily for him. "About this . . . sofa. . . ."

"You can call it a couch if you want to, I don't mind."

She sat back in the opposite corner, the two of them sitting there on the dark lawn as the wind continued to blow and the trees swayed and the distant sky flashed a white underbelly among black clouds. Down the block Jamie had retrieved his bicycle and was running it around the back of the townhouses, his mother still calling to him to hurry up and get inside. In the house beside it, a group of guys stood in the open doorway, the members of what appeared to be a poker party, looking out at the approaching storm, debating when it would start and who left their car windows open. Dickie scratched his chest through his T-shirt, as if checking to see that he was still there.

"No, it's a sofa, and that's what I should call it. But thanks. . . ."

Pamela shrugged, as if to say No big thing.

Why is it so hard to say nice things to someone you care about? Guess I'm out of practice. "What I'm trying to say is . . . I didn't mean to upset you by getting this for you. I wanted to do something nice for you. . . ."

"I know that and appreciate it. And my reaction to it had nothing to do with you or your doing nice things for me. . . ."

". . . but you were right, I shouldn't have gone ahead and done it like that. Maybe I was trying to act like a big shot or I was being too protective or something, maybe I was overreacting to that phone call you got from that other guy, I don't know."

She cocked her head and looked at him a moment, as if studying a new facet of him. But there were still some things she wanted to get straight.

"My reaction to your buying this sofa had only to do with me. There are things that are important for me to do on my own, so I know I can do them and I don't have to feel obligated to any-body. And as for 'that other guy'—Jack—I would have tried to prepare you about him if I thought it would ever come up or be an issue. Yes, I was involved with Jack at one time, as you well know; and you should also know it's over now. Whatever we were to each other, that was then and this is now. But Jack's an old friend, he always will be, he's an old-er friend. We go back a long way and we care a lot about each other, nothing's going to change that, I won't let it. He's in the hospital and I always told him if he ever needed anything he could call. And he did."

"Is he very sick?"

"He's probably not going to make it." Pamela looked away into the darkness, for a brief moment appearing as if her emotions for once might get the better of her, before she recovered.

She really cares for this guy. But that's what she's telling you, that it doesn't mean she cares any less for you.

"I'm sorry. About your friend." Dickie was amazed to think he might actually mean it.

"So there are going to be times I'm going to want to be with him. When I will be with him. While I still can."

"And now that you've told me, I can understand that. I'll work to make sure I understand that."

"You just can't waltz into my life all of a sudden because you've decided it's convenient for you and expect me to drop everything and be at your beck and call. I've got my own life."

Dickie watched a leaf cartwheel in the wind across the grass. Careful. A wave of anger swept over him but he fought to keep it in check—Wait till it passes, she's right, what she's saying to you, what she's saying doesn't mean anything more than it is. The poker players in the doorway were still debating the pros and cons of closing their car windows. One of their fellows, the tail of his polo shirt hanging out, stood in the middle of the front walk, his arms outstretched, spinning in slow circles, his face to the sky; it was evidently a poker-and-drinking party. After a moment Pamela said,

"If nothing else, you've still got obligations to Tinker."

"That's going to change. . . ."

Pamela shook her head. "I don't want to talk about it."

"We don't have to. You probably wouldn't believe me anyway."

"That's the type of thing a married man says to a girl."

Got me. But she's right. "You're right. I'll just have to show you differently. I will, too."

She appeared to soften a little, as if aware that she was being hard on him. And no longer wished to be. The first drops began to fall.

"It's starting to rain," Dickie said and stood up. "We better get inside. I don't want you sitting here if that lightning gets any closer."

"It really is a shame about the sofa," Pamela said, standing up and looking at it. "It's going to get ruined out here."

"Another good intention that's all wet, or soon will be," he grinned. "There's no way the two of us could carry it. . . ."

"Do you suppose we could drag it. . . ?"

"What about getting it in the front door?"

"We could try. . . ."

The drops were coming faster, harder, large drops. The poker players were whooping and hollering as they made a dash for their cars to close their windows.

"What the hell," Dickie said. "Grab an end!"

With Dickie at the rear and Pamela in front they tried to make a run with the sofa to the house, but lifting his end only made her end dig into the grass.

"Change ends!" Dickie said, and they hurriedly switched around, almost running into each other in the process, giggling at themselves and ducking against the raindrops. A couple of the poker players came running across the grass to lend a hand, their buddies in the doorway yelling encouragement as they helped Dickie lift the sofa and run stumbling with it toward the house, Pamela hurrying on ahead to unlock the door.

"It's never going to fit through the door," one of the guys yelled against the wind.

"We'll make the sucker fit," the other called, and directed hoisting the sofa on end and edging it around the doorframe. Once inside the door they left the sofa standing upright in the entryway as the rain started to come harder; the poker players yelled good-bye and ran back outside again into the pouring rain and back across the lawn to their friend's house.

Dickie and Pamela, still giggling, eased the upright end of the sofa down to the floor and baby-stepped it into the sparsely furnished living room, Pamela directing where she wanted it in front of the fireplace. Then the two of them collapsed on the sofa, laughing at themselves. Pamela got up again to turn on the lamp that sat on a crate across the room, when a loud crack of lightning struck somewhere close by. They looked at each other startled, wide-eyed—Wow, that was too close!—as the light in the hallway flickered, dimmed, and went out. The only light came from an occasional flash from outside. Pamela went over to the window and peeked through the curtains.

"The lights are out everywhere and it's really coming down. Now aren't you glad we brought that sofa inside?"

"I'm more glad that we're not still outside sitting on it."

"Stay where you are," she said, closing the curtains again. As she moved across the room, her form stop-timed with the lightning as if lit by a strobe light. "I've got some candles in the kitchen. I'll get them."

"That's like you," Dickie said, settling back. "Prepared for an emergency."

"Who said anything about an emergency? I got these for romantic candlelight dinners. In case somebody special ever came along."

"And did somebody?"

"We'll see."

He watched her dim form disappear into the darkness toward the kitchen. As he sat there listening to her rattle through the cabinets, he felt himself begin to let go, the first time in he didn't know how long. It had been quite a day . . . the dynamiting of the old blast furnace . . . then finding this sofa earlier on the lawn . . . his talk with Julian out at Berry's Run . . . and later the talk with Harry Todd. We're not going to be friends. And his thoughts returned to the memory that had come to him earlier, when he and his father and Harry Todd went to meet their mother and Kathleen at the train station, this time following it out to its conclusion . . . there was smoke and steam everywhere and he couldn't see a thing along the platform with all the people bustling around and the railway express wagons trundling by, and then the smoke and steam cleared and there she was, holding Kathleen by the hand, his mother, he was so happy to see her, he and Harry Todd left their father behind and ran down the platform toward her as she broke into smiles to see them, see him, Dickie realizing as they got closer that she was looking only at him, only at Harry Todd, his mother grabbing Harry Todd when they got close enough and hugging him while Dickie stood beside them not knowing what to do with himself, looked around wildly for something else to look at, pretending to be totally un-interested in the goings-on, his heart breaking once and for all time, his mother finally reaching for him and hugging him too, hugged him along with Harry Todd, but by then of course it was too late. . . .

And he thought, Of course she's always loved Harry Todd more, what did you expect? That's no big surprise. Harry Todd, her first-born. Evidently all the theories about mothers and first-borns are true, any child after the first being an addendum, an afterthought, a letdown. But he also understood that he was okay with it, he had always known it and had learned to adjust, he had learned to live with it. Tomorrow or the next day, he'd have to sit down with his office manager and figure out where he could slot Harry Todd into the company. It'll have to be someplace where I won't run into him all the time, maybe out here in the Seneca office, and I'm not sure what he's fit to do these days, we'll probably have to train him, get him his Realtor's license, but he's a personable enough guy, I'll take care of him, it's what

I do. I don't care what they say about you, old friend, I think you're all right. . . . As he sat there, Pamela came in from the darkness of the kitchen, holding a lighted candle in one hand and two bottles of Rolling Rock in the other, the candlelight haloing around her nurse's uniform. He reached out to help steady her as she started to sit down, taking her elbow, taking some of her weight as gravity started to pull her down. Pamela looked at him and smiled as she got herself settled in beside him.

42

He promised to bring me a basket of posies,
A garland of lilies, a gift of red roses,
A little straw hat to set off the blue ribbons
That tie up my bonnie brown hair. . . .

Was someone tapping on the window? That's what it sounded like. It would have to be a pretty tall someone, this is the second floor. Kitty put down the pair of bell-bottom trousers she had been modeling against herself in front of the mirror and followed a path through the stacks of storage boxes and green plastic garbage bags to the window. Or as close to the window as she could get; a cedar chest with a collapsed playpen lying across it and several cardboard boxes blocked her way the last few feet. Leaning around the edge of a wardrobe, she pulled back the drape and looked out.

The rain earlier had splattered against the screen, clogging the old mesh like black honeycomb; though it wasn't raining now it felt like it could, should at any moment, the air heavy with moisture. I wish it would rain, maybe it would break the hot spell. I'm tired of wilting. I swear the heat and humidity are harder on these old joints than the cold. Another little feature of growing old they don't tell you about beforehand. That and the joys of losing control of your bladder, walking around wearing a diaper, an old babe in swaddling clothes. I wish I thought that was amusing. She let the drape fall into place again and threaded her way back to the bed. But she was in no mood to continue sorting through Kathleen's clothes, she had had enough for tonight. It all seemed rather meaningless now, whether to keep them or throw them away, she really didn't care at this point; they could all be gone or stay where they were, it made no difference to her.

She supposed she should be glad for her talk with Harry Todd tonight, and she was, without question, but it made superfluous much of what she had based her life on for the past dozen years, even further back than that, an exercise in futility. At one time she felt it was almost her duty to preserve these artifacts, not only of Kathleen but of her husband and Harry Todd and Dickie as well, the keeper of the flame, the high priestess of the Sutcliff Cult, that the memory of Kathleen, of the family, not necessarily as they had been but as they wished they were, would die if she threw away so much as one drawing made in grade school or training bra or pair of mismatched socks. But talking to Harry Todd this evening, opening all the secrets, or most of them, had been like exhuming the body of an ancient mummy that disintegrated into dust as soon as it made contact with the light, the air. In addition to the answers she hoped he would find for herself, she had prodded Harry Todd to find out what all had gone on in the family, what had happened with the death of his sister, in order for him to reach some sense of closure, to reach the peace with himself that she sensed he lacked; and having accomplished that, or at least providing him with every opportunity, she felt as if her mission was over, these once treasured memories returned to what they were in the eyes of the rest of the world, meaningless junk. She thought *Dust ye are, and dusty ye shall remain, as far as I'm concerned.* She certainly hadn't saved all this stuff for her own benefit, no matter how crazy the town thought she was. Her own treasured memories were based on more ethereal, more enduring stuff.

Slowly, feeling very much an old woman now, she made her way through the clutter, pausing at the door to survey the room once more—I am leaving quite a legacy once I'm gone, quite a mess for somebody to clean up, which no doubt will be Dickie, I can't see Harry Todd having anything to do with it. Dickie the Competent, he never understood that, I suppose, that I never had to worry about him because I knew he was strong and resourceful enough to make it on his own, it was his brother and sister I had to worry about, twins born ten months apart, locked in spirit in each other's embrace, joined at the heart, sadness waiting to happen—before turning out the light and stepping out into the dark hall. Lightning flickered dully from the open doorways along the corridor; she could hear thunder rumbling somewhere far away, the wind in the sycamores behind the house. On the landing of the stairs, the stained-glass window, the pattern of gold cords and blue and green diamonds, was barely visible from the darkness outside. Kitty continued down the steps, into the harsh lights of the downstairs.

She went to the kitchen and worked her way back through the first floor of the house, turning off the lights as she went, leaving a trail of dark rooms behind her. The last light was in the side sitting room, one of the lamps she had had made from a metal statuette, Magellan or Ponce de León, someone pointing the way toward a distant horizon, standing on the end of the baby grand piano. She reached up under the shade and switched it off, waiting for a moment while the darkness of the house wrapped about her, her old friend. Then she made her way back across the hall to the living room and sat in the old rocking chair. Outside, the storm seemed to have blown itself out before it got started; she had expected sheets of rain, storm and fury, but if it did anything more than sprinkle she missed it.

She sat in the chair rocking slowly back and forth, one leg outstretched, the way Doctor used to always rock, thinking about him again, as she often did these days, thinking about the time she left Furnass, packed up her things and took Kathleen with her to her parents' house in upstate New York, only to turn around a few months later and come back.

"So, here you are again," Doctor had said, the first night after she returned when she appeared at his office, sitting with him in the evening as they had done for years, in the lower level of the house, in his office on the main street of Furnass, with his wife moving around distantly overhead.

"Yes, here I am again," Kitty had said. "Here *we* are again."

"You know nothing can come of this, don't you?"

"Yes. Of course."

Doctor was in his shirtsleeves and vest, sitting in his rocking chair in the corner of the room behind his desk, rocking slowly back and forth, one leg extended, smoking a cigarette. Kitty sat across from him, in a straight-backed chair usually reserved for patients. The smoke from his cigarette curled around his head, the blue haze filling up the room from the top down. It was several moments before he spoke again.

"I didn't hear why you left. It was all very sudden."

"I'm sorry. It was the only way I could do it. Otherwise, I knew I couldn't do it at all."

"I naturally assumed it was because of me."

"No. It was because of him. Because I felt I couldn't stand to live with a man like that any longer."

"You married him."

"Yes. I married him. But that was before I found out that in some way all women are the same to him. We're interchangeable to him. He can't help it, that's just the way he is."

"I know what you say is true. But it's also true that you're different to him."

"Yes. I know that. But in order for him to feel that way he had to lift me out of the realm of his appetites. I became his pure love. It was unfortunate, because by that time I would have settled for being just the object of his appetites, as long as they were directed only at me."

"But you came back."

"Because of you. Because I found I missed you too much. I missed these times with you too much."

"I certainly can't provide that kind of appetite toward you. Or at least do anything to fulfill it."

"I would never expect you to. And that's the point. I would have settled for the appetite from Harry. Because my love it turns out is for you. Whatever it was when I first met him, I've come to love him in a married way. The way married people do. Married love."

"What about Kathleen?"

"What about her?"

"You said it was only a matter of time before you thought something would happen between them. Between Kathleen and her father."

"Yes. So I'll have to make sure it doesn't."

"I'm an old man, Kitty. You know I won't be here much longer. After I'm gone, you can take Kathleen and get away from here."

"But I won't. I'll stay here. Because this is where you were. And by that time Kathleen will be old enough to decide she doesn't want to leave here either. She'll want to stay here to be with him, the same way that I want to be with you. You see, that's why I understand her so well. We're very much alike in our loves. I'll stay here to the day I die. And there won't be a day that I don't think of you."

"This is crazy. This is against the natural order."

"I know, you told me that. But it doesn't matter. I'll redefine the natural order. Or I'll learn to live in the unnatural one."

"But what can come of it?"

"Nothing. And everything. We'll be together like this, whenever we can. We'll sit together down here or out on the back porch in the summertime and talk about books and the weather. And there will be the once-a-week family dinners, and the holiday get-togethers, and the times I can think up an excuse to stop by the house."

"I can't do the examinations anymore."

"I know that. That's all right. You don't need to. We had that once, no one can take that away from me. And those few times together. . . ."

"And you know we can never speak of this again."

"Yes, I know that too. That's why I have one favor to ask you. That you kiss me. Or let me kiss you. On the lips. Not on the cheek like we always do. This one and only time."

When he didn't say anything, she got up and crossed the room. She had thought she would kneel beside the chair but he surprised her: he stood and took her in his arms and kissed her, enveloped her in his arms and the smells of his cigarettes and the tweed of his vest and the smell of him alone, kissed her as if she stepped through a door and fell through endless space forever. Thirty years later she still carried the feel of that moment with her, the feel of his lips on hers, sometimes that moment seeming more real than anything else around her.

And it's oh dear, what can the matter be. . . .

Out of her line of vision the windows flickered dimly. But when she looked all she saw was darkness, the dark glass. Oh dear, what can the matter be . . . She supposed she should be getting to bed soon, it was late. But she continued to sit there in

the darkness, the stillness of the old house, singing softly to herself . . . Oh dear, what can the matter be . . . rocking slowly back
and forth, the joints of the wooden chair squeaking softly, the
way they always did when Doctor sat in the chair rocking, rocking . . . rocking . . . content within her memories . . . Johnny's so
long at the fair. . . .

43

Once I was lost, and now I'm found. Good grief, Harry Todd
thought, where the hell do you suppose that came from? Next
thing I'll be attending church and Sunday school, Mother and me
sitting in the family pew. Calvary First U.P. Church. Calvary;
Cavalry. Bugler, sound the charge. First U Pee, then you poop,
Kathleen and I used to giggle. Ah. Yes. Of course. Mother said
Kathleen thought she lost me. That would be amazing, Grace.

His bedroom was stifling, the air heavy like walking into a
moist blanket. Without waiting to turn on a light, he hurried
over and opened the tower windows. At once a warm breeze filled
the circular area with crosscurrents; the little rain wasn't enough
to break the heat but the movement of air was refreshing, the air
seeming somehow cleaner. Out the windows, the night sky appeared torn to shreds. The distant lightning of the faraway storm
showed the breaks between the levels of clouds, webbing in all
directions, tatters of gray and black, the dim quick light tracing
patterns as they rent through the cloud cover, gone again as
quickly as they came. After thirty years in the Bay Area, he had
forgotten the severity that could come with a summer storm here,
lightning strikes, tornados even. But this storm had passed without incident, only a brief shower as it turned out, a letdown if
the truth be known. More *Drang* than *Sturm*. After standing
there a few minutes, he climbed up on the desk and sat crosslegged on the blotter. Looking out over the black landscape, the
lights of the town below, the hashmark patterns of the

streetlights, the dark river curving to the lights of the bridge across the end of the valley. This place that, whether he liked it or not, was home.

His mother acted like she thought he was surprised when she told him that Kathleen felt she had lost her older brother, but it wasn't new to him, Kathleen had told him that herself, the time he came back to town after he graduated from college. They were on the front porch, Kathleen was on the swing, gliding slowly back and forth, Harry Todd sitting with his legs stretched out balanced along the railing, the sunlight coming through the balusters beneath him like gold bars across the floor, talking about his new life in California, all his plans for the future, and he told her that she should come to California too, that he'd help her if she was interested. Kathleen's hands were clasped in front of her, as if she could barely believe, barely hope to dream about, what she was hearing. There was only a whisper of the asthma in her voice, a wheeze like a backdraft when she inhaled.

"And I thought I lost you."

"Why would you think a thing like that? Don't be silly, you're my sister."

"But where would I go? I don't think all the fog in San Francisco would be good for me."

Harry Todd had trouble holding back his excitement that she would even consider what he had in mind. "I have friends in Tempe, at the University of Arizona. You told me once that you had thought about going there to graduate school."

"For speech therapy," she said cautiously, studying his face. "Arizona has one of the best programs. . . ."

"That's what I thought. So here's my idea. I could take you there on my way back to California. I could hang around for a week or so, help you find an apartment and get settled, and introduce you to the people I know there. You could get a job until you get into school, and there would be people around to help out if you needed anything or started to get lonesome. What do you think?"

"It would be like a dream come true," Kathleen said, her face full of wonder.

"And you'd be able to get away from all this dirt in the air."

"What would Father and Mother say?"

"You let me take care of that." He swung his legs off the railing and leaned over to clasp her hands in his. "Dreams do come true. You'll see. I'll make it happen."

That evening he waited until after dinner and Kathleen had gone upstairs. He called his mother from the kitchen into the living room, where his father was watching a summer repeat of *Maverick*, and explained his idea to them.

His mother, still wearing her apron from doing dishes, sat on the sofa across from her husband. Her toes in a pair of low-heeled sandals peeked out from beneath the hem of her long gingham dress. "We've talked about this with her before, Harry Todd," she said, smoothing the wrinkles from her lap. "We discussed it with her when the doctor first diagnosed the asthma and told us she needed to be in a better climate. Kathleen was always very definite that she didn't want to go away."

"Well, that's not what she says now. She really wants to go away and start a new life for herself. But she's afraid you won't let her."

His mother looked concerned; she looked to her husband. "What do you think? Has she said anything to you about any of this?"

His father had been keeping an eye on the TV as he listened to them; now he turned to Harry Todd and his wife. "There's only one way to find out what she wants. Call her down and ask her."

"And you'll let her go, if she wants to?" Harry Todd said, looking from his mother to his father and back again.

His father shrugged. "Why would we stand in her way? If that's what the girl wants?"

"Yes, of course," his mother said.

As Harry Todd called up the stairs for Kathleen, his mother looked deeply troubled. Harry Todd smiled to himself . . . She knows the game is over, even if Father doesn't. She knows there's no way out of this one, no way he can hold Kathleen back now, no way he can keep her as Daddy's little girl, he'll have to let her go this time, they'll both have to let her go.

Kathleen came down the stairs and stood in the doorway, one bare foot resting on end with the toes curled under. She was already dressed for bed, in what looked like an old pair of her father's pajamas. Harry Todd told her the news.

Kathleen looked dumbfounded. "But I don't want to leave here."

"But you said. . . ."

"I said I thought about it, that's all. I wasn't really serious about it. Why would you think I would want to leave here?"

"Kathleen, you don't have to be afraid. . . ."

"Afraid? What are you talking about?"

Harry Todd went to her but she dodged by him and sat on the couch beside her mother. Kathleen was starting to breathe heavily and her mother put her arm around her. Kathleen burrowed into her mother's side.

"Who are you to come around here and try to tell us how to live?" Kathleen said, starting to cry. "Why would I be afraid of anything? This is my home. My home."

His mother hunched over and buried her face in the girl's hair, petting her, trying to console her, almost as if she shared her daughter's grief, almost as if she were trying to console herself. His father looked at Harry Todd, his businessman's smile on his face, and spread his hands as if revealing a truth.

"Well. It looks like you don't know so much about what goes on in this family after all."

He had run from the house, mortified, furious at her, vowing never to come back here again. I blamed her all these years, told the story of that night over the years to someone I wanted to impress, girls I wanted to sleep with, as an example of small-town minds, how people here were stuck in the mud of their small-town lives, but that wasn't it at all, I wasn't mad at her for refusing the opportunity to broaden her life, I was mad because it showed me up in front of Father and Mother, it wasn't about Kathleen at all, I didn't even want to help her for Kathleen's sake, I wanted to get her away from here to get back at Father and Mother for what they'd done to me, for sending me away from a place I guess meant more to me than I ever realized. And Kathleen . . . my interest in helping her must have seemed like a reprieve from my earlier turning away from her, but she was only telling me what I wanted to hear, what she thought she needed to say in order for us to be close again. To prove to herself that there was nothing wrong with her, that she was lovable, that she could be loved by one of the two people in the world she cared about most, whose love she needed most—poor Dickie, alas poor brother, I'm afraid you weren't even in the equation of male love for her, always the little brother—and then when confronted with the choice of me or Father, it backfired terribly on her, she knew then whose love was most important to her, and it wasn't me, maybe never had been. Because as Mother said, the real loss of her brother-love was back in high school, back on that summer day when we ran back to the house after playing tennis; as she went upstairs to take a shower I sat in the old rocker close to the doorway in the living room wanting to go upstairs after her, hoping something would happen with her like that story of the brother and sister that Julian passed around in school or that I could at least see her naked but then after she was done she came downstairs with only a towel wrapped around her to get something from the laundry and as she was heading back upstairs I thought it would be funny and I grabbed the towel as she passed the door and pulled it from her but she held on to it and I ended up pulling her on top of me and we rolled onto the floor and before I knew what I was doing but I knew very well I got my pants down and tried to stick it in her and for a moment I thought I had but I wasn't even close, I came all over her thighs and up on her stomach and I guess it surprised her and she gasped and that helped snap me out of it, or snapped me into what I was doing or trying to do and I pulled away from her and got my pants back up and ran from the house—Wait—what did she have to feel bad about, I was the one who made a fool of myself, coming like that almost as soon as I touched her—Wait—I was embarrassed and stayed away from her as much as I could after that, I didn't want anything like that to happen again and I didn't want to be reminded of it seeing her looking at me after that and I spent the rest of that summer and my last year in high school trying to get into as many girls as I could to try to get that memory out of my head—Wait—I thought at most it was a just a joke gone bad and maybe just maybe I did something I shouldn't have but then it was over and I thought I forgot about it but maybe for Kathleen it wasn't over like that, maybe she blamed herself for it—Wait—was that the start of it? They thought Kathleen and I were too close as kids and they thought that was the start of her problems but maybe it wasn't that at all, maybe it was there, that day, what I did, and then what I didn't do, I ran away from her and stayed away and she thought it had something to do with her, that there was something wrong with her that it ever happened, I'm an evil, evil girl, Mother said Kathleen said, oh my God. . . .

He looked back into the room, his chin tucked into his shoulder. Heartsick. Ashamed. They were unfamiliar feelings for him. Oh my God, what did I do? I never once thought what that day might have done to Kathleen. Not once. That what I thought at worst was a joke that turned out not so funny left scars that marked her for life. Kathleen, I'm so sorry. He looked around the room, at the row of wardrobes against the wall, the shelves of memorabilia his mother kept from his high school years, the pile of boxes and suitcases from his life in California in the center of the room, flickering occasionally from the remains of the shower outside as if from a strobe light gone bad. Wishing he could in fact see her ghost now, some sign, so he could tell her, so he could be sure she knew. But there was no one there. Only the room of his past, the boxes that held his future. He turned back to the black windows. The breeze brought a few drops of rain, the start of another shower perhaps, sprinkling him with spray, the gauze curtains reaching for him like wings. He thought he should probably climb down, close the windows. But he continued to sit there, folded into himself. Looking out at the lights scattered below over the dark hillside, the darkness where he knew the town must be.

Acknowledgements

There are four people—friends, really; dream catchers—without whom I could never have brought these books to publication:

Barbara Clark

Kim Francis

Dave Meek

Jack Ritchie

I also thank Eileen Chetti for struggling through my quirks of punctuation; Jay Tuttle who long ago did his best to help me understand financial structures; and Bob Gelston, who is always around to answer questions and take on anything else that's needed. And then, of course, there's my wife Marty. . . .

*

Richard Snodgrass lives in Pittsburgh, PA with his wife Marty and two indomitable female tuxedo cats, raised from feral kittens, named Frankie and Becca.

*

To read more about the Furnass series, the town of Furnass, and special features for *Some Rise*—including a Reader's Study Guide, author interviews, and omitted scenes—go to www.RichardSnodgrass.com.

Made in United States
North Haven, CT
28 August 2023

40826772R00193